WHISKEY WHEN WE'RE DRY

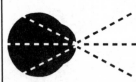

This Large Print Book carries the
Seal of Approval of N.A.V.H.

WHISKEY WHEN WE'RE DRY

JOHN LARISON

WHEELER PUBLISHING
A part of Gale, a Cengage Company

Farmington Hills, Mich • San Francisco • New York • Waterville, Maine
Meriden, Conn • Mason, Ohio • Chicago

**LIBRARY OF CONGRESS CIP DATA ON FILE.
CATALOGUING IN PUBLICATION FOR THIS BOOK
IS AVAILABLE FROM THE LIBRARY OF CONGRESS**

ISBN-13: 978-1-4328-5786-8 (hardcover)

Published in 2018 by arrangement with Viking, an imprint of Penguin Publishing Group, a division of Penguin Random House LLC

Printed in the United States of America
1 2 3 4 5 6 7 22 21 20 19 18

For Ellie

There are two moons on the horizon and
for you
    I have broken loose.

                    — Joy Harjo, *Two Horses*

I

I heard it said God moves on the water. Well, I have looked for Him there. My thirst grows with his flood.

Our kin homesteaded where desert met lake. The hills in the near distance wore blankets of pine. Patterns of aspen marked the water. Beyond them the mountains stood blue on clear days and devoured the sun long before it left this world. From the home Pa built us we couldn't see the lake but we could see the willows along its edge and we could hear the wingbeats of doves. Bison calves still wandered in with the heifers and arrowheads clung to their shafts. This autumn air delivers me there still.

They arrived in 1864 by the deed I once held in my hand. Pa was fresh from the war and on a horse he took off a Johnny Reb. Pa told us he was a Yankee sharpshooter through the first two years of that war. He come home after to his family and found his own father's grave and his mother under the watch of a new man and his kid brother dying of infection. He stayed until the brother passed and then rode west.

Pa killed many men. I know that for certain. But he wasn't the kind to talk of it. The stories he told of that war was his histories. If Pa ran the schools pupils would memorize the names of each man killed on both sides.

Ma was dark skinned and Spanish speaking. Her kin was at some point subjects of Spain, France, Mexico, and the United States by the time they was forced from their home by Sam Houston and Santa Anna and the thousands of American settlers coming for what had been theirs. They fled the only direction without guns and come to settle in Kansas, peaceful land-rich Kansas. By the time Ma was of marrying age the war was kicking and the raiders come from Missouri and John Brown come from within and soon it was bloody torn-to-bits Kansas. Her intended was shot one night for no good reason at all and her brother who had joined the fighting returned ill of mind. Kansas wasn't Kansas no more. They rode on.

She was twenty-two and walking with a load on her shoulders somewhere in the plains when she heard a horse gaining and turned to see Pa slowing on her. Course he wasn't Pa yet. He was a stranger who introduced himself as Milt Harney. She said folks called her Rosa, her mother's name. I don't know what she thought of him but I know he memorized her details. There was sweat through her dress and flies so thick from the oxen she give up waving them off. A rare sight, a shapely girl without child or man. To hear Pa tell it there wasn't no west after he saw her, just the direction she was walking.

He took up with the uncle and the leader of the clan. Traveling poor as they done was slow work. No riding for those with legs. Folks now talk like everybody rode west but not many could afford a riding horse. So it was footwork and loads and dust so thick it turn your lungs to chalk. Pa had that horse and her uncle must've been looking to slip out from under his burden. A week on they was married by the book of a revivalist in a circle of wagons as a church.

After crossing the divide they broke off on their own for the valley that would become our home. "A barrel of sugar by autumn," he promised her. Pa would be a cattleman and to him that occupation promised wealth and maybe a mountain to name as his own.

To start he got homestead acres and unspoken grazing access to the nearby Indian lands. There was a lake and the valley held its green long after the hills went to brown.

When they arrived she was already growing with child. Ma wept when she saw the valley. Cranes danced at sunrise and wildflowers shone like embers in the grass. Here no view reminded her of someone she had lost. Noah come along that autumn.

Noah. My brother's name.

Even now I turn and expect to see him riding hard for supper. How many times did I push back the cowhide flap and see him leading a string of dust down the valley? Never late for grub and never one to show up on a dry horse, that brother of mine.

You knew him best but you didn't know him then, before. Sure you've heard the stories folks tell. They make him a killer and hellion. Little children hear his name, Noah Harney, and they see men falling from stagecoaches and smoke rising from a barrel and they think a man is made real by the violence he wields.

Noah was a killer, that is certain. I ain't never been sure if he was right.

Ma didn't live past my entrance to this world on account I wasn't no good at getting born. I set Ma to bleeding.

Pa knew right off there was trouble. She was twenty-seven and her color was slipping and her lips was going purple — her life was draining from her and there wasn't nothing Pa knew to do. He wanted to ride for help but she held him back. She asked him to build up the fire. He did as she asked. Under the rest Pa was a good soul, full of respect for the women in his life, which might be the

14

straightest measure of a man.

Ma pulled little Noah close. He was five then. He put his head on her shoulder and touched his fingers to my dewy head. "Ma, how come you so cold?"

She pulled up the quilt around them, us. "Don't worry, my child."

"Milt?" she asked of Pa. These was her final words on this earth: "Play me our song."

As Pa put bow to string, Ma put her nipple to my lips. She gave me my mother. Some things in this world you don't never forget even if you ain't got no memories of them.

The one time he spoke of her passing, Pa talked most of the storm that night and how the snow climbed the door. It blew in through the slats and flakes drifted toward the fire and turned to rain halfway. The water and her blood turned the dirt floor to mud.

After a time with her gone I got to shivering. It was my brother who wrapped me in a blanket and sat with me before the fire and gave his finger to my gums so I might stop crying for her.

I asked Pa what he done with her remains.

What choice did he have but to put her to rest in the snow outside until spring might allow a shovel to crack the earth. He must've carried her there. I imagine he took a final moment together. Come inside and stood a piece looking on us. A cattleman alone now with a too young boy and a baby girl.

15

I suspect he looked on me a long time trying to feel something different. I never did
know what Pa felt, not even when I knew him
best. When he come inside from leaving his
young wife in the snow and saw the thing
that put her there, what did he feel? How
could it have been love?

Pa hired a wet nurse who'd been a whore
over in Clayville. She had her own baby boy.
Pa wasn't in no state to judge character. I
don't remember her none, she was with us
just one season, till she located his savings
and rode off with it. After that it was just us.
He grew me on chewed venison, bone marrow, and pulped tubers, as was the method in
them days.

Pa did right considering. Most men
would've turned to stone and been a mountain between the table and stove. Nothing to
do but overcome a father like that. No, Pa
was tender for us. His hands was leather and
his eyes was gray and he might've been short
on words but he wasn't short on feeling.
Music turned him to butter.

He must've sought a new woman. He
must've considered putting us to another
family. The Mormons down the valley already
had a couple of their own. Handing us off
would've been easy enough, and expected in
that time.

But he kept us and did right by us, right as

he could. He had nearly two hundred head that spring. Most he'd ever have. Tending to us kids was the reason.

Most what I know about Ma come from Noah. He was five when she passed but might as well have spent a lifetime in her lee from all the stories he told. They come from him with no more thought than a belch. It was my brother too who taught me to dress, to squat over the night pot, to grow my hair long and braid it before sleep. These things he learned from watching her be a woman.

I ain't got no recollections of her voice but I'd know the sound. As a child I went about my chores in silence so as not to miss her when she come. I was certain she would come. Each time I think of our family place I feel her. She is the water brought inside by the camas, you don't see her none but without her there ain't no flower.

I did the woman work while Pa and Noah labored the spread. I longed to be with them, in truth. I dreaded my lonely washings and stewings and mendings and tendings. But need better breed enthusiasm or you in for a tough go in this life. By six I was doing a half-decent show of laundry. By eight I could skin down a buck so long as there was a stool I could stand on for reaching. Little me had to hang on the hide to get it to peel. My cooking wasn't much seeing as I learned from Pa but it was hot and it kept. He only complained if I skimped on the meat, and in that age the hills was still flush with meat.

I kept on Ma's pattern of things. Mondays was churning, Tuesdays baking, Wednesdays canning, Thursdays jerking, Fridays mending, Saturdays baths and laundry, Sundays cleaning. Most times when alone I pretended I was Ma. She wouldn't stand for a misplaced stitch or a stain left to dry. In every task my burden was the perfection she would've delivered had I not took her.

I slept under the near-finished birth quilt on my side of the bed Noah and me shared. This is how we'd slept since the beginning and so we kept on sleeping like a mother and child, me curled into him and his warm breath in my hair all those cold desert nights. In my slumber I dreamed her with us and understand those breaths to be hers and so lived what never was.

If Pa and Noah was working a long way off and I missed her painful I might pull out her things. Pa kept them in a trunk under the bed. There was a dress, a calico. There was shoes polished black. The left one had a scrape that cut into the leather near the toe. I never put them on or let them touch the floor. They was hers and I had taken enough. But I did allow myself to touch them. That's how I come to find a chain and a locket made of silver folded inside that calico. The locket

18

held the image of a young girl. I assumed for years the girl was Ma. That girl is still the mother I see. But the picture wasn't Ma at all. Pa told me years on that it might've been her younger sister who died of fever, but it wasn't Ma.

In the bottom corner of the trunk was her Good Book. She knew how to read and she taught Pa. Pa told me, "A woman's best chance in this world is to know the Good Book better than the men in her life." He said as much but he wasn't spending no time teaching me to read.

Under the bed beside the trunk was a box long as an arm. Pa's fiddle. He drew it out only on Ma's birthday, in April, when the camas pushed up from the green meadows. He would set it upon the bed and then sit back from it and put his fist to thigh as he was wont to do when he thought of her. One year he caught me staring on him, and he drew me between him and that box, maybe so I couldn't see his wet eyes. His fingers passed over the wood.

"Pa?"

"Your mother couldn't get her fill of music. She wanted me to play any chance. She kept time with her heel. She never forgot the time."

Inside was a vivid red cloth. It was an age when men and women in town wore browns and olives and dusty white. Colors belonged to the hills in autumn, to the sunset and wildflowers and trout that rolled in the lake, the Indian paint we saw less and less of. I felt Pa quit his breathing at the sight of that red.

He had learned during the war and brought the fiddle west. It was his music that won Ma over those nights among the wagons. Noah remembered him playing. Noah said in them days every dark was warded off by Pa's song.

The lament he played on Ma's birthday I never heard outside our family. I do believe he made it up. Or maybe he and Ma together made it up. Either way it was theirs. The song leaned on mournful drawn-out notes and two steep climbs into high emotion. It was in no hurry to conclude, and neither was its audience. I am haunted by that song.

I remember staring up at his great shape with the fiddle to his chin and the bow cutting back and forth and his song slicing me open. I can't forget the word "Rowhine" burned into the body of that fiddle. It was branded like a beast, and so I come to think of the instrument as its own animal and Pa as its handler.

For all his tenderness Pa was quick to anger and it was the little things that set him loose. Regular enough I caught the back of his hand. Noah took whuppings too. I think that's how he got so quick with the stories. He knew his best luck was in talking Pa cool. He bent the man's mind. Pa wasn't slow but

I don't reckon he was ever as keen as his boy.

Folks often wonder how I got so good with the pistol. We passed our evenings watching Pa practice pistol work. He had two Colt 1860 front-loaders from the war, and he taught himself to quickdraw. Pa loved to hear talk of gunfighters, we all did. Gunfighters was not bound by children, market prices, drought, waning graze, grief too immense to touch. Gunfighters lived as they pleased. They rode over them mountains and into the valleys beyond and on again but always into the same promise.

Pa once told Noah he wouldn't be doing his fatherly duty if he didn't teach his boy to shoot good and shoot quick. Noah come to pistol play like fowl to water. I carry many memories of them drawing on each other, then Pa coming close to reveal a subtlety of technique, finger placement or the angle of the elbow. It might've been the only time they ever touched, other than in conflict.

I don't recall Pa being all that fast with a pistol, honest. But he knew lead and how to send it.

Pistols wasn't no use for a woman, according to Pa. He was so sure about this fact he didn't even bother telling me to leave them be. I only took up the spare Colt when Pa and Noah was away working and only fired it when I had poured my own lead and was sure they was outside the limits of sound.

Pa kept his bullet fixings in a pouch over the mantel. In it was a form and a pot and beads of lead the size of tears. I would watch him and Noah ride away over the hill and then I'd pour some tears into the pot and put the pot over the morning fire and when it went to silver soup I took it up with Pa's leather mitt and poured the liquid into the small hole on the form. If all went right I could have myself a few rough balls in the time it took to make flapjacks. As the balls cooled I put the fixings back in place and then took up a boning knife and went to trimming off the edges of the balls until they was smooth and clean. All this I learned from watching Pa teach Noah, watching them do it in the evenings. Down each cylinder of the Colt went a spoon of powder which I packed with a brass rod. Over the hole went a circle of thin cloth and then the ball. To place those over the powder took the same rod and all my might. Those balls was a snug fit. All this labor so once outside I took my time with the shots. I walked by the barn and out to the lake and brought up the Colt and sighted down its barrel fifty times for every ball I set loose. There was Ma's voice in the report, instructing me. Never mind Ma probably never shot a pistol.

The Colt was heavy and slow but when you learn on heavy and slow it comes to be steady. In later years my hands grew wide and veins rode over my forearms. House duties was my calling, but there was something else growing in me too. For those hours I held the Colt I was more than me.

When there was time to be had Pa and Noah took the Sharps breech rifle to the lake's edge. It was Pa's duty rifle from the war and he didn't let nobody else carry it. Once they crawled up to the rise Pa might slide it over to Noah and coach him some. I was supposed to be inside tending to things but I was usually there hiding in the bushes, listening. That rifle held my attentions. It was tall as me, and if that little pistol could be so fun my mind turned on the possibilities of a rifle that size. Its bark come back from the hills for two breaths if the wind was right.

Most days on the skyward image of the lake sat a million ducks and geese paddling and talking. Pa might point to a gander on the far edge way out yonder and whisper about yardage and windage and elevation. No shooting the body — that was his rule. "Just feathers fluttering over the mud if 'n you hit him square. It's head or nothing, son."

I only ever saw Pa miss a gander once. Noah wasn't no good with that Sharps though. He missed most every shot. Pa said Noah was too excitable. "Distance shooting is for the quiet man," he said. "Your brother tells too many stories to be good with a rifle."

Noah and his stories. He could twist yarn around a flea. A thousand men have that skill. My brother was the only one I ever met who could make a doubter believe.

Once when he was thirteen and me eight we was sitting under the eave. His boots was upon the rail as Pa's would've been, except Noah was slouching to make his legs reach. He looked awful uncomfortable. But he went on and on about the gunfighter he would be someday, turning over a thread of grass in his teeth like it was a smoking piece.

"And that's when I bust in with my pistol and shout 'Wooha!' and fire a round into the ceiling just to show I am for hot. Nixing Noah, I'll nix you faster than a half-broke mule!"

"Faster than a half-broke mule" was something we'd heard Pa say. Don't reckon neither of us had ever seen a half-broke mule.

"What you looking off at, sister? Don't you hear my story of cunning and gunfightery?"

"Course I do. You talk loud as hog at breakfast." I knew plenty about hogs at breakfast.

He sat straight and let his feet hit the ground. "Did I ever tell you about Ma and the wicked owl?"

I looked him sideways. "This for real?"

"Course it is." His smile said otherwise.

I will admit I relished the made-up Ma

stories. The real ones I cradled in my hands until I found the proper place for safekeeping. Each one was the earth's last egg and so demanded full attention and a raw heart. But the made-up stories was just wide-out fun. I could dwell in them with her, without fear of losing something.

"A storm come on during the night," Noah began, "and winds was cutting through the house and stirring the coals. The air smelled of old fire. Ma woke at that smell. Ma had the nose of a panther."

"Was you in their bed?"

"Shh, I'll tell it." He went on to say how Ma had left the cabin in the dark and he had followed with the pistol, to keep her safe. Pistols was in most the stories he told.

"What'd she smell like?" I asked.

"Smell? What's smell got to do with it?"

"Be more particular in your telling if 'n you don't want my questions."

"Mint. Mint and honey. Now shush and listen." He told of how together they saw an enormous owl with black eyes. "It had fangs like a wolf and it shrieked so loud we put palms to our ears. I busted off a round to scare it."

Most of my brother's made-up stories went like this. Somewhere along the telling he rose from the kid to the hero.

"Fangs? I don't like this story. It gives me goose pimples."

"It ain't a story. It's history." Noah spat like Pa when buying time. He took off his hat and wiped the sweat from his brow. The sun was sliding south and had found us now where we sat. "This owl left behind a skull. Deep scratches lined the eye sockets from the bird's huge old claws."

"That ain't true. Ain't no owl carrying no skulls."

His eyes settled on mine with high drama. "Honest. A human skull."

Bones was always something I avoided. Even cattle bones. My young mind didn't know no better and so believed they was hers.

My brother knew how I felt about bones. He was always joshing me as big brothers is wont to do.

"You didn't find no human skull."

"Put a wager on it."

"Where's this skull then?"

He pointed at the sage. "Yonder."

"Then let's go see it."

He laughed. "Bones don't last in this country. Silly girl. You act grown, but you still young of mind."

"If it's true, we'll find some part of it. Skulls don't just disappear entire. Like them wolf teeth you found last autumn, no bones attached." I stood. "Unless you's joshing."

All at once he was on his way, and I was trying to keep up. "I never josh," he called over his shoulder.

26

We spent some minutes toeing around in the brush of that draw. It was just one of many on the hillside, nothing particular about it. Antelope pellets at the bottom. Coyote scat stuffed full of mouse bones. Little yellow flowers and flakes of obsidian.

"This country eats bones."

"Wasn't no owl with fangs," I said as we walked back to the house.

"Was too."

"Was not."

Noah saw it first. The door to the house was open. Not much, only a crack, but we had left it closed. Noah looked spooked now for real. "I give it a pull before we set off. I shut that door."

"Should we hide?" Indians was still about in them days. We all heard the stories of raiding and butchery.

There was a commotion inside. Like what you'd expect from a red going through your belongings. "Let's go!" I pulled on his sleeve.

I was surprised by Noah then. He didn't move. I had believed the two of us would flee to the willows by the lake fast as fawns sent by their doe. But he just stood in the open. He didn't move a step. He didn't say a word. I thought him stupid for wanting to see this Indian up close.

But a little sister is her big brother's animal. I didn't leave him when it made sense to.

The commotion began again. Dishes was

falling, glass breaking. Noah drew his knife and shouted like a Reb and pushed open that door.

The image of him standing before that black doorway is the image of my brother that comes first. It is what I saw when I read your letter and learned of his passing. My big brother standing before a dark too deep for light. All these years on, and still I am a little girl scared for her brother, scared for herself without him.

Our Indian turned out to be an owl, a real one. It swooped past Noah and my brother hit the earth and the bird lifted into the bright light of day without a whisper of wind through his feathers, pure smoke rising toward blue. Of course I believed it to be the owl from his story. How could I believe anything else?

After that I didn't much ask if his stories was real or made up. Maybe I'd lost my belief in the difference.

Sometimes I wonder if he did too.

The lake was about as far as we would go. Noah and me spent many afternoons along that muddy shore. We was both drawn to water, as our mother had been. We shed our boots and he rolled up his pants and I tucked my dress bottom into my pockets, and we took spears to the weedline. The mud squeezed through our toes and gave off the smell of primal origins. We hunted the edge for the big trout that lurked there but never speared one. In time we grew bored with the hunt and sat on the shore and let the mud dry.

Whatever it is between a boy and his old man had already set to crumbling by then. Noah was quick to undercut Pa soon as the older was outside earshot. "Should be running sheep." "Tell me one good reason for not fencing our lake?" "He just ain't keen enough for ranching." At supper they put their faces to the stews I made and didn't look up until their bowls went dry. Honest, there was trouble between Noah and me too, on account I didn't think he was giving Pa due respect. A girl alone out in that desert has got to pick sides, and I was the kind to pick her old man.

One morning we was waiting for Pa to wake up, he was spending more and more time in bed then, and Noah and me took our coffee to the eave and sat watching the dawn light walk down the western ridge. I pointed up at the strange pile of rocks on the summit that had a manner of holding our gaze whenever we looked yonder. "How big you reckon them is?"

Noah spat. He was buying his own tobacco by then. He was fifteen. "That stack of stones? That's easy." He held his hand about chest high off the ground. "Yea big."

I took in some coffee and thought on it. "Well, that would make the whole dang mountain big as our barn."

He took down the remainder of his coffee and adjusted his plug like Pa would do, and then he put his boots on the rail. No slouching now. He wore a man's boots. Hair grew from the corners of his lip. "God made big brothers older and smarter for a reason, sister." He took to invoking God the winter before. Pa didn't like it none. I think that's why Noah done it. "It's my duty to set you straight when you's foolish. Maybe you and me take a ride up that ridge and gander those stones from beside them, then you'll always remember that I'm right when I say I'm right."

"You think he's sick?" I said with a nod toward Pa inside.

Noah shrugged and looked to the bottom of his empty cup.

We went in to town once a season with the wagon and spent the night away, the three of us together. Always done it that way. But now Pa was going more often, couple times a month even. He took a liking to the syrup a dentist give him after pulling two bad teeth. That was the year before and now he hardly went a day without the stuff. It cost him plenty. Our herd was down to thirty-five head. He stayed in bed most mornings. Sometimes he didn't get up until the sun cut silver blades through the slats.

When Pa did rise that morning he took down his coffee and lifted his bridle, which I done fixed for him the evening before. "Back soon," he said. Then he stopped and turned to speak to his son. "Don't leave your sister. Never know what scoundrels might be about. And patch that henhouse."

We listened to his mare lope away.

Noah didn't wait long enough for water to boil before he was reaching for Pa's fiddle under the bed. "Don't," I said from my dish-washing. "That ain't —"

"I won't hurt it none," he said. He had never before touched the box. It was the one thing we didn't molest in Pa's absence. That instrument held the power to make our father weep. "Besides, I aim to get good on it. Better than he ever was." Noah was working on the keeper nails with his folding knife. "I hear a man can make a living playing music. Imagine that, a gunfighting musician."

"Stop," I said. "Pa would tell you to stop."

Noah chuckled. "Why you always standing up for him?"

I dried my hands on the ratted apron. It was the same apron Ma wore. Pa had given it to her at their first Christmas, then to me on my previous birthday. He said I was ready for it. Now I took the apron off and folded it and set it upon the clean table. Then I drug Pa's chair to the door and climbed up and

31

lifted the Sharps from its rack.

"Give me that." He seized the rifle from me. "You too little even to hold it proper. Girl don't know the hammer from the trigger."

"Pa's got casings on the mantel."

"I know that." He parked the rifle over his shoulder like Pa would and said, "Fetch me one."

After he took the rifle out into the morning I slid the fiddle back under the bed just as Pa would leave it, and then took up an extra casing for myself and followed my brother toward the lake.

That day we found the fowl gone, flown on already. Trout was breaking the glassy surface and sending rings in all directions. I so longed to angle one from them waters and put it a pan. I wanted to see its colors. I never did get to hold one of them trout.

I turned to check again for Pa. The horizon was clean. He'd been gone long enough to shoot the Colt without him hearing, but the Sharps was ten times that pistol.

Noah had the rifle over his shoulder, a hand on the barrel just like a man. He pointed to the trout and spat. He was feeling rich with that rifle, and dwelling in the pleasure. Wasn't everyday a Harney felt rich.

"Best take a lay," I told him. "You won't hit the county shooting on the fly."

"You be quiet. Don't forget I'm your big

brother and thereby boss of you." He held the rifle to his shoulder but it was too much gun for him. He grew tired and let it down. He nodded at a spot of dirt. "Been figuring on this place as a shooting bench for some time."

We went about looking for worthy targets. Soon enough I caught a flash of pewter on the far side. Then a coyote come out from the sage. In them days wolves and lions and bears was a regular sight and a coyote wasn't nothing more special than a common tumbleweed. I pointed him out to Noah and Noah set to breathing hard. I could see the barrel moving with his chest. He was touching the rifle too firm and in too many places.

Pa didn't grip the rifle, he folded his body into a platform the rifle could set upon. Before he shot he took a big breath and let it halfway go. He squeezed with the tip of his finger. He let the rifle do the work, was always surprised by the kick. One night he said to Noah and I didn't forget, "Don't shoot for the critter, shoot for a single barb of fur."

When Noah missed I said, "My turn."

"Shut that yap of yours, making my bullet stray."

We listened to the blast still echoing back from the mountains.

For me it was the sound of dreaming. Most nights I went shooting. Sleep slowed it down. I could see the lead in the air, how it fell up through the sight's line and then down through a second time on the way to the earth.

"Should've brought an extra casing," he said.

I showed him the one in my hand.

"Give me that. Dog near on got away already."

"Only 'cause you missed," I said. "You got a turn and now I get a turn. Or I tell."

"This ain't no schoolhouse. We ain't taking turns. I'll —" I didn't let him finish. I knew sooner or later he'd wrestle me and take the casing for his own self. I wasn't no match for him body to body. So I give him a quick fist in the armpit to settle things now, and he set about whining and rubbing and I took the rifle as my own.

I caught a fist to the shoulder but I kept the Sharps. His punch sent lightning across my body, but it was less blow than the rifle was about to deliver.

"Waste of a cartridge," he muttered.

I reloaded like I seen Pa do. By then the coyote was onto us. He ran to the top of the ridge above the lake, another two hundred yards on what was already a long shot. There between clumps of short sage he turned for a last look and I settled on a dark patch behind his shoulder. Except I elevated for the distance and shifted a touch for the wind. In truth I had no desire to kill him, coyote meat ain't nothing worth skinning for. My only desire was for a target, and to hear that rifle's voice echoing back, louder than mine could ever be.

When the rifle bucked Noah said, "You missed," before I even recovered. It was the kick of a mule for a child. I thought I might be dying, but then my breath come back and my ears started singing. I wiped the water knocked out of my eyes and looked and saw nothing but light.

Noah was looking off at where the coyote had gone. "That bastard," he said. "Bastard" was one of Pa's words. He'd leveled it on the dentist when the man run low on the syrup.

I was rubbing at the welt forming on my shoulder from the recoil. The skin would go purple and then brown and then yellow before giving way to my dusty. I had Ma's color, more than Noah.

We didn't hear the horse until she was near on us. Pa had heard the first shot and assumed a raid. His Colt was drawn.

Noah took the Sharps for himself. He stood and held it at his side. That was my brother protecting me.

Pa's jaw went hard at the sight of us by the lake. He charged nearer. He come off his mare before she stopped and flipped the Colt so he had it by the barrel. I saw the wilderness in his eyes then and knew what was coming. Noah must've known too. But he didn't flee. He blocked the blow but it was little use. He fell to his knees and blood spilled from a split in his ear. That wound would never heal right and remained in evidence long as I knew him.

I understand now but at the time I didn't. I only saw the cruelty of it. Hitting a boy with an open hand was one thing. Hitting him with a pistol butt was another thing entire. But see, Pa was trying to right his fear the only way he knew how.

He kicked away some paces. He cursed his mare for eating while saddled. She trotted off and turned to inspect her rider. She raised her tail and took a shit. Ol' Sis was his mare's name. Smartest horse that ever lived. She had her own manner of conversing.

Noah was wiping at his tears with one hand and pressing his bleeding head with the other.

Pa come back for us and at first I was unsure of his intentions.

He took down his hat and knelt beside us. He touched Noah's ear and rubbed the blood between his fingers. "I . . . I ain't this man."

Noah turned from him.

Pa sat in the dirt with us. He wore a red beard in them days, the cheeks gone gray. He rubbed the soil between his hands and it carried off in the wind. "This life has a habit of reducing a man."

I tried to speak but no words come. I was still red with anger at him for cutting down my big brother, and now I was madder yet to see him cutting down himself. I would've preferred he stay righteous and free and wrong.

"I lived a different life before I come here," Pa said. "That ain't no excuse but maybe someday you'll understand. The bad things that happened to a man can get between him and his now."

Noah watched Pa. I don't reckon he felt nothing but heat.

Pa said, "Well, ain't you going say nothing? Or you finally short on words?"

Noah spat and said, "The Lord sees what you've done."

"I hope that's so." Pa stood from us and cleared his throat and spat. He offered Noah a hand to his feet, but Noah didn't take it.

Pa put in a plug of tobacco. He looked in his pouch. He handed his pouch to his boy. After a time, Noah reached up and took it and put in a plug.

They both spat.

Pa's eyes inspected the Sharps in his hand. "Well, did you hit something? Don't look on me sidelong. I shouldn't have struck you, but you sure as shit shouldn't have gone and took this here rifle without my approvals. I figured you was getting took by reds."

I said without thinking, "Noah done hit a yote. Looked square to my eye. Five hundred yards easy."

Noah turned to me. He could've corrected my words.

Pa studied the slope. "Where in particular?"

I pointed to the place on the ridge where I took my shot. Pa pulled off his hat and wiped the sweat from his forehead. He spat. "You been shooting regular when I'm not around?"

He was asking Noah. I thought about the lead I'd sent into this countryside.

"Gonna do it again?"

"No, sir." Noah's answer was but a whisper.

Pa brushed clean his hat and put it back on his head. "Girl, you best get on laundry. Son, you go dig a hole."

"What do we need a hole for?"

"We don't. Once it's as deep as your naval, put the dirt back. Think about your wrong while you's at it."

From the open doorway I saw Pa riding along the ridge, up where I had missed the coyote. I was troubled by how easy I had lied to my pa. Seemed a lie should burn you on the way out.

I set about boiling water for the laundry. I wasn't done stoking up the stove when Pa come back holding that coyote by the hind legs, a bloody swath of hide at its middle and a string of maroon from its nose.

"Boy!" he called, happy now.

Noah come around the corner with the shovel and saw that dog. By then I was standing in the sun. Noah and I shared a look of bewilderment.

Pa hit him on the back. "Nice work, son. That was an uphill three seventy-five. And this ain't an easy wind neither. You done hit something for once! I'm still mad as hell, and you shouldn't have done what you done, but that don't mean . . . Well, maybe there's still hope for you anyhow."

Noah could've said it was my shot but he didn't. He didn't say nothing. He just looked at that dog dangling at Pa's side. It might've been the closest Pa ever come to saying he was proud of Noah. I'm glad he kept that one for himself.

"Well, best get to skinning him down. And cut it small, girl. Remember yote got a chew to it." He looked at the sun. "I best get on if I'm to catch that bastard dentist."

Pa rode off and I was left with the fact. I done hit my mark with the Sharps! Pure luck, but that didn't matter. There comes a holy rightness after a bull's-eye, and the first one is a downright revelation.

I took that glee to Ingrid, my mare.

Ingrid was broke about the time I was ready to ride. Noah joked we come up sharing a tit. We was like siblings in some manner, reckon. We was the only two girls out there minus the heifers and Ol' Sis, Ingrid's ma.

She was a pinto, chestnut and white, but smaller than her mother, a stout thirteen hands. Her sire was an Indian pony and he blessed her with dark hooves, which are harder than light hooves and so less prone to cracking on rock. She was strong in the hindquarters and quick as a bear on the uphill. We didn't always get along on account she was stubborn like me but we understood each other.

When the work was done we roamed. We both liked the same places, the antelope meadows on the mountainside, the thin ridges where falcons perched, the hollow along a creek bend. In spring wildflowers spread their blankets across meadows and we could ride all day without hitting an end. It was a land between stories then and when Ingrid and me come together we wrote our own.

I rarely had to rope Ingrid or hobble her, even on the trail in the years to follow. If I had me an apple or a handful of huckleberries I'd give her half. If she wanted to go someplace she'd invite me along. She wouldn't leave me no sooner than I'd leave her. We knew each other's minds, and she knew I carried feed if I was wearing a smile.

The day I hit the yote, she whinnied when she saw me coming. I delivered carrots from the garden and told her the whole thing. She chewed and bent to lip fallen pieces from the dirt and then raised her head to look eye to eye with me. She half blinked. She put her nose to my cheek and drew a breath.

That was the way between us. We could just stand together, without a chore.

In time Noah and Pa quit talking but to fight. It grew through the winter. The next April I found my brother in the barn holding a bedroll thick with a winter's coat. He was sixteen. "You can't leave."

"Who says I'm leaving?" Noah took a plug and offered me one, so I knew I had him pegged. He was generous when trying to change the subject. Noah spat. "He is dim and mean and I'm afraid of what I might do the next time he gets stupid on that syrup. The Lord don't intend a father to be dim."

"He ain't dim."

"He is, and you'll see it your own self. Dim and selfish and mean as hell. And a fool for his syrup."

I spat out the plug and swore off tobacco forever. "Don't leave," I said with heart, on account I knew this might be my one chance to keep us together. "Brother, don't leave me."

"You'll be fine. You always pick him anyhow."

I took hold his bedroll. He held it between us. "I pick you."

He looked on me and I could tell he hadn't thought of it from my eyes. He crossed the barn to the tack wall.

41

"I pick you, brother. Please."

I must've convinced him, or he was shy of hitting the trail alone, because come supper, Noah was still with us.

Might've been better if he'd left, in truth.

Over the next year they had some good days, but mostly their arguing turned to hollering. They took to moving about each other, one near the house, the other out on the range. At supper it would be me and Pa. Noah come around after to get his. Noah started going to town and staying overnight. When he come back, he hid his eyes from Pa. He didn't look down at the man's scoldings like he had as a boy. Now when Pa lectured him, my big brother looked off in the distance like he wasn't even hearing.

On the night of their last fight I was the one who said they had to sit together. It was supper time and Noah was fixing to go to town. There was heavy clouds toward the west. "It ain't right for kin to eat apart. Ma would say so, so I'm saying so."

Pa come to the table first. Noah pulled out his bench without a word. He put his hat on his knee and took out his knife for cutting the meat. He checked its blade. Noah was a man now and about to leave his home for all time. He poured himself milk.

I reckon Noah was intending to pick a fight, that's why he brought up the fence. He said we needed barbed wire to police the boundary between us and the neighbors. The Mormons was doing well for themselves, and now they had more land and a bigger herd and their cattle kept wandering up our way and eating our graze and drinking from our lake. With the drought the lake was shrinking each year, and we got to worrying it might dry up entire. We wasn't keen on sharing our family water with Mormon cattle.

This would've been our first fence. We heard about them in town regular now. The merchants was always trying to sell you barbed wire. Great rolls of it sat under tarpaulins behind the store. Noah repeated what the salesman at the mercantile had said: "It ain't yours if it ain't fenced."

Pa let his spoon fall into his bowl.

Noah waited. "Ain't you gonna say nothing?"

Pa looked on him. His voice was slow as syrup. "Words don't do shit. That's what you ain't learned yet. You will. Trust me. World turns on blood. Just hope you learn that an easy way, since you working so hard not to learn it from me."

"I got more than words," Noah said.

"What you know about this business you learned your own damn self and wasn't taught by me? Or in the fat-chewing at the mercantile? What fool believes the wisdom of a salesman, huh? You's in a man's britches, but that's about all."

"You's too dim to know that you dim."

"What'd you say?"

Noah finished his milk. "Sheriff Younger is getting a fence."

"That ain't what you said. Younger ain't all he thinks he is. You ain't neither."

"Younger got a spread three times the size of this one. Everybody got a spread bigger than this one. What do you think *you* is? From looking around, ain't much of a cattleman." Noah said it but he couldn't look Pa in the eye when he done so.

I knew Noah always believed Pa should be the big rancher in our valley. His heat rose from disappointment.

Pa pushed back from the table. "Boy, you best —"

"I ain't a boy," Noah said. "I'm seventeen. Maybe if you put that 'medicine' aside a time you might actually make something of this place, ever consider that?"

Pa's face dawned red. "Don't talk about my medicine."

"You a drunkard for the stuff. Look at you."

Pa's bowl slid across the table and into Noah's lap. Golden stock I'd spent the day making. Noah was up and back from the table and wearing a stranger's face. I knew enough to get out their way.

Noah was full size by then, taller than Pa. His beard wasn't in yet but he was strong in

44

his shoulders. When the cattle had gone to sale that autumn Pa bought Noah a Colt of his very own with some of the money even though there wasn't no money extra if you counted it. I know Pa wanted a pistol like that for his own self and he could've handed one of his down to Noah and taken the new one, but he didn't.

Noah had gotten himself into a fair number of rumbles on his trips to town. I had tended to his swollen knuckles and split brows and so I knew my brother was no stranger to fists. I had no doubt Pa would take him, it was only a matter of how much damage might be done before that certain outcome. I went for the aid supplies.

Pa seized Noah by the collar and drug him across the table. They went down in a clatter of boots and wood and the table come down after them. The stew was lost to the dirt. A leg of the table broke clean off.

Pa was on top and drove his fists into Noah's chest. The chest is nowhere to wear down your fists, but he couldn't hit his boy's face. Noah rolled him quick.

He clocked Pa with an elbow. There was fumbling of arms and grunts both ways and then Noah clocked him again with that elbow. It was a dirty trick, one he'd picked up in an alley. Brother got one hand pressing on Pa's cheek, and the other coming back to hit. I saw the blow would be square to the temple.

The punch come down on Pa's head with a hollow crack, and then Pa went soft under Noah. It was done. A lesson in how quick this life can change.

Noah stood. He tripped on Pa's limp legs and fell hard onto the floor. He righted himself and looked back upon our old man who still had yet to move. He shook out the fist that done the damage.

Noah's eyes was full of water now and he wiped the tears before they could run. He stepped back until the wall caught him. Pa still hadn't moved but he was breathing.

I shook him. "Pa? Please. Pa, hear me. Pa?" I turned my heat on Noah. "What'd you do? What'd you go and hit him for?"

Pa moaned and sat partway up. Then sank back. I could see his eyes wasn't right. There wasn't much blood but he was hurt all the same. I put my hand under his head to soften the ground. I took my apron and put it under his neck. He looked up at the ceiling and blinked. He looked at me but I don't reckon he saw me.

Noah turned away. He seemed to be taken by something then, taken somewhere else. "Help me," I begged.

Instead he seized his new Colt and belted on the holster. He set about grabbing things from the cabin, his sleeping things, his coat. He found his knife upon the floor and put it back to his belt. He did all this without look-

46

ing at us. He went to great effort to avoid turning his eyes toward where his family lie on the floor.

It was dark out and windy and not much in the way of moonlight, but he put on his hat and his riding jacket and pushed open the door. He had his saddlebags slung over his shoulder. That bedroll under an arm. He stopped there and turned and his eyes found mine. Noah said to me in a whisper, "I am sorry, sister."

When the door fell shut between us, I heard his feet on gravel outside, quick and away.

He come out the barn at a full run. The last I seen of my brother for five and a half years was him in moonlight, leaning forward into the speed. Around the bend and only the sound of hooves disappearing.

Pa's eye was filling with blood when he got up and sat before the fire. With some shaky effort he packed a pipe. The table was still overturned and I saw then one of the bowls was broke. I set about cleaning up.

Pa finally said, "Where's my boy?"

I brought a wet rag to his swollen temple. I put my hand to the center of his back and said, "Does it hurt?"

"What happened?" Pa muttered. He asked it like a boy asks his mother a question.

I sat beside him. I leaned my head on his shoulder. He didn't put his arm around me like typical. He only looked into the guts of the fire. "It'll be okay, Pa. I promise."

When I woke in the morning the house was empty and the door was ajar. The dawn light was coming in orange. The Sharps was missing from its pegs on the wall. I rose and walked out and saw Pa on his horse as he rode the last yards over the horizon to the north, the opposite direction of Noah's tracks.

I hoped Pa had taken the day to check on the cattle and maybe hunt up some new meat. I hoped this meant he awoke well and intended to ride off his heat. Pa used to ride off his heat regular, sometimes twice in a day.

Ingrid and me took a long roundabout that morning, an aimless and fast ride. Speed always set the two of us right. Ingrid wanted to ride to a marsh where the mud smelled like cheese and so we did. It was a place Noah liked to hunt for deer, he come often to sit on the hill in wait. I took off her saddle once there and she heaved over on her side and then her back and twisted, her feet bent toward the sky. She lay on her side breathing. I took a perch on a rock.

Ingrid rolled and come to her feet. She walked near me and put her nose to my neck. Mud dripped from her mane and slid in gritty sheets down her legs.

"You reckon he coming back?" My mind was on my brother.

She nudged me and I put my arm up under her chin and knuckled right where she liked. She huffed, and then nipped at the nearby flowers.

When Pa come home that evening he rode into the barn and turned his mare out, and when he come up to the step he didn't ask nothing about his boy. There was a bulb of purple on his temple and his lip was so swollen he had trouble spatting. There was spittle down his shirt on account. The blood in his eye had turned brown.

"Howdy, Pa."

"Dear."

He sat down beside me and patted my knee. The bottom lid of that hurt eye hung low. This wasn't my pa's face.

"You feeling right?"

"Found them bulls near the forks."

"Them critters do like to travel," I said. It was his own words fed back. When he didn't finish the thought, I did. "They was buffalo once, before men got their hands on them."

He shrugged.

I asked him of the changing weather, when the rains might stop for summer. He didn't offer much for answers. When I served up our supper, Pa said without looking, "Good grub."

"Thanks, Pa."

It was still light when he poured a mouthful of syrup and laid back in his bed. He still had on his riding clothes. I had never seen him in bed in his dusty old riding clothes.

"Night, darling."

"Night, Pa."

Pa got to snoring in that particular manner brought on by the medicine. I put his quilt about him. I tidied up some and then put on a pot of water and bathed my face in it.

In the darkness after, I allow myself a few tears.

Pa and me spent those summer evenings sitting on the porch after supper and watching down the road even when the thunderheads hid the stars and lightning sparked on the ridges. Neither of us said what we was waiting on or even that we was waiting. We didn't speak his name. I was afraid to say it. "Want your medicine, Pa?"

I took to helping him with it. I was helping him a lot now. Helping meant we shared something.

One night like so many others I poured a tin cup of the black syrup. He took it and swallowed and sat back and shut his eyes to this world. I thought he was on his way to sleep. Then he said out the yonder, "We'll get you married off."

I had just started bleeding. It had come on sudden as such things is wont to do. I awoke one morning to the shock of it and Pa told me to clean up and put a rag in my drawers and he saddled up Ol' Sis and Ingrid and we rode on down to the Mormon's house. The Mormon ma had answered and they exchanged some private words and she looked at me sidelong and nodded. She put an arm around me and took me in the house and led me to the wash bin so she could keep on working as we talked. Her children played in the field and her eyes flashed over them. She explained God's purpose for my body and told me how to manage the flow. She had said, "This is your burden as a woman. This is your privilege. God entrusts us with His holiest work." When I left, she put her hand to my shoulder and squeezed.

Now I said to Pa, "What use do I got for a husband?"

His eyes opened. The left one hung low as it always done after the blow. I could see the effect of the medicine on his gaze. "You've missed some womanly opportunities in this life. I done the best I knowed how but I'm failing you, girl. It's time you move from me. I'll just make you old."

"Don't talk like that, Pa."

"A husband will tend to you. A husband will look out for you best."

"I ain't leaving you, so don't waste your breath."

There was quiet for a time and again I

thought him to be asleep. His voice stirred me. "Boys sometime or other fight their old man. It's the order of the world. I'm only sorry you had to bear witness. I'm sorry I wasn't keen enough to settle it before it rose up like it done. I ain't been much of a man."

"He is in the wrong," I explained. I'd been waiting months to say it. "He forgot his place. You ain't got nothing to apologize for."

"Boys need to earn their own trust. That's the way of this world. Same way that says a girl ought to be married and tending to her own children, not her old man. Your ma wouldn't have you become a spinster."

I considered what he was telling me between the words he was saying. "We need another man on the spread, is that it?"

Pa shrugged. "Some truth to that. But I want you to marry off. Rosa was never as happy as the days we arrived here together. That's what I want for you."

Her name from his lips shook me. "I'll do better, Pa. I'll do more. This here's my place. Beside you. Don't make me leave."

He didn't answer. He had drank more syrup and now his eyes was shut. I touched his shoulder but he didn't stir. I put my fingers to his nose to ensure he was breathing. I covered him in the quilt.

Pa took two bottles of medicine with him that autumn when it was time to ride to market, and we drove our steers to the new rail line where we sold them in an afternoon at auction. I watched as rail men loaded the animals into a steel container bound for hungry mouths to the east. We wasn't players here. Nobody turned to watch us pass. Some cowboys no older than Noah rode all the way from Texas with a thousand head. Pa leaned against the chute and looked over those longhorns. He watched them until each one was loaded and then he listened as they kicked in the cars. The last time we was here, Noah was telling stories.

I pulled his arm. "Come, Pa. Let me warm you up some grub."

He looked down to me but I wasn't sure he saw me.

Cowboys was hollering, loose on the liquor they bought with their earnings.

"Come, Pa."

"Them boys only drove those cattle and they still walking with more than us." He squinted against a pair of them pissing where they stood in the street. "I'm taking you out. We got something to spend, and damn us if we won't blow every cent."

These words scared me, but I wasn't of no mind to contradict him.

He took me out for my first ever supper cooked by a stranger. It was roast pork with honey sauce. He ordered us each a whiskey. I laughed at the burn in my throat and swore off the stuff for life. Pa thought that was funny and finished mine. A fiddle player started in the corner and Pa watched the man and ordered another whiskey. He didn't speak a word during the three tunes that man played, and when the musician come around the tables for coins Pa give him a whole dollar.

Pa studied me a time. "She'd be pleased by the sight of you," he said like we'd been talking of Ma this whole time. "She'd be proud at the woman you is."

"Pa. I'm only thirteen."

The folks at the next table paid their bill and stood and their chairs scuffed the floor. It was three men, all of them Pa's age and one of them still wearing his Yankee cap though it'd gone brown with years and dust. This man stared until Pa met his eyes. Pa tipped his head in the greeting of a hard man who ain't sure of the specimen before him.

The Yankee put in a plug. He offered one to Pa. I knew Pa wanted tobacco in that moment but he waved it off. He wasn't the kind to make himself beholden to a stranger.

The Yankee looked on me. He said to Pa, "Remember the trick shooters that come through the camps in the war?" He must've noticed some evidence of the war in Pa's face or manner.

Pa didn't answer.

"Ever hear of Straight-Eye Susan? Better

than anybody who come through the camps. Shooting tonight across town. Why don't you bring your daughter and join us? We got a bottle."

"Trick shooters don't interest us," Pa said. It was a plain lie, but I saw why he said it. Something about this man had Pa on guard. Something about the way he said 'daughter' raised the hair on my neck.

The Yankee shrugged and followed his friends through the batwing doors. Pa watched him go and said, "Susan sure a funny name for a trick shooter. What kind father name his boy Susan?"

We found a wide glowing tent on the edge of town with a crowd at the door. We could hear the merriment of a hundred people inside, all loud and drunk on their earnings. "How much?" Pa asked when it was our turn at the door. He paid the three dollars without complaint and I felt sick at the thought of so much money spent in so short a time and on nothing more permanent than spectacle.

Straight-Eye Susan wasn't no man, of course. She was a woman some years past marrying age wearing a white dress with flowers embroidered on it and a showman's hat and a golden revolver to match the golden action of her Winchester repeater. The men in the crowd called at her and said things they might only say to a whore, and she picked these men from the audience and dared them to stand still while she shot matches from their teeth and casings from their hats. Not a taunt rose from the crowd after that.

Straight-Eye Susan shot plates from the air, first one, then two, and then four. She shot the rifle behind her with a mirror affixed to its stock. She shot high and low and quick and steady and shot and never missed and all the while she joked with us, and about us, like she was too big to be reduced by anyone. At the end she took free her hat and curtsied and the men leapt to their feet in applause.

After, Pa and me walked back into the night air and he guessed what I was thinking. "Don't you go getting no notions."

"About what, Pa?" I played the dumber.

"That ain't no life for a woman. Even if you could learn to shoot you wouldn't never be able to talk like she done. Dirty mouth like that. A crowd of faces looking at you. You a ranch girl, a wife, someday a ma. Them is good things, them is the best things. Shooting ain't no life for females."

"Yessir."

Pa never again practiced with his pistols.

I on the other hand waited until I was sure the medicine had taken Pa into sleep and then rose and stoked up the fire for light and practiced what I'd seen. I practiced even though I knew I was to be a ranch wife in this valley and wouldn't never have cause to know such skills. I practiced because I knew in my bones I could do what she done. Sometimes when it got real late I gave in a touch to the fanciful notion of Straight-Eye Jessilyn. "As quick with her tongue as she is with her revolvers, and at home anywhere she can find a target."

Come the snows I awoke earlier and dressed against the cold and started in on the chores Noah would've done. I began each day at the lake breaking open a patch of ice so the cattle could get at the water. In the barn I milked our heifer and checked for a stray egg or two among the cold chickens. Then I forked hay in a path for the cattle. The bright ones trotted in for first bites while the sad few got to the hay late, and so I led the healthy ones away with fresh forkfuls and then returned to give the sickly feed of their own and time to eat it.

Some nights I heard wolves and cattle stomping the earth and rose in the dark to holler at the darting shapes of dogs. By firelight I mended the leather works with a hand punch and rawhide.

Mostly Pa just sucked for breath from his bed.

A blizzard hit on Christmas night and the snows kept on for eight days. Pa and I was pinned inside with only our minds. I tried to distract him from his medicine with games and stories. It was of little use.

He took the syrup in surprising pours and thereby hastened its shortage. The day it finally depleted he stormed the house as if I had hid bottles from him. He cursed me, then he cursed the Lord for laying snows so deep, then he cursed the sky for listening to the Lord. This was Pa at his smallest.

He set off into the winds despite my pleading for him to wait. He and Ol' Sis was turned back before the edge of our land by drifts so deep the old mare couldn't push on. He had to climb off her and lead her to the barn. Pa come back inside and stomped off the snow and said things that I will do him the favor of not repeating here.

A sickness come over him in the day after and he shook and dripped and cursed. I couldn't get him to take no sustenance. I understood then why he was so set on that medicine.

The sickness passed before the snows cleared. When a warm spell opened the road, he spent a long morning looking toward town. He was eating again, and done shaking. He called me close. "I want you to go," he said. "This house needs things and I figure you best learn how to dicker."

It was true we best stock up before the next snow, and I understood why he wanted to avoid going anywhere near that dentist. He handed me the Colt. "Keep this in your bag and don't take it out unless you intend to use it."

"Yessir."

He then took some care explaining how the sights worked and how I had to remember to aim before pulling the trigger. "It's so heavy!" I played my part.

I waited for dawn before setting out on the half-day ride. It was my first travel off the ranch by my lonesome. I will admit I rode with the Colt in my hand pretending to be a gunfighter on the way to a rich bank. I took aim at birds that flushed and imagined them to be bandits. I didn't shoot it off, not once. Even then I knew how quick my life might come to depend on a single ball of lead.

At the mercantile I found my tongue for haggling by imagining Straight-Eye Susan was doing the talking. At home I was quiet on account that's how I imagined Ma to be. And because Noah had filled every crevice with five words before I might muster one. But here I was flush with the knowledge of the Colt in my jacket, and words come tumbling out with rhythm and order. When the shopkeep high-priced the goods, I cut his words short and his eyes widened in surprise. I liked how he looked at me then, like he didn't know what I might do next. Men always seem to think they know what a girl is thinking. What Straight-Eye Susan showed me was that seeing men unsure is its own fast horse.

But then the shopkeep would not hand over my bill of sale. I tried to take it yet he held fast. His moustache was yellowed and his teeth was rotten in the gums. "You act like you something but I know you. You just a mushhead's daughter. Your coward Pa ain't no better than a Chinaman for that syrup."

The pistol was so close and I wanted to see this man on his knees, begging forgiveness, kissing my pa's boots, and taking it all back.

I swiped the bill from his hand. I folded and tucked it in a pocket and heaved up my saddlebags from the floor. "Bastard."

"Such a waste for your kin to sit on all that water. Everybody says so. A shame, they say, a mushhead and his half-breed daughter wasting that fertile spread. That land should be putting out two hundred steers a year easy. There's a dozen men in this town better than your pa who ain't getting no lucky breaks. So don't you come in here acting like you some queen."

On the ride back I felt the world as if for the first time, big and in all directions and with its cruel eye on me.

I didn't tell Pa nothing about what the shopkeep said. I tried to put it out my mind. But his words lingered like grease smoke sticks in your nose, tainting smells long after. When I looked on Pa from then on I was fighting to hold on to the man I remembered, not the man they scorned.

Things improved for a time after Pa quit the medicine. He was up by daybreak again and out tending to chores. He was always the last to sleep, which impeded my pistol play, but I enjoyed pulling Ma's quilt over my ear and falling asleep to the sight of him and his pipe before the fire. By day his eye still hung low and his conversations at times revealed ravines inside his thoughts, but he was my pa and he was out trying again and we come into a rhythm of our own. I figured it would go on like that forever, and one day Noah would return with a wife, and we'd set to building this place up together.

The spring of my fourteenth year I drug out Ma's chest. I felt Pa's eyes on me when I did. When its top opened he said, "There ain't nothing in there." As if I hadn't studied its contents hundreds of times in his absence. "Go on, put it back."

I lifted the Bible and showed it to him. "A woman best know the Good Book better than the men in her life." It was his own truth and he couldn't refute it.

He looked to the book. "Come on then. I'm a bit rusty myself."

That was the first night of many we spent before the fire working on our words. He gave me a letter at a time, and soon I could sound through a stubby word, and then a long one, and then I could piece a few together. The first sentence I ever read on my own was, "Let there be light."

By summer we was rolling, half a page a night working together. It was the joy I looked forward to all day, being close to Pa and figuring the sounds and meanings together. The first work I ever done that didn't require sweat and scuff. I thought I might have a skill for words, though Pa never said as much.

Summer got busy and Pa give up on the effort of learning. I didn't hold it against him. He preferred to smoke his pipe on the porch and listen to the darkness settle upon the desert. A cattleman works his body hard all summer and ain't got much left come those purple evenings. I took to reading the book myself in candlelight. Sometimes I read it out loud just to hear the words. I carried them all day like music to my chores. My thoughts dwelled with kings and floods and men wandering the desert and who begot who. I liked Moses best, I liked how he led those in his keeping. He was always so sure the Lord was on his side, and not playing him as the fool.

What I read troubled me too. One night over supper I asked Pa about Genesis. "It say here, 'The imagination of man's heart is evil from his youth.' Does the Lord really believe that?"

Pa hung over his bowl of grub. "A girl shouldn't be thinking so heavy." He spooned up a bite and chewed.

I ate. I ate and then I asked, "How come we don't go to church? Huh, Pa? Everybody go to church, even the injuns got church. I ain't intending to be contrary. I just wonder is all. We got something against church? Or is it the Lord we got issue with?"

Pa's eyes found mine. "We got issue with men. There's a shortage of answers in this world. It's the fool who thinks he got them."

Autumn turned to winter and winter to spring and Pa got three months older for every one that passed. He was slowing down and his slips was commonplace now, two or three a day when he seemed to be waking up from some dream that was only his. One time I come into the house to find him looking into the ceiling. He didn't answer at his name. I believed him dead for a moment, and then his eyes blinked and he said, "Just resting, dear." I checked his old places for a bottle of syrup but didn't find none.

Around Pa there wasn't no dodging talk of husbands now. I was fifteen, though my body wasn't growing much curve. The marrying talk come most days, sometimes morning and night. "We'll get you fancied up and go into town and show you off," he said. "Won't take a hour to find you a man." I would nod and say my yessirs and then proceed with my chores like regular.

I had been to town enough times to know men didn't turn to look on me. I wasn't nothing that held their fancy. That troubled me some, but not in the manner it should. I wasn't turning to look at no men neither. I was turning to look at their sidearms.

We was up to forty-eight head in my sixteenth autumn, the last autumn we was together. The garden was taller than ever and the chickens was laying two eggs a day apiece. The fowl was less on the lake, just as there was less lake, but still we ate goose and duck as much as beefsteak and pork. I was tall for a girl and my muscles was strong through the shoulders like Noah's had been. My voice too was deep, I thought. When Pa was around I tried my best to sound girl-like. When he was gone I let myself be.

What I knew by then was a woman is her place. Straight-Eye Susan was the big tent with all them people watching, and I was our valley. For all the talk of marriage I didn't give the notion much credence. Marrying meant moving onto another man's spread, and I didn't intend to become anybody new.

The last time I spoke with Pa was the morning before he set out for the high country to bring back our wayward head. It was a morning like every one before it. I cooked us eggs in lard and potatoes. Pa's beard was more gray than rust now. His low-hanging eye had taken to watering continually and out of habit he wiped it with his knuckle between bites.

"Patch that coop while I'm gone, can you?" Pa asked.

"Yessir." I was glad he remembered the coop. It needed work.

"Leave it another week and we'll wake up with a bobcat shitting one of our hens."

I laughed at the curse. Pa smiled with me, and I was grateful to see some lightness in his eyes.

After breakfast I followed him outside. He put on his hat and slid the Sharps into the scabbard on Ol' Sis's saddle. Her spine drooped with age now and her hips punched at flesh. He would need a new riding horse come market, if there was money for one.

He turned to me. The sun was warm against our cheeks. "Might be a night," he said. "Not two."

"I'll have hot grub when you come over the ridge."

He looked off toward them mountains. In the months after I wondered if maybe he suspected his end was near. "The war took me when I was your age and my brother a

65

year younger. It took all the men from our valley."

"Yessir. I remember. Sixty-one. You was in the field with a rake when word come of Sumter."

"Good." I saw he was about to quiz my knowledge. Pa had again taken up his histories of the war. He talked of it regular. I had genuine interest because I saw my father on every battlefield, and understood each fight to be a window onto this man I still could not decipher. He asked, "What started the war?"

"Sir, the first shots was really in Kansas in the fifties. And the war was all but certain when Lincoln took office." These was his own words but I could see he wasn't pleased.

"No. What started it? That's what matters."

I thought on that point. I could remember all manner of queer detail of that war fought in forests and pastures I would never see.

"Slaves? Who was going to make the rules? I guess I don't reckon. . . ."

He wiped his leaky eye and I saw his hand was shaking.

"Pa?"

"Every one of us believed he'd come home bigger than when he left. The war was like the start of forever to us. A desert and all we had to do was cross it and all the green on the other side would be just for us, and forever. My brother and me stayed up nights in worry it'd be over before we got our chance. My brother and me." Now he wiped at tears.

My hair stood. He was before me but a thousand miles gone. "What started the war, Pa?"

His eyes settled on me. "Stories, Jessilyn. We tell ourselves the wrong stories."

He didn't come home the next day. I started searching the day after but the tracks was smoothed by the hard winds of the previous night.

Took till day six. I found Ol' Sis by vultures. Ingrid and me was moving through some sage when she got to throwing her head and trotting sidelong. "There, girl," I patted, but she snorted and looked off into the timber and backed in that stiff way of hers. I swung down and walked into the smell and found Ol' Sis a short distance in the timber, near devoured. The ravens come off and rest in the trees overhead and made a racket and the vultures rose from their perches into the winds above. A magpie saw the opening and swept down and landed on her ribs. I shooed him off and threw a stick at him and cursed his race.

There was sign from what you'd expect, coyote and bear, but I also saw a lion track. Lions ain't prone to scavenging, so I reckoned her end was swift. There wasn't no evidence of Pa.

I backtracked Ol' Sis and found where the lion had got her and saw she had been dragging a broke leg before that.

I took to hollering his name. I took up running every which way like some manner of fool.

A mile back I come across what was left. The story was written out in the tracks.

They come down out of the timber at a trot and to the edge of a great expanse of broken rock, black and sharp and laid out like spilled glass. Couldn't take a step anywhere on it without a rock rolling underfoot. It was raw earth, the last land the Lord made. Pa's choice was to risk a crossing or trace its edge for some miles. He aimed for the narrowest stretch and made the wrong choice. That's how it happens in this life, in a quiet moment.

I imagine it was getting on evening and he was tired and Ol' Sis was smelling the creek on the far side. A rock probably rolled and her leg broke and he went down. His skull was broke. Maybe she rolled over him.

I had got to Pa too late. Animals don't eat hair, about the only thing. They drug him off in all directions, it was on me to find him and put him back. It was on me to collect him. It was all on me.

I try to focus on the Sharps. The rock had

left parallel lines and sharp gouges in the metal. Engraved on the barrel was ".54 caliber." It had the peep sight installed by the Union army. I put Pa's rifle to my cheek. The wood was polished smooth where his skin had held it for a lifetime.

There wasn't nothing to do but bury him under stone. I know Pa would've liked being nearer to Ma.

My hands bled from the black glass that deepened over him. My blood was in smears and drips among his tattered clothing and gnawed bones. I buried Pa in rock.

I remember the first snows was falling when I finished, dry flakes from charcoal skies. The land had lost its water and was ten shades of dry.

Ingrid put her nose to my ear, and I rested against her. We was alone now, together.

Without my brother there, what choice did I have but to go to town to get myself married? I couldn't run the land by myself. It was part a matter of hands. My two wasn't enough. The cattle had spread far and we would be missing the market next week. Things was careening toward desperate.

I washed up proper and braided my hair. My first attempts was a touch loose for courting work so I done them again. When Pa had seen Ma he knew right out she was the one for him. He saw something in her form that stirred him deep, that's how he talked of it. I looked over myself in my finery and with my hands clean of dust and wondered if a man might see something worth keeping in me.

I started at the sheriff's office. Sheriff Younger, he was nothing of the sort. Grayed and old enough to remember when St. Louis was a frontier town. I didn't go there to ask for his hand, I figured a sheriff would know every boy and man in the county and could steer a gal in the right direction. I told Sheriff Younger simple, Pa had sent me to inquire about marriage.

"Your pa wants you married off?" The sheriff sorted some papers before him. "What kind of suffering is you?"

"I'm no suffering at all, sir. I'm damn fast with supper and at churning and I hold my own with the ranch work. I keep our garden free of varmints and I jar venison with a touch. I never had no ma so I've been doing the woman things since I could walk. I'll make a man a damn hardy wife."

"You got quick words about you."

I shrugged. "I like to read."

"Is that so?" Younger was old but his eyes hunted me and his age did not diminish his size. I looked into him trying to decide if I could trust him.

"Some men like a woman who can read, some don't." He lit a cigar. He leaned back in his chair and looked out his big window. It

70

was the biggest window in town. A sheriff needed a big window to see trouble riding by. He smoked and I glanced about his office looking for some sense of his person. "Why didn't your old man come down here his own darn self? I never heard of such a thing."

"It's just the two of us and it's market season. Ain't time for him to meddle with my future."

"Typical father wants a hand in choosing his heir, especially a father whose only son has run off into a short future."

This was the first I'd heard of Noah. He didn't know writing so we didn't expect letters.

"Short future, sir?"

"You don't know."

"Know, sir?"

"Your brother has partnered with the devil."

"I don't know nothing about no devil, sir." I had enough trying to figure the Lord.

"All men long for a rich life filled with easy days and hearty drink."

This was news to me. I figured all men longed for what Pa did, land that turned a comfortable profit.

"But the good men know enough to temper their longings. That's what the Lord has given us that He hasn't given critters or injuns or niggers. But your brother is light on these faculties. Maybe it's the Mexican in your line. You half wet, ain't you?"

Two legs of the sheriff's chair dropped back to the floor, and he pushed through some papers on his desk. He extracted a leaflet and held it for me to see. It was my brother's face, sort of. "Can you read this?" I didn't get past the word "dead." A wanted poster with my brother's likeness. It offered $350 for him or his corpse.

"Your brother is wanted for his crimes."

Since burying Pa my hours in the book was spent hunting guidance. In a fit one night I carved two lessons into the wood of the kitchen table. I can't explain why I done it but I'd seen them every day since and they was a comfort.

Put on the full armor of God.

I had been a daughter my whole life. I wasn't one no more. Now they was trying to make me not a sister.

By standing firm you will gain life.

Sheriff Younger spat into his spittoon. "Your brother leads a lawless band of marauders and killers and thieves."

"Killers?"

"This is the truth." Younger's cigar was burning crooked and he turned it against a fresh match. "Where'd you say your pa gone off to?"

"Ain't gone off."

"Maybe I'll swing by and say my howdies."

I looked toward the bright window. The noon sun was low. Winter was nearing. I said,

"Keep an ear out anyhow about good boys or men on the prowl for a wife, would you?"

"I will. But if you hear from your brother, be sure and give me a report. If you lead me to him I'll promise to bring him back alive. You have my word on that. Bounty hunters won't be so generous."

I stared at the sheriff. No doubt Younger wanted that reward for himself. I put on my hat and tipped my head and turned to leave.

"Miss Harney?"

"Yessir."

"Tell me, what's that there under your coat?"

The barrel was so long that its point come clear of my riding jacket. A girl with a front-loading Colt was something men tended to take stock of.

I turned back toward the sheriff and something about his expression made my heart pound. "Thank you for the help."

"Who taught you to dress and such? Look at you. You don't got no one, do you?" He sighed and puffed his cigar. "Fine then. I won't say it twice, so listen. Old men will take anything young. They ain't picky so long as it's fresh. But you don't want an old man. A young man, well, you must catch his eye. Flashy speaks to the young man. You got to," he pointed his cigar toward my hair and hips and what lay between, "flare them parts up some, if you get me."

73

"Yessir."

"Don't look crooked. I don't know how women do it. I just know they do it, and you ain't doing it. Get yourself a woman somewheres first. Have her school you on these matters. Them women got ways, and any fool can see you ain't learned them."

"Yessir."

"I'll be by to see your pa."

I'd planned on checking in at the store and the hotel to inquire about sons that might be of marrying age, but my time with the sheriff had left me mindful of all I didn't understand about the man business. I wanted back in the barn with the smell of hay and other matters I knew so well. So Ingrid and me turned north and rode out on the road we come in on.

I intended to ride out again in a day or two's time, to the Mormon ma. Maybe she would show me the female arts. But each morning I woke I thought to myself, "Tomorrow. I'll go tomorrow." But then tomorrow would come and I'd still be at home turning over what the sheriff conveyed with his eyes.

I reckon I wasn't keen on giving over nothing that was ours. I wanted a man on the spread but I didn't want it to be *his* spread. Maybe I knew there wasn't a man alive who could work land without calling it his own.

By the time the snows laid their first carpets

I'd only retrieved half the cattle, and I knew the rest to be dying hard deaths in the headwaters. It pained me to think of them, and to think of Pa's face when he learned how I'd let him down. Presently my efforts went to keeping the rest alive.

The air got colder than I could ever remember. Each morning Ingrid and me rode out to the lake where the winter was coldest and broke a hole in the ice big enough for the cattle to lap. If we skipped a day the ice might grow too thick for me to break through the next time and the cattle would perish.

The lake didn't used to freeze so hard when it was bigger. But now it wasn't much more than a pond surrounded by mud froze to stone.

I was just starting to find a pattern to the day when Ingrid and me took a cough around New Year's. My dreams was haunted and I couldn't hardly breathe. Ingrid had mucus running loose from her nose and eyes and she stayed in the barn with her head hung low. She didn't eat what I give her. But still we rose early and made the haul to the lake, walking with our heads into the wind. We walked together onto the ice. Just so happened that the deepest cold come when we was sick, a stiff gale from the north that blew out the clouds and let all the earth's heat go into the stars. On the morning I felt my sickest, the ice was too thick to smash with my regular rock. I rolled out a bigger one, but then I was too weak to lift it. I turned to Ingrid. She looked toward the barn. She knew I could get myself to the lake without her. She was there because I was lonesome.

I drew the Colt and give Ingrid warning and fired without really aiming. The bullet fractured the ice and a second widened the hole and my rock did the rest.

I knew then that a ranch requires two. If I had been any sicker, we would've lost the cattle.

In the evenings once we was well I kept on with the book and eventually come to its ending. "And let him that heareth say, Come. And let him that is athirst come. And whosoever will, let him take the water of life freely. For I testify unto every man that heareth the words of the prophecy of this book, If any man shall add unto these things, God shall add unto him the plagues."

I found some comfort in them words. This book was the truth and the whole truth and all I had to do was decipher it. But I found cause for worry in them words too, and in the book in general. It give me the feeling the Lord don't trust us much. It give me the feeling I shouldn't trust myself.

Wasn't until Ma's birthday that I felt the full weight of Pa's absence. Darkness brought the worst of it. The wind howled against the slats and the stable door banged in random. I lit a big fire for company and set out a stew upon the table as if it wasn't just me eating. But then I couldn't spoon a bite. Some of my tears was for him, some for her, but mostly they was for me. I ain't never been the kind to pity myself, ain't no profit in it, but on that night I made an exception.

I went to the bed and dug out Pa's fiddle from beneath. I used a knife to pry the keeper nails and then looked down upon the red velvet cradling the instrument like some manner of holy infant. I stared into the red and felt him in the room with me and saw him too as he had been when I buried him. The black holes where his eyes had been, the tendons still holding the jaw.

I shivered as I brought the fiddle to my chin. The horsehairs was so limp they let the strings touch the wood of the bow, and it took me some moments to remember I was supposed to tighten those hairs. At once I remembered watching Pa tighten the same knob. I remembered him putting the fiddle to his chin, how he shut his eyes and his fingers knew right where to go. I had studied that man I could never decipher while his eyes was closed to all but music. Now my fingers began to hunt his same notes.

When drawn across the strings the bow brought Noah into the room with me. The air was again full of his breath. My sounds set Ingrid to whining and a pack of coyotes howling, but when you live in a world of wind and hooves even a wrong note carries an eerie magic.

My whole life music had been sacred and forbidden, and then one day song was mine without boundary but for my own ineptitude. It was as if a levee had broke and filled the whole desert from ridge to ridge with sparkling mountain water, and on the edge grew waist-high camas, and all I had to do to linger there was play.

Two of the Mormons found me practicing one warm April day, the oldest son and his kid brother. We was in the midst of the thaw. The creek was up and the sun was warm on our skin. Plenty more hardship was ahead but it was easy to let those worries go for the afternoon. "Howdy," I called to them as they rode near.

Considering they was cattle people, the Mormon brothers was pale folks with soft hands. They come with fresh biscuits, which I devoured before I even thought to invite them in. Isaac, the oldest and only a year shy of me, was wearing a new hat so I knew they must've done well at last autumn's market. Isaac was nearing the marrying age but still a child, I didn't trust him to drive a wagon let alone run my spread.

"Ma wants you and your pa for supper," Isaac said. His eyes wouldn't look me straight, they kept wandering to the roof, the barn, his toes.

I ate through the biscuits, their airy white centers still warm against my fingers. I hadn't bothered with baking since learning the fiddle. My mind was on them biscuits, more of them. "What's your ma gonna make?"

The boys shrugged. Isaac added, "Pork, I reckon. She do enjoy baking that pork. Whole house smell on account."

My mouth watered at the thought. "I do got a hard fancy for pork." I'd lost the hog to coyotes while out burying Pa. I'd failed to can the garden vegetables before frost set in. Under this dress, my legs was going boney.

"Ma invited you for Friday," Isaac said.

"Okay, then. I'll come Friday. I'll come any old day for pork."

"You and your pa?"

"Yeah, me and Pa." What else could I say?

Without looking me straight, Isaac said, "Is it true? What they say about your brother?"

I spoke with a full mouth. "You seen the posters?"

Isaac was all lit up at the notion now. "They say Noah Harney might be the fastest gunfighter who ever lived! He shot six marshals before they could draw their guns. I heard he got away with twenty-five thousand dollars."

Sheriff Younger called him an outlaw, but

twenty-five thousand dollars? How could one man hold such money? At once I saw my brother as Isaac did: riding fast through town, a pistol in hand, bullets bending around him. A gunfighter.

I handed back the empty basket, the last biscuit saved in my dress pocket. "Friday then."

Before dinner with the Mormons I washed my dress even though it wasn't wash day, set it to dry on a line hung near the hearth, and put juniper berries to boil. I washed out my hair even though it wasn't bath day and put in braids. Then I dipped a cloth to the juniper water and rubbed it along my neck. I thought it might make me smell fancy. It only made me smell like liquor, so I washed it clean again.

Them Mormons was clean people. I knew how I trusted clean people to be honest, and here I was fixing to lie about Pa. No way around it. I couldn't let word spread that I was alone on this ranch without inviting trouble. So I scrubbed up to shining clean.

My body hung below me like a stranger. I had nubs and hip bones but when I looked down I half expected to see muscles and a member. This didn't concern me much, as a body is little more than a horse you don't need to stable. But it did strike me as queer to find my mount so unfamiliar.

Ingrid and me rode down as the sun touched the rim of the mountains. She was feeling sprightly with the trip, and the air was uncommon warm and she had springtime energy about her. She looked to the field and I knew what she was thinking.

"Nah, girl. Not now. We cleaned up."

She threw her head.

"Quit that."

The mother greeted me in her long black dress. It went from her neck all the way past her shoes, and her black hair was back in a tight bun no bigger than a baby's fist. I wondered how she got all that hair back into so small a space.

She looked past me, and her smile went to a frown. "Where's your pa?"

"In them mountains, Mrs. Saggat."

"This early?"

"Queer year."

"Indeed. Well, I know the mister was hoping to talk business."

"Pa feels the same. Passes on his sorrys."

She sighed. I reckon she'd gone to some trouble to host us and was thinking how without Pa here she'd have to do it all again. But her grievance wasn't with me and so she mustered a smile. "Thanks for making the ride anyhow." She nodded to Ingrid. "You forgot to hitch."

"No need. Ingrid knows her place is with me."

"I won't have her getting into our feed. Tie her proper and come on in. Kick the mud off them boots."

I did as Mrs. Saggat asked. But I apologized to Ingrid for the low treatment.

When Pa brought me down on account of the bleeding I had kept to myself and let Mrs. Saggat do the talking. I was overcome first with her smell. Just being so close to an actual ma. I couldn't help but watch her hands, how they was always tending to the children as they come by, picking off dirt and twigs or fixing a lock of hair. It was like she had two heads, one for talking to me and the other for looking after her offspring. I longed then to be one of her children even though I didn't feel no special warmth from her. I just wanted to live a day like those children lived every day, a big woman looking down on me and keeping me clean and telling me what to do to stay safe. If you got a ma looking out for you, all you got to do is grow up.

That time I had been still and listened. This time I was to shepherd my lie. My heart wouldn't quit its gallop.

Their home was two stories, the only one like it I'd seen, with glass windows in most rooms, and ceilings so high a tall man wouldn't need stoop. The board floor was swept and there wasn't one woodstove but two, one on each end. I never did get to see the whole house but I reckon they had sleeping rooms upstairs. Seven children fit there, the youngest was born that summer.

Mr. Saggat wasn't a rancher so much as a boss man. He rode well but his hired men did the real labor. Mr. and Mrs. Saggat arrived to the valley late, but when Pa come inside to mother us, the Mormons got to the better graze and soon could hire men to stay with their herds and so keep the bears and Indians in hiding. Now Mr. Saggat's hands was clean and he was round in the belly and his neck jiggled when he spoke. He called us to the table with a bored voice.

There was a white cloth covering the wood and plates for each of us. I'd never seen nothing like it. I took the hands of my neighbors, and Mr. Saggat started with his fancy Lord words, which he mumbled so low I couldn't hear them myself. There was no pork but a roast turkey, a huge bird that must've weighed fourteen or sixteen pounds. There was squash and a bowl filled with beans. I bet they come from a jar, they was that fancy. There wasn't no biscuits but there was corn bread. More corn bread than I'd eaten in my whole life, just sitting there, giving off steam. I was late saying my "amen."

There was no hiding the lengths they'd gone in preparing this meal. Slaughtering a turkey is a holiday event for most. And so I got to wondering what my neighbors had in mind.

We sat together and I waited with my hands in my lap. I wanted to give off the right sense about me.

Mr. Saggat pointed at my food and said, "Go ahead now, Miss Harney, eat. A shame your father couldn't join us. I was hoping to gain his counsel on matters."

Mrs. Saggat hadn't eaten yet, so I didn't know the proper way. I tipped my head and smiled like I imaged she would.

Mr. Saggat said. "Go on now, eat up. We wait for our guest to commence the eating."

I raised the corn bread to my mouth with one hand and used the other to bring a slab of turkey into position. I took care only to touch the food with two fingers and to lean my face well over my plate in case of drippage. It seemed the fancy way to go about eating.

The children laughed at my manners. The middle boy said, "She eats like an injun." My face felt to be blistering.

Mrs. Saggat shushed the laughter. "There now, dear, use your utensils. Like this."

I did exactly as she showed. "Sorry, ma'am. I ain't accustomed."

"So is he often away from home?" Mr. Saggat asked.

I understood this to be a sliding question. If I said yes, then Mr. Saggat might get to thinking he could take advantage of our lower lands. If I said no, then he might figure Pa

84

had chosen this day to be gone and thereby avoid this conversation. "Sir, we got cattle far and wide this spring." It wasn't the best answer but it was the one that come quickest.

"Is that so? Why would you keep them spread wide so early? Ain't they still on feed?"

I imagined I was Pa. "Shallow snows this year up high."

"Is that right?" He looked down his nose. I saw it then, he was smiling at me but there was a shortage of smile in the man.

I was sweating under my arms and I drank down all my water so as to hide behind the cup a moment and collect myself.

Mr. Saggat turned on me. This time he spoke of Noah. "It was a sadness to learn he has chosen sin. It must trouble Mr. Harney fierce to know his only boy has turned heathen."

My blood quickened at his contempt. I said, "Sir, I will believe in my brother until I learn otherwise direct from him."

"But you can't deny his actions? You've seen the newspapers, I assume."

"My brother ain't no heathen." My heat had revealed itself.

The room went still. Not a child breathed and I could see the surprise in Mr. Saggat's eyes.

I crossed my arms. "But yes, sir, I worry. I pray nightly for his soul. May you lead us in a prayer now for him? It is rare I am among people as godly as yourselves and the Lord knows my dear brother could use the divine influence either way."

"Yes," Mrs. Saggat said. Her eyes sat heavy on her husband. "Let us pray for our child neighbor and her troubled kin."

Mr. Saggat put down his fork and swallowed his bite and pulled his napkin from his collar. He did all this without joy and I could tell a prayer at this moment was not to his preference. He mumbled to himself for a time and his eyes remained shut. Then he said, "Amen."

"Amen," the other voices sounded. My own come a beat behind theirs, so surprised I was to amen a prayer I hadn't been privy to.

The little children got to talking and Mrs. Saggat got to helping the littlest. These girls and boys would grow to be mothers and fathers and they would populate this valley with wholesome little families that ate supper on white tablecloths.

Mr. Saggat was chewing an especially large bite of turkey. "Your father is in dire financial times, no?"

"Zeke," Mrs. Saggat exclaimed. "Jessilyn is a girl alone without her kin."

"What I say is no slander. Harney missed market this year. Came in low last year. Now his cattle are scattered in the mountains and he's sure to fail this coming summer. I do not mean any offense but only to clarify the reality. The time has come to sell."

"Please." There was heat now in Mrs. Saggat's voice.

Mr. Saggat lifted his napkin and wiped his brow. "My men tell me your father has been tending to his herd by himself since your brother rode off. It is no wonder he is coming up short. Cattle require a payroll. I have seen this countless times before. I am more than just a cattleman, you understand. I am also invested in the efforts of others. Our people work together and so rise together. That is the way with the Saints."

"Yessir."

He leaned closer to me than he had before. I could smell not only his breath but also his perspiration. He smelled of moldy dough put to the oven. He said low like it was just the two of us at the table, "I can help you and your father. You tell him as much, okay?"

Just as soon as dinner was over Mrs. Saggat packed a plate for Pa.

"That's awful kind of you, ma'am. I worry about staying late on account of the ride."

"I'll ride with you," Mr. Saggat offered. "Maybe Mr. Harney will be returned."

I didn't have to refuse. Mrs. Saggat said, "The girl knows the way, and Isaac is counting on your help with his reading tonight, Zeke."

Mr. Saggat looked at his wife. The moment

sprawled, until Mr. Saggat began to laugh. "Seems my wife is intent on making me rude."

Mrs. Saggat led me toward the door. Outside the night was complete, the moon near full. She handed me the plate but it was her embrace I so desired. I was in hard need of the most basic sustenance. She picked up her toddler to her hip and said, "Bundle against the cold, dear, and give your pa our kindness."

Over her shoulder Mr. Saggat was fiddling with something in a desk drawer. He rose from his work and crossed the room and took my hand in his and I felt him passing something into my palm. He smiled. "Give Mr. Harney our blessings," Mr. Saggat said.

Ingrid was waiting for me where I had hitched her. The Mormons watched me from the stoop.

From the windows at the top of the house I could see candles burning and children's faces peering down at me. All them children was gathered there together to watch. So many children. At night I doubt they needed quilts for all the warmth they shared.

I pulled on my riding jacket and flipped up the collar against the wind. Two minutes before I had been in a warm room with roast turkey. Now I rode into icy darkness.

A mile down the road I checked what Mr. Saggat had given me. It was a slip of paper.

But when I unfurled it I saw it wasn't paper but paper money. He'd slipped me a dollar.

Back at home I lay in bed. Sleep was slow in coming. I kept thinking of that dollar. Neither friends nor thieves just up and give a girl a dollar and expect nothing in return.

I rose and relit the lantern by feel. I carried it to the door and pulled in the latch string.

When sleep did come it was Noah who visited me. We was riding side by side across rolling plains. Just wind over our ears and hooves in grass, and both of us together, running from something.

The next day I awoke late. The sun was already up and the cabin smelled of ash blown out the fireplace by the morning breeze.

I finished what was left of the Mormon's supper and then carried the dollar out to the holehouse where Pa kept our savings. I reached through the hole and up onto the bottom side of the wooden seat to a box sitting on a shelf there. It was a long reach for me and the smell was as you'd expect. As I did my business I added the dollar to the box and counted. There was twelve dollars, including the California gold piece Pa had carried with him since the war. I put the box back in its place before leaving.

When I come around the edge of the house, I saw a saddled buckskin hitched to our post.

The front door was open.

I thought to the location of the Colt, still under the pillow.

I knew my only advantage was surprise so I stalked to the edge of the house.

I heard spurs on the dirt floor. I looked and saw Sheriff Younger appear in the doorway.

The sheriff saw me then too. He put an arm to the doorjamb. He had his hat on and his pistol hung low. "Ain't you a silly-looking sight." I was still wearing long johns from the night. "Where's your pa?"

"Out."

"Out where?"

"He comes and goes."

"Is that right?" he asked while touching a match to a cigarillo.

"Yessir."

He waved out his match. "Ain't you gonna offer me coffee or nothing?"

"Don't got no coffee."

"No pa and no coffee."

"I got a pa, he's just out. Ain't got no coffee."

"He makes a habit of being out, don't he? Stopped by the mercantile and his name come up. Seems he hasn't been by in some months. Seems you've been running up his debts."

"You want me to pass along a message?"

He took a seat on the bench by the front door. He watched his smoke blow away in the breeze. "Maybe I'll just wait a piece, see him when he returns."

I caught myself before I could say he would be gone a while. I didn't want this man knowing I would be alone here for even the hour. "I'm going in to get dressed. I'd appreciate some distance."

I walked past the sheriff. I shut the door behind me and dropped the juniper latch and pulled in the string.

Inside I put on my dress and my sheepskin coat. It was a touch more coat than necessary given the day, but it was thick enough to conceal the Colt I hid at my back.

I looked around the room, this time from the sheriff's mind. There wasn't a thing of Pa's out, not his sleeping things or his tobacco. On the table was my one dish. I set out another, then decided to clear both.

I opened the door and stepped into the sunlight.

I took a position out in the open. The sheriff was smashing the rest of his smoke on my bench.

"Think your pa'll miss his saddle? Saw it hanging in the barn."

I spat, though I didn't have no tobacco, Pa's habit when asked a question he didn't want to answer.

The sheriff reclined and looked off toward the hills. The magpies called from the willows. The fowl was making a courting ruckus on the lake, and the breeze carried their cackles our direction. The creek was milky with runoff and in the meadows the purple camas was up and close to bloom.

"Looks to me like your herd is down. Probably doing the best you can without your pa around to help. Did he go and die on you? Or'd he finally turn to mush and run off?"

"You full of crazy thoughts, sheriff."

"There be cruel people passing through these parts. A girl with fat cattle? A lush spread to herself. There be people who would see this and think they found themselves an opportunity."

"Let Pa's rifle talk some sense into them."

The sheriff laughed. He took off his hat and brushed it on his knee. His hair was silver and clean. He was a bathing man. He said, "Your pa probably let on he was some kind of hero with that Yankee rifle."

I didn't take his bait. I knew Sheriff Younger had fought for the Confederacy.

"Your old man was a low-down, dry-gulching son of a bitch. He tell you that? His kind hid like cowards and shot good men in the back. I seen what they done. They ain't no heroes."

I felt mean as a bear now. I might've mauled that smile from his face. "I'll tell him you said so, sheriff."

Younger picked something from between his teeth. He examined his clean fingernails.

"I can help you, you realize. We can get your head sold at fair prices. We can get this burden of a ranch out from under you. You'll have good money. You won't have no problem marrying yourself a well-to-do man. I know a widower up Malheur way with five sections who'd do real well by you."

"Why would you want to help me?"

"My position requires I offer assistance to all citizens of the county, even the kin of a yellow Yank."

Younger seen something in my eyes then. His forehead furrowed. He put his hat on. "Your brother been around?"

Younger scanned the near hill, the barn. "Maybe he come home to help you, now that your pa turned to mush?"

My power rested in what he thought he knew. "Appreciate you coming by, sheriff. Now you best get on, I got me plenty of work to do before Pa come riding back."

He took his buckskin's reins and walked him from the house. He swung up and wheeled around on that antsy stallion. I could see the horse trusted him as much as I did.

"You know I rode a long way this morning to come see you," he said, looking down at me.

"I know the distance."

"Could've at least offered me some coffee."

"Can't offer what I don't got."

He raised a finger. "Little girl like you

might want to trade what she got before somebody come along and take it."

The buckskin hopped and the sheriff made no effort to stop him. I watched them gallop past the barn and along the spring and onto the road.

Ingrid blew her nose and I knew she felt the same about Younger. She trotted up beside me and I took a grip of her mane and ran three steps and bounced up onto her back. She knew where to go.

We broke through the sage to the top of the ridge and stopped in the shade of a juniper. From there we could see the sheriff and his trail of dust. We watched until he crossed our line sometime later, and then we watched until we couldn't make out his shape from the general green and gray of the valley floor.

The heifers went missing soon after, twelve of them. I noticed right off in the morning on account the numbers was down. I grabbed the Sharps from the pegs. Ingrid and me rode a loop around the meadow and cut their tracks, a mess of cattle and two shod horses.

We followed them on a run over the ridge and down across the next valley and up the other side and still we kept on. I was pushing Ingrid too hard I knew, but I believed we would catch them because a lone horse and rider will make ground on cows with calves.

Ingrid was lathered and parched and begging to walk and still I pushed her forward. Then before us was the county line. The sage thinned out to sand, and here the wind had already blown out the tracks. I could see all the miles until the sand bent into a gray slab of mountain, and there wasn't a rider upon it. We was beat. I pulled her to a stop and swung down.

Ingrid's head hung low. She was spent.

Those tracks didn't come from Younger's big buckskin, I was sure of that. They wasn't from no horses I recognized, but that didn't mean I didn't know their riders.

We had dealt with thefts before, of course. There was a tough winter when Noah was still around when Indians stole steers in three events. They was stealing for food, and red as Pa got, we was grazing on their lands after all. We come to see it as a tax. But we'd never been rustled by shod horses before, white men.

I walked back to give Ingrid the relief of my weight.

The sun wore on us and Ingrid moved between islands of juniper shade. In the dream state of travel I felt dread at the prospect of confessing to Pa what I had lost, then remembered all over again I didn't get to confess nothing to him no more.

I took the Sharps to the ridge and picked out a cow pie on the valley bottom. I leveled the rifle over a rock and adjusted for distance and windage. I remembered Pa teaching Noah that shooting downhill or up meant the bullet would be affected less by distance, so I readjusted. My shot was low. It would've struck a man's horse square through the guts. My second shot was high, clean through a man's hat. I was distracted by emotion. It was a lesson I had to learn again and again when shooting for distance.

The next night and the night after I done the only thing I could muster, I brought the cattle in close and lay out in the sage with the rifle and wondered if I had the stones to kill a man.

I wondered too after Noah. While I hunkered here alone, he rode on whim, a man free of earthly chains. Not even the law could contain my brother. In this world a man could set any course.

I tightened my grip on the Sharps and shivered against the cold. Pa would kill a rustler. Pa would expect me to do the same.

Days passed and I couldn't walk to the holehouse without thinking somebody was stealing what I had left. Couldn't look to supper without thinking I was hearing footsteps off yonder. Twice I come out the house with the Colt drawn believing there was a prowler peeking in my windows.

The concern leaked into my sleep, which I was taking at random seeing as I was up half the nights on watch. One dream come on me like an attack. A faceless man was roaring in my ear and his weight was pinning me to the earth and I seen his face, a gaping black hole and an eye dangling over his cheek by a vein. The blast of a pistol woke me. I was wet with sweat. The pistol shot was in the dream but still my ears rung from it.

In the dream, my brother hadn't come when I called him.

We rode fast down to the Mormons. I was no more sure of my intentions than the elk as they circle before a wolf attack. But I knew I was in dire need of what only a neighbor can deliver. Maybe I didn't realize how dire.

We come down to find the children playing chase. Isaac stopped cold when he saw me. He fixed his hat and pushed his siblings aside without a look. "Howdy, Miss Harney."

Mrs. Saggat come onto the porch with a basket of wet laundry and stood looking.

"Howdy, ma'am."

"What a surprise, Miss Harney." She was less than pleased to find me before her, that was plain.

"Might I offer you a hand with the hanging?" There was a line in the yard already with white shirts rustling in the breeze. Mr. Saggat's shirts was brown under the arms. "Ma'am, I come for your counsel."

She fixed her grip on the laundry. The

children was watching. "Yes, of course," she said with a little sigh. "Come near. I can see you are in some distress."

I approached until I was within proper confiding distance.

"Is it your pa? Is he hurt?"

"No, ma'am. He don't hurt."

She whispered, "Some woman trouble then?"

"Not that neither, ma'am."

She changed her grip on the laundry basket. "What then? Out with it. It's laundry day and I ain't likely to finish before supper as it is. If this is . . . If my husband come to your pa . . . Did he?"

She didn't give me time to answer. "You must understand. The Lord intends my husband to have this whole valley and all the Indian land too. He puts what is fallow to good and proper use. That is his charge upon this earth."

"I'm here because I'm on sorry times. I believe we might be of help to each other. We's neighbors, Mrs. Saggat, and I ain't got no ma and you ain't got no daughter old enough to help. And I was just thinking . . ."

Her eyes squinted at the notion.

"You's alone here among these mouths. I know alone. I know the chores too, I do. We might talk about the weather and dresses. I would listen and do right by you, I promise. I'd earn my keep, ma'am. I ain't begging charity. It's you I come here for. To be part of what's yours. To be yours."

She set the laundry on the porch and wiped her hands on her apron. "Oh, child, come closer."

I did and my knees grew weak with hope.

She put her hand to mine but she did not draw me near. She was making a study of my eyes. "Is your pa cruel to you?"

"No, ma'am. That ain't it at all."

The baby began to cry from within the house. Mrs. Saggat was slow to act on account her concern was with me.

"I'll tend to her." I rushed past to demonstrate my helpfulness. The baby was among blankets in a cradle. I lifted her to my shoulder and hushed her but I was unpracticed at these arts and the baby only wailed louder for her mother.

When I turned she was there. Mrs. Saggat took the child from me and lifted free her apron and with one hand unbuttoned her dress and I watched as she squeezed her breast and drove her chaffed nipple into that baby's scream. It descended into a wet silence.

She sat in the chair and covered her breast and baby's face with her off hand and studied me. "You come here because you're want for motherly wisdom."

"Yes, ma'am. I am starved for it."

She looked out the window. She rocked and

hummed to that little baby. "I can't take you into my house, Miss Harney. There ain't room for a girl here. Someday you'll reckon my meaning. My husband is a good man, and I aim to keep him that way."

I drew a breath to temper my disappointment. "Ma'am."

"You might've heard things about the Saints, but those things ain't true anymore. Our elders were again visited by angels and learned from them that God changed His mind on the matter of plural marriage. The Lord wants families to look like this one, and so ours will continue to look like this."

I started to explain I wasn't after her husband, but then the idea come to me. "Let me have Isaac. Please, ma'am. I want to marry your boy."

"Oh, child." She smiled this pity smile on me and I nearly broke in two on account I could see she didn't think I was good enough or pretty enough or white skinned enough for her son.

She passed her fingers over her baby's cheeks. It was a little girl and she was now humming upon the breast as she slumbered. Mrs. Saggat's words come out gentle as a lullaby. "I speak to you now, girl, as your mother might've. The Lord asks us women to make sacrifices He don't ask of men. Our reward is to be the bearers of His creation, to do His holiest work on His behalf. And so we stand tall and don't let our suffering show. You must prepare yourself, child. You must bolster your trust in His divine wisdom and count on Him to deliver on His good word. Can you trust in Him?"

"I'm trying, ma'am."

"What is it, child? What ain't you telling me?"

The truth come from me at once. I reckon I had held it as long as I could. My hand was in hers and the air smelled of milk and I couldn't draw a full breath. "My pa passed on, ma'am. I buried him. I am alone and I've been alone every night since and all day too and I'm so worn thin being on my own. Ma'am, I won't take no money, but call me an employee. Please, ma'am, let me stay, as your help. Let me stay with you."

"Oh. Well. Oh, my. I should've seen it. You carry such a burden in your eyes. When did he? How?" She shook her head and took a breath for resolve. She tightened her jaw. "You must pray."

"I have prayed."

"Well, you must continue to pray and trust in His wisdom. If you trust, He will deliver."

"But will you take me in, ma'am? I am bare before you."

She watched six of her seven in the yard through her big glass window. "The other Saints will misunderstand. They'll shame us, don't you see? The elders will believe you are

his second wife, against all divine revelation."
She shook her head. "Besides, if the Lord
wanted you here, He would've sent a sign."

"Ma'am, didn't He deliver me here now?"

Her rocking had gained pace. She shook
her head in that quick way of hers and said,
"The Lord subjects us all to His trials. . . .
He doesn't intend for you to be here. He
intends for me to deliver His wisdom to your
ear. That is all. Please don't look on me like
that. Please."

"I've listened, ma'am. I've listened and
prayed and read His whole book and I ain't
never felt Him guiding me. Not once. Is there
something wrong with me? Can a child be
born outside His favor? How do you make
Him love you if He ain't?"

The children rushed around us like a hive
of bees returned. Mrs. Saggat rose with the
baby still asleep against her chest and commanded Isaac to slice bread for the table.
She took me in her free arm and embraced
me. Then she held me at arm's length and
said, "Stay for a piece of bread, Jessilyn."

I passed a forearm over my brow. The air
wasn't hot but sweat was pouring from me.

Out the window my eye found Ingrid at the
hitching post. The sight of her delivered my
breath and with it returned my balance.
Ingrid was waiting on me.

"Thank you, ma'am. I won't bother you no
more now."

■ ■ ■ ■

On Ingrid I forced myself to sit tall. I patted
her neck. I bent to her mane and kissed her.
We rode up a ridge and back down. We rode
across a meadow and back. Anywhere but to
our lonesome home.

In the distance cranes walked amid the
purple camas. If Ma had lived and Pa had
kept on building, all that was Mr. Saggat's
would be ours. We'd have glass windows
overlooking the lake. It'd be the four of us
and probably more, a proper clan of peoples.
Noah would be Pa's foreman. Maybe with a
wife and children of his own up the valley. Pa
would play his fiddle and Ma would braid
my hair, and I'd be a big sister to a mess of
little ones and an auntie to more.

I buried my nails into the flesh of my arm.
Pain on the outside, pain where I put it.

At home after dark, winds swirled inside me
and I didn't trust myself around blades.

I started tidying, smoothing the quilt,
sweeping out the wood box, lifting each item
from the mantel and brushing the dust clear.
If only I could be clean enough.

Then I bumped Pa's bullet mold from its
place. It hit the ground and the arm broke
free. At the sight of it something come over
me and I drew my hand across the mantel

and knocked everything else in the dirt.

I overturned the table. The water tin tipped and the earth floor went to mud and I stood over it, looking into it, looking for something. My knees hit the mud and my hands tracked it across my flesh. I dug at this earth that had caught Ma's lifeblood and smeared it over my skin. I would bury this girl who set her to bleeding.

I seized the shears and went at my hair. The blades cut it short as a calf's and its tatters fell about me.

The hair was itching inside my collar and I put the shears through the fabric and down the length and cut loose that dress and tossed it into the fire and stood naked as it flamed and still the itching was everywhere and worse.

I lay in the mud. I dared Him to come take me as I was, prone and shivering and dark. Do it and be done with this girl, you bastard.

Yet come morning I still breathed. I awoke to a mourning dove sitting upon the overturned table. It cooed and flew toward the slice of light at the roof seam but found the passage too narrow and so returned to its perch. For a moment she hovered in the middle of the room as if on dangle from above, flapping. Then she banked and lit upon Pa's hat.

A gust of wind held the flap of cowhide and the bird swept across the room and out the narrow gate.

I rose with the quilt about me and took up Pa's last hat. I had not dared touch it since resting it on this peg last autumn. I knocked free the dust. Smelled it. I wondered and so put it on my own head. It fit well enough.

The idea had been coming to me for weeks. I just then set about doing it.

I drew out the chest from under the bed, not Ma's but the one that held Noah's belongings. I pushed past some articles and found what I remembered being there. Noah left when he was a full-sized man, but only a couple years before he'd been part grown. I held those pantaloons to me now and saw they would do. The shirt would be a touch long in the sleeves but I could roll them.

My height come from Pa and I could see eye to eye with a typical man. But my nubs pushed where a man's don't. They was little and always would be but still they was more nub than any man. I got a notion and so dug deeper yet into Noah's chest. I come up with his boyhood wools and pulled on the top. The arms stopped at my elbows and was too tight for comfort so I drew a knife and cut the arms free at the seam. What remained held me tight. I buttoned the shirt overtop and now when I looked down I saw only the muscles of a man who knows hard labor. That was the species of man I intended to be.

"Howdy," I said to the empty room. It

come out too deep and coarse for my age. "Howdy, young lady," I tried again.

Now I was lit up with the notion and so worked fast. I wrapped the pemmican I had left in cloth and took the canvas sack with its jerky and packed them into a saddlebag. There was salt venison and curds. The curds I ate down as they wouldn't keep. I rolled the Sharps in my bedding and tucked in the shells and bullet fixings.

The deed to the land, the grazing rights, and the twelve dollars that was mine went into a satchel.

I looked about the room. There was something else.

I drew out Pa's fiddle. The box was awkward and cumbersome, but he had brought it all the way from the war so I would bring it the miles that existed between me and Noah.

He was out there somewhere and he was all the blood I had left and I would find him and convince him home, to his duty, and together we would resurrect our family place. We would finish this story as it began, us two together.

■ ■ ■ ■

II

■ ■ ■ ■

We rode across sage and along stands of timber and paused to watch deer wheel and bound, and to listen to the croaking of frogs near still water, and toward evening we arrived at the edge of a rich meadow new to us both and alive with all manner of butterflies. The grass stood to my chest and the wet ground caved to my feet and a thousand blue and yellow wings fluttered. I pulled the saddle free of Ingrid and let it hit the earth and watched as clouds of butterflies rose ahead of Ingrid punching through the grass, then disappearing into a roll. The old girl had been waiting on rolling all day. I was glad to give her the chance.

There was wood to gather and a fire to start and salt venison to eat, but I didn't move. I just stood there gandering at this new place without a cattle track or wagon trail. Untrampled country.

A hoof rose from the grass and vanished again and mud careened through the evening light and butterflies stormed.

The resolve come to me then. I was done letting hard times govern me. I might be orphaned but that didn't make me no orphan. I was Jesse Harney, and I had a brother who knew me.

In that moment I didn't feel like gathering no food or warming no supper. I felt like playing the fiddle while my mare rolled off her sweat. So that's what I done. I played us happy notes while the light went orange and climbed up them mountains. For the first time in my life there wasn't a chore within a million miles.

We set out the next day only when we was good and ready. Our course led up the ridge and we climbed higher than I'd ever been before.

We stopped where a sheet of snow ended, where winter was still turning to spring. Ingrid drank from the trickle pouring off the snow. From there we could see past tree line, all the way to the top of that mountain. I recognized its craggy summit. It was one of them peaks I'd spent my whole life looking at from afar. It had been the edge of the world to me then, but here I was only a day from home and standing within rifle distance of its top.

I recalled that morning so long ago when Noah had sat out under the stoop, his boy-legs reaching for the rail. We looked upon those rocks and he guessed them to be no higher than a grown man. Now I saw them to be as tall as fifty of our barns stacked one upon the next.

The enormity of this country settled on me then. Pa and Ma traveled four months to reach our valley, a hundred and twenty days. Noah had been gone five years.

Up until then reconvening with my brother had been a simple fact of this journey. I hadn't given the how much thought. Just follow the news like I'd follow tracks in dust and eventual-like I'd find him at trail's end.

Now there was no escaping the expanse of my foolishness. In a land as wide as this one, how was a lone girl to find a single man? Let alone an outlaw who made his living by not being found?

I sat down on a rock to catch my breath.

By the end of the fourth day I'd eaten down the stores to only pemmican. Ingrid was eating the best graze of her life, thick green grass at every stop. But I dreamed of a mercantile in the mountains, just some front where I could get biscuits and preserves and maybe some bacon.

The fifth day we come into a gulch wet with spring and cut our first horse tracks. I leaned to check. They was shod, and some days on. We fell in line. I knew Blairville had to be somewhere uphill. From there we could pick up an easy trail along the rolling counties.

I wondered as we rode if Noah himself had been up this gulch years before. My hungry mind dwelled with my brother, the possibility of the two of us stepping on the same dirt.

It wasn't Blairville we rode into but a camp of miners working the stream. Ingrid had them first, by scent. We rode up onto a ridge of aspen for a safe look.

Six men and two wall tents, a cooking fire, a long table built beside the stream. A rifle leaned against the table. Looked like an old Springfield. The men was carrying buckets to one end of the table and letting the water run down the length. I didn't see any horses, which struck me as queer.

I saw a blue coffeepot on the fire and a Dutch oven, and there had to be food. I imagined a whole storehouse of food inside the tents. Not just biscuits but ham and potatoes. So much grub I could eat until I fell asleep and then start again.

I patted Ingrid on the neck. "What you think?"

She looked off up the valley.

"Reckon you right." I wasn't ready to put my manhood to the test, especially not on six lonely miners who might smell a woman like a hound smells a hare.

I dismounted and led Ingrid through the aspens until a bend in the valley allowed us to drop down unseen.

The hunger didn't let up, and come the seventh day we still hadn't found a town or mercantile. In late morning we come to a fold in the hill. The draw wasn't much but I could see stub willow and lush grass, and I had myself an intuition. Ingrid picked up a trot when she saw that graze.

There wasn't no mining in this draw and the water ran like ice. I looked for trout first but didn't see none. So I set Ingrid to grazing and started up the willow with the pistol. Willow is something I trusted from home to hold edibles. I was hungry and I always shot my best when I was hungry.

Yet nothing stirred from the willow.

There was a mess of rocks on the treeless hillside, and I thought about the rock chucks back home that hide from the sun in such stuff. It was still a good way up but I took it slow.

Soon enough I saw them, grouse as big as fry hens. One stood up from its bed and I drew quick and shot its head clean off at close range. That sent the flock into the air. I tracked one, winged it, and lined up on a third flying straightaway. It gave up a mess of feathers and fell all the way down in the willows at the bottom. The winged one was on the run below me and I drew and took a moment. The first shot missed, so I gave chase. The second bullet rolled him and he quivered before going still.

From starving to flush in a breath.

Ingrid was looking up from her graze. I hollered to her, and she bucked her head. We was some happy people now.

Right there I started a little fire of dead willow. Once the feathers was off, I flipped the guts out and ran a green switch up and through. That I put on two stakes over the heat where I could turn it slow. I salted the meat from a small pouch I'd carried from home. The bird dripped juice into the flames, and when I ate I laughed with gratitude.

We dropped into the next valley and found the creek flowing red. It wasn't the water but the rocks themselves. They was stained. Ingrid wasn't much for crossing that water. She wouldn't drink a sip. So I didn't neither despite a mean thirst.

Farther along we saw the red coming from the mine shafts. They shone on the mountainside like black mouths and red tongues. The whole place put me at unease.

Toward afternoon, we come to a junction. I could see trails heading up three creeks, two of them heading more or less west. I checked my shadow and thought hard about direction.

Soon after we saw a man on foot leading mules our way. He was alone, and this seemed as good a moment as any to try my manself. We waited a step off the trail while he walked down into the valley bottom and to us. Even from a distance I could see the Mexican in him. His mules was loaded down, the cargo covered in tarpaulins, yet he walked.

"Howdy," I hollered when he got fifty yards out. I shown my hand.

He kept coming without a word.

When he got inside ten yards and still hadn't looked at me, I said again, "How do you do?"

It became clear to me then that this man intended to walk right on by without so much as looking at us.

I put Ingrid in his path and his eyes studied the birds. I could see the hunger in his face. His man was delivering provisions for the mines yet he wasn't supplied even a riding horse.

"What you got to eat?" He didn't respond. I put fingers to my mouth.

He shrugged. *"No comida."*

I tapped a dead bird. "Which trail for *el norte*?"

He thought about that. Then he pointed up the steeper of the two trails. "Too much, *pero el norte, si.*"

I tossed him the bird because he was hungry and I was full. He looked at it there on the ground.

I said, "Cooks up good enough."

He lifted the bird and tucked the lead rope under his arm to free both hands. He took to squeezing the critter, checking it. I reckon he figured it must be ruined by lead, but this was the one I head shot. He studied me with a queer look. He nodded, and I understood that to be a thank-you. Then he gestured at the other trail. "Farther but more easy."

He set to work starting a twig fire while Ingrid and me rode on. We stopped along the ridge for a look back. The valley was without a tree, just rubble and willow and gray slabs of rock. At its heart three creeks the color of fire met and vanished into a black gap between the mountains. Where the creeks met grew a shaft of willow smoke.

He never doubted I was a man.

If that trail was more easy, I'm glad I never saw the other.

It led along the water, then up on cruel switchbacks, and broke out on top to a world of rock and snow. The fog took us in. There was no seeing the cairns left by earlier travelers. I did my best by dead reckoning but the terrain got me twisted.

It was evening when we found the path down, and we both lightened. I had begun reconciling myself to the fact we would spend the night upon that peak, no fire for me and no graze for Ingrid and no sleep for either of us. So when we found that trail, Ingrid broke into a trot and I let her.

We rode into a grove of pines the likes of which I'd never before seen. The ground was soft, old needles with mushrooms sprouting through. It was the first time we'd been off rocks all day. It was like walking on a mattress. I was sleepy by then and so was Ingrid. This forest felt like a place we could let down our guard.

I didn't see the men until they hollered to us. I don't know how Ingrid missed them.

Across a thin meadow was a tarpaulin lean-to and two men before a small cooking fire. They had a skinned-down deer hanging from a tree, the firelight flashing on it, and I could see a hindquarter roasting above the flames. A man was waving us over.

Ingrid threw her head.

"Get, girl."

She didn't. I assumed it was because of the deer. I often wonder how this life might've gone different had I trusted Ingrid and just kept on down that trail.

One of the men hollered, "That animal of yours needs some discipline."

I crossed my hands over the horn.

"You come down from there by your lonesome? You can't be more than fourteen years old." The one speaking wore a thick moustache. His nose was too big for his face and his skin was scarred with pocks. He had a big

117

Dragoon pistol tucked in his belt. A Dragoon by then was an old-time pistol, and I had only seen them carried by dirty drunkards. I didn't require Ingrid to take another step toward these men.

"A whole group of us coming," I said in a voice too deep.

"At this hour of the day?" I reckon they figured I was a boy playing the part of a man.

The other one was clean shaven and middle-aged. His hat was off and he had blond hair and a thin face. His Spencer repeater was within reach. He poked the venison with a silver blade. His eyes paid me no mind.

Their horses whinnied, and Ingrid got to backing away.

The moustached man with the Dragoon said, "Care to join us? We're about to feast on this here roast. Room to roll out a bed, if you care to. Hobble her up with the others. They might teach her a thing or two about heeding her master."

I tipped my hat like a man, and let Ingrid spin us and trot back to the trail. The moustache man called after but we kept on.

We rode until it was too dark to see. We paused in a cluster of young pines and as a precaution watched our backtrail. We held for a good while, then carried on in the moonlight until we hit the next meadow. It was so dark I had to ride with an arm across my face to protect against wayward limbs.

The meadow had been grazed down by cattle, but it would do. By the creek I rolled out my bed and started a cooking fire. I could hear Ingrid chomping in the darkness, her lips working at fresh starts near the ground. Soon the last bird was sizzling. When the moon emerged a pair of coyotes opened up from the timber.

The air was warm. We'd been in cold country since leaving home and I was on bad terms with my smell. After eating I shed my hat and my coat, my shirts and pants, and tiptoed about that creek until I found a soft spot where I might lay and rub myself clean.

The coyotes howled again, this time a touch closer, and I wondered what words they was saying with them calls. Pa always claimed that critters each got their own language and men who can make sense of their tongues got all manner of sentries about them. He was the one who taught me to know the approach of the bear by the caw of the raven, to look for a lion at the silence of the squirrel.

Took some minutes before I realized Ingrid wasn't chomping no more. I stood from the water. "Girl?"

She kicked the earth in the warning of her kin and so I knew she was on to something. I grabbed for my pistol and listened.

I pulled on my pants and boots and then my shirts, first the small wool I had cut to contain my nubs and then the flannel overtop. I did this right quick. I was finishing my belt when I heard a stick snap and looked up and there was the figure of a man in the moonlight, fixed on me. The man with the Dragoon.

"Look at you. Queer breed that washes up in the cold of night."

My pistol was in my hand, and I held it away from my body so that he might see it silhouetted against the silver water. " 'Preciate you moving on."

"Name's Carl. What's yours?"

I didn't answer.

"What? You too simple for a name? Or you fancy yourself royalty and above some friendly conversation with a fellow traveling man?"

He pulled a bottle from his back pocket, took a swig, and offered it to me. It glinted in the moonlight. "Let me tend to your fire while you put up your feet and help me with this here bottle."

I waited a moment then said firm like Pa would, "I prefer you move on, stranger."

"Or what? Come on now. Don't you got no mountain hospitality? We the only folks for twenty miles, minus my mule-face relative and he don't count. This is lonely country and I'm offering you a drink. You got enough friends in this world you can turn this one away? What if I happen to know something that could make you a million dollars? Huh?"

I could see Ingrid now in the meadow, watching this man and blowing steam. I took that as confirmation he had come alone.

He sat down beside my fire and took another pull. "Put that pistol away, for chrissake. Makes me nervous to see a boy your age wielding a Yankee-issue Colt. You seen what that ol' thing will do to flesh?"

I didn't answer. I was still working out what to say to this man who wouldn't leave. I stood some distance back from the fire but the cold of the creek was in me now.

"Let me guess. Your pa fought in the war and after he died you ended up with his pistol? Don't look so surprised. You ain't the first kid I seen with his daddy's Colt. Ah, kid. You're just like a thousand others. Hate to be the one to say it, but you ain't special. This country will eat you up. You could die tonight and nothing would change, not a thing."

He smelled his fingers. The fire glinted in his eyes. He patted the Dragoon in his belt. "This here pistol come by way of cards but before that it belonged to a dead injun. That savage had wrapped it in hide and there was brass studs in the grip. Smelled like a skunk. What kind of fool treats his pistol like that? That's why they couldn't hold this place. That's it right there. No thing is more important than its purpose. What's your purpose, son?"

"I ain't your son."

"There we go. Good to know you got words. What's your work? See, I'm trying to be friendly. Go on, sit. I see you got the chill. It's your own damn fire. You ain't afraid of a little conversation, is you?"

I sat. I rested the Colt across my thigh.

He pointed at the remains of my bird. "Mind?" He reached and tore free a drumstick and smelled it. "Trade you for some tobacco?"

"Eat it on your ride back."

He took a big bite. He spoke as he chewed. "Your Colt and my Dragoon could've knowed each other in the war. Ever consider that? My pistol killing the owner of yours, or the other way? These instruments got stories to tell. My relation and me be headed up past the company land. We hear there's new gold. Idiot or not my relation has a connoisseur's taste for the ore. We have that in common. He was born in fifty-one and me in fifty-two along the American River. Ever hear of it?"

"Nope."

"Californy. We was born couple years too late. Forty-eight was the year for getting it. By fifty-one the Chinamen was thick as fleas and the Mexicans was everywhere you wanted to be. No, forty-eight was the year for it. Pa said he could kick the stream bottom and clouds of gold would drift on. If there's a rush for metal I'm there. You got the fever?

What's your business?"

"Cattle."

"Cattle. You don't say? You ever consider mining?"

I didn't answer.

"Now is the time. It's starting again. It's like forty-eight right now if you know where to be, and I do. We're gonna pan the first weeks and save our scores and then buy up all the labor we can — I won't hire no Chinamen, I got principles. I'm gonna sit back while the injuns do the lifting. You know you can get a brave to work all day for a meal? Makes me think we killed them off too quick." He flicked the remains of the drumstick into the fire.

"You good with that Colt? You don't look like you ever swung a pick before but you hold the Colt like you ain't afraid of it. I bet we could find a purpose for a cattle boy."

When I didn't answer, he cocked his head. "I don't see no cattle here."

I thought on the fly. "I'm after a bounty."

He laughed. He filled his mouth with liquor and passed it back and forth between his teeth before swallowing. "Who you hunting, Mr. Bounty Hunter?"

"Harney."

"Noah Harney?"

"That's the one."

He lost himself in laughter. He laid back with it and convulsed.

123

"What's so funny?"

He sat up and brushed himself clean and give up a last couple chuckles. "Just so typical is all. How many boys your age think they hunting Noah Harney? How many on this very night is claiming to be a bounty hunter? Shee-it."

I took up the last shreds of my bird and commenced finishing it.

"You're either way behind or way ahead of all the other bounty hunters on Harney. Last I heard he was holed up in the red rock country. So which is it, behind or ahead?" He looked on me and drew from his liquor. "I bet your old man threw you out. Am I close?"

I looked up from my eating.

"Ain't your fault. There's only three stories in this whole wide world. But see? You ain't nothing I ain't seen a hundred times before. Here now, gone tomorrow. Nothing changes. The creeks still run and snows still come and another boy like you is going to tell me he's a bounty hunter."

He looked up at the stars. He howled. He offered me the bottle again. "Last chance to be sociable before I depart."

I didn't take the bottle.

The man stretched his back. "Well. Figure I'll get on anyhow. Long day tomorrow and you ain't good company." He stood. "Hey, whatever happened to the rest of your party? A party of bounty hunters? All of you?"

I didn't answer.

He took down the last of the liquor and looked down the barrel of that bottle and tossed it in the creek. "Well, night to you anyhow. Good luck and all. Thanks for the dead bird."

I was so relieved he was departing I said, "Luck to you, mister."

He turned and walked away into the night. I stood to watch him go, and when his footsteps fell away to the darkness I took my first full breath since I seen him on the bank.

I half turned to put a hand to Ingrid, to comfort her. I patted her neck. I knuckled the itchy spot between her brows. I saw it first in the startle of her eyes.

The man was on me before I knew. We both hit the earth hard. I was on the ground and his weight was crushing me.

"You ain't nothing!" he spat in my face. "Dumb and soft and stupid! You'll die and no one will know and no one will care. Don't you get it? I own you!"

His knees got on my arms, all his weight pressed on my ribs and I couldn't get a breath. He was slapping my face and laughing and there wasn't nothing I could do.

Ingrid was stomping the earth and whinnying. Her feet was so close. Kick him, I willed. Kill him, girl!

His fist collided into my nose and I fell through the dream.

Ringing ears and blood so thick I can't get a straight breath. He is strangling me and licking my face. Him everywhere and not a breath to be had and stars come down from the sky and into my eyes and I look out into the gaps between and beg my brother to come, and the gaps grow until there ain't nothing left but their calamitous darkness and I have no brother and I am no different than the dirt about me and I don't want nothing no more but stillness.

When I come to, his weight was off me. He was going through my pockets.

I didn't think, I just done. Pa's counsel like a whisper in my ear: *Steady is quick.*

My fingers found the first thing. A burned sharp stick.

I sat up and drove the stick through the bottom of the bastard's chin. There come the crackle of wood against bone. The warmth of his skin against my hand. The release of his bastard heat down my arm. I feel yet his blood running through my sleeve.

He ripped to the side and staggered to his feet. He couldn't make no sensible sound on account the wood was through his tongue and he was choking on the blood. The stick had popped one eye and left a cavern in its place. His other eye searched about him but could not settle upon me.

He tripped over my legs and then stumbled through the fire. His pants caught flame, and then he wheeled and I saw the Dragoon in his hand. Fire barked from its barrel, fire clawed up his legs. He went backward to the ground and the Dragoon sent a geyser of sparks toward the heavens.

I stood and found my hat and put it on my head, and then I looked on that man still writhing, and that's when the shaking started, the wondering, the worry.

All at once I thought of the fire luring the man's kin, showing light on what I done. I drove my hat into the creek and filled it and ran past the gagging man to dump the water onto the flames. I did this twice and the fire only steamed.

Right away I knew I should've saved the flames until I was packed on account of the light. I threw together my belongings by the dim moon. I thought of his gun and kicked it free of him and then picked it up and tucked it in my belt. His smell was all about now. He had shat himself, and his flesh was smolder-ing, and his gags come slower now, almost at random. I had put him there.

I heaved and upchuck splattered my boots.

"Girl?" I whispered toward the dark. Ingrid had run off. "Goddammit, girl!"

I rolled the Sharps in my bedding and tied it quick to the saddle.

I remembered Pa's Colt. My holster was empty. On my hands and knees I set about searching for it. I felt the earth with my bare hands.

The Colt had landed under the boughs of a nearby spruce. My fingers found it by touch.

His gagging had stopped, my shaking had turned to something else.

Steps behind me. Ingrid walked into the moonlight and I ran to her. I wrapped my arms around her neck. I tested the words against my only friend, "I killed that man."

We rode through the night at a gallop. I was blind to the world and so trusted entire in Ingrid's eyes to guide us. Her body extended and contracted and I could hear the long moments when we took flight over the earthly terrain.

I'd been a girl hiding as a boy. I had deepened my voice and learned to walk with a male swagger. But that bastard hadn't come at the boy or the girl, he had come at *me.*

When we reached the town of Scarletville I was in awful need of a rest behind a locked door. Before we entered I smeared charcoal to my face and hands to better conceal my age.

At the livery I paid to give Ingrid a stall and all the feed she could eat. It was a little boy working the door, and I tipped him a penny to make sure Ingrid got his best.

The only hotel in town had rooms available, and I paid extra for one with a locking door. I was studying every table for the relative of the man with the Dragoon. The mistress asked if I wanted a bath. She was three times my age and plump and the sun had turned the skin of her chest to something like dust. She leaned on the bar. "You look like you could use a bath," she said to me. I could tell from her eyes what was meant, and I told her no, I wasn't interested in no bath.

She looked at me cross. "You don't even want a warm towel?"

I was dirty and I got to wondering if I'd misunderstood. "What good's a towel?"

She laughed. She leaned lower, her bosom like a deep canyon. "One of the girls can towel you *off*, if you like."

"Just a room."

"Do you want a meal?"

"I don't want no damn favors!"

"A meal is just a meal, Mr. Ornery. It's beef stew with carrots and corn bread."

I hadn't eaten much. The toll of hunger had gotten past my mind and into my bones. "Two orders. One now. One toward evening."

She sucked something from her teeth with a hiss. "Ain't yet seen a buck your age turn down a towel."

The room wasn't much, but the bed did have two pillows. Which was good on account I needed one over my head to smother the

129

grunts and bedsprings. There was a shared holehouse out the back door. I took my things when I used it.

When my stew arrived the girl who brought it sat down on my bed.

She was my age and she was smaller than me but plumper, and she told me her name was Lily Flower. Her face wore freckles over flushed cheeks. Her red hair was clean and brushed and it hung past her shoulders in wavy curls. There was a purple ribbon in it.

"I don't want nothing. I just want to be alone with my stew."

"You poor dear. I can see your hardship." Without warning she put her hand to my groin and I jumped to my feet and the stew went every which way. I cursed.

She was looking at me different now. She was squinting at me like I was a sunset.

"I lost it," I said quick.

"All of it?"

"Just leave me be." The stew was leaking away through the floor boards. There was a holler and cursing from the room below. I proceeded to collect the beef and carrots from the dirty wood and place them back in the bowl.

"You mean like stripped and snipped all of it?"

I didn't answer. I wiped a piece of beef on my pants but it only got dirtier. I ate it anyhow, grit and all.

Lily Flower was sitting at the end of the bed. She was smiling and her eyes was warm on me now. She whispered, "You're a girl, ain't you?"

"I am not."

"It's okay." Her hand appeared on my back like Noah's used to when I was sick. "You ain't the only man to pass through here who ain't a man."

"Don't."

"I promise I won't tell a soul," she whispered. "Not even the girls. Are you running from the law? It must be terrible risky."

"I think it best you leave."

My words deflated her. She looked to her lap. "I thought we was just talking. But okay, I'll get on if you so desire. But if I leave," her eyelashes fluttered, "I'll be back to the floor. There's a man down yonder waiting on me. He's got a coarse manner about him. He comes here just to see me. I'm the youngest. The worst of them always want the youngest." She was looking at me now in a manner that spoke to my deepest reserves. Her face was potent as song. "Please let me stay? I'm just so tired of being hurt on."

She was playing me but I saw the old scar below her ear and the bruise on her wrist. My own hand touched my sore neck. Something let go inside me, like a dragrope busting free. "Why do they want the youngest?"

She touched my hand with hers. She

131

smelled of spring and thunder. "Do you want to know my real name? I want to tell you my real name, since I know a secret about you. Nobody here knows my real name, not even the lady."

We was sitting side by side on the bed now. Our shoulders touched. She brought her hand into the air like she was cradling something of value for me to see. "Elizabeth Annalee Montclair." She let the name take flight about us. "It sound hard fancy, don't it?"

"It do, some."

She smiled but there was only sadness in it. I believed the name reminded her of a time she could no longer remember. "If you don't like it here, why don't you get on?" I asked.

"And go where? It's the same in each place. I've traveled some, I know." She smoothed her dress. "This here is a whorehouse. There are rules here. There ain't no rules out yonder.

"I used to think someday a man would take me from here and make me his wife. I would be a good ma, I know it. But I'm old enough now to know some things ain't never going to happen even though there ain't no rules against them."

Her eyes found mine. Her flush cheeks had gone pale and she looked built of paste. Her fingers rose to touch my neck. "He turned you black and blue."

"Don't."

She didn't take back her fingers but let them caress me. "What name did your people give you?"

I wanted to tell her. I did. We was the same age and I had never known a girl my age. "My ma called me Jessilyn."

"That's nice. What's your middle name?"

"Ain't got one."

Excitement flushed her face. "Oh, you should make one up! How about 'Daisy.' Jessilyn Daisy. Got a bell to it, don't it? Or 'Anne.' Sounds like you from a big city with lanterns lit all night and children rolling hoops and eating soft candy. I do enjoy naming. Ain't it queer the Lord lets us assign names? So much we can't touch in this life, and yet He give us the power to pick our name. Now that's something."

"I'm going by Jesse."

"I'll keep you safe, Jesse. Jesse. The name ain't as pretty but I understand your thinking. You don't want nobody knowing you're pretty. You're running. Can I see your arms?" She pulled back the sleeve of my shirt and she held my hand as she looked. "Strong for a girl. Strong for a boy. Don't you miss people knowing you're pretty?"

"I ain't never been pretty."

She blew air from her lips like I was joking. "It's just these clothes you done sewn yourself into. We should doll you up. Can I? Right now. Please? Oh Jesse, let's! Let's be Elizabeth and Jessilyn just this once." She laced her fingers with mine and squeezed. "Let's doll each other up!"

"Nah."

"Come now, don't be a hound. . . ."

I took back my hand. "Pretty brings trouble, don't it?"

"How can you say that? Pretty ain't nothing to fear! Pretty is all we got, girl. How you going to find yourself a mister without your pretty? Huh? Tell me that." She commenced pinching my cheeks. "There. We'll get your blush on yet."

"Quit it."

"I'm giving you some rouge, that's all. Damn pretty if you want to be. You look like you was raised by timber wolves but I see your pretty fighting to get loose." She rested her head on my shoulder. Then she rose again at once so I might see her face. "Do you think I'm pretty?"

Her eyes was half open, like her lips. "Yes. Terrible pretty."

She rested her head again on my shoulder. "You probably think I'm a bad person. Do you? I didn't make a decision to come here, if that's what you're thinking. I come into this too young to know of a choice." She told me the story of losing her parents to fever on the trail. "The Lord spared my brother John and me. I ain't never been sure why."

When she finished she looked on me and I

understood it was my turn. "I'm hunting the only kin I got remaining, a brother."

"Thank the Lord for brothers," she said. "I knew this about you. I could see it in your face. I seen it downstairs, right off, even before I seen them bruises on your neck."

She smelled so clean. Her hand was upon mine. I asked, "How'd you end up in this place?"

She sighed. "We reach for the familiar drink when we run dry."

There was a knock at the door. "Lily Flower? You have a special visitor."

"Shucks!" Elizabeth Annalee Montclair stood in the middle of the room. She whispered, "That's the lady. Make a man sound."

I coughed like a man.

"Do a moan."

I did my best.

"Lily Flower?"

"Yes, ma'am. A touch busy here." She said it with a pant in her voice.

"You almost done? Your mister is waiting in the lobby."

I said like I was mad because I was, "Enough already! This is my hour."

The voice on the other side of the door was quiet a time. "Come downstairs when you's done, Lily." The floor creaked as the lady moved on.

Elizabeth Annalee Montclair sunk back to the bed. I thought she would be elated. "I shouldn't have asked you to moan."

"Why not? It worked."

"Now I'm going to have to bring her money."

"How much?"

"I could say it was a mouth job. That's fifty cents."

"Fifty cents."

"If I tell her it was the whole thing, I can stay longer. The whole thing is a dollar."

"What happens if you . . ."

"If I don't bring her money?" She looked off in a way that wasn't herself. I knew I was being played. I wondered if any of it was truthful.

I dug out the dollar. It was in my fingers. I looked on it and decided I did not want to ask if Elizabeth Annalee Montclair was her real name. I gave her the dollar. "How long can you stay?"

She giggled. "Oh, you're so good to me! Oh, Jesse, we're fast friends. I'm so glad you're here!"

I was damned wore down. "I got a question for you, for that dollar."

"Ask me just anything."

"How do the bad ones pick? You know what I mean."

She laughed like it was funny. "Most of them is kind. Some of them is downright tender. Afterward the sweet ones feel sad for me and that makes me feel sad, so I reckon sometimes I prefer the middle ones, not too sweet and not rough. The slow, fat ones usually." She twirled her red hair about a finger. "The mean ones want the youngest. I don't reckon they got any issue with me. I reckon they got issue with young."

She passed her fingers through my hair. She was humming a song. No one had ever touched me like this.

"How much for the whole night?" I asked.

"From now until morning? Four dollars."

"I don't want to leave this room and I don't want you to leave neither."

She kissed the top of my head like a mother. "We won't go nowheres, sweetheart. I promise. Just like this until morning, okay? Now why don't you tell me what you's running from."

"No," I said. "Tell me a story about your ma. Tell me the longest story you got."

When I awoke I found Elizabeth Annalee had pulled the covers up around us and had dangled her arm around me. We was sharing a pillow. Her mouth was open and a track of drool ran from the corner of her lips. I smelled old booze on her breath. In the dawn light her teeth was browner than I recalled. Her skin was dry and flaking. She wasn't as young as she looked in the lantern's glow.

I left before she could wake and leave me.

I tipped the stable boy another penny out

of my remaining monies, and Ingrid threw her head and kicked the wall she was so glad to see me. I had bought two dollars and twenty-two cents worth of provisions from the mercantile, and I slipped Ingrid the first of a dozen molasses candies I purchased for her. She chewed crooked and then her tongue come out to survey her lips for more. "You's a funny eater," I said and rubbed her face.

Her ear swiveled, then swiveled back.

I put my forehead to hers and said, "Only wish you could talk. You and me together till the end, girl. You and me forever."

I climbed from the muddy street and stepped into the saddle. Ingrid didn't need the heels. We rode out at a run, just us.

Once on the grassy flats Ingrid slowed to a trot, then a walk, and I took a cheek of the chewing tobacco I bought. I didn't intend to be the kind of man who don't chew tobacco, even if I despised the stuff.

I unrolled a wanted poster I'd taken from the sheriff's office and spat.

Ruthless Noah Harney, leader of the Wild Bunch, wanted for murder and mayhem and thievery during the New Moon Heist. $2,000 reward for his delivery, dead or alive. Reward guaranteed by the Union Pacific Railroad.

They had a sketch of a man looking mean, but it wasn't my brother at all. Part of me got to wondering if there might be two Noah Harneys. Maybe my kin had made himself a family and found a spread near some water. I could only hold my belief for a half breath.

I unrolled the other poster I had took. It had another man's face, this one narrower and meaner. *The Moonshine Kid, sidekick of Noah Harney, henchman and murderer. $500 reward, dead or alive, for his role in the New Moon Heist.*

The small print on both posters mentioned Pearlsville and so that's where I figured we'd start our search proper. The man at the mercantile had said Pearlsville was a seven-day ride.

We kept on and I lost track of the counties.

We stopped in wholesome towns when the chance arose and watched the people going about their business. I remember a child holding his mother's dress and pointing for the sugar treats in a shopwindow.

In such towns as Cottonwood and Sweet-water I paid money for a bed and a stable and the provisions I craved when in the wilderness. Coming up as I done, town was the place for spending money, so I had little trouble handing a man fifty cents for a supper of fresh meat and potatoes or a breakfast of onions and fried eggs. What was fifty cents next to a full belly?

In Sweetwater I took a plate of lard biscuits and hog gravy to the porch and watched as people arrived and entered the town's church. It was a ceremony with music and charm and Ingrid and me enjoyed listening so much we took up a seat in the shade by the open window to hear the words of the preacher. He was a fiery man. I don't believe love was the fuel lighting his lantern.

"And so it is the Jews who wage war on Jesus Christ! The Jews who seek to erase their own prophet!"

I did not know what to make of his claims, and in truth I quit listening a couple turns in. It wasn't the words that mattered. It was the strength in his voice that held me, the surety of it. This man with answers.

The farther we went the more people we encountered. With those who stopped I practiced the manly arts of introduction. I tried rocking forward in the saddle in that way men do to straighten their back and stretch their muscles. I tipped my hat without giving nothing away with my eyes. I chewed tobacco in big cheekfuls and spat it with no concern for the slop.

The man part come to me natural enough. It was the seasoned part that took pretending.

I recalled how Pa carried himself that night we saw Straight-Eye Susan, when that Yankee called him out in the restaurant. Pa turned on that man, Pa looked like he had once stood before a thousand lives and opened the Lord's floodgate. That Yankee left and did not trouble us when we again saw him and his people at the show. Hard men speak a cold language, and though I did not yet know its meanings, I understood its temperature.

The men I could handle. It was the women who I believed saw through me.

We come to a desolate section of the trail without even a juniper for shade. It was sagebrush and flat, and the sun beat on us from early to late. The distance quivered in the heat. Dust on our skin baked into a hard crust. Seeds that clung to Ingrid's mane roasted and give off the smell of fresh bread. For a day and half we barely spoke. There wasn't no energy for even daydreams. We pushed on because that's all there was to do.

Around noon one day we was on the storm side of a mountain, in the dark timber. We was off course but didn't yet know it. We come around a corner of rock to see a boy before us. He was holding a double-barrel and looking at me as if he'd have to use it. He wasn't twelve years old.

Behind come four more just like him, all boys, only smaller. Clear as day they was relations. I raised my hand to them and called my howdies.

That double-barrel didn't flinch. It was pointing at my face.

" 'Preciate it if you'd lower that scattergun. I ain't trouble."

He didn't answer. The weapon did not redirect.

"You got folks, boy?"

"Don't do nothing." His voice quivered. He was just a child but I saw more season in his eyes than in half the men I passed on the trail. Sure as hell more season than me.

"I'm gonna put my horse in the shade. If 'n you don't mind. And let you pass."

He didn't answer. I give him a moment to think about it, then stepped Ingrid off the trail and put her behind a thick tree. I climbed down. "Where's your folks?"

Around the corner come a woman in a brown dress. On her back was a sack that was bending her crooked with its weight. When she neared I saw a baby wrapped tight and tucked in a sling against her chest. Hers was a white dress that had gone the color of earth.

Her five boys looked on me without words.

She swung her heavy load to the ground. She pulled her baby tight to her chest, and I saw in her belt a long bowie knife. "Just passing on," she called to me.

"As am I," I replied.

She was looking at my pistol. I realized my hand was resting on it. "You got grub?"

142

"Not enough to share."

"No, I mean, you need grub? I see a lot of mouths here."

She blinked at the thought. Some of the boys looked on one another.

"I don't got much, but I do have me some dried venison." Ingrid had spooked a forked buck some mornings before. I neck shot him and we dragged him downwind of the trail and went to work building a rack and drying up what we could. I'd only eaten the last of the fresh meat the night before.

I filled my arm with the jerky strips from the saddlebag and brought them to the boys. The youngest took his first, then the next youngest, then the next. Finally it come time for the oldest. He held the scattergun with one hand and reached with the other to take the meat. His eyes stayed on me as he ate.

I brought the remainder of the jerky to the ma.

She was a worn woman. The sun had turned her face and hands to buckskin, and her eyes had lost their color. I could see her hair was falling out in clumps. The baby stirred and she shushed it by putting the sugar rag back in its mouth. She smelled the meat, then tucked it away, for her boys, I reckon.

"Where you heading?" I asked.

"Somewheres else. My man is coming up behind us any minute."

143

It didn't make no sense for a man to send his woman and children first up a trail.

I took off my hat. I pointed off up the trail. "Hard desert up yonder. Two days to cross on horseback and only one water along the way. Got to dig it out."

This news got her looking sick.

"You got something to hold water in?"

She nodded.

I searched for good news. "Could be hotter yet. Least these nights is cool. Summer ain't on us square."

She waved the flies from her baby's face. "The Lord shall guide."

"Yep, that's what they say."

That night I built up a small fire some distance from the trail and stared into it until the heat dried my eyes. I picked this spot as I done every spot now, with defense in mind. I put a cliff against my back and a dry creek bed before me and the Sharps and its charges was waiting behind a pile of rubble I imagined I'd use as my retreat. But on this night sleep would not come.

I couldn't shake that woman. She had all those babies to look after, and the passing of any one would be an impossible suffering to endure. But she had to endure because the fates of the remainder hung in the balance. She couldn't even retreat into her own death, for her babies would be lost and alone and without a hope. Nothing was hers, not even her own lifeblood.

I had to do something so I took Pa's fiddle and give it a tune and then looked about the cliff and the creek bed. I took out the bow and give it fresh resin. I drew the horsehair across the A string and then I held perfect still and listened for its return.

The next town was called Bastion. Even from its outskirts I could tell it was different. It was a highway town, built at the confluence of trails, and its services was for travelers, not loggers or miners or cattlemen. Wagons was circled and oxen corralled and little children chased each other with sticks. I saw women tending to cookfires and men leaning against barrels spatting tobacco. There was the smell of meat sizzling and lard potatoes roasting. Some drunk fools danced to a Jew's harp and harmonica.

On the town's edge was an army encampment of maybe twenty-five men. Their rifles stood in threes and the soldiers lay in the shade with pipes and cards. The reds was warring again in these parts.

This was a day on from my last proper meal. But a look in my pouch revealed I didn't have enough money for even the stable. Fact was I was near on broke.

"How far to Pearlsville?" I asked one traveler.

"Six, seven days maybe."

"That can't be." I had heard that same figure six days before.

He shrugged. "Okay then. Can't be."

I rode straight into town and to the sheriff's office. On the wall I looked for the likeness of my brother. Noah had a new reward, five thousand dollars, and a new, better likeness. In this one I could see the shape of my brother's eyes. No mistaking those eyes. Even on paper they pulled you in. The money was being put up by the "Good Governor and the Friends of Industry."

I pulled down the poster and folded it into my coat pocket.

There was also a different type of poster on the wall. This one was for a traveling trick shooter. His name was Lightning Lance and he was charging fifty cents a man to witness the spectacle he pledged to put on.

We rode back to the families gathered on the outskirts of town. The cooking fires was sending gray smoke into the still air, and children chased a dog about.

I rode toward a ma with a particularly large caldron. She caught my eye and hollered something over her shoulder. That's how I come to be greeted by five weathered men, standing between me and that stew over the fire.

"What's your business?" one of the men said. His teeth was brown as dirt and several was missing. He wore a buckskin coat and a thick leather belt and in it was a short-barreled Remington.

"I come to see if you might be interested in a show, a little quick shooting." It was as good a starting line as I could muster. I will admit I was fearful of this crew but their stew smelled heavy on the meat.

The tallest man took a step toward me. His shirt was off and his chest bare. His blue eyes was kind and I guessed him to be a father to daughters. He had narrow shoulders but arms of sinew and muscle. He had a healed-over burn or bullet wound on his shoulder. He said, "We ain't interested."

The one with the Remington said, "Quick shooting?"

"That's right. I'm putting on a little show this afternoon. In trade for a bowl of that stew."

"We ain't interested," the tall man repeated.

The one with the Remington was looking at my front-loading Colt. The Dragoon I had taken was in my saddlebag. If these folks didn't bite I was gonna try selling them that Dragoon. "I'll be shooting on the fly."

"On the fly? With that old thing?"

"Two targets."

"What is you, eleven years old?" Remington said and had a good laugh. That his friends seemed to have the same opinion of me only emboldened him. "I bet you a dollar you can't hit two targets on the fly with that old iron." He hollered to the remainder, "What do you say, boys? You in for a dollar?"

The tall man with the blue eyes put a hand across his friend's chest. He said to me, "Are you some kind of trick shooter?"

"No, sir. My brother is west of here and I'm aiming to find him before winter. I'm hungry is all."

He considered this. He spat a stream of tobacco. By now children was gathering around us. A ma wiped her hands on her apron.

The tall man said, "Let's make this interesting then." He picked up a stick from the firewood stack and busted it over his knee. Now he held two sticks, each about as long as my forearm and as thick as my wrist. Targets. Maybe he knew that sticks are harder to shoot on the fly than round objects. The spin confuses the eye. He said, "I'll put a dollar to Jimmy's dollar, so that's two. Can you cover it?"

I nodded. That was my mistake.

"Make it three," hollered another man.

By the time they put their money together they had five dollars.

I should've declined but I had no doubt I would hit those sticks. "One condition," I said. "I pick my throw. If I don't like it, I don't draw."

The tall man looked at his partners and

shrugged. "Fair enough."

And so it was on.

We walked some distance from the edge of the camp and when I looked back I saw cooking pots with lone women over them stirring, their eyes following our commotion.

We come to stop near the edge of the meadow. Here the ground dropped away to the creek and the forest offered a dark background. They had picked the location because it was a safe direction for shooting. I was glad because it offered me an advantage. The downhill slope would buy me an additional moment of flight should I need it.

I stepped down from Ingrid and asked one of the kids to hold her lead. I was worried she might spook on account of all the strangers.

"Ready?"

"Not yet." I stretched my hands. I checked the weight of the Colt then let it slide back into its holster. I knew I wouldn't shoot the first throw. "Now."

The tall man threw the sticks and I watched them rise only fifteen feet over his head and then drop down the bank.

"You didn't shoot."

"I didn't like that one."

"Picky eight-year-old, ain't he?" Remington laughed to his buddies.

A boy returned with the two sticks and handed them to the tall man.

"You gonna shoot this time?"

I wiped the sweat from my forehead. "If I like your throw."

In a quickdraw everything has to be smooth and steady. There can be no jerky movements or stops in the motion. The target must be led a distance commiserate with its speed and distance from your person. Some use a quick logic of yardage and speed, but these shooters never master what is a pure body experience. The best shooters have no trust in logic. Pa once said, "No sounds, no time, no thoughts other than the sight of your bullet center punching the target. Your eye pulls the trigger."

I shot the first stick when it was two feet from the man's hand and rode the recoil into position for the second. When it paused at the apex of its climb the round went off and I saw it knock dust from the stick's edge. I'll admit it wasn't a solid hit. By the time I realized another shot was warranted I was too far behind its fall to catch up. I was surprised.

The crowd erupted in cheers. A chill went through me.

"But I hit them both," I said. "I hit them! Look at the stick. You'll see the mark of my bullet!"

A boy was sent to find it and he returned to hand a stick to the tall man.

The tall man said, "The stick is clean."

The crowd circled me. Ingrid whinnied.

The men would entertain none of my offerings for another round of competition.

"Pay up, Mr. Big Trick Shooter."

"But the boy found the wrong stick!" I was
backing away from them.

"He don't got the money, look at him," a
man said.

Once this notion got loose in the mob there
wasn't no hope.

I looked toward Ingrid and willed her to
run away before they might thieve her. She
threw her head and whinnied.

The tall man was coming for me. "Is it true?
You cannot cover your wager?"

"I can trade a Dragoon pistol in fine shape.
It's worth —"

He delivered a punch directly into my
abdomen. It was the first time I had ever been
punched like that. I went down in a heap. I
lay there looking at their boots and the tall
man leaned over me and lifted Pa's Colt from
my holster. Even now his eyes looked kind.
"Your people should've taught you better."

I couldn't muster no words on account of
not having the air for them.

"Get his horse," another man said. I heard
Ingrid's feet on the earth and her voice calling out over them. They was holding her and
rummaging through my saddlebags. I heard
the fiddle fall to the ground inside its box. I
heard the Sharps come free from the saddle.
The contents of my bags was dumped to the

dirt and men picked through them and when they was done, children run off with whatever was left.

I tried to rise, but now it was Remington's turn. He drove his boot to my ribs and I rolled onto my back. I was gagging and coughing and he said, "Let's have some fun for once. Hold him still."

Remington drew his knife and showed me and said, "We's just gonna mark you a little, so nobody will again be fooled by your mischief. A thief must be branded, ain't that right, boys?"

"Do it, Barrow. Do it good."

I fought but it was no use. I quit fighting because every motion only made the knife slide deeper.

He cut two lines in parallel on my cheek and then stood and wiped the knife on his pants. "There we is," he said. "Just like back home when we catch a thief."

I sat up and watched them go and got hold of my breathing and checked the wound with my fingertips. Ingrid come to me and put her lips to my forehead. It was only because of the tall man that I still had her and the saddle upon her back. He had called to stop the crowd of them from making off with her. They had taken just about everything else. The blood was upon my shirt and pants and still coming. I rolled to all fours and then stood.

When erect I saw the soldiers watching from their camp. Some turned away at my attention.

Ingrid led me to the doctor.

He was an Englishman and his own apothecary. The sign on his frontage read:

Freedom from What Ails
Doctor Massy at Your Service
STRICT CONFIDENCE AND AFFORDABLE RATES

Doctor Massy was young for a man of medicine. He wasn't dressed like the old doctor back home or any doctor I seen after. He wore a felt hat, and about his neck was draped a white scarf of silk. There wasn't even no sun marks on his face. I could've seen him five days' ride up a river and known in a breath he was physician or taxman.

Doctor Massy took me into the back room and asked first about payment. There was a queer smoke hovering about that back room. I figured it to be of some foreign tobacco. "The consultation is one part and the medicine is another. The healing is free, and the direct result of the first two. Therefore, I would recommend a prompt payment so as begin with the recovery straightaway."

"I done just got beat and robbed, sir. I ain't got nothing but my hands. I can work for your services."

He lifted an empty pipe to his lips, and just as soon pointed it at me. "I remain wealthy in labors owed. I could build a czar's castle upon a craggy cliff if all the labors due came paid." He pulled back the curtain on the window and saw Ingrid at the hitching post. His pipe ticked his teeth. "I admit I don't frequent the auctions, though I'd wager that little pony would not garner two bits if she were the only horse to survive the rapture."

"She ain't for trade."

"And why would she be? You only grip your chest like there's a bullet lurking within. Look at you. Unable to draw even the shallowest of breath without a quiver. And all this blood upon your face."

"I'm broke, Doc, two ways."

"Ah!" He raised his pipe. "A witty cowhand then. Tell me you're a poet as well?"

"You mock."

"Don't pout, dear boy. Beat and robbed, you say?"

"Yessir."

"And cut rather severely." He set his pipe aside. "One does not enter the field of medicine for the profit contained therein." From a box he withdrew a new pipe, this one carved to look like some manner of serpent. Only its bowl was brass and too small for even a pinch of tobacco. He blew a puff of air through the thing and then drew a seashell from a shelf. I had never before seen a shell and so I didn't think to notice the black paste within its center until the doctor spooned some and set it upon that brass bowl.

He pushed the pipe to me. "Here. You better take the first. Once I begin, there is no telling."

"Have we arrived at some manner of bargain?"

"Don't stall, dear boy. At this very moment I careen toward boredom, and with it, a lack of the sharing spirit."

I took the queer pipe in my hand. "Will I feel better? Is this the treatment?"

"Ah, the worthiest question and one without an answer. Yet tell me this magic vapor isn't already helping you improve, just knowing it exists? Now posthaste, good man."

The pain in my side had brought on a fever sweat and I would've tried moose dung if he'd advised it. I put my lips to the strange pipe and drew in the hot breath of that flame. The smoke come out as brown and gray. I felt it coming now. My forehead was melting over my eyes. My heartbeat drummed in the near distance, growing ever louder.

The doctor took one for himself and then another and then two more for good measure. He saw me watching and stopped midway through yet another to say, "Fear not. I have only established a precedent." The word grabbed his attention and he said it again to himself as the smoke left his teeth. "Prec-

155

edent." He drew more from the pipe. "What the American mind fears most."

My breathing rose within my ears like a thousand whispers, and my pain was just where it always was but now that seemed a hundred miles from here in a place too small to affect a god like me. I remember knowing sudden-like that this was how Pa must've felt each time he swallowed his medicine. If I could be this free-riding smoke, why go anywheres else?

The doctor was speaking but I could hear no words over the thousand whispers. On the counter was a flute of black syrup.

I don't recall leaving the doctor's storefront but I do recall waking in the morning to slicing pain. Ingrid and me had taken our rest in the lee in a revivalist's tent, and now the sun was up and my rib cracked new with each breath.

We discovered the travelers was already gone and with them Pa's fiddle and his Colt and the deed to our family land. Their fires smoldered and their tracks led onto the muddy road where they was swallowed by a hundred others going all directions.

I had to make a choice about which trail this company took. They had carried implements for wheat harvest, so I wagered them to be of the High Plains. The drought had dried their lakes as it had ours, and families of the plains was headed deeper west to find where the clouds dumped their water. I had encountered their kind already. But two trails headed general west.

We rode fast and for the first time since leaving home I rode without a gun. I did not enjoy the sensation. Just short of noon we overtook wagons that was not familiar to my eyes. It was a clan of Irish and I spoke to them from the high seat of my saddle. They was brothers, just the pair without women, and they had not seen the party I was after. They had a single scattergun between them. The older of the two looked upon me and said, " 'Tis a hungry land. Don't ye fear the reds?"

"Should I?"

"They off the reservation. And you're about carrying no weapon. Maybe you don't place much value on your pebbles?"

"That's what the reds do," the little brother confirmed. "They cut off your pebbles and hang you by them from the nearest tree."

The older brother squinted. "How could they cut the pebbles from your body and still hang you by them?"

The younger one thought this through. He got eager with a new idea. "They hang you by your pole. You know . . ." For clarity he took meaty hold of his groin.

"Then you's safe," the big brother said of

the little. To me, he added, "He ain't long enough to tie no knots with."

Ingrid and me turned back late that day. We rode while the moon was high and then broke for the night in a lush park where Ingrid could graze. The pain was on me fierce then and I could not lay on my back or on either side but for the point of an arrow going in with each breath. The wounds on my cheek took turns burning and itching.

I drew out the flute of syrup I'd stolen from the doctor's supply. I shook it. I hadn't never stolen anything in all my life, but I'd stolen this without a thought. I drew the cork and smelled the contents.

All those nights I poured for Pa, and some of them, after he fell into deep slumber, I rose and poured a little for myself too.

Now I put the flute away without a taste. I was afraid of its freedom.

By afternoon of the next day I come to decide I had chosen another wrong trail. I still hadn't seen the company of travelers, and now the day was fading and what hope was there of ever recovering Pa's things?

We took a break near the creek. It was a low moment. I give in to the tears for a time at the weight of all I lost. Pa would never forgive me.

His voice come to me there by the creek, as

it had years before when he found me crying. *Quit that blubbering. It don't get nothing done.*

I passed my sleeve over my eyes. I locked my jaw. If only I had the fiddle. I would've traded five Colts for that fiddle.

As is wont to happen when the sun leaves the valley floor, the wind reversed to blow down the creek. In it I caught a whiff of wood smoke.

A group was ahead of us on the trail and not that far along. I dusted myself off. I muttered, "Please," and wondered who I was talking to.

I tied Ingrid to a spruce. She took this treatment personal.

"Ain't risking you a second time, girl."

I found their camp on the edge of a great meadow that continued up the ridge to the mountain's rocky top. I took a hide on the edge of the forest. They was unloading from the day's travel. Even from this distance I could see this was indeed the company I was after.

I walked out the woods and hollered and showed my hands so they would know I meant no harm. At the sight of me, there come some ruckus from the camp. The tall man was holding a crate, his eyes overtop and on me.

I just barely made out, "Ain't that the buck we done kicked on?"

"Lookie here!" another shouted. "The trick shooter come back for seconds!"

The tall man handed off the crate he was holding. He set his gloves upon it and come walking out from their camp toward my approach. The others watched. Behind them the children was hiding in the lee of their biggest, a boy with a man's hat on. The women kept at the work.

"I come for my family's things," I called as the tall man neared.

He spat a worn plug at the grass between us. There was still that kindness in his eyes. I was right to have seen it the first time.

"I admit I done you wrong. Ain't right to wager what you can't cover. I ain't here to argue nothing about that other than to say I deserved to get beat. And I done learned a lesson in it."

He took a fresh plug.

"I won't argue the pistols. Seems only fair you keep them, seeing as I used them in my attempt to cheat you. But the Sharps, see, my pa carried that in the war and now he's dead and gone. It ain't only a rifle to me, understand, and I didn't use it against you in no way. Also the fiddle and the deed to our family land. That's what I come for. You ain't got no claim to them things."

He spat. "You got some brine walking out here telling me the way it ought to be."

"It ain't brine, sir. I serve my kin is all."

He cracked his neck with a fist to his chin. "You realize we could beat you again and this time there ain't a witness for ten miles. Ain't a reason to stop. Hell, we could stake you out in this here meadow and let the coyotes chew you apart."

I didn't buy his bluff. He was a farming man and what he cared about was his company getting to whatever valley held their hopes. Still I wasn't of a mind to test my theory.

"Give me my rifle and such and I'll be off and you won't never see me again."

"Now why would I do that?"

"On account you know it's right, sir."

"Is that so?" He laughed. He turned to the others and hollered, "Go get us a rope."

"What kind of rope you want, Boss?" one of the men called.

"What do you mean what kind of rope? Get me the dragging kind." The tall man shook his head. To me he said, "I'll tell you what, next time I ain't building me a company by calling on strangers. Next time it's my kin and the neighbors of my kin, and no blasted fools from Missoura. You know Missoura? Refuge of idiots, I'll tell you what."

I caught my fingers testing the cuts on my cheek.

He said, "Now I suggest you get while you still got legs for getting. I'm sure Barrow would like to finish the job he started on your face."

"But it ain't right," I said. "You know it ain't right. How come you ain't doing nothing to make it right?"

"You dim, kid?" the tall man asked. "You tried to take from me, so I done took from you. That's the way of it. You ain't one of mine, and I got to look out for mine. You'll come to understand, you live long enough. If there's rules, you done broke 'em when you come back here for seconds."

He tipped back his hat. "Now go on, boy. You won't find what you're looking for, not in this meadow."

The men was coming now, with ropes enough for a herd of mustangs. I saw the one with the Remington. His eyes was hungry on me.

"You don't know me," I said.

"I know you. I was you once. So hear me when I say get on, before my crew takes hold of you. They bored with travel and will relish punishing you. I ain't willing to test my command of them here and now by ordering them off your body. You got me?" He pointed to the timber. "Get, boy. Get, or I'll stop trying to help you."

So I got. I turned and ran into the trees.
But I didn't go far.

I watched from the other side of the creek as

the evening come on. The water there was slow and I could hear the families chatter in the calm air. With the animals turned out, the men mostly sat. It was the mothers I watched, in their evening labors.

I was drawn to one in particular, the tall man's wife. She wore a yellow bonnet and I could see from her laughter with the children that she was their favorite. They sat about her as she worked, and the oldest ran her errands without complaint. She was telling them a story I could not hear.

When the meal was ready and they ate, I sank back into the brush and stared up at the sky. There come the clink of spoons on tin and I saw the first star appear against the purple heavens. The earth still held the day's heat. My stomach moaned. I hadn't eaten in days and beetles and crickets was starting to look worth a taste.

I sat back up to see the woman in yellow staring my general direction. I held dead still. It wasn't possible she had seen me, yet she was looking this way. She walked toward me a few steps, but then her husband called her back.

The cooking fires was now stoked up, and the people lounged about them. A couple played instruments but with no skill. A man and his son plucked at Pa's fiddle, but they had even less talent than me. When they grew weary of it, they passed it along to others.

The woman in yellow was probably twice my age. She now wore a shawl for warmth. While the others reclined in the firelight, she was tending to her children, brushing their hair and readying them for sleep.

Maybe an hour passed, and twice during that time she looked up across the creek. She was the only one.

With darkness complete the tall man rose and gave his wife a kiss upon the brow, and I watched as he walked back into the meadow where he and I last spoke. His jacket was on against the cold and a rifle was in his hands. The first watch was his.

In time the others took lanterns to their wagons and they laid out under the tarpaulins stretched to the earth. Their shadows moved about the fabric in the lantern light. The whole world was dead dark but for the golden glow of those tarpaulins.

The woman in yellow was now in her sleeping place with her children. The light cast the shape of her Bible upon the tarpaulin, and I moved closer. Even at the creek's edge I couldn't make out her words, but I could hear the up and down of her voice and I could for a moment imagine the experience of falling asleep beside such a magnificent woman.

To know the Word by the voice of your mother, that has always been the path to salvation.

In time the lanterns went out and the fires turned to smoldering, and there rose only the occasional mutterings of a sleeping child. It was then that I took my chance to cross the creek.

I had kept a keen eye on Pa's fiddle and knew which wagon now held it. I hadn't seen the bow, but I could replace the bow.

I used the moon shadows cast by the trees to conceal my approach, and I stepped as slow as I would if stalking a bedded antelope. All the while my blood swished through my ears and my breath was quick.

I don't believe I made a sound as I moved ever closer to Pa's fiddle. So how did she detect me then if not for the silent plea all children emanate in hope their mother will hear?

"Don't move," she whispered, and I nearly leapt from my boots. She was crouched on the edge of her sleeping children, a pistol in her hands. "Don't you dare take a step."

"I'm sorry," I said without thought. I had steeled myself to fight if it came to that, but her voice cut through me and left me bare. "I don't intend no harm, ma'am, I swear it."

She rose in her white nightdress. She stood between me and her brood. She was barefoot in the summer grass. The moonlight glinted from the barrel. She was holding the pistol with two hands. "They said you would come. You or Indians. This is a thieving moon."

"I ain't here to thieve, ma'am."

"Yet you risk life, for what?"

It occurred to me that she hadn't yet sounded the alarm. I took off my hat so she might know my honesty. "I only come for my family's things."

"Shush," she said. "Quieter or you'll wake the children."

"Yes, ma'am."

"I thought you looked hungry in town. Have you eaten since then?"

"No, ma'am."

She looked about, and then waved to me to come nearer. She held the pistol on my knees now. "What is your name?"

"Jesse."

"Come, Jesse."

I followed her to the rear of her wagon and to the cauldron that had held their supper. I was so close I could smell the old sweat under her arms. She held the pistol in one hand and with utmost care lifted the lid of the cauldron and set it aside without a clink. She handed me a bowl and spooned out the still-steaming grub and whispered, "Quick now. My husband will wake the next watch soon and return to me."

The stew was warm in my mouth and its taste and her kindness released something

166

bound up inside me, and all at once I was shaking, though I wasn't sure why. "Sorry, ma'am, for waking you and all."

"I will feed you, child, but then you must go."

One of her children stirred and for a long moment she held a finger to her lips. Only once she was sure the child was back asleep did she speak again. "You're without folks then, Jesse?"

"Yes, ma'am."

"Where is it you intend to go?"

"Pearlsville, ma'am. I seek to rejoin my brother there."

"Good, so you have family then."

"I do. That fiddle you seen tonight, that was my pa's and I already lost him once."

"Finish the stew," she said with sternness. "Then go. I cannot help you with your fiddle. There's no allowing you to go prowling through our wagons. These men shoot first. You should know that."

"Your voice, ma'am. It's so kind and learned."

She looked on me now for a long moment, her arms crossed about her chest. "It was the strangest thing, Jesse. I laid there exhausted, every muscle worn weary, and yet sleep would not arrive on this night. I could feel you out there watching us. Jesse, do we know each other from elsewhere?"

"No, ma'am."

She took the empty bowl from my hands. "We've never met before? Not once? I used to be a schoolteacher in Ohio. Maybe you've passed through Ohio?"

My belly was stuffed with potatoes and meat. The warmth spread through my arms and down my legs. "I'm sure of it, ma'am. I would remember you."

"You must never come near us again, do you understand? Never. Not on this trail, not three weeks farther along, not this winter. To see us again would only bring trouble upon you. Do you understand? Your pa would not want you hurt for the sake of his fiddle, I promise you that."

"Yes, ma'am."

She looked on the pistol in her hand. It looked like Pa's Colt. "I believe this belongs to you. My husband gave it to me this evening and told me to keep it near in case of attack. But I don't want a short gun near my children, we talk daily of the accidents that have claimed so many children along these trails. You'll see my husband loaded the empty cylinders from his own supply of powder and lead. You might check them. He is not skilled around firearms." She withheld the Colt. "But if I give this to you, you must promise to ride far from here. You must promise never to do wrong with this weapon. My husband will not agree with my returning it to you."

"Ma'am, I'm without resources. I may

starve or worse if not for that pistol."

"I know. Do you swear to me what I ask?"

"Ma'am, I have no wrong intentions. I swear, and I would do so with my hand laid open upon the Good Book if you desire. I am honest and bare before you."

"There is something familiar or peculiar about you," she said. "What is your full name, Jesse?"

I understood that I couldn't say Harney, not without her thinking of my brother's crimes and linking me to them. What choice did I have but to lie? "Jesse Montclair, ma'am. That's my name."

Come full morning we broke free of the valley for obvious reason and followed the high ridge. It was a grassy spine with rims of rock and we made good enough time along it. The view was its own distraction. My eye followed the hawks on the wing, and I imagined what the world must look like from their height.

We camped that night along a high meadow bordered in aspen. We picked a spot among some rocks that would offer cover in case of attack. I advised Ingrid to stay close.

The spruce nearby held a chattery population of red squirrels and I set about gathering some for supper. I wasn't keen on spending one of my shots on so small a meal, so I threw stones instead of lead. When the rocks failed I tried building a deadfall but the critters wouldn't come close.

It was getting on toward dark and my stomach was singing its lament.

Overhead two squirrels hollered at me and then chased each other to a new branch, where they sat again to holler some more. I drew the Colt. It come from the holster like silk.

To fire a round would be to announce my location to any soul in the valley. Still, I took aim and aced the bigger of the two squirrels and he flipped end over end to the earth. The shot echoed back from the basin wall and then a half beat later from the far side of the valley.

I built a fire and skinned him with my knife and ate his meat before he was full cooked. Squirrel ain't nothing but a rat of the branches and they taste like it. I cracked the bones for their marrow and sucked dry the stems.

After, I leaned back and licked my fingers and felt inclined to offer thanks for this recent turn of good fortune, the Colt and the mother from Ohio. It was a high feeling, to feel grateful for something again. I tried to hold it, always the child bottling smoke.

What happened next is the part I wasn't going to tell you. It's the part I don't touch. Even in my own mind. It's the only piece I don't pick up from time to time and turn over and consider and reconsider and put back just where it belongs. This part built the vault within me and then climbed inside and slammed shut the door.

You should know I ain't confessing on account I fear my Maker. Ain't nothing that could happen to me that I don't rightly deserve. But I know what I done that night can't die with me.

I remember I was dreaming of butterflies. Of a great big bowl of turkey gravy and all about me orange and black butterflies on the wing. I was dreaming so deep I nearly missed Ingrid's snort of warning.

I woke to hear hooves moving through the aspen. I called and at the sound of my voice the animal broke into a trot.

I gave chase by sound alone, still half in dream, the leaves about my face the wings of butterflies. When I cleared the aspens I saw what I believed to be a man swing up on Ingrid's bare back, and I understood. Ingrid was being rustled from me.

I tried hollering but it didn't do no good. They was twenty yards away in the crisp moonlight. The Colt was already in my hand.

Whistling didn't work neither. A rider don't never teach his horse the truth, that all control is hers.

They was past thirty yards now and gaining speed. I was losing my Ingrid, and then I would be alone.

I heard no burst but the echoes returned, and I was surprised at what I done. I was relieved too, even in that moment before the echoes finished returning, relieved to own an instrument divine enough to reset right.

The thunder of Ingrid's feet upon the earth. She was running my way and I was still flash-blind. The Colt had barked fire into the night. She found me and bowled me over, she was so happy. She nibbled at my cheeks, and I took hold of her neck and she lifted me to my feet. We put our noses together.

I swung up on her back and we walked across that dark meadow to see the bastard laid out.

Even now I struggle against it.

In the moonlight I saw it was a boy I killed. He was lying facedown. I could tell he was a boy right off just from his size and dress. I could tell he was dead too. My bullet done hard damage to his head.

I bent down beside him. He was an Indian, maybe fourteen or sixteen, one of the few hundred that summer refusing to move to a smaller reservation on land foreign to his people. He smelled of smoke and grease and wet soil. There too was the warm iron smell of blood.

How could I be older than a rustler?

Ingrid and me walked back to camp in darkness. We loaded what little we had, and sat a time, pondering the event over and over, and then walked back to the body while the dawn was arriving. I recall praying it had all been a dream.

The body was still there. It hadn't moved. Somehow that felt queer, that it'd been there this hour, unmoving.

I remember a potent urge to roll him over. Ain't sure why, but it was there like you feel the urge to help an old woman who has stumbled. The body was stiffening by then.

His eyes wasn't there no more on account the bullet broke apart his face and so he could not look on me.

He wore elk skin with white and blue beads sown in. His feet wore a white woman's boots, toes showing through a gap of one and rawhide for the lace of the other. One of his arms was snapped from the fall and I could see where the bone poked at the sleeve.

He done this to himself. I was trying to believe that. He done this when he decided to steal from me.

Ain't sure how I didn't see it sooner. Eventual I come to notice something wasn't right about his chest. I poked his rib with the barrel of the pistol on account I was afraid to touch him.

This boy had nubs. This boy was in fact a girl.

In my tellings of these events I have all but

once left out the girl. When I told Noah I left out the girl. When I told the court. I always leave out the girl.

If I don't fire the Colt maybe I die alone in those mountains without a horse, I don't know. So why do I leave out the girl?

In truth it was smallness that moved me to fire on her, not fear. I didn't think about the chances of my survival without Ingrid or about my rights to my animal or any such justified notions. I only cringed to be reduced, and I pulled the trigger, and I felt relief at the sound of my hit.

Say I don't shoot. Say I follow Ingrid's tracks and keep on them even if it takes me all summer. What's to say I don't find them in some canyon with peaceful intentions? Maybe I enter with my arms held high and she asks me to join her in a supper of venison and camas. Maybe together we confess all we survived and all we done to survive, and maybe we decide to join together and survive as one.

Us riding Ingrid together across them mountains, me forgetting my brother and her forgetting her people and both of us riding for the safety of some far-off valley where girls can't be seen by other eyes.

Always, I leave the girl out.

I was drowning after, the struggle of a body at the river's surface. I gasped for the story I had believed all these miles. Same as when I was a girl and used to breathe the stories Noah told of Ma. The made-up ones with the real ones.

I was a Harney, dammit, and my destiny was to find my brother and bring him home and thereby save our family land. The journey would be fraught with struggle, and to manifest my destiny I'd have to put on the strong armor and persevere no matter the hardship.

So that's the coffin the girl had to fit in. That's all she could ever be, a hardship on my journey. She wasn't a girl who dreamed of a land with chest-high grass where bison still followed the spring. She was an adversary hell-bent on taking what was intended for me.

What kind of girl comes in the night to steal a horse from a lone traveler? What manner of father sends his daughter to thieve? This was *their* fault. Indians did not value life as they should, as the Lord intends life to be valued. They was beneath the Lord's lessons — they could never make good on all His gifts.

I drew my knife across my cheek in parallel to the lines the man with the Remington had sliced. The blood ran but I did not wipe it clean.

Instead I drew the flute of syrup from my pocket and pulled the cork and swallowed a mouthful. It wasn't pain I wanted free of.

In the days that followed I drank that syrup

instead of foraging food. I drank as I swallowed air. I drank until the only fact that remained was my westward motion.

III

When we arrived in Pearlsville I was starved and in no mood for honest labor. I bet a boastful man outside a saloon he couldn't shoot his empty liquor bottle from ten paces and guessed right and so made a dollar. That I put up against another man, his pistol verses mine with four targets at fifty paces. I said four because that's how many balls I had remaining. He went one for four while I erased all. With the proceeds I bought myself supper and new powder and lead for the Colt and then went looking for another game.

After I exhausted one saloon I rode to the next and began again. I found no shortage of men with a predilection for gambling and an unfounded confidence in their own abilities with a sidearm.

Pearlsville had plenty of saloons. But soon enough word got around and no one would bet against the kid with the slashes on his face.

In three days' effort I had twenty-six dollars. This sum was more than I had personally made accumulatively in my life, yet I wasn't buoyed none by the success. One patron had missed when I had hit and he called me a son of a bitch, an insult I took to heart. Maybe I was looking for a beating. I cracked him on the bottom of the chin with the butt end of my pistol. It caught him in surprise and his eyes dazed and I watched as he fell stiff to the ground. His friends was on me then and I took a blow to the back and a knee to the same damn rib before the barkeep's pistol ended the thing.

Pearlsville was the biggest city I ever saw. It was where the gold and timber and beef that drained from them mountains met the straight current of the Union Pacific. The railroad had spawned wealthy businessmen with employment to offer, which done brought workingmen with their families, falling to this after their dreams of homesteading had worn thin. Now there was great swaths of shacks and lean-tos across the city, vast patterns of browns and grays with tendrils of smoke rising from rusty pipes. There was women hanging laundry on lines strung over the dusty streets, kids running between the legs of stallions, shouts in languages I never knew existed. There was Indians dressed like whites, blacks dressed like Indians, Mexicans every which way, even

Frenchmen.

These was folks who didn't grow their own crops or raise their own beef cattle. Not even a heifer for curds. Everyone of them, far as I was concerned, had locked themselves into some queer manner of prison.

I couldn't stop looking at the rich people. I'd never seen rich people before. Pearlsville had ladies with two-foot feathers blooming from their hats who rode sidesaddle and dodged the sun with umbrellas perched like sails. There was rich men whose watches dangled from chains of gold and whose boots shined like they repelled dust. The rich didn't hurry nowhere. They strolled and then stepped into polished coaches. When they rolled down the street, haggard mothers shuttled their children to the sides.

I saw mothers sitting on steps working laundry and smoking. Mothers pulling their kids from wrestling matches. Mothers with swelling bellies and sweat-stained dresses.

There was Orientals too. Lots of them in their confines on the outskirts of the city. They wore sky-blue gowns and a tight little braid from where some men go bald. They wouldn't never look at me straight. Their eyes didn't seem to move from the earth before their next step. I never saw an Oriental woman, just the men. Folks claimed they stored their women and children underground for safekeeping.

■ ■ ■ ■

The sheriff's door was locked. Noah's likeness was in ten places on that wall, the same
poster. No missing it. His corpse was worth
ten thousand to them now. I tore the posters
down and crumpled them in a ball and set
that mess in the dirt and touched a match to
it. It burned up and was gone from this earth
in but seconds. That's what I wanted to happen to me when I died. I didn't want to be
left out. I wanted to be sent into nothing on
a plume of smoke.

I turned around to see a group of lawmen
coming up the far side of the porch. There
was the sheriff with white hair, dressed in the
apparel of a businessman. His badge gleamed
and a new Remington was on his hip. He held
a ring of keys in his hand. Behind him come
three younger deputies, halfway between my
age and his. They was big men, clean shaven,
and dressed as cattlemen. One still wore his
spurs. Their badges was over their hearts. I
thought this queer, that a man so frequent
the attention of gunfire would offer the
advantage of a bull's-eye.

The deputy with spurs looked on me but
did not alter the content of his pronounce-
ments to the sheriff. I was a shrew on the
ground who had caught his eye but not his
attention. The sheriff pointed at the near-

empty wall and said, "I don't know why we bother putting up them posters."

They walked inside and shut the door behind them.

I pushed open that door for myself. They was taking seats at four desks in the room.

"Let me guess," the sheriff said. "A bounty hunter."

"You seen others?" I asked.

"You're the fourth come through that door today. The first we just found dead in a shitter across town." He nodded to one of the deputies and the man shuffled through some papers on his desk, rose, and handed me a sheet of paper with printed words on it. The sheriff said, "This here is the paper we give him."

I looked the note over and saw that it was the latest news on Noah's movements. He had last been seen here in Pearlsville the month previous. But since then he was blamed for the robberies of three shipments and the killings of eight men two counties east.

When I looked up their eyes was on me. The deputy with spurs said, "I'm sure you can find someone to help you make sense of it."

I looked him square and said, "I can read." His gaze narrowed and he spat and I learned how quick a soul can make an enemy of a lawman. "It says here the Governor has raised a militia to war against Harney."

The sheriff was putting a match to a rollie. "Ain't nobody rooted out that injun yet, but I'm sure you'll be the one." He waved out the match and tossed it at the wall.

"The Governor lives in this here town?"

The sheriff puffed, his eyes studying me for the first time. "What's your name, son? Who gave you that mark? You part Mexican?"

The deputy with spurs said, "What's your business with the Governor?"

I could see there was nothing to be gained by counsel with these men and so I did not answer. "How does a man sign up for the militia?" I was figuring the fastest way to Noah was to join the army hunting him.

The men laughed.

"Get out there, squirt," the old man said. "But do me a favor and get yourself kilt outside the county. We worn thin for one day."

I found the Governor's mansion upon a bluff overlooking the city. At the edge of town a gate bisected the roadway leading up that bluff and there was a guardsman holding a Winchester repeater and smoking a rollie. I nodded to him, but he only looked on me. Everybody in town was smoking rollies. In the city there was too much standing around with bored hands.

"Can I pass?" I asked the guard.

"You on the list?"

"Could be."

"Doubt that."

"Check for me?" I wanted to see how long this list was.

The guardsman took a moment to study me and then flipped his cigarette into the dirt. He wore a duster and a black hat with a silver band. He was young with green eyes and red hair and I thought he looked a touch soft for such work. That made me sure he was dangerous. He unfolded the list from his pocket.

I told him my name was Jesse Montclair. It just come out like that.

"You ain't on the list."

"How do I sign up for his militia?"

"You." He looked me over. "You got army experience?"

"No, sir."

"The militiamen all got army experience."

"How many of them is there?"

He hefted his holster back onto his hip. "Round about a buck fifty, I reckon. What you say your name was?"

Over his shoulder, near the mansion, I saw a gleaming carriage driven by two white horses, each bigger than Ingrid and Ol' Sis put together. They was waiting on someone.

The afternoon was bright and unnatural hot. The light shone red through the smoke of cooking fires. Each breath was rich with creosote and manure.

I'd been hearing a train rumbling to a stop. Then that whistle and at last a great release of steam. I ducked the gap between two buildings and arrived in time to see another release from the train, this one men, women, and children with trunks and bags and wide eyes. Merchants glazed in dust befell them holding steaming corn and strips of meat on skewers. A boy peddler held a whiskey bottle and offered pulls for a dime. Others was shouting about horses and wagons for sale and rides for rent "to wherever your dreams will take you."

"Welcome to the pearl of your future!" That was the city's call. The words was writ on the arch over the train yard.

Railroading settlers was still coming off the cars. I couldn't help but hate them a little, how they likely covered more miles today than I suffered in a week on the trail.

I wondered what traveling that fast did to a soul.

Ingrid and me spent the evening together. I took my supper to her stall and the bottle of ale that come with it. We didn't much talk. We stood close, as horses is wont to do when full of belly. "So long as your feet is on the ground, you the boss of the man on your back." Her eyes hung half open. I passed a hand along her neck. "I should've taught you that. You knew it once but Pa broke the notion from you so you might wear a saddle. But I want you to have it back. You gotta remember, girl. Nobody else decides nothing for you no more."

I woke early and walked to a local sit-down and was the first patron through the door. The owner was sitting at the bar with a paper when I come in. I ordered his hot breakfast and asked if I might take a gander at his paper while he made it.

My brother's name appeared on page 2. He was blamed for a holdup in Wyoming and another in Nevada on the same day. The reporter raised the possibility that Noah had broken his gang into two to confuse the authorities. Didn't say nothing about the possibility Noah was getting blamed for crimes he didn't commit. The article mentioned, like it was old news, the New Moon Heist. It said, "Harney is known to have escaped with $50,000 in fresh-printed cash."

Fifty thousand dollars. I said that figure out loud. I wondered what fifty thousand might look like if laid out on this table before me.

The Governor himself was on page 1, with a picture and all. The article was about his support for the Chinese Exclusion Act. "This brave law is curing the woes of the family man by opening employment across this triumphant state." I read the article in its entirety, but it was the caption to the picture that held my attention.

Governor enjoys some shooting
sport last Sunday.

In the picture the Governor watched a man fire his pistol from the hip. The motion was blurred with speed.

I paid for my meal and paid extra to take the paper with me. With it under my arm I crossed the city. A new guard was at the Governor's gate. I took a rest below a cottonwood. As the sun grew hot I moved from its rays into the shade. I finished with the paper and then started it again.

It was past noon, and the wind was picking up dust and spinning it in a loose circle before letting back to the earth, and I hadn't seen hide nor hair of the Governor. Deliveries went past the gate with some regularity. I took note of that.

I walked about to put blood in my legs again and in the distance to the west I saw a white building being built all by its lonesome. There was scaffolding along it and the tiny black dots of men at work. It must've been a half mile from the edge of town, but even from this distance I could see the twin flags flying overhead, one the stars and stripes and the other the freshly drawed-up banner of the state.

188

"What's that out yonder?" I called to the guard.

He took a gander for himself and squinted against the sunlight. He was older than the first guard, twice my age plus some. "That there is the state capitol."

"Why ain't it in the center of town?"

"They aim it to be. That's the direction they building."

I grew thin with waiting. "Governor ever come out of his hiding place?"

The guard rested his Winchester on his hip. "Why? What plans do you have for him? What's your name, son? Come near. I seen you here before, ain't I?"

I wasn't getting nowhere sitting at the gate and so I started down the road back into town without much of a plan. I caught a ride with an open wagon drawn by a sole quarter horse. Its driver was a minister in black cloak and round hat and he was picking up walking men and giving them rides in exchange for listening to the Word. He preached as we crossed town and in truth I wasn't much interested in his message, though I played the part well enough that he delivered me all the way to the capitol building. I hadn't planned to go that far but as we neared I saw them two white horses out front tethered to that same polished carriage I remembered from the mansion.

A deputy stopped me from entering the capitol grounds. I didn't make no fuss but just sat down on the side of the road and tipped my hat to the sun. Wasn't long this time before I heard hooves and the smooth runnings of carriage wheels. I looked up to see the white horses punching dust. A guardsman sat beside the driver.

I understood this to be a chance worthy of risk. I stepped into the path.

The driver reined back and the carriage rocked forward with the stop. I heard the occupant curse. The guardsman was up with the two black eyes of the scattergun leveled on me. He was cursing and shouting. Another guardsman come off the back and levered a shell into his Winchester. He circled behind me, and I put my palms out where all could see.

"I mean no offense. I only request an opportunity to speak. I done been waiting all day."

"Get out the way or we'll roll you over," the guard shouted down the length of the scattergun.

"I won't get until you hear me through. You'll have to pepper me if 'n you want me gone sooner."

At this the guard from behind put a boot to my ass and I tumbled face-first to the earth. He was upon me at once, a barrel to my neck. The Colt was pulled free of its holster. I didn't dare breathe. The speed of this guard impressed me.

"What's your business!" the guard with the scattergun shouted. "Tell me or you'll tell it to your Maker as you done suggested."

"I . . . I just want a minute with his governorship."

There was silence.

"His governor. Ship?"

"I got a question for him."

"What kind of fool sits the road with a quest —"

"What is this delay?" I heard a new voice from within the carriage.

"Sir," I shouted, "I'm here to talk with you."

The guard with the scattergun called to his younger counterpart, "Get this bandicoot out of here. Have Sheriff Wilhelm put him on a train for St. Louis."

Desperation shoved me back on familiar tricks. "I bet you five dollars against an audience with the Governor I can hit a target of your choosing. Right now."

At this a head appeared from the side of the carriage. It belonged to a young man with a thin moustache. A narrow cigar hung from his lips. His face showed not a sign of sun or weather. This was not the Governor of the state. "A shooting wager?" His voice was rich with dignity.

"Sorry, senator," said the guard with the

scattergun. "We're sending this horn on his way."

I dug up Straight-Eye Susan. Except now my words come out with the resolve of a killer. "I'm a better shooter than any of these men. I can outshoot your best gun or I'll give up trying."

The senator turned the cigar in his mouth. "You are not flush with humility. A showman then? Are you some manner of weapons performer?"

"No. I look at something and then it gets center punched with a nugget of lead. That's all."

He pushed open the carriage door and stepped out into the light. He wore a maroon suit and a silver vest. "Any man can speak such bravado. Demonstrate your skill and I will judge its merit." His eyes scanned the middle distance for a target.

The older guard called, "This ain't a prudent idea, sir."

The senator ignored the guard. He pointed at a bird on the wing. The sun was in his eyes and he held a hand to block it. "That raven. If you're so good, hit that raven."

"The one on the wing out yonder? The eagle?"

"Whatever its species. Kill it and we'll see about this audience."

"You want to see my five dollars first?"

He chuckled. "Hit the animal or I'll let Tuss

192

put you on the next train east."

"It's some distance for a sidearm. Them birds is tall as a man up close. Can I have two shots?"

Turning to the guardsmen, the senator said, "What think you, boys? Two shots? Yes, why not. Have two, but not a third. The day is already well aged." He nodded toward the guard who had kicked me to the ground. The man spat and withdrew the Colt from his belt and handed it to me.

The senator put his clean fingers to his ears. His cigar glowed and a cloud of smoke drifted over me.

I cocked the Colt and sighted and led and was surprised when the pistol leapt in my hand. I was not surprised to miss low and behind. I shot again with calm. Pa's voice in my ear, *A real shooter don't miss twice.*

Feathers fluttered off in the breeze and the eagle beat his wings faster and away, but then slower and then the bird was spinning. I felt the impact on the earth we shared. Dust rose up and was taken by the wind and I wished the senator had picked an ale bottle or a standalone stone as our target.

His cigar lay smoking on the road. He turned to me and then we both looked down at this tobacco. I picked it up for him. He said, "I am persuaded."

"So you will take me to the Governor?"

"I like that you're small too." The senator

squeezed my shoulder like I was some manner of animal at market. "And frail for a man. Look at you. The Governor will underestimate you and wager high. You say you can shoot on the quick?"

He opened the door of the carriage and pointed. This rich man was inviting me inside. His shave was so fresh he seemed not to grow facial hair anywhere but in a thin band on his upper lip.

"This ain't keen," the younger guard said. "I advise against it."

"Well, lucky for us we don't pay you for your counsel. Now tell me everything. Where did you garner those marks upon your cheek? Go on, climb inside. They won't shoot you for doing as I say."

The younger guard took back the Colt and tucked it in his belt. He ran his hands over my sides and down my legs and then stood and spat on my toe.

I climbed inside and took a seat upon the polished leather. We set off at once. I had never been inside a carriage before, let alone one with braces for a smooth ride. The senator lit a new cigar. As an afterthought he offered me one. I declined. I was smitten by our transportation. We was within a cloud during a windstorm.

"Tell me, will you win this competition?" He was not of this place and spoke with the accent of his education. "I suspect you will but I must know, have you won competitions before? Are you a gambling man? What is your history? I should know this and more because someone may ask. You aren't a criminal? Is there a warrant someone might uncover?"

"I'm just a nobody. But I'm fixing to get myself a job with the Governor."

"First you have a job for me. Have you wagered and won before?"

"Yessir."

"Brilliant. I will wager four hundred on you. That should capture our Governor's attention. Don't you think? Whether you win or lose, I still win so long as we compete as equals. However, I would much prefer you not lose. At this particular juncture, honestly put, my coffers would feel the sudden deprivation of nearly a half thousand."

I didn't answer. Four hundred dollars would never fit in one man's pocket. I wondered if rich men carried different bills than us regulars.

He lectured as we rolled at great speed through town. Before us folks jumped free of the road. His talk took a turn for the personal. "I am to be his son-in-law. But you probably already know as much. We are in the papers often. His daughter and I will be married this fall and will travel to the nation's capital where our home is nearly completed. I am the new congressman from this infant state.

Maybe that is why you recognize me."

I in fact did not recognize him. I couldn't have told you then the difference between a congressman and a whore. The word "congress" was something I most associated with breeding.

"You may wonder why I would stake such money on you and against the father of my intended. Well, he is a man who values his friendships, and being privy to the subtle dynamics between him and his closest allies, I have learned that for him friendship and wagers go hand in hand. It is the wager that builds the esteem and history, two vital ingredients of any contemporary friendship between equivalent men.

"Don't have the wrong impression, however. I am not yet dusty enough, if I may, to find personal enjoyment in the coarse outlets of the Governor. I retain the dignities of my eastern forbearers — the very founders of this nation, I might add. Nonetheless, when this western man offers me a whiskey, I take it even though I do not normally imbibe libations more callous than, say, gin. I am a Lutheran, you understand. We prefer service to vice. Alas, sometimes our fates require a sensible and controlled excursion through the wilderness, do they not? Is that not the lesson our nation's history so prescribes? What is your name after all?"

"Jesse Montclair."

"Jesse Montclair." He rubbed his chin. "Not of the Georgian Montclairs, I hope."

"No, sir."

"Have you been graced with a jovial nickname? Something cocky and bullying, perhaps? I would prefer not to employ 'Montclair' in the company of his governorship. The Montclairs are most spiteful Southerners, and their conflicts with the Governor predate the war."

"I ain't got no other name."

"Then we will call you Jesse Straight. You strike me as a straight type. It is a handsome nickname. You can carry it proudly. In years to come you can report that Senator Scott gave you the name just prior to the moment you won him four hundred dollars in a shooting wager against some forgotten, comelately, western governor." He smiled like we shared a secret. "As you tell it, may our fortunes allow that you shall say 'President Scott.'"

I was without words when the Governor's gate opened for us. Just like that, we rolled through. The feeling was like the first bounds of a horse coming to speed.

Our ride took us to the shade of that white mansion on the bluff. It rose from the sage as if placed by the Lord Himself. White columns towered from the stone porch to the stone roof. I saw an armed man on top. I saw a stable bigger than any I had imagined, and beyond a white-fenced pasture and two herds of tall buckskins throwing up dust. It was more than I had ever thought to dream of.

A powerful mare was in the lunging circle. I watched her bound, the muscles casting crescents of shadow across her flank. A woman was there holding a rope in one hand and a whip in the other. She wore the divided skirts of a rider. When she looked our way I saw she was young in the face.

We disembarked. The leaves of a thick cottonwood clattered in the wind. The senator placed his hand on my shoulder and hollered orders to the well-dressed black at the door.

Boots appeared under the arched doorway and I saw then a tall and thick-shouldered gunman in the same duster and black hat as the others. But I recognized this one as the man from the picture in the paper, the shooter who so held the Governor's attention.

The man stared on me as he put in a plug and positioned it proper in his cheek. He wore twin Peacemakers with pearl handles and silver metal and not a patch of rust. When he drew them later I'd see the one on the right hip had a cut-short barrel so it might clear the holster in quicker time. The one on the left hip had a longer barrel for better work at distance. The guard's eyes did not flinch from me.

"Am I pretty to you or something?"

The senator said, "Oh, I do enjoy banter between the fighters!"

The gunman spat. "You carry a load of earnest considering you're but a half-pint of a man." His voice was deep and as seasoned as his eyes. I will admit he reminded me some of Pa. The thought put me in silence.

The guard enjoyed my hesitation.

Disappointment arrived now because I had lost the momentum and revealed to him that I was young in the manly arts of bullying. That would be a deficit I could not overcome. And so I decided then to bend it to my advantage. I didn't look to him again but to my feet. I played the part, which is all manly games ever is.

The senator had noticed my loss and was on the cusp of saying something when we heard a great number of feet on the marble floors of that palace. There before us come the Governor himself.

I knew him from the photographs I'd seen in newspapers and campaign posters and I will admit the man in person was command-ing of attention. On his lip was a bountiful moustache matched only by his thick side-burns. He had two inches on the next-tallest man and a full foot on me. He was thick throughout but not weighty and he walked with a speed uncommon among men with gray hair. The step from the stone porch did not slow him, he didn't even glance down, just took it in stride.

"Is this your man?" he asked the senator. His voice was rich like gravy and I wanted at once for him to approve of me. "He is liable to blow away."

The Governor shook his son-in-law's hand but his eyes never left me. "What's your wager then, Reginald?"

"I will wager," the senator looked upon me with new eyes, "two hundred dollars."

The Governor snapped his fingers. "To the range then. Brandy this time, Charles."

We walked all of us at the Governor's pace and the senator hopped his steps to keep up.

I was back some from my competition and I saw now the shooter walked with a rider's limp and carried his shoulders with some unease. He worked out his fingers as he walked. Age was stiffening him, as it had Pa.

We crested a small edge in the topography and I could see across a well-used firing range. A younger black they called Will was sent at a run to deliver two white plates into the dirt of the bank. I thought his fine cloth to be a queer sight among the sage.

The Governor hollered, "Enough, Will. Place them some distance apart." It would be a distance of ninety-five paces. I had counted Will's steps as he traveled. I confirmed them as he returned. The plates faced us from the dirt wall. The wind had built up gusts with the resources to lift my hat. Bullet drift would be a factor.

It was not a situation I would've selected for myself. But it was a situation I had practiced since my girlhood.

The shooter spat at my feet. Out of strategy I turned my eyes down. If I played the timid he would continue to underestimate me.

The shooter pulled back his duster and hooked it over his holsters. The fingers of his right hand danced over his sidearm.

Will took up a stack of plates and come to stand between us shooters. There was little communication between him and the guard or the Governor or anyone else for that matter and so I knew this was a game they had played often. In the dirt before us was the shards of a thousand shot plates.

"My boy here, upon a timing of his choosing, will wing a plate downrange," the Governor called. Men was accumulating along the periphery behind him, taking positions on the hill above. I turned behind me and saw the girl with the divided skirts watching. She was being addressed by an older man in a rounded hat but she seemed to be paying no attention to him at all. She seemed to be paying attention only to me.

"Another plate will be released before the first has landed and you will fire upon that one as well. Then you will take aim downrange on the stationary target. You will have three shots and three shots only. A fourth will disqualify you. He who destroys the most plates wins. In the event of a tie, we will move on to a second game with a doubled wager. Did I leave anything out, boys?

"Reginald," the Governor addressed my patron, "care to conduct the coin toss?"

"It would be my honor." The senator removed from his pocket a single piece of gold. He said, "The home man calls it in the air." I was spellbound by the auburn color fluttering up against the desert evening.

"Tails."

The senator caught it. "Tails it is."

All eyes looked to the Governor. He nodded to his shooter.

My competitor said, "He goes first."

I felt the weight of their eyes on me. I had never before held the attentions of the sober and wealthy.

The how shapes the what, and good shooting comes from good form. So I did as I always do. I stretched my hand and lifted my pistol to check its weight. I rolled my shoulders and settled my mind with even breaths. Hunger rumbled through my abdomen and my focus come into keen attention. The entire galaxy existed downrange of my position.

Will lifted a plate from the crate of them and I saw then the fine design on its middle. Such plates I'd never before eaten from and here I was about to bust one. Will twisted with the plate held flat in his hand and come forward in speed.

The plate didn't travel up as I expected but rather out and away and soon began to plane to the right. I was following and unsure of the trajectory on account of that turn, but I could see the black blur of the design in the plate's middle as my sights passed it and bucked.

The plate was dust.

The next one was already in flight and already banking. It wasn't open to me as the first one had been, it was maintaining its thinnest profile. The pistol erupted and I was blinded by the smoke that drifted back into my face. I heard the gasps of the viewers behind and so I knew I had hit.

I leveled the old Colt on the distant plate and exhaled half a breath. I fired too soon, I knew that, and I saw the dirt implode at the bottom of the plate and it rolled free and disappeared into the gulch. I had an excess of confidence after the initial success.

Everyone clapped. It was the most civilized sound I ever heard. It did little to alleviate my regret at missing. I'd come all this way only to miss.

The Governor proclaimed, "Fine shooting!" Then in a changed voice he said to my competition, "Be true, Drummond. Be true."

The plate rose up and hovered there for

him and he easily knocked it to the earth. The second was caught in a gust and banked hard and his shot was behind it.

I could barely contain my relief.

He brought up his second hand to steady the pistol and took a long aim downrange. His bullet fractured the upper half of the plate.

The clapping commenced.

"A draw then," the senator said. "How lovely. We now double our wagers."

Will erected a metal apparatus some thirty paces away, placed four plates within the space of a man's chest, a fifth where the man's face would be, and a sixth where his genitals would hang. This contraption was lowered to the ground.

This time Drummond would be shooting first. He readied himself. I was pouring powder and jamming balls. The spectators behind could be heard snickering at my old-timey ways. "Rustic, isn't he?"

The Governor's voice called over the field. "The pistol must remain holstered until the target hinges up. The shooter has a three count to unload his shots. He who breaks the most plates is the victor."

Will stood a distance behind us, a string dangling in his hand. "Are you ready, sir?"

Drummond nodded.

Before Will pulled the string he braced and I heard gravel beneath his boot.

Up come the targets and four of them went to dust. The audience commenced its clapping.

Drummond cursed. He wanted more busted.

I was impressed. A three count is no time at all to release six shots and he had done so with time to spare. His misses had been near.

Quick shooting is a different skill. The pistol is held at navel level, where it can be fired faster. The right hand holds the aim while the left is made to work the hammer. In practice the shooter must always hold the pistol in the same manner and at the same elevation, and true mastery only comes to those who can reckon distance to the foot. As with any shooting skill muscles must be built. I had earned coarse calluses from my hours working the heavy-hammered Colt.

At the sound of gravel under the man's boot I drew.

I didn't fire at the plates. I fired at the bend of cursive in the design at their center. The first two shattered clean, then my confidence sent a wide miss. I recovered from the surprise and destroyed a third and fourth, then rode the recoil up the face and felt the revolver jump at the shot. The fifth plate wobbled but did not fall.

The audience gasped.

It was the Governor himself who marched downrange. He took the plate from its position and a smile come over his face. He walked back toward us. I was sure I had missed.

"Another doubling of wagers then?" asked the senator. "Not that it's a problem."

The Governor tossed me the plate. I caught it and saw a chip in the rim the size of a pinkie nail. Only the scarcest edge of my bullet had made contact.

"The day belongs to the kid," the Governor announced.

The audience rumbled. When the Governor clapped they did too.

Drummond spat.

I worried this victory would put me at odds with the Governor, seeing as I had just cost him four hundred dollars. But his arm come around me and he offered a cigar. He asked, "Now tell me, son. Where did you complete your tutelage?"

I took his cigar. "My what?"

"From whom did you learn the fine art of shooting?" He snapped his fingers and Will touched a match to my tobacco. I had never had a cigar before and so began to cough.

"There now, son. Take a breath, but not of the smoke."

"Thank you, sir."

"The name of your mentor then?"

"My pa." It was one of the few questions he would ask that I could answer honest. "He was a sharpshooter in the war."

"And so you know the long guns?"

Drummond said, "Son of a Yank."

"Oh, leave the kid be," the Governor said to Drummond. "This isn't about your old war. He wasn't even alive then." He took his arm from me and offered Drummond a cigar too. "Don't fret, old boy. Our history is long and gloried." Drummond walked away and left the Governor to return the cigar to his pocket. "He will recover. Son, tell me you know the long guns?"

"I know the Sharps. I don't know the Spencer."

"Or the Winchester then, I take it," the Governor said. "You must join me for a meal. Will you?"

I was fluttering now. He was a leader of men and the high officer of the state and here I was a counterfeit before him. "I am most interested in joining your employment, sir. That's why I come."

He gripped my shoulder in his thick hand and smiled. "Join me for supper and we'll discuss the rest."

In a house as high and mighty as the Governor's, a man don't just eat in his day clothes. I was given a suit of fine wool to wear and a bath was poured. The attendant stood rigid in the corner holding a bar of soap in his open hand. He was waiting on me to undress.

207

"I ain't likely to need no help with this business."

"Of course, sir." He set the soap on the edge of the tub and bowed his head and spun on a heel and pulled shut the door behind him.

The door didn't have a lock to turn so I shed my coat and rolled it tight and wedged it into the crack of the door with little confidence it would hold. I checked the view from the window and then pulled the curtains until they overlapped. I waited and listened. Finally I give in and unbuttoned my shirt and slid free of my trousers.

I shed the old shirt I had doctored to hold tight my nubs. It was rank now with sweat and grim. I took the soap to it and ground the fibers against the edge of the tub. Wasn't no washboard but it did remove some stink. I rinsed the cloth and then set it upon the windowsill where the sun might beat on it.

I held my chest with my hands. My nubs had withered on my journey. I felt too my hips where they punched at the skin barely holding them in. There was a small oval mirror but I didn't dare look in it.

The water went brown at once upon my entrance. I took the soap to my skin and lathered and rinsed. I worked fast on account I was sure some fool would burst in any moment.

When I rose from the water and toweled,

my eye caught the glass of whiskey waiting on the bureau. The attendant had left it before I asked him off. I took it up and held it in the light and smelled it. I swallowed the contents down like any man would do. I had tasted whiskey before but this was my first introduction to its effects.

At once the drink amplified the charms of my present situation. I pulled on the old shirt even though it wasn't all the way dry. Then I dressed in the attire they left me and laughed instead of gagged at the pinch of the collar. I took up the whiskey glass and waited on the last drop to touch my tongue, and then I turned the mirror so I might see my face in it.

I blinked at the sight.

The wounds to my cheek was a shock. Three straight lines, one along the next, each as long as a finger. They was red but not oozing. I would never be free of them.

My hair was short and uneven and looked fitting of a cowhand who trims it by knife alone. I used the scissors on the bureau to even what was left.

Then I stood there before myself.

My eyes had sunk into my face and built an armor of glass between them and the world and I wasn't even sure of their color no more but for the red about their centers. I worried my brother would not recognize me. I barely recognized my own self.

All this time I had understood myself to be the same girl who dwelled with Pa them years at home, only now in hiding. But my eyes. Them eyes didn't belong to that girl, and there wasn't no pretending otherwise.

It is the burden of the survivor to wake one day and discover in yourself a stranger.

A black led me up to the middle level of the house and along a glorious table of white finery and crystal and china and drew out a chair near the head. I knew enough to wait for the Governor himself to sit beside me and then I began to sit and felt the attendant slide the chair forward. I thanked him.

Across the table from me and beside Senator Reginald Scott was the girl with divided skirts. Except now she wore a dress the color of a trout's side. She was introduced to me as Constance. She said, "You are new to such tables."

"I am, ma'am. Hope that ain't too obvious."

"To Mr. Jesse Straight," the Governor proposed. He held his drink high and all others at the table did the same. I was surprised to see so many faces, most of them men, all of them near on the Governor's age. "A prodigy who has yet entered his prime."

Drummond was not present, nor did I see a place set for him.

Around us the black help was dressed in

formal attire. The old one I'd come to know as Charles stood in the corner. He too was about the Governor's age. Will, who had run the plates out on the range, appeared with a platter and brought it first to the Governor, who waved it off, and then to Constance. She looked upon the platter and then up to Will and said something so quiet I couldn't hear. Will moved along to the senator.

"We have found with great trial and error, mostly error, that the best help remains the freed slave," the Governor was speaking to me in private tones. "This father and son we imported from the estate of a Virginia planter turned secessionist turned corpse. Today the Negro, who has just witnessed the closing of the seas upon his old masters, finds himself burdened by the boundlessness that is his freedom. And so it is the Christian duty of the established and capable to build a system of merciful employment for the freedmen, one that recalls the firm walls and narrow gates of his earlier existence but still pays proper homage to his equatorial dignity. Here we pay them a fair wage and offer them quarters fitting of English attendants. If we were to advertise, we would be overrun with similar men. I have put their bucks to great use in my camps. They swing a pick as if their very lives depend upon it. A charming attribute in a workingman, you must agree."

He smiled. His face was deep wrinkled

around his eyes and his skin wore sun bruises. His hands was thick and well calloused and more powerful than mine would ever be. He might've been the leader of men but he was no stranger to hard labor himself. I reckon he was downright fancy to gander at in a former decade.

Constance was entertaining a whisper from her fiancé. She had never worked chores in the dead of winter or sat alone by a fire worrying on her missing pa. She giggled and pulled a tendril of hair from her cheek with a pinkie. I wondered if I had been born into this house would I possess her charms, or was they straight from the Lord and so would've found her even in a hovel beside a shallow lake.

The Governor's hand seized my shoulder. "Tell me, son, all you have done in your life. Tell me of your people. Northerners, I could tell by your manner alone. But I want to know where you have been and where you plan to go. Well, don't keep me waiting."

On my plate was a great proportion of beef loin with a rich red gravy overtop and I held my fork at the ready. The smell had my mouth leaking. "I been a hand my whole life."

"Cattle?"

"Yessir. To hell with sheep."

The Governor smirked. "Indeed. Though I fear we may all be running them and their shepherds one day soon. But you shoot for money?"

"Been making coin by wagers lately, sir. Traveling west since the spring thaw."

"Looking for land, no doubt. You aim to be a homesteader like everyone else of your position?"

"Not particularly."

"What do you want from this life then? Tell me it is not gold."

I shrugged. "I have no interest in swinging a pick or rolling a pan, sir."

"A wise mind then. There was a time, but now gold is a cluttered business. So what then? Land? Riches? Women? You have ambition beyond the immediate. I can spot intention within a man. Have you heard the talk of dams? It seems your generation will stopper this nation's largest rivers with barriers of rock and build fertile valleys in the hottest of deserts. That sounds like the making of a land rush to me. The wise man is making acquisitions as we jabber."

"Someday I hope to return to my family spread and —"

"Now let me ask you," he leaned over his plateful of food and clasped his hands. "Do you prefer the fifty-four Sharps or this newer forty-five? I have been told by my hunters that the forty-five is too diminished for heavy game, but the men in my militia prefer this newer weapon because of its merciful weight. Do you have thoughts about accuracy?"

I had never fired the newer forty-five but I had seen its shells, and I knew what Pa had taught Noah about lead. "I will always prefer the smaller round flying faster for accuracy work, especially in the field. The flatter trajectory will aid yardage estimates. The trouble is knockdown power. I suspect the forty-five still offers plenty for targets of man size."

"Yes, yes, well." He took a sip of his red wine. I could see I hadn't said nothing he didn't already know.

I finally put the fork to the meat.

"What are your thoughts on barrel length?"

I held my bite aloft. "My experience on the matter is limited and Pa taught me not to overspeak."

He smiled. "Your father offers sage counsel. Not all do."

I opened my jaws to consume the meat.

"Do you have any schooling?" Constance asked me.

I lowered the bite and my mouth watered its objections. Constance's hair was brown and rich and she looked upon me with blue eyes. She was small in stature but large in them eyes. Her gaze would not move on before it was ready. I felt small within it.

"Let the man eat," the Governor said.

"What about the marks on your cheek?" Constance asked.

The Governor pointed with his chin. "Forgive my daughter, but I must admit I too am curious. Though, dear, it is less than ladylike to inquire so directly after a man's wounds."

"How did you procure such branding?" she asked, her eyes unwavering.

"To look on it is worse than to wear it."

"I think it lends your face a mysterious quality," she said. "Is your family east or west?"

"My kin has passed on," I said. The liquor allowed the statement to emerge without its bite. So like a child who continues to poke at the numbness to confirm what he already knows I added, "My ma died in childbirth and my pa fell from a horse last autumn."

Constance reached at once for her wine. But she didn't lift it from its place.

The senator turned from his conversation with an elderly woman beside him and said, "What have I missed?"

I took my bite. It was the finest roast I had ever devoured in my life. It was the first of many that summer. I would also consume a great deal of the Governor's liquor. He was a man who believed in meat and spirits each day for health.

The Governor was still thinking weaponry. "We must put a Winchester in your hands. Imagine the midrange accuracy of the Sharps with the speed of a revolver." He hit me across the back and I gagged on my meat. "Maybe you are wondering why I was so happy to lose today."

He didn't wait for my reply.

"Drummond has been my best man for some years now. And I say you beat him handily given the disadvantages you faced. The unfamiliar games and that rusty sidearm. That was the state's congressional delegation you so entertained."

This conversation caught the attention of Senator Scott. He raised a finger to the old woman beside him and interjected, "I found this young man on the streets."

"Your driver said he mistook your carriage for mine." The Governor's eyes remained on Scott's.

The Senator put a finger to his collar and chuckled. "Yes, well."

The Governor's attentions returned to me. "I am happy to see you beat Drummond because Drummond has made me good money over the years. This spring, however, his shooting has slipped. His vision, I believe. He is aged, not aged for labors of the mind, but aged for a man in his line of work. Shooters, in my experience, peak at thirty-two. How old are you, Mr. Straight?"

I felt compelled to lie upward. "Near twenty-one."

"Exactly." The Governor smiled. "I trust Drummond entirely in matters of strategy, he is a cunning architect of combat. His mind goes calm when the bullets come at him, but I have watched him lose too many shooting wagers of late to count on his pistol when real money is on the line."

"Drummond is the Governor's preferred shooter," Senator Scott added for my benefit.

"I'm confident Mr. Straight is savvy enough to piece that together on his own, Reggie, but we appreciate the sound of your voice." The Governor took the fork from my hand and set it beside my plate. He said, "You mentioned you would like to enter my employ."

"Yes, very much, sir."

"Your arrival is serendipitous for a number of reasons. As you may know, we have a wedding approaching. I could use another skilled gun around." He lifted his napkin and wiped his lips even though he hadn't taken a bite of his dinner. He tossed the napkin beside his plate and leaned back in his chair. "I would like you to come to stay here and practice your shooting at my expense. I will supply you with a pair of balanced pistols to replace that thing you used today, as well as a Winchester straight from manufacture. I have ours built with custom modifications. I will of course cover all expenses you incur and you will have room and board. At the end of a week, we will revisit the issue of your long-term employment."

I considered what he was proposing. "I have a mare," I said.

"Of course. She will have a stall in our stable and all the feed she needs. I have a boy who will tend to her." He smelled his wine but it didn't have his attention. "If I like what I see, you will accompany me across this territory, as I complete my official charge. We will find ourselves often in the company of other dignified men who also have their own shooter. They will look at your age and your" — the Governor gestured with his pinkie at my body — "smaller than typical stature and assume you to be incompetent. They will bet large against you. When you win I will ride home triumphant. We will be victors together. There is no pleasure more savory. Would you like that?"

Constance watched me over the rim of her wineglass. "Father enjoys winning more than his health."

"Winning is the only story worth telling, dear." The Governor leaned toward my ear, "Of course you are concerned with compensation. We will discuss that at the end of the provisional period. Now is the moment to express your gratitude."

"Sir, I ain't a trick shooter. My mind is set on settling an old debt with a certain felon, Noah Harney."

At the sound of the name the Governor cringed as if in pain. He drank down his wine.

"I hope to join your militia and ride out after him. I must find him, on oath to family."

The Governor sat back. His gaze became

hot. He roared, "A thousand men have been unable to find him! You are talented with a firearm, but, son, you can't also have a preternatural talent for tracking. That bastard will knock you from your horse at five hundred yards and your talent will leak into the dirt."

"He couldn't hit a barn at that distance." I shot from the hip, emboldened by my drink. "He don't got no skill for the rifle, never has. I know Harney, see. He and I come up in the same county. We roughed some as youths, though he was years my senior. He turned to vice about the time I turned to learning the pistol."

The Governor had gone to ice before me. I noticed the silence. All conversations had turned our way.

"We parted on sorry terms, Harney and me. See, there was a skirmish. My father was struck in the face in his own house. The blow left him diminished in capacities. He never full recovered. Now Pa is dead and I am to be his agent of revenge."

Senator Scott said, "Why would you risk your future on that felon?"

"I will take the reward money and I will return to my family spread and buy out our debts. For my kin, only land in the free and clear qualifies as a future. Mine is people who prefer working their own dirt."

The Governor pushed back from the table.

He still had not touched his food. But now he wiped his lips and excused himself. The men rose as he departed.

He was gone a breath before conversations bloomed anew and glasses was raised toward Will's decanter.

"You should never mention that name around Father," Constance said. "That criminal has taken a great deal of —"

The senator took it upon himself to finish her thought. "He is a thief and a bugger and he has disrespected many prominent men of the West."

"Especially Father," Constance said.

"What is Harney's claim with the Governor?" I asked.

Again Constance began to answer but Senator Scott finished. "His claim lies with all men who have earned their money. As you will learn, ours is a land of givers and takers. The great Governor is a giver of the highest order and that makes him a target of the most loathsome takers. It is that simple."

There was a voice beside me. "Sir?"

I looked to find Charles awaiting my attention. He was three times my age and yet had called me "sir."

"The Governor asks for a moment."

I rose and followed Charles and his gray woolen hair down the hallway and up the stairs and looked out the glass windows as we walked. The evening light was just now leaving the rock promontories and I was overtaken with the thrill of being inside and outside all at once. I was still new to the luxuries of glass, and the effects of whiskey.

He opened the door to a private office and directed me to enter. The Governor was standing before a window big as a wall. Above the mantel was a great elk stag and beside it a pair of deer with symmetrical horns well past their ears. I had seen such critters in the wilds but never before affixed to a wall. I wondered how they did not rot. On the floor was the hide of a magnificent grizzly. It looked to be at least ten feet long. I had to step on it to cross the room.

"Is there anything else, sir?"

"No, thank you, Charles. That is all."

The door closed. I was alone with the state's most powerful man. A clock ticked the seconds.

"I am but a servant to the people," the Governor spoke to the glass. His eyes held either the mountains beyond or his own reflection, I could not tell which. "I have devoted my life to turning rock and timber and grass into employment so that hardy men can support good women and this great land may be populated with righteous, decent, hardworking people. My calling has been to turn wilderness into America."

He lit a cigar and returned his gaze to the glass. "Mine has been a campaign against evil itself, which prefers to see this land go fallow and populated with an order of slothful people, Mexicans likely."

He turned sharp to me. "Am I right to see color in your skin? I am not a bigot, Mr. Straight, only a realist. A pinto will never achieve what a buckskin can, no fault of his own."

I knew the answer this man sought.

"This land was not always like you see, Straight. I left the States in forty-eight to wade the ungovernable West and arrived in California to rumors of gold. It was a fortunate moment. But everything else after I have labored tirelessly for. I have come into nothing by charm alone. Candidly, I am the reason we now live in a state. I am the reason the territory did not pick sides in the war. I am the reason this town below exists at all." His voice was nearing a shout. He turned his cigar.

"The name you mention . . . He would turn this place back to the barbarians, to the savages, to the Spaniards. He is . . . He is . . ." The Governor put a hand to the glass to steady himself. His breath was slow to catch up. "My physician advises I do not. . . . Let us speak of another matter. If only until my breath returns."

"Sir, my honor lies in avenging my pa. I have ridden many weeks to arrive at your feet. I offer you private knowledge of this man.

Who else has grown up with him?"

"You have not soldiered. Have you seen death? Have you caused it?"

I saw myself in the glass. "I have killed a man."

"Tell me of it then, if it is true."

The liquor bolstered my reply. "He was attacking me and I was without a weapon. I put a stick through his face. I didn't think about doing it. But I did it. His legs burned in the fire."

The Governor turned the cigar in his mouth and maintained his gaze on me. He was looking for my lie. "Is there a warrant that follows you?"

"I am followed by other troubles but no warrants, sir. The killing was within my rights as a man. It transpired without witness."

"The killing affects you."

"Some, but that bastard is beyond my sympathies."

"Yes, good, sympathy is a most disadvantaging quality."

"Pa's humiliation weighs heaviest on my soul, sir. He was never the same man after Harney. His debts fall on me to repay, and as I see it, so do his reprisals."

"Losing your father," the Governor said to the window, "that is when a man is born."

"Yessir."

"I lost mine to cholera in forty-seven."

"I'm sorry to hear that, sir."

"It is a long time past. And it was his death that sent me west, so I must assume there to be some order to the Lord's will."

"The Lord intends me as your agent," I said. "I know this in my soul, sir. The Lord has sent me to you for use as you see fit. It is on me to convey my talents in honesty so you may know how best to govern them."

He studied me. "Your talents would be wasted with the militia. They are a club and you are a lance. But I understand you. It is admiration of your father that drives you forward. I can think of no quality more deserving, more American, than that one."

"Yessir."

"I have an intuition about you, Straight. I have been made rich by trusting my intuitions." He stepped to this desk and poured two whiskeys from the crystal flute. "Forget the militia. Join me now as a full guardsman. You work for me through this coming winter, and when the moment is right, we will put you on the hunt." He handed me one of the whiskeys.

I held it aloft but did not sip. "I aim to find him before autumn, sir."

His drink went to mist. "Before autumn! And then what? Take Mexico by spring?"

"I will bring him to justice."

He laughed. "Yes. To justice."

"You find me humorous."

"No, son. I do not. I am sorry if I have

224

given that impression." He looked at the whiskey in my hand. "I have offered you a position as a guardsman and you throw it back at me. Do you know how many men approach this house each day wanting to clean my halls? My guards are salaried and they are taken into this family. You live in this house. You eat this food. When you are sick, you are visited by my doctor and I pay his bill. Do you understand what I am offering?"

My mind was busy turning over the words "taken into this family." "Yessir."

"My guardsmen start at four dollars a day. In addition, when you shoot a wager you'll receive a percentage of any winnings we procure. Do you see? I will build you into a proper citizen if you can keep yourself from running off and dying. Will you still turn me down?" He rang a bell that had been sitting on his desk.

"No, sir. I appreciate this opportunity, sir. I have only a minor request."

The door opened and Charles entered. "This way, Mr. Straight."

The Governor raised a finger toward Charles. "A request. I will try not to be offended."

"If you do apprehend Harney while I'm in your employment, I want to see him. Can you promise me that?"

The Governor took his cigar in his teeth. He studied me and smiled. "You carry the

225

rocks of a bull. Yes, Straight. I can't promise he'll be living, but if I see him, you will see him. I can promise you only that much." He held up his whiskey. "Are we agreed then?"

I touched mine to his and we both took them down.

Will waited while I changed out of the dinner wools. Once I was again dressed in my dusty old clothes, Will led me into the lowest reaches of the house, where I was to bunk with Greenie, the next youngest guardsman at twenty-five. I'd seen Greenie before, at the gate my first day of waiting. He was a few inches taller than me. He had a freckled face and appeared younger than his years. His name fit. "Howdy," I said.

He just looked on me. His green eyes revealed nothing. There come a tapping on the door and he opened it without inquiring who might be there at such a late hour.

By now the blacks was tidying and the Governor and his kind was smoking upstairs.

Drummond entered. Behind him come another. Three men now intent on me. "What's this?" I asked.

The Colt had been taken after the wager and not yet returned. I pulled the knife I'd taken from the dinner table. I said, "Then die trying."

But these men were trained in hand-to-hand. Greenie stepped past the knife and seized my arm and twisted it behind my back and then there wasn't nothing I could do to protect myself. I might've been their match with a pistol but I was just a kid without it. Still I kicked and caught Drummond with the first blow and he went to the floor holding his stones.

They took turns on me. The blows was to my belly and chest and thighs, not one to my face. At first they was holding my arms back, then they was just holding me up. I heard the sound of the hits as if they was across a hall.

When I finally went down it was Drummond who lifted me from the floor and heaved me into the wall. "My turn now, Yank." He put a knee into my groin. The pain was fresh. Then he went to work on my guts. He only stopped because I upchucked on him.

They left me to my suffering on the floor.

A fever come over me and I shivered. The pain only increased as the liquor faded. I watched the moon track across the sky and still I laid there in the dark, unsleeping, allowing only the shallowest of breaths and aware of every moment.

Despite the pain, my good fortune was not lost on me, and I was grateful for this opportunity to bleed on the floor of the Governor's mansion, a step closer to salvation beside my brother.

■ ■ ■ ■

Come morning Greenie lifted me gentle-like and helped me to the bunk. He had brought me some whiskey. I took it and felt the stuff pull a quilt over my wounds. He sat down on his bed and set his hat on the covers beside him. It was but some hours since he had driven fists into my flesh. Now he offered me tobacco.

"You manned up and took it proper."

"To hell with you." The words hurt.

"You ain't chasing me off."

"That's the spirit. See, someday we'll be drawing fire and might as well be just us in this whole damn world and we'll know you the kind to stick. You'll likely get it worse on account you're taking Drum's commission work, but that will pass. Drum hasn't been making many commissions anyhow. You'll know you're past the worst of it when they give you a nickname."

"More whiskey."

"Boss knows you'll be laid up today. He's sending me down for your horse now. Boss took a special liking to you. Ain't seen that before. Boss ain't the type to take a liking. The rest of us, we had to earn our spot with some dirty work. That fact will keep the boys sour for a time. Especially Drum. But not me. I'm glad not to be the youngest no more."

"Ingrid is my mare's name." A cramp cut me off.

"I'll tend to her good. You got my word, Straight. How old is you anyhow? Where'd you get them marks on your face?"

"Bastard's knife."

"Your old man?"

"Nah."

"Bet you cut loose the bastard's nuts in return." Greenie smiled. "Those marks likely helped you, honest. They make you look more seasoned than your years. What is you, eighteen?"

"Twenty-one."

"You know what they say, a Yank at twenty-one is a Reb at fourteen. You look like you put that notion to the test. Governor took a chance, I reckon, building us of both kinds. He's a Yank himself so you got that going. Drum will probably say that's why. But the truth is the Governor might be the only man in this here whole Republic to've put the war behind him. He talks like this state is the step forward. The real trouble is the shortage of females. I'd like to say you get used to it. But, shit. You got a girl?"

I shrugged.

"You into girls?"

"Course."

"I ain't asking if you a fish or nothing. Just a warning. Whatever you do, don't you get caught looking on that Constance. She is quick with the tongue and her eye wanders but that don't mean she taking any fancy in you. Governor's keen on getting her married before the natural troubles come. Drum and Tuss and I head to the whores on payday. You can join. Governor gifts us each a trip to the top house on payday. Ain't like the girls you see on the trail, old dogs and witches. These ones is, well, don't get me thinking on it. Payday still a long ways off. I got a powerful hunger for the females, myself. Ain't a fish bone in this ol' body."

He rose and put on his hat. He offered me his hand, and I took it. "Well, I'll go get your mare."

I gave him my bandanna. "Let her smell this and she'll follow you."

Sleep come to me around midmorning and by the afternoon I found my way outside and was pleased to discover a posture that didn't hurt if I held perfect still and did not breathe. I was left with bruises under my shirt and mounds of swelling, but nothing that wouldn't heal.

Ingrid was waiting for me in the stable and bucked her head when she saw me coming. I smiled at the sight of that perfect animal. I slipped her a biscuit from the table.

"Pretty sight you is, girl."

She put her lips to my cheek and knocked my hat free.

■ ■ ■ ■

We walked a short distance to the cotton-
woods and I took a seat against a log while
Ingrid rolled herself clean in the grass. It was
the kind of bright, no-sun day when you keep
an ear for thunder. Down below smoke rose
from chimneys and lingered low over the city
in the still air.

I brushed Ingrid out and she ate heartily
from the Governor's grain. With feed like that
she could fatten up proper.

Like me Ingrid had aged on the trail. I
pushed her too hard most days and we got
too early a start most mornings and now her
hips shown through her skin. She deserved a
long rest with good feed. I told her as much.
I waved a fly from her eye and put my
forehead to her cheek.

Ingrid's ear swiveled and I turned likewise.

Constance hurried by in riding clothes. She
was leading that black mare of hers. She saw
us and tipped her hat in the manner of a
cowpoke. I wasn't clear if she was mocking
me or the world in general.

She reminded me some of Elizabeth Annalee, not in physical form or color or de-
meanor. Maybe it was merely that she was a
woman who wasn't yet a mother. Or maybe
it was that I couldn't tell where the show
ended and she began. I watched as she led

her animal to the lunging ring.

Her big mare got to trotting circles in connection to a rope that hung from Constance's left hand. In her right was the whip. The mare trotted with an eye back on that whip.

I put Ingrid back inside the gates and then walked near.

"What's her name?" I called.

Constance kept her eyes on her work. "Enterprise."

"Queer name."

"Father named her. He insists on being the namer of all things. Your animal is terribly small."

I hung my arms over the fence like a man is wont to do. The motion hurt fierce on account of my bruises. "She is quick for her size."

"Do you enjoy a small horse? She seems better suited to a girl. Or maybe a demure little Paiute."

I spat. "She's the only horse I ever knowed. We got plenty in common. We come up together."

"I agree you both fit together nicely. Only it seems a man would want a bigger horse is all. I haven't met a man yet who doesn't buy the biggest horse of the herd. Men are always so concerned with the dimensions of things. Are you in pain? You look like you are in pain."

"Your mare don't trust you."

"She respects me. Well, she is learning to respect me. She is of Carolina stock, and her sire is well regarded for his leaping capacities. Moon Shadow is his name. You've heard of him if you keep current with riding."

"That ain't respect she's learning by your whip."

"The whip is only for show. She rarely needs a lick. She was tamed by Sir Edmond Huffington. He is masterful with these animals. Father sent for him from London."

"Well, he must know his business if he comes that far to conduct it."

"She will be made to jump for me. I only agreed to go to Alexandria if Mr. Scott agreed to build me a stable and a course. I intend to become a well-regarded rider."

"Do they let girls jump horses?"

"If not, I intend to be the first. Have you ever sat on a horse as it sailed over a beam? The feeling is the closest humankind can come to flight." She pursed her lips at the thought. "If I was someone else I would load this animal and disappear among those mountains. To leap real timbers fallen across a trail, to be united in speed with a beast of four legs and a thousand pounds as it dodges through the timber . . . I have this dream in which I outrun a band of Comanche." She glanced my way and then sent a flick down the lead rope. "I so envy you men. The world simply awaits your explorations."

"Sometimes it feels like it's waiting on us to make a mistake."

Constance nickered and Enterprise's ear cocked.

I had walked down here for a reason. "I don't see your ma. Did she pass on?"

Constance waved a fly from her face. "Mother is in New York. Mother moved back when I was two years old. She was no match for this place."

I must've looked confused.

"Their marriage is political, you understand. There is little joy in the union. Out here she was prone to lie about for weeks on end with the curtains drawn. Mother is the type to need brick walls to shore her dainty energies, as well as alleys to tempt her figurative mind. She is of the old class. They don't believe in dirty hands. I visit her each summer. The train makes the voyage quick enough, and in truth I rather relish the adventure. Or the notion of the adventure. Rest of the year I am on this estate. Father brings the tutors to me here. Mother was right to leave my upbringing to a nanny, and these mountains, and these animals. That is the only thing mother has been right about."

Senator Scott hollered from the barn. "Constance. There you are." He walked to the fence beside me and said, "Hello, Mr. Straight. A surprise to find you here."

"Mr. Senator."

"Senator Scott, please. I have collected your share of the winnings, good man. Would you like them? Then come with me and leave poor Constance to her lunging. That mare is a problem, despite her terrific expense. Too headstrong for good work, I fear."

Enterprise regained her trot. She was as strong and beautiful as any horse I had ever been close to. She held her tail high and controlled her feet with prancing precision. She seemed to float about the ring. Her eye held mine as she made the turn.

"Mr. Straight," the senator said in a quiet tone as we walked toward the house. "That mare has been promised to me. It would not be looked upon favorably if a man such as yourself complicated that. I would take even greater offense, given the primary role I played in bringing you here."

"I have no interest in a new horse," I said. "I got Ingrid."

His face revealed nothing. "Yes. Well. Here is your percentage. You will see I added a touch more than the standard two percent, as a token of respect. Respect, Mr. Straight. That is all I ask in return."

The paper money was thick in my hand. It filled me with good spirits. "Yessir. I understand. I didn't mean no offense watching your mare."

"And no offense was taken. Now, how about we toast our little victory yesterday?"

The thought wet my tongue. "I would like that very much."

I found myself in the parlor with a gin listening to the senator's thinking about the future of our western state, labor, prosperity, harmony between the races — he had ideas on everything and didn't expect me to offer much in the way of response. He was testing himself before me like I was some manner of mirror. The whole while the black who poured our drinks stood nearby in case we needed another.

I had been nodding to the senator's subjects for three drinks when he at once grew solemn. "What did she say, anyway?"

"Who?" I shrugged.

Senator Scott's eyes narrowed. "Don't be coy with me. I am not a fool. I see how men look at her. I am more than a decade her senior but that is how such marriages are arranged. A man must prove himself to be a worthy suitor via the challenges of the marketplace, while a girl is best plucked from the vine early so she might ripen in the presence of he who will best look out for her.

"I apologize. I have been put to . . . Well, I hear things, false things no doubt, yet they are enough to occupy my mind. Even to sour it in moments." He sipped from his drink. "I am deeply invested in this marriage, you understand. It would not be a simple prospect to step back. Even if honor necessitated a prompt exit, I would be bound to follow through by certain . . . financial realities." He seemed to decide better of this subject. He took down the remainder of his drink. "I joke. These are life's great excitements, the infinitely unknowable aspects of any worthy endeavor. Ours is a continent built upon the worthy foundation of promise and courage. Is it not?"

The drinks had me in a haze and I took their liquid to the servant's holehouse out back. I pulled shut the door and found it had no system of locking from the inside and so I was inclined to peek out the door before I drew down my britches and got to it. Pissing had a manner of putting me off my game. I might play the part of a man well enough that at times I done forgot the truth, but there wasn't no pretending when it come to pissing. Someday I would be at work with the men and far off from any holehouse or trees. What would I do then to relieve my stores? Best to keep myself parched.

When I was through, I bound my winnings in twine and affixed them to the underside of the bench as Pa would've.

As I crossed the yard I swore to myself I would put liquor at a distance. I enjoyed it plenty, but my aim drifted when I was drinking. I hadn't hardly thought of Noah since taking my first drink of the day.

But when I come inside Greenie was there with a bottle. "This is for you, from the Governor. To heal your bruises. We work tomorrow, so let's get to it today. Also he said you was to share a healthy portion with me." Greenie fixed his hat. He wasn't much of a liar. "Okay, maybe I added that last part my own self."

When I awoke in the morning I found a new set of clothing on the bed beside me. There was new boots on the floor. On the coat hook was a duster like Drummond's and a clean black hat.

I pulled back the wool and felt the full force of my first drought. I vomited into the spittoon and lay back in the bed, too dry for thought. A whole night had been lost to me and I feared what damages I may have inflicted while still standing. Ain't wise for a man with shallow secrets to drink deep.

Last thing I remembered was Greenie and me singing to the empty bottle.

Too soon, there come a knock on the door. "Yep?"

"May I, sir?" It was one of the blacks.

"Come in, but quiet-like if 'n you would."

The door inched open and Will entered. He was dressed in his finery. His eyes did not demur. He looked upon me like we had some contention.

"Last night, did I wrong you?"

238

He only said, "The Governor wants you upstairs."

"Okay."

Will did not leave. His jacket could not hide the contour of his muscles. Veins rode high over his hands. Now I said to him, "You look on me like we got beef."

"Don't keep the Governor waiting. Sir." The door shut behind him.

I dressed in my new clothing and found the articles well starched. The britches was a touch tight in the hips. My new boots was stiff and dead set against my feet, I had never owned a new pair. I bent to stretch the tightness from my bruises.

My mouth was ash and acid and so I stopped in the kitchen to dip three cups from the bucket. Dizziness passed over me. I resolved then and there to never drink another drop of whiskey.

I arrived in the foyer to discover the Governor had already departed for his appointments in town. I found instead Drummond. He spat when he saw me. "You kept the Governor waiting."

"I'm a touch ill."

"What is you for real? Fifteen?"

"And you one hundred and fifteen?"

"I would kill you now if 'n it wouldn't put me in bad favor with my employer."

"So I am safe then. What is it you hold in

239

your hands, old man?"

Drummond let the woodbox fall directly to the floor. It landed with a substantial racket that echoed down the corridor. "The other is in the corner," he said and walked from the house. He left the door open.

I took a step toward the box.

"Let's go," Drummond said.

I knelt to the ground and pried back the box lid. Inside was a double holster and two silver Peacemakers. One was short barreled and the other long, just like Drummond's. I lifted the short one and knowed right off I'd never before held a pistol with proper balance. I lifted the weapon into the light. It was a sight to behold. Its workings was smooth as butter, and I cocked and released the hammer a dozen times to relish its music.

My eyes fell on the corner. There was a new scabbard and in it I found not an old Sharps or Spencer but a new Winchester repeating rifle. This had been the very weapon Pa hoped to own from the moment he saw it hanging in a shop. I lifted and worked its action. I squeezed the trigger and it cracked like glass. It was gold and blue and its stock didn't have even a briar scratch.

These was new weapons, three of them, for me. Common folks didn't ever own new weapons. Even the pistol Pa bought Noah was aged a season.

Drummond hollered from outside, "Well,

you gonna breed 'em or shoot 'em?"

I buckled the belt around my waist and tied each holster tip to my thigh with the leather already cut for the purpose. The scabbard went over my shoulder. I paused before the fancy mirror. I had on my black hat and duster. I saw myself as I would be seen. By and by I was a damn gunfighter.

"You worse than a woman," Drummond hollered.

A crate of ammunition sat upon the shooting bench. Drummond loaded his rifle from it. Then he opened his pistols and filled them with the same shells. The novelty of a six-shooter eating shells would take me some time to overcome. All summer I would be reaching for my old fixings.

When Drummond finished he racked the action on the Winchester and let the rifle rest on his hip. I will admit he looked like no man could touch him, and I was in awe.

I stepped past him and took aim down-range, and missed the mark. The sun was hot on my skin. The report echoed about the ravines of my drought.

Drummond brought up and destroyed what I left behind. "You let your steam get the bet-ter of your form. Think first of your feet and work your way up to your fingertips."

I hadn't never thought of my feet, but I knew enough to understand Drummond was right. Balance starts in the feet or it don't start at all. Pa never mentioned feet.

"This trigger likes the whole finger. Ain't like that Sharps." He demonstrated with his own finger. "Like this, see? Now take aim and exhale and let that finger fall asleep on it."

"Why you teaching me?"

He took aim and fired twice in under a second. Both bullets hit their mark. "You ain't nothing but farty air, I don't know why Boss don't see that. But much as it grinds me, you'll be riding with us. Your bullet might just be the bullet that saves Tuss or Greenie or Boss himself."

I took aim downrange but Drummond put his mitt over the action and forced the barrel toward the ground.

His eyes was on the sage past the range. There was a shape moving there, a woman in a black dress. Her white hair wasn't bound in bonnet, it tossed in the breeze. She walked across our shooting without a concern for us or our lead.

"That's Lady Mildred. The Governor's mother."

"Mother? She must be ancient." The Governor looked to be sixty.

Drummond spat. "Near on ninety and I reckon she outlives half us."

She disappeared into a fold in the land and then reappeared on the next rise. She made the uphills quick as the downs. "Where's she going?"

"That building yonder. That's her residence."

"That hog shed?" It was a one-room thing. But now I noticed the rocking chair under the eave. The chair faced away from the mansion and toward them mountains. "Why don't she live inside with us?" I wondered too why she hadn't joined us for supper.

"Boss don't bring his momma around. You stick here long enough you'll see why."

When the Governor was home his guardsmen took rotation on various posts. The gate, the roof, the Governor's office door. The work didn't come natural. Guard duty was the hardest labor I ever done, occupying ground with no other task than that. Always at war with time. But I was a lucky one. Each day I went to the gun range, usually with Drummond.

We guardsmen also drilled. They taught me to take a man at gunpoint, bind him, and search him, all without him gaining the upper hand. They taught me to grapple and roll someone twice my size. They rushed me with knives when I didn't expect it, and then explained errors in my form. If Drummond could think it, we drilled it. Then drilled it again. He never let a mistake go unpunished.

Drummond wasn't an easy man to be

around, honest, but then neither had been Pa.

My first shooting wager on the Governor's behalf wasn't no wager at all. The Boss summoned me to the range on the first hot afternoon of the year. Drummond was already there, dropping shells into his pistols. Will and the other servants was erecting a white cloth to block the red sun. Underneath sat four upholstered chairs.

"The both of us?" I asked Drummond.

"It'll be trick shooting. The men coming is some of them Mormons. Won't wager nothing but they enjoy a little shooting sport like the next man."

I will admit my mind worried that one of the men might just be Mr. Saggat. I pulled my hat low and spat. But Mr. Saggat wasn't nobody who could hold the Governor's attention. The men who come was the ones that ruled their city on the Salt Lake. They was serious men without a smile to offer, and they wore their beards in the manner of easterners before the war. Their clothes too was cut in the fashions of thirty years bygone. They looked fresh out some history too boring to talk about.

I was introduced by the Governor. "This is Jesse Straight, gunfighter and trick shooter. If you read the papers of my city you will soon be reading his name. A preternatural talent for the sidearm." I tipped my hat to them and tried to rein in my pride.

Drummond and I shot plates on the fly and plates on the roll, and when we made clean work of those Will put the plates away and brought out the saucers. These we got with equal ease and so our finishing act was a pair of silver dollars produced by the Mormons themselves. It was all an act Drummond and the Governor and Will had put on before. I just followed along. Except when the silver dollars flew, Drummond missed low.

The trouble for Drummond was his hands. They just wasn't nimble no more. His joints was swollen and slow to keep up with his mind's eye. He cursed when that silver dollar hit the dirt.

The Boss showed high pleasure after they left. He put his arm around me. "That was damn fine work, son. Did you see the look on their faces when you handed the man back his center punched dollar? Word is going to spread about you."

Drummond picked up his scabbard from the bench and walked back into the house.

The mountain behind the mansion was flanked in sage but that give way to mahogany and rock near the top. It bore the Governor's name.

That mountain held my attentions when I shot or when I stood duty on the roof, and so my first afternoon off I saddled Ingrid and rode the ridge up until the earth grew so steep we had to cut switchbacks. A pair of tall horned bucks jumped from the bitter-brush in a draw and I could've shot them both with ease as they high stepped to the edge and stopped to see about the ruckus. But the Boss was clear on the rules. His employees wasn't to do no hunting. Them bucks was all his.

So Ingrid and me rode on until we crested the ridge and found a pass where the wind hummed a song through the rock. I saw at once the tracks. A shod horse. Soon I heard her voice from up yonder. Constance was balancing upon a rock that stood like a pillar from that mountain.

I looked around and saw we was alone. Still I knew I should turn and go somewheres else.

"I watched you see me," she called. "There's no pretending I'm not here."

"Howdy, Miss Constance."

"You navigated the steepest route. I use the long arm of that ridge. There's a clean trail most of the way, deepened now by our frequent hoovings."

I looked off at the distance.

"Come now. Your job is not at risk for talking to me. Why did you come? You didn't follow my tracks."

I spat. "I saw this here rock and took a guess on how big it was. I been watching it when on duty."

"Were you right?"

I leaned and patted Ingrid's neck. "They's always bigger than I reckon."

Constance's riding skirt fluttered in the wind. She outstretched her arms like a bird. The rock she was balancing on was no bigger than a saddle and yet some fifty feet off the ground. If she stepped forward and did not take flight, she would fall to her death. "Would you like to see the view from up top?"

"Nah."

She frowned. "I would think a man your age would want to climb the face and show me he isn't governed by fear. Don't you males relish fear and test yourselves against it at every opportunity?"

"I listen to my fear. I trust its vision."

"You are a peculiar specimen then, Mr. Jesse Straight, especially so given your choice of employment. Tell me, what do you know that the remainder of young men don't?"

I shrugged. "I reckon most of us males fear smallness above all else. I'm built small." A raven sailed over the pass and cawed. We watched it sail out and over the ravine. "Senator Scott has a good instinct for preservation."

"Yes, that might be his only instinct." She pulled a ribbon of hair from her mouth. "Father says love is a luxury not available to the political classes. He questions the very utility of the enterprise." She dropped into a deep voice, a bad mimic of her father. "What mountains has love reduced? What wars has love won? Where's the profit in love?"

She put a hand to the top of her hat as a gust of wind rose up and then died away.

I studied the distant ridges for the shape of someone watching us.

She turned her back to me. She put out her arms and tipped her head back toward the heavens and called, "Tell them I died in peace." She leapt and was gone from sight.

Ingrid and me come around the back of the pillar to find Constance jumping down from the last step. The back side was a giant's staircase. She untied Enterprise and swung up on the animal's back. She was royal in her movements, always. "Did I deceive you?"

"I best get on."

She puffed up in mockery of me now. "Best do what's best." The air come out of her. "Do I bore you, Mr. Straight?"

"Ma'am, I live downstairs in your house."

"Downstairs, upstairs. Father can pretend but . . . We all live together in God's garden. Is not that the premise west of St. Louis?"

"Maybe that's the view from upstairs."

I turned Ingrid and we started back the way we'd come. "Safe ride to you, ma'am."

I was still thinking of Constance the next afternoon as I stood duty before the Governor's office, his voice inside and my eyes on the mountain out the window. Her mother *chose* to live far away — how could that feel?

When the Governor put his hand upon my shoulder I nearly jumped. "Glad to see you're so attuned to your surroundings, young Straight. Man this door as I step down to send a telegram. Maybe you would notice a burglar if he stepped on your toe?"

"Of course, sir. Sorry, sir."

I watched as he descended the steps with Charles behind him, the butler transcribing the telegram even as they walked. A black who could write, I didn't know such men existed. But that wasn't what impressed me. To walk and write at the same time, now that was a damn skill.

I shook such distraction from my mind and resolved to think of nothing but my brother. I'd been with the Governor over a week and still had learned nothing of Noah. My belly was full and my mind was taken with fancy and somehow all this felt like a betrayal to my kin. So I stepped inside that office and narrowed the door behind me.

I set about my project with haste. The papers on the desk was well ordered. The stacks went deep and I thumbed through them for the name Harney.

After some minutes without finding any sheet that had more words than numbers, I paused a moment to listen. I heard nothing and so kept on.

It was all paperwork concerning companies the Governor owned. I gave up and instead pulled the handle to his desk drawer. I found it locked, and so set about looking for the key. I looked under his ashtray, his humidor, even the buffalo hoof he used as a paper-weight.

I didn't hear no boots on the stairs. I didn't hear nothing, not even the banister creaking. That banister creaked when the wind touched it, so I don't know how Will got so close without making a sound. The door opened, and there he was, looking on me.

"Oh," I said, a breath behind. "I was . . ."

Will stood straight as his father Charles, an arm bent around his back. In his other hand was a silver platter with a crystal bottle of brandy perched on top. His eyes narrowed on me.

I understood then I had to change course. I had to believe he was the one being caught. I stiffened tall. "What's your business here?"

His platter rose and settled with a breath. "Shouldn't you be guarding the door?"

I pointed at the half-full crystal already on the Governor's desk. "Who sent you with that bottle?"

He swallowed. That was all.

There come the creaking of the banister, and Will was the first to take a step back. I followed him out of the office and closed the door.

When the Governor and Charles emerged on the landing Will and I stood on either side of his office door as if we had been in silent contemplation all these minutes. The two of them walked between us without a glance.

I turned to Will and him to me.

Charles appeared again between us. "Will, I told you to deliver the brandy to the Governor's quarters, not his office."

"Of course, Father."

I did learn about this New Moon Heist. I caught the arm of the man who delivered our dairy, and when I mentioned the name Noah Harney, he started talking at once.

Noah and his Wild Bunch had hit a train in Wyoming in the dead of night. Two of them had stepped onto the tracks and waved lanterns in the signal used to warn a conductor of a faulty bridge crossing.

"They didn't hit this train at random, no sir," the dairyman said. "It was coming from Pennsylvania, sent by the old boys who run the world. The men who got the rails, the banks, the cattle herds — these men don't like Harney, not a piece."

"Why? What's a gunslinger to a high name back east?"

He leaned closer with a big smile. "Harney keeps kicking the hive and somehow he don't get stung. Some say the Lord is on his side. You know Harney has more money than the president of these United States? Now that's a fact. I read it in the papers myself. They say he's got whole caves filled with gold. But it ain't for him. He spreads it about the people. That's why the ranching folk hide him as they do."

I didn't full understand until after, but all across the West families was being pushed from their homes by the dropping prices of what they produced — wheat, cattle, timber. These people who'd bled for their new day was now being forced to move again, and most went to cities where they was paid a day rate that left them in the hole, and this time with no view to stir their souls.

It was just like I'd seen with Pa at market, each autumn the price was lower than the year before, driven down by the men who owned ten thousand head and so could afford to take a lower price for their beef simply to drive off the competition. Just as soon as the family man quit, the very baron who had forced them out bought up their holdings for a dime on the dollar. Just good business, they said.

Everywhere he went my brother was being treated as a hero by men like our pa. The dairyman whispered, "They say his Wild Bunch is five hundred men now. Imagine that. Could be a real war coming."

The night they stopped the train, a gunfight ensued between the Wild Bunch and twenty-one Pinkerton agents who had taken an oath to defend the cargo with their blood. It went on for an hour, until too much dynamite burst open the armored car like tin.

The fifty thousand in new-minted money was intended for the Governor, to help finance his militia.

"Could say the war is already kicking."

I rode with the Governor often and always highly armed. As I was the cherry among the crew I was left the seat in the carriage's rear and ate our dust as we traversed the mesa and climbed the mountains to a company mine owned by the Governor.

The carriage come to a stop in a mining camp and the Governor went with Drummond into the manager's office. Greenie and I moved to cover the back of the building while Tuss manned the front. In the bright sun my eyes was of little use and I leaned in the only shade I could find, a thin band thrown by a pillar. The Winchester was in my hands.

In the distance I could hear picks hitting rocks and the chants of blacks at work. In the near I heard the pleas of a white man who had done wrong by the Governor. His words was no more clear than them chants, but his fear was conveyed clear through them walls.

Greenie was passing a knife blade under his fingernails. "Makes you glad to be on his good side, don't it?"

Some minutes on, the white man come flying through the back door. He was fat and dressed well but he landed like a sack of grain. Drummond was the one who kicked him. He spat and nodded at Greenie and disappeared back inside. The door slammed shut.

Greenie swaggered over and leaned an elbow on my pillar. He grinned and showed me a bottle inside his coat. "You gonna tell Drum if I offer you a pull?"

One night in the bunks Greenie and I lay awake in our room passing a bottle back and forth and trying to invite sleep. It was slow coming. It had been a day of watching and not much else. The bottle went dry and then we just laid there.

"You asleep?" I asked.

"I ain't drunk enough yet."

Splitting a room with a man was less trouble than I'd expected. The room had a bed on either side. I slept in my long johns and I took measures to change when he wasn't near. If the morning was chilly I concealed my chest, as my nubs hardened like no man's and might show through my button-up. I did have to suffer some manly business. Greenie did little to tame his formidable flatulence and in the mornings he was more likely to fill the night pot than make his way to the holehouse. But all in all he give me space and I give him plenty of the same.

This night he lit a match and touched it to the candle and threw back the covers and said, "I'm finding us a bottle even if I got to go to the Governor's bedside."

He returned minutes later empty-handed. "Nothing worse than sobering up from half drunk. Tell me about your girl, Straight. You ain't never told me about your girl other than you got one."

"She ain't really my girl no more."

"She leave you?"

"You ain't told me nothing about your home," I asked. "You got folks?"

"Yeah." The thought only deepened Greenie's mood.

"Tell me about them."

"I'm their only son. Seven years in September since I been home." He thought on it a time. "I worry Pa has passed on and I don't know it. Maybe I'm still living like he's here on this earth and he ain't. I ain't sure I feel him no more. You think I'd feel him if he was still breathing?"

"Have you sent a letter?"

"I ain't much for writing."

"My skills ain't practiced," I admitted, "but I can scribble. If you find paper and a pencil I'll write your letter."

"Why help me write to my folks?"

I shrugged.

He rose and took the candle into the hallway. I heard him out in the kitchen and then going up the stairs. He was gone long enough my mind began to slip in the mushy snow that comes before sleep. His feet stirred me back. "Found them in a desk drawer."

I took the writing things from him.

"Guess what else I found?" A big smile spread across his face. He pulled a pint bottle from his pocket. "Brandy. It was stashed in the same drawer as the writing utensils." He took a long pull and passed it to me.

"We gonna get in trouble?"

"Maybe. Worth it."

I took the bottle and felt its comfort spill through me.

"How is these things started?" he asked. "I mean do I ask after them first or do I tell them about me? I ain't much experienced with correspondence. Getting or sending."

I hadn't read a letter home in my life and so didn't know how a man was to start one. I imagined Pa opening a letter from Noah. I could see what he would want to know first and second, and what he wouldn't want to know at all.

"Tell them that you are well. Then wish them good health. From there we'll read it over and see where we stand."

Greenie was a good-looking man but words

slowed him down some. I did my best to follow his dictation but I had to fill in some gaps on my own choosing.

"Okay, read it back to me."

"Dear Folks, This is Joseph, your youngest boy. I am in good health and in better spirits. I have grown some since you saw me last but I still wear the boy-face you give me. Because of it my friends call me Greenie. Are you in good health and spirits? I hope so. I think of you often."

"Now what should I say?"

"Tell them what you have been doing for money and what dreams you got for your future. Tell them you will return home soon."

He took a sip from the bottle we was sharing. "Will I?"

"Sure you will. A man owes it to his folks to return from time to time. Anyhow they'd like to hear it, I reckon."

"Add to it something pretty sounding at the end," he said. "Like what a good church boy would say. Say something about the savior. My folks is Baptists."

I give this some thought. "May the good Lord bless and support you until I might arrive home to take up the efforts my own self."

"Yes, that's it. That's right. Damnation. You good, Straight."

I handed him the letter. "Now sign your name there."

He was slow to touch the paper. "I ain't got

nothing but my initials."

"Then that's what they'll want."

When he was done he looked the letter over in the light.

My writing wasn't nothing fancy but I believed it to be legible. I learned it copying the Good Book. It pleased him plenty. He give me the remainder of the bottle. "What's your girl's name anyhow?"

I said the first name that come to me. "Elizabeth Annalee."

"What's she like?" He was sitting on the edge of his bed looking at me in the candlelight.

I told him of her orphan background and how she dreamed of a wholesome marriage. I told him I wasn't the type for marriage so I left her. It all come out sounding very manlike, the way I laid it.

"That's not what I mean. I mean, what is she like?"

Men save a precise tone for conversations about love acts, and I had come to know that no matter the meaning of the words spoken in that tone, the content was lust. I summoned the manly elements within me. Men always spoke first of shapes. "She's about yea tall and her hips come out like this and her chest is, well, just about proportional."

"Proportional. So big then?"

"Big? Good size. Healthy. Plenty of milk."

"I like good-size tits."

"Yes, me too. Good-size tits is nice." I tried to fathom what it was men did with good-size tits. "They make a kind pillow."

"You should get her to bouncing on you. You ever done that?"

"Course. All manner of bouncing."

He looked at me sidelong. "You been schooled proper?"

"Course I been schooled. Proper."

"Bullshit! I can see it in your face! You ain't never rode your pony into that girl's stable. Lookee here, we got ourselves a frosty!"

"A what?"

"Straight is a frosty! Don't be ashamed. I was a frosty till I wasn't no more. Round about the time I turned twelve!"

Greenie laughed and blew out the candle and lay back on his bed and laughed some more. "We's gonna get you a proper hayride come payday."

Late morning the next day we got word of the Wild Bunch from a man on a near-dead horse, he'd ridden all out since dawn.

The Governor looked to Drummond. "Well, move! Don't just stand there!"

We rolled fast and in the afternoon we come through a wide valley with no trees and saw the bloating bodies of two dead horses. In the ash was the metal rims of wagon wheels. There was pools of brown blood baked into the earth. The bodies of four men was then being piled into a wagon by the deputies.

The sheriff took off his hat to speak to the Governor through the carriage window. "The ones that fought back was killed. The ones who surrendered was stricken of their footwear and firearms and left to walk. The story they're telling will have folks buying them drinks for some years on."

The Governor spoke through clenched teeth. "The gold?"

The sheriff pursed his lips. "Every ounce of it, sir."

I imagined my brother in this very spot of earth. Him wheeling around on his horse, gun smoke leaping from barrels, bullets straying around him. A gunfighter.

"Straight!" It was the Governor. "Get down here!"

I climbed down from the top and the door was opened for me to enter the shade of the carriage. The sheriff cocked his head at the sight of me, but he could not remember where we'd met before. I tipped my hat to him. "Sheriff."

I put a foot to the step, and entered the carriage with the Governor and he pulled shut the door behind me. I was expecting a conversation about Harney.

"We're making a detour," the Governor said. "Put your feet up and rest those eyes. I have a business associate over in Buckstooth who will gamble large against you. He has a thing against little men with big mouths. So run that mouth of yours."

I nodded. I pointed at the tracks. "Shouldn't we get after the Wild Bunch?"

The Governor passed a cigar below his nose. "And what would you do, young Straight, that the posse already in pursuit would not?"

I thought for an answer. "Well . . ."

The Governor called to the driver, "Move quick. We must catch Mr. Cliffpatrick before he boards his train." The Governor lit a cigar and looked me over. "You will find that I am the type who prefers healthy distraction when the moment doesn't allow for decisive action."

The driver's voice responded through the carriage wall. "We will arrive back after dark, sir."

The Governor roared, "By God, I know the distance in terms more nuanced. . . . How many of this territory's features bare my . . . Just for this once do as I say and drive, and leave the thinking to men born for it."

We arrived in Buckstooth to learn that Mr. Cliffpatrick had left the preceding day, earlier than planned due to concerns for his safety. This set the Governor in a worse mood, and I was glad to return to the top of the carriage for the long ride back in the dark.

In the days ahead I lost my first two wagers when my bullets passed behind their saucers. The problem was all mine. My mind was on my brother, even when I took aim.

After the second loss the Governor was down nine hundred on me, and didn't so much as look my way for three full days. I was sure my time in his employ was coming to a fast end.

I asked Greenie about it the night of my second loss, as we laid out in our bunks. "Think he'll cut me loose?"

"Oh, he ain't gonna do that over a couple losses. He just gets in his moods is all. You's safe until he finds a shooter he likes better."

I was on the range practicing when Charles brought word the Governor needed me down at the capitol building. Ingrid wasn't saddled but one of the big buckskins was, and I had to lead the animal alongside a rock so that I might reach my boot to the stirrup.

We thundered down the road and I understood all I was missing riding a small horse. I didn't even know the buckskin's name but he was the trustful type and he knew just where to take us and what speed. As we crossed town all eyes followed me and my tall horse and the Winchester I perched on my thigh. I was riding with the Governor's brand and wearing the duster and cruel black hat of his guard. No man dared look me in the eye.

That was some potent medicine.

I found the Governor standing beside a teardrop of a man. Mr. Hershel was his name and he was the owner of the rail line, in town for a meeting about Harney. He wore a brown suit with a cut so particular it couldn't fit another man on this earth. There wasn't no jaw to Mr. Hershel at all, just flesh drooping from his eyes all the way to his collar. He wore spectacles and leaned on a cane.

When he saw me Mr. Hershel tapped his cane to my right arm. "Your employer was quick to offer a wager this day. I wasn't two minutes off the car when he proposed a shooting. Now I wonder if I'm here to discuss Harney at all or if this isn't all a ruse to arrange long-sought retribution. I've known the good Governor three decades now and can say he's rarely shown such enthusiasm for one of his guns. Which has me worried about my money. Yet if you're as good as he seems to believe, a thousand may be a fitting ticket price. How much have I taken from you over the years in these wagers, good friend? Your Governor keeps an exacting total."

"Two thousand one hundred and fifteen dollars," the Governor said. "But it is Mr. Cliffpatrick who holds me deepest."

Hershel's shooter was Shamus Wilbur Pickett, better known as Famous Shamus. He was a beanpole of a man, whose long arms unfolded like a vulture's wings. The contest was the standard for wagering men at travel. What made it less standard was the newspaper boys who showed up.

One stood about with paper and pencil while the other asked us to pose for pictures. They witnessed the moment I bested Famous Shamus on the quickdraw.

Afterward the Governor slapped me on the back. "I knew the pressure of the newspapermen would help your aim! You are the rarest kind, Jesse. Like Drummond. The question is, will you turn to stone when the bullets come at you."

"*At* me, sir?"

He laughed, his big hand wrapped tight about the back of my neck. "Don't worry, Straight. You're too valuable to risk."

The next day the paper was sitting in the foyer. There was my image beside the joyful Governor, my hand still holding the Peacemaker. Behind us was a droopy-looking Hershel and Pickett. All our eyes was downrange on the target I just hit. The caption read, "Faster than Famous Shamus, but is he faster than Harney?"

The Governor went red at the sight.

That afternoon the editor of the paper come to the house with the man who wrote the caption. The stone walls could not contain the Governor's wrath. We heard a brass spittoon go bouncing down the hall. The editor and his man left with their hats in hand, but the Governor wasn't done. He chased them out. "How is Harney news when he wasn't even there? Huh? Tell me that, Straight? How can a low-down bandit hold so much attention when great men are each day building a nation from dust? Am I the only man on guard for such inequities?"

I admit I was in awe of the sway my brother held over the untouchable Governor. But I played my part. "Let me near him, Boss. Put me up against Harney and we'll see who's still standing."

At this, the Governor pulled the cigar from his lips. "If only he could be lured here by a wager so big . . ."

"Charles!" The Governor was calling down the hallway now. "Charles!"

A door opened and out stepped the butler. "Yes, sir, how may I serve?"

"Charles, we must draft a letter."

"A letter to whom, sir?"

"To that blasted felon."

"Of course, sir. May I ask, where will we send it?"

The Governor turned his cigar. "We could place the letter in the paper!"

"Yes," Charles said. "That could be done. However, sir, might it send the impression that you two are on equal footing? Might your constituency —"

"Good point, Charles. I rushed ahead of myself. Never mind. I was, but for a moment, a victim of emotion."

I spent my first ever payday standing guard outside buildings in the hot summer sun. But no heat could turn my thoughts from that pile of money I would gain come nightfall. I was learning money can be its own whiskey.

I was wet when we returned to the estate. Even my new hat was soaked through. Greenie and the others went to the bath. I stayed behind. "Come on, Straight," Drummond called into my room. "You smell like a burned pig."

I made like I was busy until he left. Then I shut tight the door and wasted not a moment in stripping down. I put a cloth to a bowl of water and set about scrubbing the sweat and dust from my skin.

I had softened up some since arriving here. My legs was like sticks below the knee but above they was getting fleshy with all the grub I was eating.

I wiped clean my thigh and saw blood mixed with the dirt. I reached a finger to confirm that I was in fact experiencing my womanly bleeding. It never appeared regular for me in this life, but when it arrived it always started light and grew heavy a day on.

In the kitchen I dug around until I found a pair of thick rags. I returned to my room and shut tight the door once again and commenced tearing the cloth into small pieces I could fold and position proper. I tucked the extras into my shirt pocket.

We took our pay to town that night, the boys and me. I was flush with drink by the time supper was through and so I didn't have my best interests in mind when I agreed to go. Probably wasn't no getting out of the trip nohow. We saddled up, the four of us, and put the animals to a canter and watched the last glow of the day fade into purple.

"You can have any one of them you want," Greenie said, "except for Miss Aberdeen."

"Greenie has been in love with that Aberdeen since we rode him down there on his first payday," Drummond said.

"She understands me is why. She comes from Tennessee too."

"Son, she don't understand nothing but what's writ on a bill. She's probably from Iowa if the man of the moment is from Iowa."

"You don't know her," Greenie said. "I won't stand you talking down on that sweet gal. She's the most honest whore I ever met."

Drummond laughed. The money had put us all in good humor. "You just get greener and greener. What's your type of ride, Straight? No, let me guess."

267

Tuss leapt on. "I reckon the bigger the bet-ter."

"No," Drummond said. "A wide gal would scare this kid."

Greenie laughed. "Should we tell them? You saggy old bucks won't believe this. Jesse here is a frosty."

Tuss slapped his leg. "Boy, howdy! A genu-ine frosty? Can't be. How old is you anyhow?"

Drummond exhaled smoke. "I didn't know they was making frosties no more."

Tuss took Greenie's tobacco from Drum-mond. "I thought Yanks was born bred by their uncles."

"Hey, pass that over here," Greenie said.

"Not before I twist me one for now and two for later," Tuss said. "Huh, Jesse? Is it true?"

I was bolstered by the bottle in my pocket. "I like me a lot of woman for the riding."

"Is that on account you ride a circus pony for a mount?"

It was partial true what they said about Ingrid. With them up on those big buckskins I felt to be looking eye to eye with their saddle horns.

The brothel wasn't like no whorehouse I ever seen. The sign on the door was in French and didn't make no sense to me. We come in past two heavies with clubs who called Drummond "Drum."

Upstairs, we was the only patrons. In its smell and furnishings, the place give off the sense that no man had been there before. The six girls was on the couches in various costumes of red and black, playing cards and giggling. They looked to be having honest fun.

"Hi, boys," one of them sweet-called. "Wanna teach us to play cards?"

I let my eye wander to their round edges, to the dark shadow where leg met leg. I will admit I felt something.

The matron welcomed us in French. She wore her gray hair in a tall bun draped in a gold chain and she greeted Tuss and Drummond and Greenie each with a kiss on the cheek and a squeeze of the hand. Greenie pulled another bill from his pocket and give it to the matron on my behalf. The Governor had paid our way in but Greenie told me it was classy to slip the matron a little something extra. "This one here is unbroke," Greenie said.

"Mais non." The matron put her hand to my cheek and studied my eyes. "Ah, so he is. We will take gentle care of him."

"Make sure he gets it good for his first time," Drummond said.

Greenie slapped me on the back hard enough to make me gag. His hand pulled me close and he whispered in my ear, "Don't be afraid. Ain't no better teachers in the whole wide world than these ladies."

He crossed the room and took up his Miss Aberdeen and spun her till she squealed. Tuss and Drummond took theirs by the hands and soon three doors shut and I was alone in the room with the matron and the remaining ladies.

The matron didn't waste no time. She gestured with a feather toward those girls still fanning themselves. Two smiled on me, a third glared. "And your preference, *monsieur*?"

"I . . . I . . . I sorta . . ." I took a step back.

The matron took me by the hand. She was grandmotherly and endowed with mountainous bosoms and a girth wider than three of me. She put her hand to my chin then passed the back of her fingers along my marked cheek. She snapped her finger and a girl stood. She was a stalk with black hair and blue eyes. She said in an accent I couldn't place, "Have no apprehension. I make good use of you, cowboy."

She took my hand in hers and walked with me across the room and to a closed door, which she drew open. She shut the door behind us and said, "You desire a drink first?"

"Sure. But I ain't much for this business. I'll give you a bill and all that but I don't want nothing from you. No offense or nothing. I just, well . . . I'll just drink some and then we can go out and you can tell the others I done good. All right?"

She poured a whiskey from the crystal on the bedside and handed it to me. Her blue eyes pierced. There was a smile on her lips but not in those eyes. "It is my business to know what you want before you know what you want. Now sit with me."

"I'd rather stand."

"You poor thing. Come here and I tend to you."

She drew me down to the bed and passed her fingers through my hair. I turned away. I sipped my drink. I was afraid to finish it and so have nothing left to do. She stood before me. There was nowhere else to look.

She took my hands and brought them to her thighs. Their heat stunned me. Together we raised her skirt inch by inch. I couldn't hear for the rush of blood in my ears.

At the sight of curly hairs I leapt from the bed and stood in the middle of the room.

She only lowered her skirt and laid against the pillows and crossed her bare feet. "Come now. Don't leave me alone. We don't have to know any rules in this room."

"I don't . . . I ain't . . ." I stumbled.

"You don't know what you like, do you?"

"I reckon I don't."

She looked on me until I broke first.

"I don't know. I ain't like them." I nodded toward the door that opened to the parlor. I put in a three-finger pinch of tobacco. "You gonna tell?"

She smiled. "You pay me not to tell."

I wasn't surprised by this turn of events. "How much?"

"Fifteen."

"Fifteen dollars!"

"You would pay more. You pay whatever I ask, so thank me for only asking fifteen. You have sad eyes and maybe I take pity on you."

I took the bills from my pocket and counted fifteen and threw them on the floor. I slid the spittoon toward the chair and sat and spat. "How long until I can go out without drawing suspicion?"

She shrugged. "It's your first time, so not long."

I pointed a thumb toward the door. "You aim to tell them?"

"The girls? You are no novelty in these halls."

"You can't tell the girls or it'll get back to the men I come in with."

Her eyes narrowed over her drink. "For fifteen more I make sure those men never doubt you."

It'd been a mistake to show her my wad of cash. "That's a crazy lot of money."

"Not for safety. That is what you want, correct? To hide and not be found?"

No doubt what I needed more than money was not to be called out. "What you offering exactly?"

"Trust. They will trust you."

I put fifteen more on the arm of the chair.

She rose from the bed and collected her monies. She put two dollars on the bedside table. The rest she tucked inside a shoe on the floor. So she was gaming the matron. "You thank me later."

"If this don't work, I'll tell your boss about the shoe."

Her eyes narrowed on me. "I make it work."

She took the glass from the bedside and smashed it to her bottom lip. It wasn't enough force to break the glass or split the lip, only enough to make the flesh swell at once. Still, I was speechless at what she done. Then she drew a thin blade from the small of her back, which she kept, I'm guessing, in case of trouble with a patron. She poked her finger and squeezed drops upon that lip until one ran, and this she smeared across her chin. The effect was convincing from a distance.

"Won't that hurt your chances with the next man?"

"Beef from icebox will shrink the lip." She sucked the bleeding finger. She waved it in the air. She smiled on me. "You ready?"

"Ready for what?"

She screamed and threw herself into the wall and let her body crash into the floor.

I was dragged through the parlor and down them stairs and thrown out the front door into the street by the two big men with clubs. The air left me on landing.

Greenie saw the whole thing, as he was already waiting in the parlor. I thought it queer for him to be so soon done with Miss Aberdeen. Greenie picked me up from the dust and manure. "You can do just about whatever you please, but you ain't supposed to hit them!"

"Yeah, well." My breath was slow in coming back.

Greenie brushed the dirt from my back. "That girl bite your rutter or something?"

"I don't want to talk about it."

"Fine then. But you done got milked, right? Look me in the eyes."

"I got my money's worth."

He punched me in the shoulder. "All right then! No friend of mine stays a frosty!" He rubbed his hands together and looked down the street. "Now where we gonna find us a bottle of whiskey to celebrate?"

After a visit to the holehouse in the morning, I found Drummond and Tuss and Greenie at the table with their coffees, and they broke out laughing at the sight of me, as if they'd just finished joking at my expense. Greenie shot me a quick wink so I wouldn't take offense.

Tuss said, "So tell us the real reason you hit that gal last night?"

Drummond rose from the table and put his arm around my neck. This was the first time he'd done such a thing. "Don't worry, kid. It'll go better next time."

"I don't want to go there again, never."

At this they all laughed anew.

Drummond rubbed his knuckles through my hair. "From now on, down here with us, your name is Little Pony. You hear? None of you's say different."

"Little Pony?"

They was laughing, and I understood. They was of the mind that I had punched that woman for laughing at the size of my thing.

"Good thing you's skilled with that pistol!" Tuss nearly fell off the bench he was laughing so hard.

Drum wouldn't let me go. "Want to complain, LP? Huh? Huh?"

I pushed free from him and picked up my hat. "Couldn't I at least be called Wild Pony or Bucking Pony or some such thing?"

"Nope," Drummond said, still smiling. "Round here, a man earns his name."

After my regular morning duties I joined the Governor and Constance on a journey into town. I was climbing into my dust-eating seat up top when the Governor said, "Straight. Why don't you join us inside?"

Drummond said, "I wonder if there is room for all of us, sir?"

275

"You ride up top, Drum. Don't pout. I already have one daughter."

Drummond eyed me as we passed.

I stepped inside the carriage and took a seat beside the girl and set the Winchester's stock between my feet so its barrel pointed up. My eyes stayed off Constance and upon the horizon as we rolled down the road. My mind was with Drummond. How easy the Governor reduced him.

They was speaking of her upcoming wedding. It was to be in a month's time so that the new Mr. and Mrs. Scott could catch the train to Washington before the snows of autumn closed the passes.

"I am going to great lengths to please you, pea," the Governor said.

"You are a wonderful father."

"You said you wanted dancers and so I have formed a troop of the most limber in the city and have flinched at no expense to train them."

"I said dancing, not dancers."

"But you can still dance. That is the point." The Governor's voice rose. "Dancers to fill the floor! This is a frontier town. I am trying, girl."

"Yes, I know. I value your efforts. I've said nothing to suggest I don't value your efforts."

"You drive me mad."

"I hope to please you, Father. That is my life's ambition." She said this while her eyes looked with boredom out the window.

The Governor said to me, "Daughters are what you live for and what will kill you, Straight."

"Don't say such things, Father. It is not kind to be coarse with words. Mr. Straight buried his own father not long ago."

"It is fine," I said. "It is but a coarse world."

"Indeed," the Governor roared. "Well put."

Constance took up the book in her lap and began to read. It wasn't the Bible. I read over her shoulder and saw that within these pages she was entering a realm of chatter and family.

"This is what she does," the Governor said to me. "She rides off into her books rather than converse with her old father who is soon to be left alone in his vast western wilderness. She is ready to be done with me."

"Father, don't be dramatic. It is a ride to the restaurant is all, and you are becoming short on words and long on emotion. Such is not your most becoming condition."

"As you can see I have no need for a wife. If I procured one I would only have but two."

"Three, Father. You would have three. Mother is still your wife according to law."

We arrived at a hotel in town and the carriage was met by a mess of employees eager to please Constance and the Governor. Senator Scott was there waiting on the porch. His face wore a smile.

We entered with them and found the floor cleared of all tables but theirs. A waiter left a pair of drinks upon the table, but Constance waved hers away. The senator then waved his away too.

In the corner of the room sat the only other occupants of the restaurant, two bearded men in pelts. The older of the two held a pole of tin cups, each one a touch smaller than the last. In his other hand was a wooden wand. On the underside of his boot was tied a white stone so that if he stood his toe would never have touched the floor. He was a queer sight. But his partner was a bound farther. A woman's washboard dangled about his chest and affixed to it with all manner of nails and twine was strips of copper metal that curled up and away. His boot too was sleeved in twine, in this case holding a metal pipe he was preparing to tap against a spittoon.

The senator raised his finger in signal and these trappers began their song. I suspect if a man was three months on a beaver line that tune might've carried some civilization. To us it sounded like pure industry.

The Governor leaned to me and said, "Tough town for wedding choirs."

Constance shook her head, and the senator snapped his fingers. The racket was stopped at once, the trappers shooed from the room by the senator's spindly attendant.

The Governor ordered Tuss and Greenie to linger behind with his daughter. Drummond and I followed him back to the carriage, but again it was me invited inside its confines. We rolled on.

"She is my only daughter, you understand. Without her I will be a man left with only his work. The prospect becomes more encouraging as the wedding approaches."

"You will have your many friends," I said.

He laughed. "A governor does not have friends. A governor has people who are friendly because they want something only the Governor can give. But I do not complain. Complaining has long been a market cornered by the French."

He looked off at the Chinamen along the street, but I do not believe he was seeing them. "A problem with prosperity is that it makes a place long on crowds and short on people."

We turned out of town and I could see his mansion on the hill and the mountain beyond that bore his name.

"A man works his whole life so that he may build something. He builds and builds and builds, and all the while he suffers. He believes that all the building is for a noble cause, you understand, some future that will begin once the building is complete. And then one day he looks upon his future and sees it shortening. He looks behind and sees

279

opportunities missed. He wonders, 'When did my cause go rancid?' That is a sorry day, Straight. It opened a hole under this man."

The daughter in me wanted to put a hand to his. Instead I shook my matchbox. He remembered the cigar in his fingers and put it to his lips. I struck a match and lit it. The carriage shook over a bump. "You have built a homeland for your daughter, sir. She may ride on, but this place will be what she carries with her. Home is its own compass point."

"She will change her name to that fool's. Constance Scott. What kind of name is Constance Scott?"

"It sounds graced, it sounds wealthy."

"I shouldn't put him down. She is lucky I found her a suitor of such stature. But now I see he is a fool who came to his prominence in this family's carriage. I cannot respect a man who didn't create his own opportunities. Definitive proof, I must deduce, the West has turned me for good."

The Governor smoked for a time. "Her mother lacks fortitude and devotion. It is for the best that my wife remain in the East. But as a result I have come to worry about Constance Pearl for a father and a mother alike. The habit dies hard."

I turned for a look back. The top of the hotel was just visible above the distant buildings. She was in there with Senator Scott, who would lift her from this place and deliver her to a new land where she would create a family of her own. I saw Constance holding her infant to her breast. I saw her cuddling her daughters back to sleep. The straightest path to a missing mother was to become one yourself.

"Enough of this," said the Governor. "We must organize a shooting."

"Yes." I remembered the Winchester in my hands. "As pleases you, sir."

"Tomorrow then. I want you to spend this afternoon at the range. Practice with that rifle."

"Yessir. A shooting of what?"

He smiled. "Oh, I like you, Straight."

I had been at the range for a round when I heard Drummond's voice and turned to see him putting in a fresh plug.

"You come to learn from me?" I joked.

He didn't answer. He sat. He said, "Shoot some. Make it look like I'm coaching you. Boss is watching."

I saw the Governor's shape in his office window. I reloaded the Winchester then held it freehand and continued hitting the targets with uneven success. I braced for ruthless ribbing upon my misses but heard none.

Drummond said, "I come up during the war and we lost what little we had to Sherman's advance. Nothing but our skin. Low-down like that teaches you poor ain't about a shortage of money. To be favored by a man like the Governor, now that answers a call from deep inside, Yank or not." He looked me in the eye. "Don't be fooled, LP. We ain't nothing more than bought souls. He asks us to lay down our lives in his defense. He pays us to exchange our breath for his." Drummond spat. "I don't reckon he sees men. He sees losses, profits, distractions. He might be a great man but he ain't no man's friend. And he ain't yours. I see now he wasn't never mine."

Drummond stood and busted six rounds from his pistol at nothing in particular and sat back down. He said, "I seen the way you look at his girl."

"Whose girl?"

"Don't lie to me. Ain't no secret the way your eyes follow that one. Natural enough, I know, but you rein back them eyes, son. Don't be foolhardy. That honey ain't worth waking the bear."

I didn't say nothing. I didn't know what to say.

"There's talk about the house," he began. "I ain't telling you this for gossip sake. When it's his daughter there won't be no jury by your peers, if you follow the horse I'm riding."

Drummond spat and pointed his chin at my arm. "Try dropping that elbow."

"My elbow?"

"When you shoot."

I took aim on an iron plate at a hundred yards and fired. The bullet hit the plate square. I worked the action and hit it square again.

I opened the action and ejected the last empty shell. "I'll take any more advice you got."

Drummond took the Winchester from my hands and showed me his preferred grip on the front stock. "You're applying pressure on them follow-up shots. You're thinking about reloading. You ain't staying true to your trigger. Follow that lead through its target."

Drummond handed me back the Winchester. He looked at me with a peculiar heaviness. "It is different when the bullets come at us. Matter of time, you'll see. When the bullets fly, it ain't him I think about. It's us."

I watched him limp back toward the house. I watched until he was near the doors and then I racked in another shell and took aim downrange. When my bullet missed the bull's-eye it was Drummond's voice I heard telling me why.

The following day a string of carriages arrived carrying businessmen and their guards. After meeting inside they spilled out to the range with tumblers in hand. Wagers was placed and cash monies counted out on the table and then I was put up against their best. He was an Indian with short hair and dressed in the fine suit of his patrons. His hat was much like the Governor's.

When the Indian offered his hand in the customary shake I was thinking of magpies on the girl I left out.

The Indian drew back his hand and rested it on his pistol butt. He spat on my boot.

My blood went to a boil without no warning at all. I just swung on the man. My fist done broke his nose.

The Governor himself pulled me off. I saw the men he was wagering against and how they was laughing and all at once I felt damn foolish. The Governor helped me to my feet and slipped the toe of his boot under my hat and kicked it up and caught it and placed it back on my head. "Straight here lost his parents to the reds."

"Yes," a rich man said. "Too many did."

The Indian was straightening his nose. He spat blood and cursed me.

The Governor commanded me inside to right myself, but he himself walked me across the yard. His arm was about my neck and he said in my ear, "Hell of a blow! Good show. But learn to swing with your left. We can't have you breaking that trigger finger."

Inside I was twisted with doubt. I couldn't explain even to myself why I had hit that man. These years on, I see I was only trying to hit myself.

Boss had to schedule a rematch with the Indian and his keepers. When it come I kept my eyes on the target. I was ashamed for my heat, for breaking his nose, for being laughed at. But I knew by then how to twist shame into its own hunger. I outshot the Indian each round and on the last I beat him two to one.

Afterward the same two media boys done an interview on me. I was stunned until I put it together that this little interview piece was how they was making up to the Governor for that earlier caption. The Governor wasn't just the subject of the paper, he was its owner as well. So the piece they wrote on me was about as truthful to what I told them as what I told them was to the honest facts of the matter. I remember opening that paper and reading that given twin pistols I could fire twelve rounds in three seconds and keep them all in a man's heart at fifty paces. This come as news to me.

My picture turned out fancy. It's the one that ran months later in all the papers beside Noah's. Him with a Winchester and peep sight, and me holding Peacemakers across my chest. This time the caption read, "Fastest man living, Jesse Straight, of the Governor's guard."

■ ■ ■ ■

In the holehouse I counted out my monies. I had over two hundred dollars. It was a mountain. Hard to manage even. Had Pa ever held so much money?

I took twenty-five dollars and folded the bills and put them in my breast pocket. The rest I rolled into their satchel and tied back in their place. For a moment I considered taking it all in my pocket just to be near it, but Pa wouldn't never do something so dumb.

The thought occurred to me then that I could simply stay on with the Governor a year and return with enough money to buy a herd and hire the hands I needed to run the place. A year here and I could take on Mr. Saggat himself.

Maybe that's when I first felt the difference.

When I thought of the life Pa had built for us, there was a boredom within me now. The prospect of those lonely days and the drab work and the worry of market prices and rustlers and lions and disease. I didn't miss it. Who was I if I didn't miss the life I was here trying to recover? I missed the land but I didn't miss the hunger, the solitude. I hadn't known when I was living it, but that life was lackluster.

Pa give his breath trying to make our spread

work. And here I was not even putting value in what he'd built up.

I punished myself by remembering Pa's remains in every detail just as I found them upon the earth. I dwelled for a long time on the particular manner of his hair scattering in the wind.

I found Drummond sitting over a bowl of grub. I placed the twenty-five dollars beside him.

"What's this?"

"Even things out," I said. "For the coaching."

He held the money and looked at me. He tucked it in his pocket. "Twelve bullets in three seconds, a mule's ass."

"Boss was the one answering their questions mostly. Can I ask you something?"

Drummond shrugged. "You probably going to even if I say no."

"You ever afraid of catching a bullet?"

"Nah. You can't see bullets coming at you. Arrows, now that's another matter. An arrow bends and falls and you gotta make a dodge. Can't think of nothing else but dodging. Hurts less than you figure if 'n you get hit, unless the point hits bone, then its god-awful, blinding, make-your-teeth-ache pain."

"What's a bullet feel like?"

"Like a horse done kicked you, then set you on fire. But you can't see bullets." His gaze narrowed. "You ain't losing your confidence, is you? I give you shit over the newspaper and such but . . ."

He pushed his bowl aside. "Listen, LP. Some men, most, I reckon, figure they the kind to miss. So they miss. What I seen right off in you, what the Governor done seen too — missing ain't in your bones. Now tell me, you hungry or full?"

"Hungry."

"Good. That's right. Hungry will put your bullets where you look."

He put in a plug and offered me his pouch. He said, "Honest? The only hit I fear is the gut shot. Gut shot ain't no way to die. But there ain't no other way around it, a bullet comes through your belly, you got a day or two of the worst living reckonable. I seen it. If 'n we talking honest, that's what wakes me up nights. Wouldn't wish it even on Harney. There ain't no turning the tables on the gut shot."

"Yessir."

He stood from the table. He pulled the bills I gave him from his pocket. "You sure?"

"Yep."

He put them back. "Promise me something. If it's just you and me and I'm hit through them guts, you put one here." He touched his finger to the space between his eyes. "I ain't joshing. Don't make no friend go on living when he's done for. End it quick for him."

He touched his finger again to the point between his eyes. "We do that for each other and we can put the fear to rest some. You understand?"

"Yessir, I do."

When Greenie returned that night I was in bed thumbing through the Bible I found upstairs. Greenie held a bottle in his hand and offered me a nightcap. His straw bed crackled under his weight.

We laid there watching the candle throw shadows on the ceiling.

I whispered, "Do you intend to be a hired gun your whole life?"

"I couldn't make half this much money doing nothing else. I'd be hermit-lonesome without the crew. But someday maybe I'll take my earnings and ride home and buy the spread next to my folks and find me a gal to be the mother to some children."

"Really?"

"Nah. I know that's what I'm supposed to want. But what woman could ever understand? You understand. I don't got to explain nothing to the crew. Do you think it's wrong for a man not to want the wife and such?"

I pushed the book aside. "I think a man gets to want whatever he wants."

"I think I used to want those things," he said. "I think I can remember being a boy and wanting a girl and a family and a spread.

Seems awful far off now."

"What do you want from this life if not family and land of your own?"

"Honest?"

"Honest."

"Most the time I'm riding around hoping some fool will make a try. I watch it in my head most the day. I see the fool first and I draw down and drop him in the dust before he gets a shot off."

"That's what you want?"

"No. I don't know. I want that as much as anything. But I know it ain't right to want a killing. I ain't a savage. I'm just a kid from Tennessee who gets bored easy."

I passed him the bottle.

He finished it. "This helps."

"Yeah, it do. Does Miss Aberdeen help?"

He sat up and looked on me. "I wish she did. What about your gal?"

"I ain't of the mind to go back," I said in all honesty.

The candle flickered. It was low and would be soon smoking. Greenie licked his fingers and squeezed the wick, and I heard him lie back in bed.

"I'm glad you're here, LP," he said in the darkness. "Now I see I was lonesome before you come."

"I was lonesome too, friend."

The next day I saw Will unloading a cart of

split wood before the shack where the Governor's mother lived. He was stacking the wood upon her porch. I walked out toward him. I shed my duster and rolled up my sleeves.

"Is she here?" I took up an armload of quarters and palmed one extra in my free hand.

Will passed his forearm over his brow. "Who knows where she is. That woman runs a mad trapline." He pointed his chin to the heap of worthless rabbit and badger pelts upon the porch. Two fresh ones was staked out on a board.

"She selling them hides?"

He shrugged. "Eating their wearers, I think."

"Badgers? Don't she got all the lamb and beefsteak she could ever fancy inside?"

Will laughed. "She doesn't come inside."

I took up a new armload and was grateful for a labor of the body for once.

Will set his quarters in place. Sweat ran down his neck and soaked his shirt. "This isn't a job of yours, so what is it you want from me?"

It is true I wanted to know what had brought Will into the Governor's office that day. Ever since, I had been seeking a cause to find myself alone with him. But now we was together, I couldn't think of no way to bring up the subject without him turning the inquiry on me. "What do you think of Harney?" I asked.

Will squinted. "Who?"

I started to explain, but then saw by his eyes he was playing me.

"It's so sad," he said. "To see a good man like the Governor getting picked on by his constituency." Will scratched his cheek.

I couldn't help but laugh a little.

Will almost smiled. "He sent you to ask questions, or something?"

"Nah. Nobody sent me. Stacking wood feels like home is all," I said.

"Is that right? Well, then, let's load you up." He stacked the wood so deep I had to feel my way to the porch with a toe.

He palmed two quarters and tossed them into place and wiped the sweat from his brow and studied me for a long minute. It was the kind of look he would not dare in the company of white men.

"I get the feeling we ought to talk," I said. "Somewheres else."

He turned back to the wood. He loaded his left arm. He said, "Guardsmen don't talk to niggers."

We finished the work in silence and then took a moment in the shade to catch our breath. Before us was the vast sage and the wavering heat. There wasn't nobody else outside. I drew my flask and offered it to him. He declined. I took a pull for my own self and wiped the sweat from my eyes.

Even the horses was sticking to the shade of the stable.

"Thanks for the hand," he said, and walked back toward the house.

My first action come that week. I was in town with the Winchester in hand and a half-empty bottle hidden in my pocket. Before me was a crowd of disgruntled laborers. I was only thinking about when I might sneak a pull of whiskey.

Greenie and me was on either side of a door that contained the Governor when a bottle broke on the wall. The shouts of the laborers climbed in volume and the whole mass of them surged toward us.

Greenie fired a shot over their heads and the mass stumbled backward as he intended. He marched toward them with no fear at all, and men fell upon one another to move out his path.

That's when a small man rushed out from the shade of the building. In his fist was a silver blade.

I know I hollered as the Winchester leveled, but he didn't stop and I fired. It happened that fast and with that much thought. If I hadn't, Greenie may have taken a knife to his back.

There was another shot then too, this one from Greenie. I heard a man in the crowd cry out in pain.

Greenie leveled his rifle on the mass of men, as did I. They was a force many times our number, they could've tore us limb from limb, but instead they dispersed before us like rats in lantern light. To see big men turn tails and run from our guns was its own pull of whiskey.

The Governor himself opened the door. "What in ruination?"

The man I shot was writhing on the ground. Greenie's was gagging in the sun, blood bubbling from his mouth. A pistol lay beside him.

The Governor paid the wounded no mind. He said to Greenie, "Must we go?"

"I believe we have it tamed, sir."

"Good. Five minutes more and this will be a profitable agreement." The door shut.

I went to my man's side. I took his knife from the ground and put it in my belt. He was hit in the wrist and the abdomen, and for a moment I believed I must have shot twice. But logic revealed it was the same bullet that inflicted both damages.

He could barely speak he was so scared. He was a man in his middle twenties with a fighting scar on his forehead and a bent nose. His hands was as long as a grizzly paw, though one was going ghost white. He sang, "I'm dying, ain't I? I'm dying, ain't I?"

It occurred to me then in full force that *I* had put this man upon his back.

Drummond arrived and stepped a boot to

the shot arm. The man roared in pain. "Who put you up to this? Who's paying you?"

"Paying me?"

"You ain't no Chinaman, so don't talk dumb like one."

The man looked up toward the blue sky. "I am now heading off to meet my Maker, ain't I?"

"This one is fit for the stage," Drummond said to me. "Look, kid. You took a bullet to the hand and a graze along the belly. See?" Drummond touched the toe of his boot to the belly wound. "The bullet didn't even hardly cut you. If it had, your guts would be bulging like snakes through a bag. Now, tell me who put you up to this or I will gladly help you encounter your Maker."

The man's head settled back to the earth and he looked up and upon the blue yonder. I could see his mind moving off with the pain.

Drummond drew his pistol. He cocked the hammer and drove the barrel into the man's eye.

The wounded voice cracked. "We heard the Governor was coming. He works us to breaking and then kicks us loose. All the while he charges for food and sleeping and even our goddamn water. Who put us up to this? Your master done put us up to this!"

Drummond considered the words. He slipped the pistol back in its place.

Greenie was standing over the man he shot.

The man was now dead. I could see his dead eyes staring off at the buildings. The ground about him was red and glistening. Greenie was looking down at him. Greenie was miles off, looking down.

Drummond said to me, "Harney is behind this. He is watching us. I can feel it."

I looked out from under my black hat and upon this cruel world and the faces watching back. I could've gone two ways then, down into a pit of sorrow at what I done to this man — or up on a horse so tall I might just ride free of it.

Drummond tapped the back of his hand to my chest. "Good work, LP. Too bad you missed but . . ." He winked.

"Ain't nothing." I was testing the words and trying to believe them.

He tipped his head toward Greenie. "What you just done for him, that there is the highest thing, LP. There ain't nothing more righteous in this world than defending a brother."

"Yessir."

Across the street doors was cracked and children's faces watched us. There was a stillness over everything now. Not a breeze. Not a murmur. A mother's hand pulled a child in by his ear and a door slammed shut. A tall man with a Dragoon in his belt looked at his boots when he seen I was watching.

A potent whiskey come over me then, all at

once. It poured from their eyes when those eyes flinched from me. In that whiskey was proof I too was made of grit and gravel and could not be blown from this earth by simple winds.

I racked the Winchester, and for once found what I was after all those times I tipped a bottle.

Greenie pushed me. I stumbled and righted myself. He was looking on me in a wild manner, and so I punched him in the gut and he slapped me across the neck and then we was laughing and he took me in a headlock and Drummond took the rifle so I could grapple with both hands.

"Right?" Greenie yelled when he cut me loose.

"Right!" I said and meant it. I was high now, so high I could let myself believe we was on the side of right.

I woke early the next day on account my guts was churning and walked into the chill of desert dawn.

Among the sage I found Lady Mildred's tracks. She was up before me. I followed those tracks until I found new blood where she had whacked a snared rabbit.

She walked with tiny steps and favored her right leg. Her shoes was the flat-sole variety of a farm wife fifty years before.

As the sun touched the mountaintop I

stood and looked the way she'd gone.

I was still standing there when the sun found me.

I played sick on payday to avoid the girls. After supper I drove my finger into my mouth and vomited in the hall where no one could miss it. Greenie helped me to bed and I stayed under my quilt until the crew left. Once I was sure the place was quiet, I rose and snuck into the kitchen for some more supper to replace what I'd given up.

By then it was dark and the cleanup was long past. The Governor was done entertaining upstairs and the blacks was back in their quarters. So I was surprised when I found someone in the kitchen in the glow of a single candle. It was Will and he hadn't heard me coming. I paused in the entryway.

He was holding a note to the candlelight. He was reading.

Will was no longer dressed in his serving wear. He wore his long johns and a pair of leather moccasins. He was bent over the counter, one foot balancing on its toe. His attention was whole given to that note.

It was too far to see its words or even its penmanship, but I could see it wasn't the thin parchment that occupied so many desks within the house. This note was written across a coarse paper with a single fold upon its middle — fancy. I had seen that paper before, but where?

Will must've sensed my gaze for he turned all at once and stood tall and said, "I'm just tidying up." Then he touched the paper to the flame and let it burn in his fingers before tossing what remained to the stone floor. He walked out of the kitchen, and as he passed me he said, "You don't look ill."

"I'm feeling better."

He continued down the hallway and I waited until I heard the sound of a door clicking shut.

I toed the ashes on the floor. There wasn't a scrap left.

I woke up when Greenie come back. I sat and shook off the dream I'd been having.

"Feeling better?" he asked. "Sorry to wake you. I was stalking, but you got an ear."

"I'm better, mostly. Wasn't sleeping hard."

Greenie sparked a match and touched it to the candle. "Got a letter from home today. Was hoping you might read it aloud. I ain't yet opened it."

"Course," I said. "How was Miss Aberdeen?"

He drew the letter from his shirt and I took it and unfolded it to the light. "What does it say? Everybody okay?"

"Dear Joseph, Your letter comes like the spring breeze and fills our hearts with certainty that Jesus holds a place for our family by His great hearth. Please send another soon. Please tell us more about your prosperity. Do you have a wife? When might you return?

Your father fell ill last year. It is his heart. He spends his days in bed rest now. Though it pains me to say as much, I can only pray he will survive long enough to witness your return. Your presence would be most valued and appreciated should you return, even for a short stay.

Maybe you don't yet have a wife. The Nelson girls are soon to come of age. Maybe you remember them from our July celebrations? Mr. Nelson would give you your pick of them if you arrive with re-sources. I will attest that men find the middle one pleasing to spectate.

Please, my dear son, stay in good health and spirits, and send word of your plans just as soon as you have them. May the Lord continue to shower you in prosperity and peace. Your loving and devoted mother."

"That ain't Ma's voice. Somebody done wrote them words for her." Greenie spat. He laid back on his bed but found no calm there and sat up. "Prosperity? What does that even mean?"

"You considered leaving for home?" I asked.

He shook his head no.

"I'll get a pad and pencil."

"Nah, not now."

"What do you aim to do?"

He shrugged. "Wire them money, reckon."

"You could ride it there your own self."

"I ain't leaving this for that."

I handed Greenie back the note. He held it in his hand and looked on the words. He folded it and tucked it under the mattress, where he kept his monies. "Can I ask you something? Why'd you play sick tonight? Payday don't roll around but once a month and Boss done treated us to them girls and most men would've gone even with the pox."

"I wasn't playing."

"So I got to wondering." He leaned and whispered, "Do you love girls?"

I laughed. "All men love girls."

He studied me in the candlelight. I looked to my hands. Greenie knew me too well.

"What I wouldn't kill for a bottle," he muttered.

I found the remains of mine in the bed and heard the last pours slosh at my shake. I offered it across the divide.

Greenie took the rest down. "One time you asked me what I wish for. Well, what I wish for . . . I can't never touch what I want. Do you know that trouble, LP?"

"I know that trouble."

For a long time neither of us said nothing.

Greenie cut short the silence. "There was this one time. We was in winter quarters and we'd lost eight good men from the company just that autumn in an ambush. Our friends not being there, it wore on us. To see your buddies, they was laid out with their hair skinned . . . quills stuck in their eyes. . . . The injuns cut the muscles from their legs while they still lived. They took care not to cut the arteries. What they done . . . it laid waste to all I'd ever dreamed. After that there wasn't nothing but killing them savages and taking every breath I had left for my own self. It was hard lonesome, you know?

"There was this one kid in the camp, youngest one. His name was Frederick but we all called him Bern. Bern was small but he could ride better than most and he and me took to bunking together on account we was both from Tennessee, him from west and me east-middle. So I heard him get up that night in the dead of winter. I heard him leave the tent. I don't know who else was out there with him, but I watched them go into the storehouse and there wasn't no mistaking the business they was transacting. Now there wasn't a gal within forty miles. You follow me? When the boys found out . . . What they done when they found out . . . The boys cut him to pieces. Our own people. They cut his man parts. That was just the start. My friend Bern died in the snow, all laid out, all alone. Our own brothers done that."

"Did they get strung up?"

Greenie didn't answer for a long while. "Captain was in on it. Report said injuns done it."

His hand was shaking.

I asked, "What did they do to the other man, the one he was with?"

His voice was so low I nearly missed it. "Never figured who the other was."

I asked, "How'd they learn what Bern was up to?"

The empty whiskey bottle clanked on the floor. Greenie said, "My point is in this world a man must be careful how he lives."

I lay back on the bed. For no good reason my breath was coming up short. "Greenie? What you trying to tell me?"

Greenie lay back too. "Nothing. Just go to sleep. I shouldn't have said nothing."

The wedding was nearing and Constance was busy with preparations and most days there was cause for her to venture into town for one matter or another. She was in the papers regular now and the thought of all them men reading about her wedding give the Governor pause. Natural enough he put the four guards he trusted most on her person anytime she ventured out. Drummond rode inside the carriage while Greenie and I rode buckskins. Tuss held the scatter-gun beside the driver. It was as we drilled in the slow times.

On this particular day we rode her down to the tailor's where her dress was being took in, and stood our familiar positions about the building while she lingered inside. The longer we stayed the more folks gathered about to watch. She was a princess to them, and it wasn't every day they might catch a glimpse.

There was a beggar calling to me but then again there was always beggars and I didn't think much of this one. But when Constance and Drum come out, this particular beggar got between us and the carriage and started making a show and wouldn't move out the way. He wasn't an old man like most beggars and he seemed too well fed for a man who made his living on scraps. Drum was the one who called it. This beggar got him thinking ambush. He shouted, "Angel! Angel!"

It was our code. So all at once we went on hot. We made quick work of it.

Drum put the butt of his rifle to the beggar's head and knocked him flat to the earth. Greenie and Tuss leveled their weapons on those about us and barked at them to lay flat or die. I was closest to Constance and so I was the one to put my hand to her back and drive her forward while shielding her body with my own. I put both of us through the open carriage door.

At once the carriage was off at great speed. The boys was coming up behind on the buckskins, and I was pointing my rifle out the window, and all of us was waiting on their shots. I was hoping on them a little, maybe.

But not a bullet was loosed.

I was now inside the carriage and alone with the holy daughter. We was rolling at such a clip that the smallest bump could lift us from our seats.

Constance was crying as I had pushed her with some force and her day dress was now tore and her elbow bleeding the brightest, cleanest red across her white skin. "And what was the point of that? Huh? That man was only begging his supper!"

"It's our charge to protect you, ma'am."

"They only long for a look. They only long to be near. I am a promise to them, don't you see? Don't you remember? This life can hold brighter days." She put a white cloth to her bloody elbow. "It is all so sad. All of this, all that we have . . . I'm not able to pretend that I am glad. Not anymore. What we have comes on their backs. This whole wedding, my entire life, it comes on their backs. And you people beat them to the ground with your rifle butts!" The box that contained her wedding dress was between us. She had clung to it with force when I pushed her into the carriage. "I should be married in some dusty calico, like any other woman in this state."

"Would you rather live in a hovel and worry over every meal?"

"You've been turned by my father. Don't deny it. I remember when you arrived. I saw in you that you didn't believe in this. You were different. I saw it that first night we dined. You were in awe, but you were not in approval. You might be the only person to ever eat at that table who didn't want all the silver and charm for himself."

She set the box and the dress it contained on the seat beside her. "I would have you know that not all men are as weak willed as you. There are men who fight right now to remedy injustice. They risk everything they have, love and life included, to overturn this madness, to create a system built on balance and equity." She dabbed a linen to her eyes, then to the blood on her elbow. "What, really, brought you here anyway? If you didn't want all of Father's silver for yourself, what is it you wanted? I know you wanted something."

"To be favored by a man of his caliber, that answers a call from deep inside."

Now her eyes narrowed. "To be favored? Is that why you broke into Father's office just the moment he and Charles were off sending a telegram?"

I glanced sidelong at her. Her heat had caused her to say more than she should, but she was too prideful to backstep.

A deep silence rose between us.

There was only one person who knew I had broken into the Govenor's office. But why had Will told Constance, of all people?

She had held this secret from her father, I knew as much or else I would not in that moment be trusted with her safekeeping. But why keep the secret?

I was turning over the possibilities when I remembered where I had seen that heavy paper before, the paper Will had burned when I found him reading it. Constance had used the very same kind as a bookmark that day I rode with her and the Governor toward a lunch with her fiancé.

I was still sorting these events the next day, even as I stood in the Governor's office, just him and me. He was watching out the window for the approach of his militia.

"We've made progress," he said almost to himself. "The fifty thousand stolen from the train. Every serial number on the bills was known and recorded. The Pinkertons monitor where these bills turn up. A brilliant stratagem — I only wish the idea had been mine. The noose narrows, Straight, and soon it will tighten."

"Where is Harney?" I asked. "Where do these bills lead?"

"Here they march!" The Governor seized me by the shoulder and led me from his office. "Little brings me as much joy in this world as looking over my fighting men!"

"Your militia? Why bring them here?"

307

"You don't think I would leave the security of this wedding entirely in the hands of my few guardsmen?"

The militiamen wore green wool coats and gray trousers. The uniforms was caked in dust and sweat. They was an old force, older than I expected anyhow. The men was in their thirties mostly and the officers on past forty. Nearly all wore thick beards and sun-beaten eyes and they looked upon me with dour intention.

Their leader's sword clanked as he dismounted and handed Will the reins to his powerful bay. He offered the Governor a Union salute. He was looking up at his commander on account of the difference in their statures. The Governor said, "At ease. Welcome back, major. I understand you have much to report."

"Sir, I recorded extensive notes on our encounters with the enemy."

"I look forward to your briefing, major." The Governor pointed with four fingers at the great many men on the road. "Order your boys to retire to that pasture and join me for a brandy. After we discuss the bandit we need to begin designing plans for the defense of the estate."

"Yessir. I am eager for your counsel, sir."

I looked out over the mess of soldiers and saw their eyes back upon us. Behind the soldiers come a great train of wagons and supplies. I heard the bellows of worn-down mules and the grinding of metal rims over gravel.

The sheer size of this militia sent a shiver through me. A force of 150 men existed to extinguish my brother from this earth, and here I was almost part of it.

I looked to the mountain. I wanted to believe he was there, above all this. I wanted to believe that even from so high he would recognize me.

That night Drummond and Tuss and the major went outside with bottles. They was old friends and laughed like it. Greenie was in our room cleaning his Winchester. "Come on," I said. "I'm going out there."

"You can keep that major for yourself. I was hoping Harney might clean the smile off his face once and for all."

I looked at Greenie anew. "You afraid of him?"

"Afraid? Shit."

"Get up, then, let's go." I had questions to ask the major once his guard was down.

We took our bottles outside. The major was leaning against the house and patting the pockets of his uniform. I handed him my tobacco pouch.

Drum and Tuss was looking us over. Tuss said, "Ain't you kids got some letters to write?"

The major was a little man but strong as a bulldog. "Indebted," he said with no meaning to the word and no warmness for me or my tobacco. He chewed the plug three times and placed it in the corner of his cheek and spat. He tossed the pouch and I caught it with my left.

We all spat.

The major sent down a pull of whiskey. He was smirking at me. "You got the look of a fish. I got an eye for such matters. He looks fishy, don't he?"

Tuss and Drummond held perfect still. I could tell I was expected to do something. I sipped my bottle.

"He is cold, give him that." The major swigged. They all swigged. "If you took Drum's spot you must be a decent squeeze with a six-gun. Never met a fish who could shoot worth a shit. Never met a kid who could shoot who wouldn't go to fists over being called a fish."

I tipped my bottle toward the major. "You seen Harney recent?"

"Only his dust. Shit, that one is some part injun, I'll tell you." The major puffed out his chest. "He's got himself squaws. Whole herd of them. They keep him hidden. They got these tunnels they use. Hide 'em with sage and you never see nothing but tracks going into a mountainside."

Pure bluster, but I liked the notion of my

brother taken in by the countryside. "I hear he's being hid by the cattlemen."

"That's bullshit," the major said. "It's the reds. Round about May, my scouts put him up the canyon from us. They was all there and we had the jump. Closest we ever come. The boys was bouncing with it. We all thought it was ours. As we slipped into position up comes a whistle like an elk bugling, 'cept its spring and I ain't never heard a bugle outside autumn. It was his squaws, had to be. It was their warning. We busted on 'em then and come up the canyon red hot and there's their fires still burning and even some half-eaten chow in the dirt. But where's them? We had that canyon tied down. No way out."

The major didn't go on. "What happened then?" I asked.

He spat.

Drum asked, "What happened, Billy?"

He pulled from his bottle. He muttered the next part. "They circled back on us. Burnt the supplies."

I couldn't help but laugh. My old brother, the trickster.

The major shoved me and I fell into the darkness. It was Drum who stopped the little man from kicking on me. "I don't rightly care if he's good with a pistol or not. Who this tenderfoot think he is?"

I climbed from the dirt and found my bottle.

"I quit the Governor once," Tuss said out of the blue, like all the while we was talking about quitting. "Course he was the colonel then. Wasn't two years later I was back at his door. You miss the work. You might hate it sometimes, but watch, you walk away and you'll come crawling back."

"What'd you do when you quit?" Greenie asked.

"Rented a fertile spread from Boss. Found myself a Methodist gal and got to thinking we'd start us a little family. She could cook, no doubt. Give me two boys in two years."

"Where's your family now?" I pulled from my bottle.

Tuss shrugged. "When you's here you want to be somewheres else. But if you's somewheres else you want to be here. Try settling down, just try it. Boring as watching snow melt. I saw it through to the youngest was born and then that was all for me."

The major spat. "Some men is farmers, some ain't. No use pretending to be something you ain't."

"So what is we then?" Greenie asked. "If we ain't farmers?"

"Braves," the major answered. "Every color got 'em. We's the lucky ones. You imagine sprouting beans for living?"

We stayed drinking that night. Tuss put us to poker so he could take our monies, and he did too. Tuss was all the time making my winnings his. When we couldn't see the cards straight no more we took to singing at the moon. The boys pulled out their trunks and pissed on the dirt.

I was so sauced by then that I pulled down my britches just like the men done and pretended to hold my thing and let loose. I will admit it got messy before it went straight. But I saw that a girl could make it go if she held herself just right and believed long enough.

We pulled up our britches and belched and Tuss's tobacco pouch made the rounds. It done fell from his pocket when we stood from the card table and Drum had snagged it before Tuss noticed. Now Tuss was the last to receive it. "Thanks, fellers. Mighty kind to share your pouch. Wait a fool . . . That's *my* damn 'baccy pouch!"

Greenie fell down laughing. Drum leaned on me for support. We both tumbled over.

Tuss was the one who saw the saturation of my pants and pointed. The lantern light was brought to bear and all the boys balanced themselves for a proper gander at my wet pants.

The major belted, "Somebody better teach this snapper to shoot!"

This was what got them howling so loud Charles was sent to shut us up.

■ ■ ■ ■

I was laying on my bed too dizzy with drink to sleep when Greenie come in and kicked off his boots. But instead of his bed he fell into mine, right on top of me though he caught his own weight.

A bead of his sweat hit me between the eyes. Our noses was touching. All at once the liquor was gone from me and I felt clean sober. There wasn't no missing his hardness.

How many moments was we locked together? For all of them I took in his breaths and he took in mine. All I had to do was welcome him. He was waiting on me to welcome him. But I just lay there unmoving.

I had come to love Greenie in that manner of young, lonesome men who see in the eyes of another no judgment. But no man ever moved me toward lust, even this one whose mood I knew by nothing more than the force of his spat.

Soon enough he pushed off me and moved onto his own bed. He rolled to the wall and was silent.

Greenie's voice come in flat and low. "You gonna tell?" His back was still to me.

"About what?"

"Promise you won't say."

"I swear to you."

"I ain't a fish," he said.

"Don't matter to me if you is."

"I just really thought you was part of this." His voice was shaking. "Don't be queer about it or nothing, I beg you. Let's just go on as we was. I'm just drunk is all, can't hardly see straight. Just fell on the wrong bed is all. Thought I saw Miss Aberdeen."

I laid there seeing everything between me and Greenie with new eyes. The only man I knew better was my brother. To tell it straight, Greenie was my first friend in this life.

The longer I thought it over, the more I dwelled on that terrible story Greenie had told of his friend Bern who died in the snow with his parts cut free. Greenie was the other man with Bern that night, I was sure of it now. My blood quickened at the thought. How could Bern have been killed like that and not Greenie?

All Greenie had to do was tell Drum it was me who'd made the move. I was the fish. The first one to tell would be the one trusted.

Looking back, I'm sure he considered hanging me to dry. Greenie feared one thing worse than death and that was being cast out of the crew. And so he must've weighed his belief in me, in my loyalty to him.

No other way but he come to decide he could safekeep his trust in me, in Jesse Straight.

Even all these years on, I lift Greenie from

those events and keep him near. I see anew his sidelong smile, that familiar glance over his shoulder before slipping me a daytime bottle. Despite what come to pass between us, I worry for him still.

What would Greenie have done had I come clean to him that night? I like to think he would have considered picking me, over them.

This life is cut with trails unrode. There was a time I resented that fact, the cruelty of being stuck to only one. But age like I got teaches you to be grateful for those trails untook. The old mind can wander their lengths and see what the eyes was never allowed, what the eyes would have missed. I've had time to wander those trails that interest me.

I only hope Greenie was so lucky.

I remember the next night in fine detail. Ain't no forgetting it. I was down with Drum and Tuss eating in the kitchen. They was arguing about the proper design of horseshoes. Never mind neither of them shod a horse in all their lives. Greenie was in his room, and that's where my eyes was, on the shut door.

Then Charles appeared beside the table. "Master desires your presence."

"Oh, shit," said Tuss, his mouth full of food. "The kid done and did it this time!"

Drummond didn't say a word. He didn't

blink. His stare sent goose pimples down my arms.

I was delivered to the Governor's office, which was lit now with lanterns on account of the darkness. The room was empty. I stood in the middle. "Do I wait?"

Charles was in the doorway. "Stand with your hands at your sides."

"Am I in some manner of trouble?"

He was an unwavering man, that Charles. All summer I'd been in his proximity and never once had I seen any side of him he didn't want me to see. "Sir," Charles said down the hallway. "Straight waits as you requested."

The Governor entered and behind him come a man dressed in a black duster. This man wore a leather patch over his right eye and his head was clean shaven. He wore no hat. His ears had long ago been cut down their middles. The top half of one curled forward.

The Governor poured brandies and offered me a glass. I took it. Still the new man stared on me. He was taller even than the Governor.

"Please, let us sit," the Governor said.

"Is there anything else, sir?" Charles asked.

"No, that is all. Thank you, Charles."

Charles bowed and shut the door without a sound.

I took a seat after the Governor. The new man sat last. I sipped my drink. I was the only one.

"Straight, I'd like you to meet my agent, Mr. Thorvald. Mr. Thorvald is just returned from Harney's home county. He carries a few questions for you. I have communicated to him that you knew Harney as a boy."

The bald man placed his drink upon the table. Now his eye turned from me to a pocket inside his duster.

I remembered to breathe.

The Governor was studying me. He hadn't studied me since the evening of our first dinner.

The bald man had a notebook in his hand and a pencil. He touched the lead to his tongue and tapped it to his book. He spoke with a heavy accent I did not recognize other than to know it was of the Old World. "Harney, he make few friends. And yet here is you."

"We ain't friends."

"No? What be you then?"

"I knew him. That's all. What's this about?"

"So, you have been to his family land?"

"Yes."

"Describe it for me, please."

"Like what it look like?"

"That is correct."

I looked to the Governor. He nodded.

"Well, there's a lake northwest of the house. A barn with two stables off to the south. Sod roof. A small place. Like they all was in the time of its building. It has been some years since I was near it but that's my memory."

"And inside?"

"Like inside the house? I don't remember. A fireplace. Two beds. It's a house, what do you mean?"

"Who lived in the house?"

"There was Harney and his pa."

"Is that all?" His eye expected something. I understood he knew of the sister.

"There was a girl too."

"How old?"

"It's been some time. But I'd reckon she would be round about seventeen."

The Governor said, "Describe her."

"She was not much to look at, I remember that. I didn't never spend time at their place. Harney come over to our spread."

"Where was your spread? Precisely," Agent Thorvald asked.

"Across the valley. Beyond the Mormons. That sister was ugly as sin, I remember that. Flat chested and raggy hair and strong where God don't want girls strong."

"There is a big house on the edge of town, white and wide. Is that the one?"

"No, not the Thurston place. It is a touch farther. The earthen one along the river. Our acres went up the draw there." I had described the place the Landcaster widow lived.

"How far was that from Harney?"

"Ten miles, on abouts."

"So Harney would leave his residence and all the work there and ride to your residence, as you say, and work for your father? Why would he do this?"

"My pa had money to pay for a time. Not many did in that county. Not many do."

"He would ride past the Mormon? The Mormon has much. The Mormon hired eight hands this summer."

"All of them Mormon. Them Mormons keep to themselves. They like Chinamen that way."

"It's true," the Governor said. "And we're better for it, if you ask me. When did you last see the sister?"

I took a moment to consider. "Two years back? I don't rightly remember."

"Your age is twenty?"

"Yessir."

"Or is it twenty-one?" the Governor asked.

"That's right," I said. "Twenty-one."

"And you lived in a place such as that one and you don't give attention to a girl who lives only few miles away?"

The Governor's eyes did not waver. His drink waited in his hand.

"Ugly as dust, like I said. Besides I had me a girl," I shot on the fly. "Her name was Kathleen. Harney done took her plum."

"Ah," the Governor said. He was set at ease by my answer. "Of course. Because paternal loyalty will only drive a man so far. But coital rights, well, they will drive a man to carnage."

"Kathleen . . ." Agent Thorvald was writing. He looked up. "Her family name?"

"Richmond."

"Richmond? I do not remember such a name in the county records." .

I didn't answer. I thought it queer that a man would think he could remember every name in a county listing. I saw the warning within the statement. Agent Thorvald was trying to bait me. I held my tongue.

The Governor smelled his liquor. He gave in to the silence first. "I have a great interest in this sister. See, Straight, she has been missing since this spring. We came looking for her only to find her disappeared. The Mormon . . . What was his name?"

"Saggat," the agent and I said at once.

"This Saggat believes she may have joined her brother."

"If she could find Harney."

The Governor sat back in his chair. He sipped his drink. He looked into the marble eyes of the great stag.

I considered why they might want the sister. "You can ransom her to Harney. Lure him out."

The Governor glanced at Agent Thorvald. "It will come as confirmation and no surprise that Harney's father was a traitor and coward. Tell him, Thorvald. You'll love this, Straight. It has kept me cloud bound all afternoon."

321

Agent Thorvald looked up from his notes. "The elder deserted in sixty-three. Harney was name of his major. His true name was Rowhine."

My breath slipped.

"He took the name and papers of the dead major to avoid leaving a trail west. It was a common act of cowardice," the Governor added.

"This ain't true," I said at once. My hand could no longer hold the liquor still. I took it down and said, "I don't buy it. It don't add up."

Agent Thorvald studied my face.

"It is true," the Governor said. "Rowhine was a coward and he fled his duties and so naturally raised a son with a lack of —"

"No," I said, despite an understanding I should remain silent. "People can't just . . . Harney's pa was a sharpshooter, no doubt. I watched him shoot."

"Rowhine was a sharpshooter, before he turned yellow."

My glass clanked on the table. I was dizzy. I was remembering the word burned into the bay of Pa's fiddle. I had believed it the name of the fiddle's maker, not its owner. Rowhine.

"You look sick," Agent Thorvald said. I saw only suspicion in his eye.

"Maybe the girl will return home," I said.

"She will find only ash." Agent Thorvald tapped his pencil to his tongue.

"Ash."

"We burned the structures, of course."

I laughed because it was all I could do. I slapped my knee and I said, "Burned them to the ground! Ain't that something."

I was the only one laughing.

"There is another matter," Agent Thorvald said. He flipped to a fresh page in his notebook. He extended his enormous arm across the table and placed the notebook in my lap. In his fingers was the pencil. "Write your name."

"My name?"

"Yes." Agent Thorvald passed his tongue over his bottom lip. "There is no Straight in the county register."

The Governor looked to the notebook in my lap. "No games now. I'm asking for your true name."

"The senator dubbed me 'Straight.' I thought you knew, sir."

"So write the name then. As you sign it to documents of county interest. Agent Thorvald has implored us to be fastidious."

"Of course." I took up the pencil. I adjusted my grip. I signed my name "Jesse Landcaster." It was a poor choice as Mrs. Landcaster never had no offspring, but it was the best I could muster under their gaze.

I took my tobacco pouch outside into the desert night. I leaned against the house and looked at the big, dark mountain that belonged to my employer. I had never called Pa by his real name.

The Governor had been west for the whole war. He'd built his fortune while boys like my pa went off with their brothers to eat bullets and walk among ghosts and return if they returned at all broke and ill of mind. And now he was claiming my pa was a traitor and a coward for walking west from that fight that wasn't his.

Had Ma known Pa's truth? Or had she died before he come clean?

Why was that question troubling me so?

I walked into the chilled desert air. My mind was on the top of that mountain.

No mountain could ever wear a man's name. A mountain rose above the plane of names and lifted the winds and with them the ravens and smoke and sent them over the earth. Only a map could wear a man's name. And what was a map to someone who had walked the flanks of a mountain for all her life and knew its every crag and spring?

I stayed that night with Ingrid but I barely slept. Agent Thorvald would soon know there was no Jesse Landcaster and then what?

I swore off whiskey for a hundredth time and really meant it. I wrapped my winnings and all the shells I could carry in a satchel and buried them in the hay of the barn. I checked Ingrid's shoes and cleaned out the old mud with a pick. When the time come to make a run for it, we'd be ready.

The next morning Constance found me in the barn. Her riding clothes was clean as they always was and she flicked the lead to quiet Enterprise. "You're readying yourself for a long ride."

"That ain't the case."

"And what's that roll of blankets then?"

I kicked some hay over them. I looked out the window toward the house. "I don't reckon we should be talking. Ain't that the senator's carriage yonder?"

"We are soon to go for a ride. He feels we haven't learned enough about each other. He feels I've been keeping aloof from him."

She picked her teeth with a point of hay. "I plan to ride him up the steep face of the mountain. These eastern men fancy themselves prodigious riders. Give them a polo club and a lawn and they may be, but they are no match for the West's uneven ground. What good is riding if you only ride manicured grass? Give me a mountain and a game trail and I will ride a thousand years."

I checked my hands. They was so dirty compared to hers. "How come you ain't said a word to your father if you reckon I done broke into his office?"

Constance put a hand to her top button. "What makes you think I didn't tell him straightaway?"

I shrugged. "On account I'm still breathing."

Enterprise called out and Ingrid whinnied in response. I settled her with a brushstroke to the bottom of the neck.

A third whinny sounded from outside. I leaned for a look and saw the senator leading a saddled buckskin.

He walked in and looked direct on me though he spoke to Constance. "Are you ready, my dear? Lead that animal of yours into the light and I will join you promptly."

I kept my eyes on the brush I was passing over Ingrid's haunch. Constance led her animal from the barn without a word.

The senator lingered long enough to say, "Don't think I haven't already conveyed my suspicions to your employer."

Drummond fetched me from my guard duties. "Boss is waiting on you. You alone." In Drummond's eyes I saw he had knowledge unknown to me. There was no mistaking something had turned him against me. I knew Drum too well by then.

"What's this about?"

His eyes moved to the distance. "You best come along, kid."

I didn't have no choice but to follow Drummond to the front of the estate. There Will was holding two saddled buckskins. The

Governor was there, the wind throwing up his jacket. When I approached, the Governor said with no humor in his eyes, "Glad you could join us, Mr. Straight."

He hadn't called me "mister" in months, and I could not temper the terror that swelled in me at that one word.

Out stepped Agent Thorvald, and on his hip was a sawed-down scattergun. His eye did not waver from me.

"Come," the Governor said. "Join me on a ride."

"Just us?" I asked. "Where to?"

Will held the buckskin as the Governor swung up. The Governor spun his horse and said, "There now, do not tarry. We have a most vital appointment."

Will winked. It was a warning, clear and simple.

He put his open hand to the buckskin's nose as I swung up, and then knuckled the animal along its brow. He knew just how this particular horse wanted to be touched.

"They call him Dash." Will's eyes held mine. "As in, dash far, far away."

"This direction!" The Governor heeled his animal and Drummond slapped the hind-quarter of mine, and at once we broke through the sage and the gulch and across the flank of the mountain, toward what fate I could not know.

The timber finally slowed the Governor to a walk.

"Where we going, Boss?" I called to his back. We was riding single file through the limbs.

"I am coming to believe, Mr. Straight, that the poor man is the quintessential American. He is the only one to possess the qualities of the soldier and the saint. He might feel burdened from time to time by what other men have that he doesn't, but in the poor man's core is a fundamental gratitude for the little he does possess.

"A rich girl will always have trouble in this world. A rich girl will doubt the Lord's order. She trusts too deeply in the permanence of her own comforts, you understand. Such trust is the least of American qualities. It is that trust we warred against in 1812. I suppose if I had been a better father I would have adopted her off to some collection of the righteous downtrodden and thereby let her loose into the lowest rungs of this world so that she might climb up on the strength of her own might. But alas, I did as her mother preferred and gave her only the best of everything. And so I should not be surprised by our current predicament. Some elements of character are not passed with the blood, I fear."

The Governor blocked a branch with his forearm. "The wedding is in three days and now she tells me she cannot marry this man. She says either I let her out of this marriage or she will flee from my keeping. A girl alone in those mountains? I doubt it strongly.

"She has changed in that manner all women change when they have known the touch of a man. Like a fruit half plucked that now wears a bruise, my Constance has been spoiled. Don't you see? That girl wants away from me but not into the arms of her intended. She has a beau, I think we all know it." His eyes looked to the ground between us. "Have you heard word?"

"I have heard such gossip, sir, but I put no stake in it."

"Yes, so rumors swirl. Some would say it has been a long time brewing. Only I believed my daughter's good sense would overrun her native impulse for the beastly and carnal. And frankly, I trusted in the permanence of due gratitude from those I rescued. I should've known this generation would default on their debts. That is the difference between my age and yours, Straight. My generation remembers that all we have rests on the struggles of those who came before. Yours seems to believe there was no generation before. There are the aged and the young, and the world will forever belong to the young, and the young will not age."

We rode through the forest without the benefit of a trail and the animals hurdled a log and put us through limbs. The Governor gripped his hat as he ducked. He was no stranger to hard rides.

"I think you know there is no Jesse Landcaster in the county registry. So think about this from my position, Straight. A young man arrives at my home. I invite him in and grace him with good fortune and kind living. Maybe I let his talent get the better of my judgment. And then he twice lies to me with the most fundamental and primary of all confessions between friends. We are friends, aren't we? I honestly believed so."

"Friends, sir?"

"Yet I don't even know your honest name, Straight."

"I can explain the —"

The Governor rose a finger. "You're lucky, son, that I can see through men. I know by your eyes that you haven't muddled my daughter. There is no doubt in me that you value your knighthood more than you value congress with the princess. Not all men are built thus, but you are. Frankly, so am I. My secret in this life, if I may, is I have never been as moved by flesh as I am by victory. Such is a supreme advantage.

"I also know that you have lied to me about

your name because you are embarrassed by the raw fact of your greasy lineage. On your first night here, in my office, I let you lie to me about your family. Your blood is not your fault, Straight. I have always been prone to trust men who are propelled by shame. It is these men who will stop at nothing to prove themselves to me, as you have done in every manner that counts for anything. But tell me now. Is it Hernandez or Delano? Both were in the country registry. No, never mind. Your name doesn't matter. In my mind, you are nameless. I prefer it this way. Only the nameless man has a future. Do you want a future, son?"

The Governor put a match to his cigar and turned it against the flame. He licked two fingers, pinched the match, and dropped it to the dry needles.

"Mr. Cliffpatrick brings his best man and a terrific sum of money. If you win this wager, I will forgive your deception. I will offer you a blank slate on which we may write your new, brighter future. Agent Thorvald, frankly, advocates I put you in the earth. But you and I share something that none of these others do. Isn't that right?"

"Sir?"

"Maybe it originates in the burying of our fathers in our coming-of-age. Maybe it lies in our ambition. We are both poor men blessed with ambition. No, I am not ready to give up on you yet. I am, above all else, a loyal man, a patriot. We are maybe the only true Americans left, you and me.

"So I want to confess something of my own. You may not consider me the confessional type, but I . . . Think of Jesus, Lord to so many but friend of none. How lonely He must have been for earthly honesty. . . . A man of my stature must select his moments of confession with keen discernment. I have never trusted the preacher as thoroughly as I have the shamed man who owes me his very right to breathe. Now that is you. After today you will owe me your salvation. Do you understand?"

"Sir?"

He drew a deep breath. It was the first time I had seen the Governor bolstering his resolve. "I told you I made a fortune along the Californian rivers in the forty-nine rush. That is true, in a sense, but I did not pan for my fortune as most assume, as I may let on in conversation. I did not pull myself up by sweat and toil, not in the traditional sense at least. In the course of one night I became the owner of three mines and the commander of all their men, and in the coming years I reaped ridiculous profit from their labors."

"In one night, sir?"

"You will never tell of this. I know that. But even if you did no man of substance would hear you. They believe in me, Straight. And nothing a hired gun says could ever change that. So what if those mines and their men came to me by way of cards? So what if the games were not level? With trickery I ruined my mentor in an hour. He died a year later from a knife when one of his debts could not be repaid. But he was not as generous as I have been. So rest assured that I only improved the world by taking stewardship of his fortune. None of this troubles me. I did the right thing. He called me 'son.' He had lost his boy as I had lost my father. I let him trust me. For the betterment of this Republic, I did what I did.

"Let me give you some advice, Jesse. Only profit — oh, yes, the salvation of earned bounty, the lordly return upon investments made — only hard-won profit can earn real redemption. It is profit that unites us. Profit is the future we share, and the reason you still draw breaths.

"So onward then, faster yet, we must not be late for our future!"

We arrived at a timbered basin far from the eyes of newspapermen. Cliffpatrick wasn't yet there and so on the Governor's suggestion I took some practice and tried to settle my mind on the task ahead. I wondered who would throw the saucers. I assumed Cliffpatrick must be bringing them.

I heard the cracking of limbs first and

turned to see two men ride into the basin. Both was on powerful black stallions. The first man wore white and was older than even the Governor. This was Mr. Carson Cliffpatrick. He called in his plantation drawl, "Ready to try again, eh, old friend? You western men insist to learning the same lessons on new days. It remains amusing, anyway, to serve your tutelage."

The Governor smoothed his moustache. "I was beginning to doubt you, Cliff. Thought maybe you, like those Southern generals you so fancy, had tucked your tail and ran."

The second rider was black and just this side of Drummond's age. He wore a hat and a sheepskin vest and upon his hips was a pair of gleaming silver six-shooters with a make I'd never before seen. They looked to shoot fifty-caliber loads. He swung down from his stallion and hitched it to the nearest tree and then took hold of his boss's ride and offered the man a hand as he climbed down.

Cliffpatrick nearly fell backward once upon the ground, but the shooter caught him by the shoulder and kept him upright. Cliffpatrick swatted at the help and said, "This here is your gunner? How old are you, boy? Does your momma know you're out here with us grown men?" He wore a thin goatee and a white hat with a black band and carried fifty pounds of extra flesh, all of it in his thighs.

The Governor elbowed me. It was a signal

to run my mouth. "Did your Negro help you up onto that horse too? Surprised he could lift you."

Cliffpatrick laughed. "He does have a tongue on him, I'll give you that, governor. It'll be a shame to see it go still in some minutes."

"Still while I count my winnings," I said.

The old man smiled. "Now isn't that something." He pointed a thumb at his shooter. "This bear here is my man Johnson. Don't look him in the eye or he may maul you."

"What's our game?" I asked.

Cliffpatrick laughed. "Oh, your employer didn't say?"

I looked at the Governor now. He shrugged. "It's a duel, Jesse."

The old man waddled close and patted my cheek with his icy white hand. "Now where'd that tongue go, boy?"

"Shall we prepare?" the Governor asked.

Both men pulled gold watches from their pockets. Cliffpatrick said, "Twelve fifteen."

The Governor corrected his watch. "Twelve twenty then?"

"Make it twelve twenty-five. I do enjoy the anticipation," Cliffpatrick said. He pointed his thumb and Johnson jogged back to the horses and fetched from a saddlebag a silver flask and two crystal glasses. He jogged in return and handed the flask to his employer and held the glasses in his two big hands.

The tumblers looked like shot glasses there.

"The finest Caribbean rum." Cliffpatrick poured the flask's contents and said, "The man who invents a method for keeping a cube of ice at a summer sporting match will rule this divided nation."

The two patrons lifted their drinks and clinked. "To being that man."

Cliffpatrick refilled their glasses and shook the flask and said, "Mite left. Boys?"

Johnson looked to the earth. "No, sir. Thank you, sir."

The Governor tipped his head toward the center of the meadow. "Go step it off. We have some wagering to do. Jesse, wait."

He approached and stood before me. With both hands he righted the collar on my shirt. He licked his thumb and cleaned a smudge of dust from my forehead. "Now, son. A win against Cliffpatrick starts us both with a clean slate. Do you want me indebted to you? Yes, I think you do."

Johnson and I walked toward the center of the meadow. If I died no one would ever know what come of me. If Noah sought me out, he'd only learn that I had vanished from our ranch in the spring of my seventeenth year and had never been seen again. My stomach lurched and I bent to catch my breath.

Johnson lifted me by the armpit. "There now." I looked in time to catch him wiping a drop from his runny nose. "Got me a fever myself. Never used to this mountain weather. Wintertime even in the hot months. Where's your peoples from?"

"I don't know."

"Been in the business long?"

"No, sir."

"Oh, don't call me 'sir.'" He glanced over his shoulder at the white men on the hill. "Mr. Cliff pays me real good and he feeds us good too. He put my girls on with his house crew so they out the sun and maybe learn a skill worth knowing. We come for that Kansas land after the war. Free acres for Negros. It was in all the papers. My woman knows some words and she yelled in joy when she read it. So we set out walking her and me, walked through our boots and it took on six months too but we made it. But . . . weren't no land at all. Not for Negros. Then there weren't no work on account of all the Negros that come for the land that weren't theirs. All for nothing but then I meet Mr. Cliff on his new beef ranch. The Lord helped me fall into this real lucky."

"Girls?"

"Yes, sir. Three, five, eight, ten, and twelve. My woman don't seem to got no boy in her, but we aim to try again anyhow, Lord willing. A man can't ever have too many daughters but he needs his son. You got family?"

I didn't know how to answer.

"It's okay. You gamed before? Not much to consider. We step off our paces and at their signal we draw. That's all. I weren't made good at this by the Lord's hand to hurt you, I promise. He'll guide my lead through your heart. These here shooters I throw got a bullet thick as a bit. You won't feel nothing but air."

I just looked up at him. My hands tingled. There wasn't no feeling in me at all but low-down trembling.

He give a sad, knowing smile. "All right to be scared. Nothing to be ashamed of."

I looked back to the Governor and Cliffpatrick. They was lighting each other's cigars.

"You don't got much choice in the matter," he said. "If you run they's gonna have me to gun you down. Best you stand proud, take it tall. The Lord will notice. I won't gut shoot you, that much comes from on high."

"Feeling dainty, are you?" It was Cliffpatrick.

Johnson whispered, "Be proud of yourself to come this far. Word is you had some talent."

"Sometime this summer, perhaps?" Cliffpatrick called.

"Yes," the Governor seconded. "Jesse, pace it off ahead of our signal."

I felt the heat rise up. I imagined Johnson and me turning on them with our pistols. The thought brought my hands back to my body.

It stilled my vision. I tested the balance of my Peacemaker. I wondered if I had it in me.

"What's to stop us from killing them and splitting the money in their pockets?" I asked.

He laughed. He put an arm around my shoulders and turned me from them. "And then what? Without them you and me just dogs in a world of wolves." He patted my back kindly. "Don't worry, I won't tell your boss none of this after."

I watched as he counted the steps to his position. He kicked away some fallen limbs and stretched his arms.

I done the same. I heard the wind in the treetops and thought of my brother when he finally returned for his sister.

"In ten," the Governor called. Cliffpatrick finished his drink and flung the crystal to the side. "Nine."

When I looked again to Johnson I saw a new face, this one steeled off from all feeling, this one not reflecting me at all. His fingers flexed in the air over his pistols. I was but a target to him now.

All the hours alone, all the sorrows and hopes, every sunset and song condensed into a single point the width of a button's eye, and I imagined my lead center punching that point on each number of their countdown.

I didn't hear no signal. I drew only when I saw his action. But I did more than draw and it's good I did or I would not be here writing these words. Johnson was the faster man. But he was expecting one thing and I give him another. As I drew I let my body fall between my feet into a squat. His bullet come so close it left a black burn on my ear.

He looked on me in surprise. He might've shot again and he could've had me, but he didn't shoot twice. He holstered his pistol.

Blood bubbled from his nose and he wiped at it and looked at his fingertips. My bullet had popped the button free of his shirt, and now blood spilled from the hole as it might from a bucket shot through. He made a blow of the blood in his nose and wiped his face with his sleeve and blood smeared across his cheek and he wobbled. Blood spilled on his chin and dripped down in long filaments toward the earth.

Johnson reached a hand to me. He was wavering and he reached out so that I might help balance him. He fell before I arrived to him.

He was gasping. It was me he was looking on when his eyes went gray. My silhouette against the treetops and the vast nothing beyond. I saw it reflected back, I was darkness over him.

The Governor was whooping and hollering and his hat spun into the meadow. Johnson's body gurgled as the muscles give in and the remaining air in his chest slipped into this world never to be drawn back.

"Hot hell and holy dickens!" the Governor's voice echoed back.

"That ain't allowed!" Cliffpatrick objected. "Ducking? The shooter can't move!"

"Oh, no, no, no." The Governor's finger was in the air. He pulled a folded booklet from his pocket and held it between them. "Check the rules yourself, Cliff. The shooter can't move his feet. Straight, did you move your feet? I didn't see him move his feet."

"I'm not suggesting he moved his feet. I'm saying he ducked. It is low. It is contrary to the spirit of the endeavor!" Cliffpatrick pulled a monocle from his breast pocket and put it to his eye. From another pocket he drew his own copy of the same booklet, and Cliffpatrick held the text at varying distances until the print went clear for him.

"There." The Governor pointed to a passage of text on Cliffpatrick's booklet. "Article seven, section four. Shooter shall not adjust his feet once positions are set."

I passed my hand over Johnson's eyes. His daughters had to know.

"There must be more." Cliffpatrick studied his booklet. "Under article four, perhaps?"

"You won't find what you seek, Cliff. Who wrote these rules?"

"And that's why I am suspicious. How can we lack a ducking ordinance?"

"You voted them into use!" The Governor's voice cracked like a boy's. "Don't sink low,

Cliff, just because my tyke gunned down your fancy nigger. An upset is always tough to stomach. We both know losing is part of the game's pleasure — it makes the wins all the sweeter!"

The older man removed his monocle and placed it back into his pocket. He folded his booklet. "Well, I will make a motion at this spring's meeting to amend the current wording. We must have a ducking ordinance. It's absurdly philistine not to."

"We will discuss it then. Now, if you'll congratulate me properly . . ."

Cliffpatrick straightened his coat. He took a breath to collect himself and then offered his hand to the Governor. "Well done, sir. Hell of a show. I'm still shaking with the surprise of it. As you so sagely point out, an upset is always hard on the stomach. A rum then? To settle us? Where is my blasted flask?" He laughed. "I almost called to Johnson to fetch it. That will take some getting used to. I liked that one."

I stood over Johnson. "How will we get him on a horse? How will we get him to his family?"

Cliffpatrick shrugged. "Oh, yes, of course. Put him on a horse then."

"But he is two hundred pounds. I can't alone."

"So don't then." He tipped back the flask and looked down on the dead man as his pink tongue passed over his lips. "Best damn shooter I ever had."

"Mr. Cliffpatrick," the Governor announced to the basin, "was on a streak of luck with this Johnson. What was it, fifteen victories this year?"

"And eight more from last autumn. Counting only the duels. I was finalizing arrangements just yesterday to sail for the Continent. Son, you have left me out to dry." Cliffpatrick looked down his nose at me. "How much to recruit this one?"

The Governor laughed. He slapped Cliffpatrick on the back.

"I'm not saying to buy him," Cliffpatrick said. "Just how much to let me lease him? I have these commitments now and no shooter, you understand. I'm thinking we split the winnings sixty-forty. What do you say, old friend?"

"We'll talk."

While they counted the money upon a saddle I bent down beside Johnson a last time. A spasm had his foot twitching. His eyes wasn't nothing but glass now. In them was my burden to live a life worthy of this man's death and all the suffering to befall his fatherless children. Every action I took from there out was an action weighed in counterbalance to those he would never take. Every moment of rest weighed against his own.

"We must bury him!"

The Governor shook his head. "So the wolves can undo our labors? Don't waste breath warring those forces that cannot be arrested."

I dug anyhow, I dug and dug and dug, with a rock for a trowel. We couldn't leave him out.

But why was I so desperate to hide that dead man under dirt? Was it to benefit his soul or mine?

We rode along the tracks we had laid on the way in, but I saw nothing familiar.

"I speak here of our Republic, of our dignity — of our standing among the greatest civilizations of the world! These Southern men I deal with. They are forever warring. Even as they move west, as they have done in droves, they yet carry their anger at being crushed before the eyes of their servants. They seek to pass their resentments to their offspring, who will no doubt pass it to theirs. It is a poison that will transcend generation. And so they must be made to know that here, in our West, each man is made not by his father's failings but by the character of his own grit.

"I hope you appreciate the depth of my affection for you. Jesse, thanks to this win I now value you more than anyone else ever has. That is love. There is no purer definition."

The Governor pulled a purse from his pocket and tossed it to me. It was thick with cash. "Your share, plus a measure of generosity. We will have many offers after today. That Johnson had a robust reputation. Cliffpatrick's reputation.

"Once Constance is married off and this wedding hubbub is passed by, you and I will make a tour. You will earn more in one month than your whole family could in this lifetime, I promise. I will get us to New York. And from there to London. You watch." He smiled at me. "Have you shot in a building? There is no rush greater. The sound! I am damn pleased, Straight. But enough of this 'Straight' business. It is time we name you properly."

I held the money in my hand. I couldn't reckon its weight against the man left behind.

The Governor said, "Embrace your moment! Ours is a new land, and such is the gift of a new land. What you do from here forward is what will define you. Son, hear me on this point.

"I hope you can look upon what I offer you here today and see it as your gateway to the life you desire. I will make you significant, I will make you a god among men. Our Republic is but a child among ancients. The families that rise up now and take hold of this place will govern it for a thousand years, until some new superior race comes from some yet undiscovered continent to supplant us. What I speak of here today is not about tomorrow, it is about forever, or as close to forever as we finite types are allowed to fathom. With this name, I will welcome you into your forever!"

He ducked a branch. "We will have you listed in the registry as 'Spartan.' The citizens of our city will know you as Mr. Spartan. Jesse works, but I'm prone to Samuel. There is something about the alliterative effect of Samuel. Samuel A. Spartan. It is daunting, isn't it? People won't soon forget a name like that. It would be an especially fine moniker should we have cause to name a river in your honor. The Spartan River. Yes, by God! Many of our rivers still bear the names of this land's previous inhabitants. Of course it falls upon us to update them." He looked at me and then again to the gaps in the trees. "I know what you're thinking. You've been in the papers, but 'Jesse Straight' is not a name to be remembered. The Straight River? See my point."

He pulled a big breath of air and said, "I cannot express the depth of my love for this mountain! Good God, what a land! Come, Samuel! Let us run these horses until they break!"

When we returned it wasn't Will who met us for the animals. It was another man who was typical seen in the garden. He wasn't a calming influence on Dash or the Governor's buckskin. Dash kicked around until he could approach this new man from upwind.

The Governor went straight inside as he intended to send telegrams in all directions concerning the victory of his young ace, Samuel A. Spartan.

Agent Thorvald stepped out from the shadows, intent on me.

Inside the holehouse I sat on the bench with my drawers up. The sun cast blades of light through the room and flies tested the seams for escape. I was panting for no good reason. All that had happened and all that still needed to happen rose up at once like a dust storm and I was lost inside.

The agent's boots cracked the gravel outside. Now his shadow erased the blades of light.

In truth, his presence was a queer relief. The dust blew free and I was holding my Peacemaker and if he opened the door I would seize him and drag him within my darkness.

I kicked open the door. "What do you want with me?"

He didn't say a word. He still wore his sawed-down scattergun on his hip. A fly landed on his brow and he didn't flinch.

He drew something from his shirt pocket, an envelope.

I watched him cross the yard and disappear

around the corner of the house. I drew open the flap on the envelope and saw what was inside. A man's ear.

I met Drummond on the road. He looked on me a long minute. I couldn't tell if he was relieved or troubled to see me alive. "Was he quick as they say?"

"You knew I was going into that."

"What did you want me to say? You know I don't call no shots around here."

Drummond stretched his stiff right hand. That's when I saw the splatter of still-bright blood upon his sleeve. Now I saw there too was blood below his eye and along his neck, small drops like those that come from some knife wounds. I handed him the envelope. "What happened to Will?"

Drummond flicked the envelope to the earth and looked to the sky. He cleared his nose and spat. Then he reached into his jacket and I did believe for a half beat he was drawing on me. But he only drew a bottle. He offered me a pull. Drummond never drank in daylight.

By now I had it figured. The Governor knew who had his daughter's heart. The Governor had sentenced his butler's son to death. Drummond and Agent Thorvald had done it together. As they would've me if the Governor asked.

He offered again the bottle.

"I don't want nothing you got." I walked past Drummond and let my shoulder collide into his. "Coward."

He called to my back, "It ain't cowardly to do your duty."

I went straight to the Governor's office. He was not present. Tuss was keeping watch at the door. "It's true! You had me worried, LP. Word was you was going up against Cliffpatrick's gun. I heard you was back, but figured it must be as a ghost."

I drew out my cash winnings. "Poker?"

"I love you, kid." Tuss looked about us. He whispered, probably the only time in his life. "But Boss don't take kindly to gambling on duty, you know that."

I looked about us and shrugged. "You gonna tell?"

A smile come upon his face. "But I don't got no cards."

I told him to go get his set and I'd keep his post. "Won't take you four minutes down and back."

He rubbed in hands together. "I reckon we can get in a few hands."

"Get them cards before Boss strikes up a notion to work."

Once Tuss was off and down the stairs, I slipped through the office doors and locked them behind me.

Right off I pulled up the grizzly rug looking

for a trapdoor. Then I got on my back and looked up at his desk. There was a scattergun sawed down in the manner of Agent Thorvald's. It was bolted on a swivel below the desk. All them times I sat across from the Boss he could've ended me with two ounces of finger pull.

I stole the loads from the scattergun.

Now I was running on guesswork. I rose and examined the pictures on the walls and then the few books on the shelves, and then I stood and thought about it all as if I was the Governor in my own office.

I went straight to the stag head and lifted it free from its hook in the wall. It sank to the ground with unnatural weight and I could barely slow it. At the back of the thing was an iron door. It had an ancient lock but time had seized the latch open. I drew the door and saw the cavern within.

What was I hoping to find? A map with directions to my brother's camp? Proof that our name was in fact Harney? Nothing in the Governor's office was worth the risk I was taking by being there. But such was the oil that boiled in me. I didn't rightly care what I found or if I was found out, so long as I could take something from that man. Something he would miss.

When I reached inside my fingers found pellets of gold. Surely the Governor had similar stashes all about his house, and maybe all across the state. This one was so rare visited a mess of spiders come pouring out. How many years would pass before he noticed this treasure's absence?

Still I stripped off my boot and drew out my stinky sock and collected the gold pellets within it.

That night I laid out in the sage and watched the sky. It was my first night clean sober and sleep wasn't nowhere for me to find.

I could burn this house down from within. I could pillage the Governor one stash at a time until I broke him. And then my brother could ride through the smoldering gates and take me home.

What a foolish notion. My brother wasn't watching me from above. And if he was, he'd look down here at me and see only a guardsman like all the other guardsmen. What was to stop him from flipping his peep and taking steady aim and dropping me like a sack of feed?

Come dark a lantern was lit inside the old woman's shack. Its light cast beams across the earth and I stepped into one and followed it all the way to the cracked curtain.

Inside I could see her ancient hands flashing over meat, her blade slicing and chopping and then herding the cuts into the pot. Only her hands and that blade, the rabbit laid out on the block and its body being turned to meat. Then I couldn't see her hands no more. The flesh lay on the board untouched. All of us, meat.

I never heard the door open or her feet on the gravel. She was just there, at the corner of the house. "What's your business?" she called. I could see the bore of a Spencer studying me. "I may be dusty with age, but don't play me for no fool. Only shady intentions encourage men to go creeping around at this hour."

"I am on my way back from the stable and I saw the light is all."

"Who you be anyhow?"

How to answer that question. "One of your son's guards."

"You the shooter I see over on the range? The little one who sometimes sleeps in the stable?"

"Yes, ma'am. That's me. Didn't know you was watching."

She pointed the Spencer at the iron pump near the edge of the shack. "I need a pot of water and while you're here creeping you might as well fetch it for me. Come on now," she called. "Don't be conditional."

I filled her pot from the hand pump and returned to her porch by the light of the lantern lit inside. I counted one more rabbit and four quail hung by their legs along the rail. She saw me looking on them.

"I don't see no wounds on them critters."

"Why folks insist on peppering supper with lead I'll never know. Die easy enough in snares that don't cost a bit and won't bust no tooth. Any reason you young'uns can find to pull a trigger. Sometimes I think your kind is afraid to let the echoes of that war finish.

"Come in here and roll up them sleeves. Knock off your boots on the porch, I ain't keen on sweeping these days. My bones protest any form of cleaning."

I did as I was told. I removed my hat as I come through the door. It was the first room fitted by a mother I had seen since visiting Mrs. Saggat's house a lifetime before. Everything was dusty and disordered. On every surface was pebbles of dawn color and branches braided by the years and wind. She collected these queer things. A wasp nest hung from twine in the corner. She caught me eyeing it. "That old thing. I just like its shape. Bugs made it, ain't that something? Bugs make something every bit as fancy as my boy's palace."

What held my attention was a tree as thick as my thigh she'd cut at the base and at overhead and wedged into the corner of the cabin so it fit perfect up and down. It was an aspen and its trunk had been scraped in wild order until there wasn't much bark left on the tree. Under those freshest rubs was the grown-over sign of more.

"The stags done that, with their horns. Ain't it lovely?" She fingered a tendril of velvet left pinched in a splinter of wood. "This here is the cloth that shields their horns as they grow. The stags take to rubbing it off on the same trees they done last year and the same trees their daddies done ripped about. I always been collecting things that put me in awe."

There wasn't a tint of color left to her skin and if a wind had come up it might've blown off like dust from a cracked lake bed. Her hair was thin as cobwebs.

But her motions, like her voice, was steady as rock. She held the lantern up to my face. There wasn't a shake to her. She couldn't have been much more than four feet tall but she was formidable. She handed me the knife. "Well, get to it. Them critters ain't putting themselves in the stew."

She took a seat in the rocking chair and put a match to her pipe. She rocked and puffed, rocked and puffed.

I rolled up my sleeves and went to butchering what was left of the rabbit.

"Why you dressed like a man anyhow?"

The knife paused its work, but then I kept it going. "I know I got a baby face."

"You wear a man's clothes and you hack that rabbit like a man but you as much man as me. Less even. Woman is water and the rivers in me is dried up."

I didn't say a word. I kept on cutting the rabbit.

Her chair creaked. Her lips worked the pipe.

"So I take it you got my son and his paid admirers fooled. That's no feat. Don't crack that bone. I don't want no slivers in my stew. Who taught you kitchen skills? You're a damn idiot around a knife."

"Yes, ma'am."

"Don't get pouty on me. Answer my question."

"Ma'am?"

"Why you dressed such? Come now. Just the two of us. Those fools don't dare venture out this way. And my son only comes on his birthday. I've lived here a thousand years without no help from them."

I was hungry to tell it straight. Not even Greenie knew the truth, and I was worn with holding it all back. On that particular night I feared that even the raw facts of my life was only an hour more with the Governor from vanishing.

It come out in its pure form. I told it with hunger. "So when Pa died I set out to find my brother by my lonesome and bring him back home. I killed a man outside of Scarletville and just recent I killed another, and it was another man who put these marks on my face, but he didn't die. When I was girl I didn't have no ma so . . ." I went on this way, back and forth through time with no logic but its own. Such relief to hear this in the air outside rather than echoing endlessly within. At last I told her of Johnson.

She said, "But you ain't told me why you dressed as a man."

I thought on it. "A man can be invisible when he wants to be."

She dug a pinkie into her ear. "I look about this world and see nothing familiar but for the things the critters make. Now I see you."

"Yes, ma'am."

"Call me my name. Mildred. Do you believe in Heaven?"

"To be honest I sometimes wonder why the Lord would suddenly care enough to offer us a heaven. I don't mean to blaspheme."

This made her laugh. "Why you worrying about blasphemy anyhow? Blasphemy is for paid admirers.

"Nah, around here we got ourselves a knife, a stewpot, a critter, and a world that makes critters. That's what the Lord give us if He give us anything at all. And if not for them things we'd sink into the dirt and every little storm and critter would go on as if you and me never took a breath. Don't know about you, but that comes to me as some manner of relief."

"Relief ain't something I got much experience with."

She laughed at this notion. "Talk to me when your bones ache and your head pounds and you can't hold your piss for ten minutes. You have any idea how much of the day I spend avoiding discomfort? I do three things here. I get my food, I build me a fire for heat, and then I spend every remaining minute trying to settle into some posture or another that don't hurt."

I laughed. It felt like the first time.

She come near and I didn't dare breathe. She passed her fingers through the hair over my ear. "Coarse as straw. Mine used to be like that, but now it is corn silk too long in the sun."

She drew new from her pipe. "Men like my boy see this rich land and turn inward. It makes them foolhardy and narrow of thought. They don't see the place but for their own reflection in it. Give my boy a hundred years and he will have rewritten the map of the cosmos to place himself at its center. You watch, girl, you beware. His is a crowded hermitage. His kind march through a blizzard and convince themselves it is a desert. Tell me, what is it you desire from this life?"

The answer was ready on my tongue. "Home. And my brother there with me."

I put the stewpot on the woodstove. There was camas bulbs and carrots and some variety of wild onion already in there. It was so very late by then.

"Take my bed. I don't sleep no more at night. I sleep when the sun is at its blinding.

So you sleep in my bed. You pull that quilt up and about you and let me keep an eye out on your behalf. I can see how worn you are with keeping guard. Let me do that for the both of us."

My eyes watered. "I couldn't impose, Miss Mildred."

"You ain't got no choice but to stay, child. Now fill up that woodbox so my old bones don't have to. It's a trade then, see?"

Mildred packed her pipe while I worked. When I was done, I hung my gun belt from the hook and shed my boots and laid upon her bed.

"I got a lot to tell you. The story begins in a logging camp by a lake. Shut your eyes now, dear. Let this old ma tell you how all this started."

For the first time in my life I drew a thick quilt about my neck and fell asleep to a mother's telling.

The guests started arriving in the morning, and wagons was delivering the remaining provisions, and builders hurried to finish their projects. The wedding was tomorrow and the last of the guests was to arrive by the evening train and so dinner would come an hour later than normal but would be served as a feast during a royal ball.

I saw the performers roll to the door in two laid-open wagons, their instruments kept safe in wooden crates, and two of them sitting upon them with a hand to the wagon edge for balance. They was met like all deliveries on this day, by a pair of militiamen who checked their paperwork and then searched through their belongings and patted their persons for weaponry.

I was still watching when the Governor found me.

"Samuel, my good man!" He was in terrific spirits. He told me I was to shoot a duel in Denver come two weeks' time. From there we would continue east. "Already word is spreading of Samuel Spartan! What did I tell you?"

He put a hand to my back and said, "You were seen near my mother's cabin this morning. Do you have a missive for me?"

"No, sir."

"Are you sure? She is a woman of firm opinions. When she's lucid. What did she say? What drew you so near a madwoman in the morning hours? You're not keeping things from me, are you? Since our fresh start? Samuel, I thought we were past the keeping of secrets. Aren't we friends?"

"She said all kind things, sir."

He laughed. "That woman hasn't spoken a kind word since the forties."

He took a fresh cigar from his pocket, and I struck a match and cupped it against the breeze. While he puffed I considered setting his moustache on fire. "As you can see, my mother has a substantial presence in my mind. I would prefer if you would help limit the damage by not visiting her. Then I won't have to hear about it and imagine all her subversions. Also, why must you do the queer? Visit my *mother* of all people? Shoot my guns, drink my liquor, wrestle my niggers, but don't visit my mother."

He drew in the smoke. The smoke escaped on his words. "I brought her here out of kindness. A son's duty and all. But I swear that woman is a burr. She can't be any other way. And watch, I promise, she lives another two hundred and fifty years. You know I tried to hire her a nurse? She wouldn't hear of it. I tried to build her a proper house. I have all the beef she could eat but she won't touch it. And the trouble she causes. Had to finally stop inviting her for supper on account of her rabble-rousing. Isn't a mother's duty to get out of her son's way? If I succeed in this life I will build giant castles in which sons can place their mothers and rest assured they are well tended. The good Lord has tested me with that maternal figure of mine. And now this daughter who won't leave her room."

As the shadows grew long and the sun less hot, the guests wandered among the garden to a guided tour. The women clung to the elbows of their men and laughed the cackles of civilization.

I was on post inside, fresh washed and in new attire, when darkness settled and the music began. In the last hour of the event I would ride out as a guest. I needed a new hat and jacket for the escape to work.

But once free of here, where would I go that was any closer to my brother? There was no home to return to.

The major was among the guests in his sword and stripes but he knew not a soul and so leaned against a wall and rolled a smoke. Two of his men stood attention along each of the entrances and exits, their rifles rested on their toes. The rest of the militia remained at the ready at their posts among trenches and dikes.

The guests held masks to their faces and wore elaborate costumes in colors fresh as spring. Even the musicians wore masks though theirs had to be tied to their faces as they needed their hands for making merriment.

I did not see Constance among the crowd. I did see the senator tipping his head in laughter.

When I saw Greenie, I joined him near the musicians.

We hadn't spoken in days. In the months before we hadn't hardly gone two hours without talking.

There wasn't no missing his swollen eye.

He'd taken a punch since I last seen him.

For a long minute we stood there pretending to consider the party before us. He was the one who offered a plug. I took it and thanked him. He said, "I don't think I can call you Spartan." He looked at me in his sidelong glance, and I understood he too thought the notion absurd, and that was all it took to put me at ease. Greenie and me was in this together.

"It's Mr. Spartan to you."

"Nah, you'll always be an LP in my book."

We spat.

"Who gave you that blow?"

"Boss always assigns us the dark business." He looked at the ground. There wasn't no one else he could tell and I could see he was in hard need of telling it.

They had told Will that a valuable delivery was due at the rail station and so he climbed into the cargo wagon without protest. He rode with his feet dangling off the back like he done any day when deliveries arrived. Except this time it was Greenie and Drummond who went with him, and he should've suspected something, but he trusted. When they arrived they rolled into the station warehouse itself and Agent Thorvald was there to close the door behind them. Will realized the score at once. He made a break but it wasn't no use. His strong arms cast Drummond aside and he swung and connected with Greenie. But then Thorvald broke his knee with a club, and Will staggered about begging for his life. They beat him with clubs hollowed at one end and filled with lead.

"You think they was lovers?" Greenie asked. "For real? A black and a white?"

Greenie sighed. "I don't really care either way. Ain't my job to care. I just do, and I leave the thinking to the guy with money enough to pay. If it wasn't me, it'd be someone else, right?"

A minute passed. "Right, LP?"

"I don't know."

Greenie said, "Folks say you lied to Boss. Folks say you is lucky to be breathing."

The Governor was approaching us with a short man at his side. The Governor's costume was a kingly red cape and a bejeweled crown. He wore no mask and yet I could not see any truth upon his face. I had once lusted for his approval.

The man beside him wore a buckskin outfit like those worn by the buffalo hunters a generation before, and positioned below his navel was a huge flintlock pistol in his belt. The man lowered his mask to shake my hand. I was surprised to see the round spectacles of an attorney or doctor.

"This is the shooter I was telling you about," the Governor said. "Teddy, meet Mr. Samuel A. Spartan."

363

The man took care in replacing his glove after shaking my hand. He said in a shrill voice, "I hear you shot down Cliffpatrick's Negro? When I heard that I had to meet you. I saw that bull of a man shoot in Denver last autumn and was surprised to see such quickness in one so large. Gladiator to gladiator, a specimen like that one would be unbeatable, I imagine. How the Lord has blessed us with the great equalizers of lead and powder, no?"

"Teddy here owns two of the finest ranches you'll ever ride and isn't half bad with a long rifle himself."

"I am a sportsman, nothing more."

"Your accent is eastern," I said.

"It is," he admitted with considerable regret. "But I am man of the West. The East is rusty and self-confident beyond good charm. Have you been?" He left me no time to respond. "Though if not for the East's money neither of us could afford to be western men, am I right, governor?"

"Every family needs its wealthy uncle."

The crowd was stopping its dancing and turning toward the balcony where Constance now stood, her gaze upon us all. She wore the dress of a far-off princess and a smaller variation of the king's crown, but she had added the black mask of a bandit.

The Governor said, "Oh, for chrissake."

The crowd clapped at her arrival.

The senator climbed the stairs and took up

the arm of his bride-to-be, and the musicians did not miss the moment. With horns they announced the arrival of royalty. The senator led and Constance had little choice but to follow.

Despite the mask about her eyes I could see the red sorrow within. There was no missing her grief.

Senator Scott raised his arms to quiet the crowd. He pulled free his mask. All fell silent, including the musicians. The man was dressed in a white suit with a stripe down the side and military honors on its breast. They was contrived, no doubt, as the senator had escaped military service by consequence of his wealth. "Thank you all for coming," he shouted. "We thank each of you for making the long journey on our behalf. My bride-to-be insists I not monopolize the floor with a speech, but then again I am a member of the senate — what else might I offer?"

Lofty laughs around the room.

"I wish to take just one moment now to thank our generous and influential host. Mr. Governor, tomorrow when I marry your only daughter I will be the most grateful man in this sprawling state of grateful men. All of us are beholden to you, sir. Constance is a refined young woman of sunrise beauty and with charms that exceed the principles of fair division we imagine for our democracy. To be considered a worthy suitor by you, sir, is the single greatest honor of my life. I thank you."

Heads turning to glimpse the Governor. I could only see the back of his crown, but I imagined he was wearing that pursed smile that revealed so little.

Teddy clapped his buckskin gloves and others joined in and the senator raised a glass of champagne toward the host. "To you, sir. The prime giver. We cherish your contributions to our union, and to ourselves."

"Hear, hear!"

In all of this Constance had remained still, her eyes upon the chandelier. Now she walked down the stairs, leaving the senator to hurry along behind.

From the musicians a lone guitar sounded, and the dance floor cleared of guests except for Constance and the senator. He offered his hand and she looked upon him. She did not take the hand.

Moments passed and not an eye could look away, not a breath could be drawn. We all waited, Greenie and me included, for her to accept what she was supposed to have already accepted. His hand could wait no more and so took hers from her side and the dance commenced at once.

Greenie leaned over and said, "A gold coin says she don't go through with it."

It occurred to me then that I knew the song played by the guitar. It rose up within me like a wind and carried with it memories of

366

long ago. My eyes looked upon the Governor's crown but my mind saw only Pa on Ma's birthday, his eyes closed to the fiddle, and Noah in the firelight working the action on the pistol.

Pa's song. It was Pa's own!

I stepped for a better look. The musicians hovered with their instruments, their masked faces upon their masked leader who now bowed to the power of the chords. Each note come through him and out of him and delivered with it a lifetime of sorrow and revelation and delight. It wasn't just Pa's song but everything Pa had hoped to convey, only cleaner than Pa ever could.

I knew then despite the mask and the costume and all sense of reason that this musician before me was my Noah.

"What is it?" Greenie asked.

"I can't do this!" Constance was shouting. "Stop, don't touch me! I won't do this! I can't . . ."

There was a commotion then at the door and eyes turned from the dancers to look. One of the soldiers was attempting to stop someone from entering and I heard Miss Mildred's voice ring out, "Let me through!"

At this all other eyes turned toward the door and even Constance herself turned and the Governor barked at the guard to leave Miss Mildred alone. Miss Mildred crossed the dance floor with purpose. She was tiny and yet a path cleared before her as it would for a lion. She put a hand to the neck of the musician's guitar. The song went still. At the sight of the player's eyes, any last doubts vanished. Here was my brother!

But here?

"This is not holy or right," Miss Mildred announced. She raised a finger and leveled it on her son.

He sidestepped from it as if that finger was a barrel.

Miss Mildred called, "There is no love here, don't you see? The premise is in error. The whole house is built upon a lie!"

The Governor moved to put an arm around his mother and laughed and showed his laugh to the crowd of masked guests and they took this to be evidence of a bizarre joke and laughed with him.

Miss Mildred pulled from her son and took her granddaughter by the arm. "Do you want to go?"

Constance nodded.

"Stop!" the Governor bellowed. At once he seemed to remember the audience about him. Maybe he thought of the headlines the next day, for in the corner stood reporters from five newspapers. A smile passed over the king's face, wide and gleaming white. He addressed all of us. "My poor mother is ill of mind. Please join me in forgiving this intrusion. Age will leave us all in a state of confusion, I fear."

Constance walked with her grandmother toward the door.

The king was nodding at me. Drummond and Greenie was already moving to block the exit.

When I looked back I saw the guitar player frozen, his instrument hanging at his side, his dark eyes upon me. One of his band said something in his ear but still he stared. My brother knew me.

The banjo player left the stage and followed a few steps behind Greenie and Drummond. The two of them now stood at the threshold, and Constance was yelling at them to let her out. The player simply drew Constance out of the way and shut the door on the men and turned the latch on the lock.

Then the man swung his banjo against the wall and the neck shattered. He drew from the instrument a pistol and shot the senator through his head.

Hot jam splattered about the room and screams erupted and a great wind blew people across the floor and shots barked from every corner and great plumes of powder smoke belched through the air and a musician held Constance from behind and her feet kicked high in the air and another placed a feed bag over her head and these men ran with her through the havoc and the agony of the wounded and the Governor crumpled with a wound, and still Noah stood on the stage, still Noah stood looking on me. A photographer's flash burst.

Noah come straight for me and stepped over the man in buckskin with the flintlock who was on his knees and covering his head to the reality, and Noah placed his hand to my shoulder. My brother touched me. He lifted the mask from his face and opened his mouth to speak and said only, "Jess."

The rest lives on in me as if from dream.

I remember Agent Thorvald on the balcony reloading both barrels of his scattergun, flipping it closed, and taking aim on us. I drew and shot him through the throat. He bucked and staggered.

Plaster rained from the ceiling and we flinched against it. The air was fogged now with too much gun smoke. My ears rang so loud I only saw the bark of fire from barrels but didn't hear their bursts.

I know Noah swung his guitar against the floor and pulled from its guts a six-shooter and shot a militiaman as he leveled his rifle. The bullet entered the eye and the life dropped out the man at once.

"This way!" I hollered.

We went down the stairs toward the kitchen and as we passed by a platter upon the table Noah took up a drumstick and ate it as we walked. We passed through the kitchen and out the side door and into a night lit by gunfire.

We emerged and saw the others firing on militiamen who now had no choice but to cling to the fronts of their defenses. They had built their structures to ward off an attack from outside, not from within. Through the mayhem rode a lone man with a string of the Governor's own buckskins. My brother said calm as dawn, "You ride with me." He leapt onto his saddle and reached a hand back toward me. A bullet ripped between us.

Constance was still bagged but now she was sitting atop a saddle and being tied with cattle rope to the horn. Another man was tying her feet to the stirrups. She screamed and thrashed but there wasn't no easy way to come loose from such a web.

"I ain't leaving Ingrid."

"Ingrid? You mean . . . ?"

"She's in the stable."

Noah looked up at the house. Bullets come at us from two directions and his people returned fire and militiamen ducked for cover. He flicked the chicken bone into the night and licked his fingers. "Well, better hurry."

I didn't bother with the saddle or reins but only swung on in the stable and gave Ingrid the heels and ducked the door and we burst into the night at a full run.

We joined them in the darkness and bolted

as bullets sliced the air over our heads and sparked from rocks at our feet, and we continued toward the mountain by moonlight, our human eyes unable to see but trusting the horse in its bounding gait. I counted eight, plus Constance and me.

We was pounding the sage when the man beside me cursed and touched his hand to his shoulder and cursed again. He lost his rhythm with his mount and fell sidelong to the earth. No one else saw but me.

Ingrid wheeled back and I leapt to the ground and helped the man stand. He was shot through the shoulder. We was outside the accuracy of their rifles now but still the bullets whined overhead and clattered through the sage. "My mare ain't big enough for two," I panted.

He drew his pistol and took aim back at the men saddling to come for us. "Go," he barked. "I'll hold them long as I can!"

But then from the dark come the sound of hooves and Noah appeared, trailing the man's gelding by the reins. "You fit to ride?"

"I think I can."

"Then this ain't the moment for your death."

The wounded man tucked his pistol in his waist with his good arm and then used the same to grip the horn and swing up. We rode on.

At the bend in the mountain we didn't turn

up as I expected. We cut across the gully and along the slope of sage and then headed back down the mountain the same direction we had come, only some hundred yards into the timber. We rode within sight of the estate and I could see smoke bellowing from the palace. Someone had set its guts afire.

We cut from the wilds and come into the heart of town by a rare-used road. We continued into the heart of the city, where our tracks mixed with the thousands of others on the dusty streets and we slowed to a walk. Men turned their horses down alleys. Soon it was Noah and me. Constance was not with us. I asked a question but he put his finger to his lips and continued walking his horse as if he was in no hurry at all.

By full moon we rode east out of Pearlsville. We kept our pace for some miles. But Ingrid could not keep up with the big buckskin. My brother called for me to leap to his saddle and I done so and caught myself by his shoulders. Ingrid kept with us now that she was lighter my weight.

So I clung to my brother and buried my cheek into his back and listened to the thundering of his heart and the hooves below us and I believed all over again in the Lord's vision.

He had been there all this time! All my suffering, all my hardships, He knew! All my sins, He forgave them!

■ ■ ■ ■

IV

■ ■ ■ ■

In the wee hours of the morning, we come to stop at a barn and turned loose the horses into a pine corral. Ingrid was lathered and worn and so didn't protest the treatment.

Just as soon as the gate was tied I jumped on Noah's back and kissed his hair and he flipped me over his shoulder and the two of us went into the dust laughing. He put me in a headlock and knuckled my hair until I begged mercy. Soon as he let go, I kneed him in the guts and climbed on top and started slapping at his face until he rolled me. Then we lay there on our backs laughing it off and watching the stars shoot.

"How'd you manage that anyhow?" Noah asked. "The guardsmen?"

"Shot my way in, brother. I might best you with this here Peacemaker."

He howled. He sat up. "No, for real."

"How else would I get on his guard?"

He turned and looked at me in the moonlight. "Who taught you to draw?"

I thought of Pa and sat up and found my hat and brushed it clean. "There's a lot to tell, brother."

I think he sensed the news and didn't want it. He stood and offered me a hand and powered me from the ground. He brushed some pine needles from my jacket. "Hell of a costume you wearing. I was up on that stage, and ain't nothing I notice in this world when I'm playing music but for the Lord's own grace, and there I seen you. Except it ain't you. It's a goshdarn guardsman, but for once I don't want to see this one bleed." The years had deepened and coarsened his voice. I couldn't get enough of it.

"What'd you think when you saw me?"

"Think? Well, standing up there, before I knew you was my sister — ah, it sounds too queer to say it."

"Say it, brother. You got to now."

He shrugged. "Even before I knew it was you, I knew I loved you."

He put his arm around me and drew me near and for a long time we leaned on the other and didn't say nothing at all.

The men gathered about the corral as they rode in. They hollered and pushed and pulled bottles from jackets. "Did you see her? She's prettier even than they said!"

Constance had still not arrived. I could see

my brother watching the darkness for any sign.

The men each acknowledged my brother with a downward nod of the head. Just the same as Greenie and me would do if we walked into a room and saw Drummond standing there. One of my brother's crew said, "Did you see the gals go to butter when you played that tune?"

Another threw his hat in the air before he was even off his horse and howled and then marched over to shake my brother's hand. "You said it would work and I didn't know but goddamn if that wasn't slick as sauce!"

"I appreciate your enthusiasm, Mason," my brother said. "But watch that tongue. The Lord has blessed us by keeping us all alive once again and we won't reward Him with disrespect, now will we?"

"No, sir!" Mason said. "Tonight, I'll do just as He asks. No premarital congress or taking His name in vain or any of that other goddamn shit." He turned to the sky. He was a big man, and powerful. "You hear me, Lord? I love you! And I love this man here!" The bandit took my brother in his arms and slapped his back. "I'd follow this man anywhere! This man has your attention!"

A third man didn't say nothing but just swaggered near and hung his arms over the corral and spat. My brother straightened up and hung his arms too and muttered so low I nearly missed it, "Nice play with the door, partner."

This new man was thin and small shouldered and dark. He was the one who had locked out Greenie and Drummond in one move. His face was familiar to me now. This was the Moonshine Kid from the wanted posters I'd seen tacked up beside my brother's. He tossed a thumb my way but didn't look. "Who's this?"

My brother turned to me and smiled. "Annette. Meet my sister, Jessilyn."

The man took off his hat and I saw he wasn't no man at all. She was lean and her jaw was sharp as Noah's. She wore a pistol on her hip and a rifle slung across her back like a brave. Her hair was shorter than mine. "You had a man on the inside all this time?" That voice was powder igniting.

My brother shrugged. "Guess so. Didn't know until the heat but never hurts to have a friend where you don't expect one."

"Jessilyn?" Mason blurted. He looked on me hard. He looked to Annette. Then he looked eye to eye with my brother. "What's happening to womenfolk these days?"

When Constance arrived I saw she wasn't no more in her feed bag. Her feet wasn't tied to the stirrups, her hands was loose. She wore a man's riding jacket over her fancy dress, and

380

a man's hat as well. Her hair was tucked up inside.

The boys all went quiet and turned toward her. She was steering her own horse.

Noah put his hand to her mount's nose and patted the animal's neck. "Smooth enough. I only wish we had got there in time for Will," he said.

At the name she stiffened.

My brother offered her a hand but she swung her legs and leapt to the ground with considerable skill. "You promised you wouldn't hurt Father."

Noah turned to the boys all watching. "Did we hurt her old man?"

There was a hard silence. The boys toed the dirt. A voice said, "I mighta seen him take a stray round to the wing."

Noah drew a breath and shook his head. "What was the one rule? Huh?"

Annette had been leaning on a pine but now she stood tall. "Was a considerable fight, but you boys knew the rules." She looked over the men and spat. "You better hope I don't learn one of you took intentional aim on that man."

Noah touched Constance's elbow and said, "Come on this way. We got a meal ready for you, dear. Your first meal in freedom. I will learn of your father's health, okay?"

As we neared the barn I could see light inside.

"Baby! You there, baby?" At the door stood a full woman in a dress with her hair down. I could see it was curly and tamed, and her voice was sweet as molasses.

"I'm here, sugarbread!" shouted Noah. "You won't believe what I rustled up."

The woman come running from the doorway and leapt in the air and Noah took her in his arms and spun her and kissed her proper. When she landed her hands could not keep off his person. One was around his back and the other she planted on his heart. Her eyes was like diamonds in the moonlight. "Is this here our guest of honor?"

"This is Constance Pearl."

"Oh!" the woman exclaimed. She was tall with an ample chest and her dress did nice things to her shapes. "It's such a high pleasure to make your acquaintance, Miss Constance. I feel like I know you from your letters. Where's your man? Mr. Will?"

Noah explained the sad news and the woman took Constance in her arms and I saw a genuine tear roll from her eye.

Noah said, "But Constance ain't the surprise." My brother pointed at me. "Jane, this little man before you, this little man be my sister."

"Jessilyn?" the woman said.

"This here is Jane Saint-Steel," Noah said. "She's my woman."

Jane put her fingers to my hand. "Oh, come

into the light and let me set eyes on you! Your brother hasn't told me enough. I've been so dying to meet you!" Then she took Constance's hand too, and the three of us crossed to the barn. "Two new friends, just like that! You just never can tell what the day will bring."

The barn was worn and weather beaten but there was room there for us all. The bandits was laughing over their steaming bowls of venison stew. A cat twisted about their ankles. One bent to pet it. These boys was hard faced but young, most my age thereabouts. They was all colors and persuasions. The only thing they had in common was the guns they was wearing. And the way they looked at my brother. This was Noah's Wild Bunch.

One of the Chinamen among them had ten years easy on Noah. His head was shaved bald and wrinkles formed about his eyes when he laughed. He flicked a man's ear in jest. He lifted a bowl to his lips and drank it down.

We had two wounded. The one I had helped, who I would come to know as Pale Jay, sat with his shirt off and hot blood soaked through the white cloth wrapped tight around his shoulder. The bullet gone clean through. He held the arm to his body and ate with his good hand. The other wounded man had took a blast from the agent's scattergun. He had six or eight trails of blood coming down his back and a stick in his teeth. One of the boys took a knife to the wounds and dug out the lead, piece by piece. He handed each one to the man to ponder. They both was laughing.

The one they called Annette sat by the fireplace with her bowl balanced on her knees. Her eyes was black and glistening and mean. I could see she too passed as a man when she wanted to. It come natural to her given her height and jaw. She wore a cowboy's jeans with sheepskin chaps. Her shirt was plaid and unbuttoned at the top. She wore a bear-hide vest for warmth.

"Be careful of Annette." Noah was holding two bowls of stew and give one to Constance and the other to me. "She bites." Then he took up Jane in his arms and the two of them shared some private language. Jane squealed in delight. It was halfway to morning and this party was just starting.

Constance set her stew aside untouched. "So you were involved in my escape the whole time? I never fancied it."

"I'm more surprised than you," I admitted. "So the feed bag on your head, all the screaming and kicking, that was for a show? Damn persuasive."

"Yes, well. I wanted to walk away and for father to know it was me who chose to leave." She looked at Noah where he stood. "The feed bag, I suspect, was for the newspaper-men."

I too looked at my brother, at all these faces glancing his way.

"This was Will's idea," Constance said. "This was all for . . ." She was quiet a long while. I let her dwell with it.

Constance continued, "Harney came to me about a year ago when I was in a piano lesson. He saw my carriage as it crossed town and said he couldn't help himself. He had to meet me. Of course I was aghast at the sight of such a wanton criminal, but your brother just laid himself bare before me, no fear at all. He was unarmed and unguarded — he floated into the room. He gave me the name of a man in town to contact if I ever needed any help. I didn't write until Father demanded my engagement. Jane wrote back, and the letters started coming by federal postage. She used the name of one of my tutors."

Noah called our attentions and all the men put down their spoons and looked upon my brother in silence. It was the first time I saw him hold the mind of a crowd bigger than me. He owned that room outright.

"We must take this opportunity to say our thanks to the Lord Himself for helping the righteous cause on this night. We all come through like the sickle blade and them the grass, and we must take that as further evidence of our lordly destiny. We walk the *holy* path, gentlemen. You, me, the man beside you, we're *one* creation, and we was created to deliver *justice* to the doorstep of the wicked. In this time of merriment, let us remember that just as the Lord willed this land to the plow, He too has *willed* it to the downtrodden. And he has chosen us, entrusted us, enshielded *us* to deliver it. Join me in gratitude. Join me in amen."

The boys banged their fists once upon the table in unison and mumbled, "Amen."

"And!" My brother had himself a big old smile now. "Join me in welcoming our new friends. This is Constance Pearl, she don't need no introduction. Welcome, Miss Constance."

The boys whistled.

"Enough of that." Noah smiled at his crew. He pointed an arm at me. "And this guardsman? This is my little baby sister. She plays the part nice, don't she? We got to get you some new clothes," he boomed. "One of the boys catches you out the corner of his eye, he's liable to shoot on instinct!"

After some laughs Noah blessed our meal, and then he reached for the salt and took up a heavy pinch and got to spreading. He reached for another pinch.

But Jane took the salt from him and set it out of reach. She said, "Pickling yourself. I swear, if it wasn't for me your brother here wouldn't be a damn mess of a man."

Noah sighed in that familiar manner of Pa's. I'd heard that sound directed at Noah a thousand times in my former life, and now I was hearing it again, and that set me right in a manner I hadn't been set right in years. I put my fingers to his back just to touch him.

"Cursing ain't ladylike," he said to Jane.

"If the Lord didn't want women swearing, He would not have given us the capacity. He intends us to name it as we see it, and, well, sometimes that requires using a gritty tongue. Annette swears all day and I never hear you correcting her."

"Annette, is you a lady?"

Annette glared over her stew. She gripped the spoon like a trapper just come in from winter.

Noah said, "Besides, when have you ever seen me telling Annette what to do?"

Jane touched her fingers to my wrist. She was the sort to always match her words with a touch. "Now, Jess, tell me of your father."

Noah looked on me, then back to his bowl. He could tell.

I stirred the heat from the stew. I searched for the right starting words. I had been telling my brother of Pa's death since it happened, and yet now I couldn't figure where to begin. "I put Pa to rest, brother."

"Oh, no," Jane said. Her hand covered her mouth.

Noah didn't look up from his stew. "When?"

"Last autumn."

"Last autumn." He stirred his stew. He pushed it away. I'm guessing he was thinking of all he had done since last autumn and how all of it had been in a world without his pa.

The news spread through the barn and soon all fell silent to turn witness upon their leader. Noah noticed no silence. "How'd he go?"

"Right quick."

"How?"

"Fell off Ol' Sis. They was crossing some sharp rocks, off on the injun land."

"Pa don't fall off horses."

Noah was correct on that score. "He didn't when you knowed him."

The voices was back in hushed volume. A spoon clanked in an empty bowl. I didn't like to see my big brother unsure. I thought to change the subject. "My brother, the famous gunfighter. You don't look famous. You look the same, just older and uglier."

"Did Pa . . . Did he hear how fast I draw?"

Jane patted Noah's hand. "Your brother is more than a gunfighter now. He has risen to his calling, a servant of the Lord."

Noah didn't look up.

"Baby? Say something."

He looked to Jane. They held eyes a time. Then Noah said, "Just as He spread the

388

waters of the Red Sea, the Lord spread our enemy and shepherded us through. We are but the implements of his His divine revolution."

"Hallelujah!" Jane called. She squeezed my hand. "Doesn't he have a way with language?"

Noah stood from the table and all conversations ceased and all eyes returned to him. "*Praise* the Lord that He kept my sister in safekeeping as she waded fire and brimstone to join our holy cause! He who harbors doubt, I *dare* he to look upon my sister now and see not the *proof* of our Lord's favor! I *dare* the doubter to think of what we did tonight and still hold doubt in his heart! No, tonight He *burned* the doubt!

"The Lord parted those men and shielded our escape and here we sit in good spirit, but not yet in humble mind. Boys, join me now in kneeling at the feet of our Lord." My brother got on his knees and then bent his face to the earth.

I watched as the boys sighed and rose from the table. They wanted only to enjoy their success, but they rose anyhow and did as my brother asked, and not a one of them voiced disagreement. Even the two wounded bent to the floor.

Jane rose and swept back her dress and knelt. She put her nose to the gritty wood. They all done just as my brother done.

Except Annette. She still sat in her chair

finishing her bowl of stew. I expected my brother to lose his temper at this, but he did not. Yet when one of the youngest boys lifted his head from the ground my brother frowned at him, and the boy put his nose back to the floor.

I did the same and heard my brother's prayer.

After supper, Youn, one of the Chinamen among the crew, lifted an instrument and tuned its strings. The rest of the men pushed aside their empty bowls and took up the instruments that had been awaiting them here in the barn. The room was at once alive with music.

Noah kissed Jane on the mouth. Jane stood and said, "Now where's your guitar? You got to play for your sister."

Jane found the box and set it on the table and cleared Noah's bowl and spoon.

He took up the polished instrument and gave it a quick tune and then stood from the table. By then the room had come into harmonious song. It wasn't the music I was used to hearing, short songs built on a pocket's worth of words. Their song started as one thing and with each person who joined shifted out away from itself and rode about hills that no one had thought to see before and my brother's eyes was shut and his fingers was leading the charge. Their music was a herd of mustangs, scores of feet but one dust and all blowing in the same direction.

Come first light the Governor's buckskins was gone, led off by one of my brother's boys. They had been replaced by dusky pintos and undersized bays. Unlike the buckskins, these was everyday mounts that nobody would remember, their brands mixed.

The boys rode off in pairs, some before us and some after, the idea being that no posse could identify us by our number.

I saw my brother give the rancher a considerable bag of gold. He was a weathered man with a bent back and his jacket was missing half its buttons. The man shook Noah's hand, then reached out to pat my brother on the shoulder. Someday his grandkids would tell their children of the time the family sheltered the great Noah Harney.

Noah, Jane, Annette, and me and Constance went together, them in a tarped-over wagon like any of the thousand others crossing the mountains that summer. Annette and Constance stayed under the tarp among a mess of hay and burlap sacks while Noah and Jane took to the driving seat. Me and Ingrid rode at the side. A shovel and pick tinged with the bumps, and water tins sloshed and collided. We did not hurry. We only rolled up that road like any other family of too late pioneers.

Noah wore a silly, round farmer's hat and a woolen Lincoln beard that was fixed to his skin, and he smoked a corn pipe. I would not have known him as my brother had I seen him, so complete was his adoption of this farmer's person. Jane wore a bonnet of a flower pattern and a dusty dress that covered every inch of skin to her neck and wrists. There was a basket on her lap with a cloth over top and inside was biscuits. Jane passed the treats around and said, "There now, children, we's near onto Pa's homestead."

"This'll be the last one," Noah said in an accent that matched Jane's. "I promise, Ma. This time they'll be wheat and barley till the world's edge. It'll be a skip to the girls' schoolhouse and there won't be another hunter for a hundred miles. We's doing it proper this time, my dearest woman."

"Can we have neighbors?" Jane asked. "Please, Pa?"

"Only time will tell," Noah sighed. "Yessiree. I got me a powerful feeling of goodness on this here score."

Annette pulled back the flap. "You two talking like that puts me in a killing mood."

"The sunrise," my brother said in his own voice, "puts you in a killing mood."

It wasn't noon when we felt the rumble of horses coming up behind us and Noah looked to me and barked, "Off in them trees!"

Ingrid and me wasted not a moment doing what Noah ordered. We rode until we come to a cluster of young pine and there I dismounted and held her still. I was out of range of the pistol and my Winchester was back at the Governor's.

The horses soon overtook the wagon and all come to a stop and I could see the green uniforms of the militiamen and the gray suits of two Pinkertons. I counted fifteen. The major was not among them. They spoke a time beside the wagon and then one of them dismounted. He proceeded to pull back the tarp and peek inside. He leaned far enough to shove a box and then stepped back. "Supplies," he called to his boss.

One of the Pinkertons walked his horse to the rear of the wagon and leaned in for a look. He said, "What you got in there?"

I couldn't tell what Noah said.

The Pinkerton drew a knife and cut the nearest burlap bag and drew a handful of beans and then tossed them aside. He walked back toward Noah and looked him square. They had some words and my heart beat so hard my head spun.

Finally the Pinkerton tipped his hat to Jane, and all of them spun their horses and rode off in a cloud of dust.

If Constance had shifted or the militiamen had jabbed a sword into the hay, I ain't sure my brother would have lived through the encounter. I reckon all of us would've gone down in bullets then. The thought of how close we come in that moment gives me chills, even all these years later. But back then, high as I was on being with Noah again, I only looked to the sky and thanked this Lord who only had eyes for us.

The road forked and then forked again and we was in some hellacious wilderness now. We took a narrow but deep-rutted path up a craggy canyon and left the water behind.

"For some months," Noah said of his dodging the militia, "we kept in their dust. We only waited for them to move on and then took up residence around their old fire rings. A man never thinks to look behind him."

"I heard tale of some of your tricks. You burned their supplies?"

He laughed. "We baited them into a maze of canyons where their wagons couldn't go. In truth we was just bored. That was good fun. What I wouldn't give to've seen the look on the major's face when he learned the news. That man has a cruel face. I ain't never trusted short men with hard eyes. There's a lesson in that for you, sister."

"When have you seen the major up close?"

"Oh, a half dozen times before last night. Twice as close as we is now on one occasion."

"He told me he hadn't seen you."

Noah shrugged. "Men like the major ain't no more complicated than a bear. If you see a bear in the pines and turn and run, he'll give chase. If you charge him, that bear will eat you for supper. But let's say you smile at that old bear and wave and then keep on your business, well, he's likely to lumber off on his own. See, a man like the major only takes interest in threats and opportunities. Anything else don't count."

The terrain grew steeper and we rode now in single file up a rare-used switchback left over from the days of bison.

The horses panted and lather grew where leather met their flesh. Ingrid was swinging her head up and down in pace with her feet, and ahead the wagon creaked under the angled load.

Near the top, the gully narrowed to a pinch. There was fresh-broken rubble upon the trail. "This here is where we dynamited our way in. A big old rock was rolled to here by some long-ago peoples to forever seal this place from all that lay below. This is the only way in and out that don't require rope ladders."

From here we had a long view over the terrain we'd just now transcended. In all directions stood rocky crags. The wind sifted the pines. A pair of jays mimicked the call of an eagle. We didn't stop to gander but kept on and soon broke over the top of the lip.

Before us was a great valley surrounded on all sides by sheer cliffs. The valley floor was a mix of green grass and sage mostly. Wasn't a tree within sight and no place to hide for nothing bigger than a jackrabbit. A party of antelope broke into a sprint at the sight of us, their hooves kicking up dust. They ran a mile and then stopped to watch.

At the far end of the valley stood a great column of rock that towered hundreds of feet into the air. We set a course directly at it.

"But we ain't just a band of outlaws no more," Noah said. "The Lord has delivered a congregation this summer, and charged me with its safekeeping. We needed a place nobody would think to look and one we could defend against a superior force, and the Lord saw our needs and so offered us this forgotten temple of stone."

The great rock was cracked and fissured and broken by the might of time. In the heat of the sun I saw design in them cracks and fissures, it was there before me clear as glass. I saw balconies, three tiers of them, one atop the other. I saw panes and batten. The whole rock looked to be growing as we neared, like a ship rising out the sea.

Our course bent around its flank and into the deep shade of its northeast end. Massive clefts lay about the sage where they come to rest after tumbling from the tower.

We rode around a corner to see a gap in

the wall. This gap and its entrance was filled with crumbled rock that shattered under our hooves like glass and sent a clamorous warning up the trail. I saw then the boards set like railroad steel over the rock. The spacing was ideal for our narrow wagons. Noah called like Pa, "Yip ha," and his team went rolling up into the canyon as they must've a hundred times before.

It was a short canyon. We went around one corner and then a whole meadow opened before us with well-grazed grass and a stand of aspen. There was a spring of water that gushed from a crack in the rock and splattered into the pond dug out by the feet of animals. The cascade filled the hollow with music. A heifer looked on us from the pond's edge and water streamed from her chin.

They called the place Lord's Rock. It was a land between names when we was there. Nobody knew it as Calamity Tower until after.

I've heard the old Indians of the area considered it their most sacred place though their name for it was not recorded in time. Still their pictures was painted on the walls, some of them placed ten men off the ground so who knows how the reds put them there. Their offerings too was about the caves, pots, and bones and beads.

We was the last people to dwell there, on a spot of land so holy it drew believers for as long as believers have wandered this land.

I will admit that I felt the Lord's presence just as soon as I entered that place. Here I was protected by walls of rock, a tower built of my brother's knowing. For the first time since Pa's passing, my mind wasn't consumed with my next play. All I had to do was listen to my Noah, and believe.

There was houses, a whole mess of them, built of rock and mortar and shingles, each house built using the cliff as a back wall. I counted the houses and made it to eighteen when Noah smiled on me. "What do you think?"

Near the living quarters stood a stone and mortar fireplace as high as a man is tall. It opened toward the houses and would throw considerable heat against the rock. Beside it was a mass of pine timbers, stripped of their limbs and bark and each the length of a wagon and a half, just enough they could be tied in for the journey here and trusted not to flip out on their own accord. Near them was a pair of two-man saws and a heap of fresh wood dust set upon layers of grayed wood dust. Seats cut of pine trunks sat before the fireplace, and upon some was the burned-down wax of candles looking like biscuits to my hungry mind.

Ribbons was strung overhead from the fireplace to the rock walls and they made the sound of bird wings in the breeze.

A great commotion was let loose upon our arrival and from the houses come men and women of all persuasions. They whooped and hollered and music echoed around that rock. Children chased hoops and dogs chased them and chickens saw the mess coming and figured it was for their flesh and went clucking through the wheels of wagons.

There was thirty-something souls, plus the Wild Bunch — too many I thought. These others was folks who had been broke by mining or driven from their homesteads by cattle barons or arrived west with too little knowledge of land and water. They had begged for my brother's charity and he was inclined toward generosity.

We rolled to a stop before the houses, and Noah leapt down and reached a hand back for Jane and already they was surrounded by people and merriment. Jane at once began introducing Constance to the women.

Annette and Youn pulled free the tarp and then the man they called Blister jumped up and began heaving the sacks of beans and grits and cornmeal and wheat flour down to waiting arms. Men hefted the sacks to their shoulders and carried them through a door into a building as big as five houses and come back out to grab armloads of feed and give it to the horses.

The bag the Pinkerton had cut was being sewn back up by a woman in an olive dress.

Her fingers moved like lightning and when she was done, two men was ready to heave the heavy sack into storage.

Noah was telling the story to a flock of children at his feet, boys and girls alike. I took notice. "Then what? Then what?" they shouted until he raised a hand to quiet them.

His hand formed the shape of a pistol. "The *Lord* spread His protections upon us and their bullets strayed *wide*!"

The children commenced firing on one another with their own finger pistols and Noah looked to me and pulled off his beard and said, "Just like us when we was little, ain't they? Kids always like the shooting parts best."

"Nothing changes," I said. "You still the storyteller."

He smiled. "Everywhere I go, sis, the truth follows."

There was Indian children, boys and girls ten to sixteen or thereabouts, all smaller than their years, most dressed in threadbare gray uniforms with their hair cut ragged. I looked about but didn't see no Indian mas.

Jane said, "Your brother shot up their school this spring and knocked down the gates once and for all. These poor children had no place to go. Couldn't remember which way was home."

"Why'd he shoot up an injun school?"

Jane said, "The Lord directed him thus.

400

Those poor children. Soldiers came and took them from their mothers, you know. Claimed it was for their own good."

Annette pushed me toward the wagon. "Don't just stand there," she said. "Work."

I took up a sack of cornmeal and drug it from the wagon and heaved it to my shoulder.

"Just one?" Annette lifted another, boosted it with a knee, and set it upon my other shoulder.

I barely held my balance under the weight.

"Maybe one more?" she said. Before I could respond, she was heaving another sack.

Noah took that sack himself. He said to me in private tones, "That's the game she likes to play. Push you till you break. She'll grow on you, or break you, one of the two."

The plan had been to deliver Constance and Will to an eastbound train. They would ride to Chicago, then onward to New York City, where they would start over under new names. My brother put his hands in his pockets when he spoke to her. "I got fresh mounts ready to go if you still want to catch that train."

Constance leaned on the wagon wheel, her dress dusty and littered with hay. She brushed at that hay but it was no good. All about us men and women went about their labors, all with an eye angled on Constance. She blew the tendrils of hair from her face. She saw nothing but the dirt before her. "I don't know what to do," she said. "I am so lost without him."

Jane put her arm about Constance. "Come this way. I'll lead you to your cottage. It's the last one, and it isn't as fancy as you deserve, but it is solid and blessed from on high. Let's find you some clean clothes, and maybe a cup of tea. Do you drink tea? Tea has a manner of setting the world right. Let's you and me have a cup and talk it through. What do you say?"

Constance wiped a tear from her cheek. "Thank you, ma'am."

"Oh, never call me 'ma'am'! Do I look that old? Consider me your sister."

Annette watched Constance and Jane cross the meadow. Her thumbs hung from her gun belt. When she saw me staring, she spat a stream of tobacco. "What you looking on?"

"Not much," I said and turned back to the labor at hand.

Jane and Noah lived in a house like all the other houses but theirs had a line of men waiting out front. I entered to find Noah sitting at the table over a bowl of boiled eggs listening to the concerns of an old man who was deaf and shouting so loud my ears set about ringing again.

Noah shouted as he chipped shell from white, "Let me stop you right there, Mr.

James. Is there a point to this ramble? Something you want me to do?"

The old man thought this over. He shouted, "The Yanks come at us by fives but there wasn't no lead left so we hacked them to bits with our hatchets."

"That's a fine story, Mr. James."

"It ain't no story a-tall." He held up his left hand to reveal three missing fingers. "Ask my digits if they think it a story."

"I agree with you," my brother shouted. "With everything. Now, maybe I could come by tomorrow after some proper slumber and hear the rest of this fascinating true event?" Noah rose and helped the old man to his feet and put a hand to his back and guided him toward the door. "And thank you for coming by," he hollered.

Then he turned to me wide eyed. "Mr. James's wife passed last month. She was twice as deaf as he. Maybe you heard their banter in Pearlsville."

Mason stood by the door. He put in a cheekful. " 'Nother one, Patrón?"

"It's like this when I've been absent." Noah took the whole egg at once.

The next man put his hat in his arms and waited to move from the doorway until Mason directed him to sit. He was older than Noah. Still he said "sir."

He took some minutes to get rolling but then come around to his point. "I just believe that maybe there's enough of us now that we need some manner of government. Like last week when the sugar arrived, folks was having a hard time getting their share. It's the injuns' fault. There's too many of them. Old Miss Wilson asked me to get hers because she was afraid of them little heathens. My wife has a fear of their kind too. Some events of her childhood, you understand. It troubles folks to mix with the reds. Maybe we could send them on, someplace else, someplace they can be their way without offending our womenfolk?"

Noah washed down his egg with a cup of water.

"I ain't faulting you in any way, you understand," the man said. "I know the Lord called you to set them free. I'm just wondering if He also insisted on them reds coming to live off our winter supplies and such."

Noah finished his water. His tin cup met the table with the softest clink. "So you desire a government to help ensure you get your full amount of sugar?"

"Well, yeah, sort of. That and other matters."

"They's children, Mr. Travis. Them injuns is but children."

"But you know their kind." Mr. Travis nodded gravely. "They could turn on us at any moment."

Noah tapped his next egg on the table.

"Listen, Mr. Travis, I like you. You're a hell of a magician and not half bad on the Jew's harp neither, but three of my boys out there is part injun. What would they think of us booting some kids just on account they happen to be red? Why not me and Jess here for being part wet? Or you for being a Negro?"

"But their kind don't heed our Lord. They don't belong in . . . All I'm requesting is some —"

"But have you considered what the *Lord* is requesting?"

Mr. Travis looked to the table.

Noah held the egg in the light and turned it. "The Lord has endowed each of us with the capacities for self-reliance, Mr. Travis. There ain't no higher calling. He who can tend to his own needs is free to give his faith fully." He offered the egg across the table to Mr. Travis.

Mr. Travis looked on the egg. He held up a hand and said he was full.

"You've been with us since April and I would like to see you remain, Mr. Travis."

"Me too, sir. Very much. I hope you hear my gratitude." Mr. Travis turned to me to explain. "We was but days from death and Mr. Harney and his people found us and took us in and filled us with hot soup and charity. We might not have survived without this man. My wife says your name still in her nightly prayer. I didn't come here to talk ill of you, sir. I hope you know my sincerity."

"Why do you stay on with us?" Noah asked. "Your fortune improved weeks ago and you could've ridden out."

Mr. Travis looked about the room. He sat a little straighter. "Because the Lord acts through you, sir. Because the Lord brought us together. Because maybe the Lord believes I can play some crucial role. If the Lord trusts you, who am I to doubt? You walk through bullets and don't get hit."

Noah smiled. "Mr. Travis, why else do you stay with us?"

Mr. Travis shrugged. "Everybody knows me as the roofer. That's a damn important job. It ain't number one, like you, Mr. Harney, but a roofer is something. Here, the Lord knows me. He sees my good work. Here, I'm an important man."

"You do make a damn tight roof." Noah looked to me. "Mr. Travis got this manner of laying slats. Ain't a drop of water thin enough to sneak through, not even in the thickest gale. I know slats and this man is gifted. It is true, Mr. Travis. No need to shy at the compliment, as any praise of a man is only praise for his Maker."

"I am grateful for you, sir. Someday when the smokes clears, as you preach on Sundays, we'll ride from this holy rock and into our own green valley with grass head high, and there we'll begin the good work as the Lord intends."

"Amen," Noah said. "That is beautiful, Mr. Travis. And that is why we don't need no government. We're as the Lord intends, humble peasants in His fertile garden. We look out for one another. We care for our fellow man. I will make an announcement about patience in the food line. Will that suit you?"

Mr. Travis was not one for disagreement. "Yessir. Thank you, sir. I knew you would know best."

"And in exchange, will you promise to do a kindness for them poor red children? I suspect the boys among them could do well by learning your trade."

"You want me to teach them to lay slats?" He looked about the room. "What use has an injun got for a roof?"

"We don't know what future the Lord has in store for them children. But here we is with time and it would only do them good to learn a skill. And maybe the good Lord will guide you to see the same sparks in them that you see within your own children. Now if there ain't nothing else, Mr. Travis. As you can see, I got plenty of talking ahead this afternoon."

Mr. Travis hadn't got what he come for but there wasn't no disappointment in his face. He rose and thanked Noah and then turned and thanked me and then put on his hat and thanked Mason for opening the door and then walked out into the summer light and called his thanks a last time. "Maybe I'll show them red children some card magic too."

"Praise the Lord," my brother answered.

The next man stepped forward.

Noah laid his head on the table and said, "Send the rest away, will you, Mason? Please?"

Mason pushed the man back out and said to the rest, "Go on, get! Patrón has had enough. Come back later."

"Do you have to sound so mean? I ain't mean, I'm just worn down is all."

Mason shouted, "Patrón is just worn down. He ain't mean." The door slammed shut. Mason looked around the room. "Me too?" He put on his hat and hit the spittoon and then stepped outside.

"Want something?" Noah asked. We was alone and I was reveling in that fact.

"I'll take a whiskey, if 'n you got one. We's due for a little celebrating." My mouth watered at the notion.

"We don't keep no whiskey in this house," Noah said.

"Why on the plains not?"

He smiled a big brother's smile. "The Lord don't want me tied to my saddle, sis. There was a time though."

"So you don't drink even a drop of whiskey? Like it's your birthday and you just come into a satchel of gold, and you's telling me you don't say yes to a bitty glass?"

He pulled his tobacco pouch and studied me. "You was such a sweet girl when I last seen you. Now you got all this . . ." His finger gestured toward my jacket and his brow furrowed. "You're as rough as a cowpoke the morning the coffee brews clear."

We sat in quiet for a time as I pieced that one through. Then I asked, "What about you, brother? How'd you go from yarn spinner to this?"

My brother rolled a fresh smoke and offered it. He rolled another in short order and then my match lit them both. He reclined and we both exhaled and I waited. So many miles and finally here we was, my brother and me together, just us.

He told me how after leaving our home that night long ago he rode hard on the notion of going all the way to California. But just over the county line he ran out of food. He set about raising money at a poker table but found himself out back getting stomped on. Broke and robbed he offered himself to the next company he come across, some old-time cowpunchers. It was them who changed his mind about California.

"Big Red was our boss and he took me on, special. He and me stayed up nights trading yarn. He wasn't a God-fearing man, but he was wise in his own way. In time he let me in on how he made his real money. See, a cattle baron off in Pearlsville or St. Louis, he expects to lose a few head each week to bears and lions and wolves. He plans for it. But Big Red knew by then the meat eaters was near killed off in them mountains. So that meant some extra head. Got me? We was doing all the work, Red said, so why shouldn't we take those extra cattle for ourselves? I worried what the Lord would think. I wasn't sure, but I was young and went with the old. He and me pieced together a good herd up a side valley. Come fall, we sold it and our wages went up tenfold. But in truth, it didn't sit right with me. The Lord couldn't approve of rustling."

I thought about what Pa would say of thieving another man's cattle.

"Big Red rode for Montana the next spring and the new boss wasn't worth a bit. He put me on fencing, and he would've left me digging posts until the new century. So I skipped out. Tried to catch up with Big Red but never could. All the ranches already had their hands and I couldn't find even day labor. I went through my money by solstice. That was a low time for me, sis, the summer of eighty-one. I admit to harboring dark thoughts. I considered coming home then, tail between my knees, but . . ."

Our eyes met. He looked back to the table.

"I had took to drinking. That winter and spring, I had money for drinking. But once the money was gone, that's when my thirst

410

grew. I missed rye like an old friend. I done things then for a drop that I ain't proud of. Whiskey was the boss of me.

"Sis, I was in Telluride looking on the bank there when the Lord come shown Himself. It was nighttime and I was alone and cold even though the calendar said August. The moon was red behind that bank and then as I watched it turned gold. It sounds crazy, I know, but it ain't no crazier than what happened to Moses on the mountaintop. See, then beside me — this is the part I've been wanting to tell you since it happened and you got to believe it — beside me appeared a man taller than Pa, taller than Big Red even, clean shaven and dressed in a suit too clean for this world. He wasn't no man of flesh, but of divine will. I listened, sis. I memorized every word. Do you know our Lord? Have you heard His voice?"

I shrugged.

"May He speak in your ear too. Them words set me right inside, and I have stayed right since. He knows each of us. He has a plan for each of us. Take comfort in that, sis. That's all the comfort we need in this life."

"What did the Lord tell you?"

"Well, that's for us. But He did mention the First Bank of Telluride!" Noah laughed. "After that night, I saw it all clear as dawn. See, in this country law don't yet come from God, it comes from money. Money is the hammer swinging about and beating down the righteous. That's what's happening to working folk on both sides of the big river. It's money that drives down cattle prices and runs family men into debt. It's money that grows kings while little children starve not two miles away."

He looked about the room and then leaned closer. "I'll tell you some of what He said but keep it here. The Lord told me, 'Noah Harney, you got to solve this problem. You got to be the one save these children. You got to be one to bring my laws to this land. If not you, then who?' And then He said, 'I hereby enshield you from lead and blades. For as long as you do my work, I will protect you.'" Noah let this settle while he relit his cigarette. He raised his eyebrows and exhaled.

I knew all about the First Bank of Telluride. It was big-time on account Noah waited until summer's end, when all the payrolls come in from back east to cover labors owed. This was the twenty-five thousand in cash money our neighbor boy Isaac had mentioned, but in truth Noah got it all without firing a single shot. No dead marshals. The genius wasn't in the heist, it was in the escape. Before the robbery he stashed three fresh mounts on a straight line toward the high country, each about five miles from the last. The lawmen didn't stand a chance of keeping up on their worn-down horses.

I thought at once to warn him of what the Governor had said to me about the cash stolen in the New Moon Heist, the only robbery more famous than Telluride. "The Pinkertons have the serials on the bills you stole from the train. They been tracking your movements. You got to stop spending them bills."

I saw his teeth glint. "Ah, robbing that train! I hope the Lord gives us another chance like that, sis. I'd like to show you how we do it. A lot to think through. You'd be impressed."

"But the serials? I heard it straight from the Governor."

He swatted the notion aside. "We traded that cash for gold six days later. The Pinkertons is likely right now swarming a saloon in Arizona."

"You know about the serials?"

"The Lord keeps me apprised."

I looked on my brother smoking his cigarette. He was a big man now, but those eyes was the same that used to ponder our lake and the mountains beyond.

"Why always hit the Governor?" I asked. "You got some special beef with him in particular?"

Noah looked at me like I was dim. "He's the one who swings the hammer in this country, sis. By now that man got ownership over just about every satchel of gold in the Rockies. He owns the land. He owns the houses. He owns most the cattle. Someday he'll probably own the horses too and rent those back like he do the houses to the men he pays to run his cattle over his land. See, the Governor is in the man business. He eats up men for a living. True though, the rail lines ain't his, about the only thing. But we hit those too. Those rail barons? They make the Governor look small time. Back east money, got me? They's the real kings. Gold enough to fill an ocean. All this out here? Just a trickle running downhill."

Noah rested his elbows on the table. "Did Pa learn of all the good I done . . . before?"

I knew my brother wanted it honest. "He never spoke of it. Pa quit going to town."

"Well, he knows now. That's for sure. He knows more than even us."

There come footsteps and the door opened and in come Jane. Noah rose to greet her, and I took up my hat and stubbed the remains of my smoke.

"Stay!" Jane said.

But I thanked her and took my leave. My brother had his own house now, and in it I was a guest.

I stepped outside and into Annette's hard glare. She was splitting wood across the yard near a cabin set off from the rest. She spat. Her eyes left me to balance a round and then she stepped back and swung the ax with force

414

enough to send a quarter of pine end over end. The clap echoed from the rock walls.

She knocked back her hat and looked on me again and this time she didn't flinch, ax in hand.

Between us the children was playing a game in the last of the sun. The light turned their marbles to beads of water, rolling over the dust but never sliding through. I thought of the lake back home, and that put me in the mood for a long view.

I climbed a thin trail along the rock until my lungs burned, and broke out onto the flat rim hundreds of feet above the earth. They had built rock walls along the edge with firing ports to allow careful shots without exposing the shooter. Crates of ammunition was stacked in the lee of the rocks. There was boxes of canned beans and pickled meat too. A drum to catch rainwater. A couple of the boys was sharing tobacco and watching downvalley, rifles over their laps.

I sat in the sun and removed my hat. The whole world was below me. Swallows shot by beneath. I longed for whiskey.

Wasn't long before I heard my brother's voice. "Knew I'd find you here. You and that mare of yours always took to the high spots." He crossed the top and sat beside me. That he'd chosen me over Jane stirred something deep within.

"Didn't figure you'd come looking for me."

"Jane understands what it means to miss your sister."

"I didn't reckon I'd find you married."

He laughed. "You and me both, sis."

He said he heard Jane before he ever saw her. "We was riding toward a rail town on the Union Pacific line, and it was near dark, and the spring light was purple over the green grass. Ah, sis. The horizon was orange with strips of crimson — storms way out in the far yonder. Coming across that was a woman's voice. Lord. Her voice. I swear, an angel's harkening. The cranes was dancing to it. Pure holy. We was married a month on."

"Her voice ain't from out west."

"No. She's got a long story, that one. My kind of woman."

A pair of rock doves swooped to a perch on the rain drum. They watched us. They was but ten paces away. They dipped their heads under the water and threw it over their bodies and quivered it through their feathers. They looked on us, then did it again. The wind passed overhead and the sounds of birds on the wing come like bursts of gale through rope.

When Noah spoke next, his voice had taken a turn for the dark. "Tell me honest."

"Tell you what?"

"Did I break Pa with that blow?"

I shut my eyes to the light.

"Don't pretend you don't know what I'm

talking about. Did I break him?"

"Nah."

"Lord forgive me for I am a sinner."

"Pa forgave you. He didn't hold no grudge."

"Pa was all grudge."

I drew a breath to defend our old man, but instead I let the silence remain.

Noah was looking over the water. "Thank you, Jess, for tending to him at the end. Should've said as much sooner. I am grateful for you. I have always been grateful for you."

Those words soaked deep. "Pa wasn't dim. Pa wasn't no fool."

Noah took off his hat. "You're right. Pa was a sad man but not a fool. I trust you said a few words from me when you put him in the ground?"

"I didn't say nothing. Wasn't nobody to hear."

"The Lord is always with us, Jess. Though I suspect He hears just the same in the language of the tongue or the heart. Just so long as Pa could spend eternity beside our mother."

I watched the birds clean themselves. I watched as they lifted their heads and let their beaks touch.

"You did bury him beside Ma."

"And how exactly was I to put him on a horse in that state?"

"You could've found somebody to help. The neighbor. What was his name? Saggat. Somebody. Jess, you didn't bury him beside Ma?"

"He died a full day's ride onto Indian land. He was worked over by critters by the time I got to him. I didn't even ever find his right arm!" My voice had rose. "You ain't seeing the proper picture in your mind. I was alone with him. What was left. You left me to tend to him alone."

He put his hat back on and the brim cast his face in gray shadow. "All I ever done is walk the path the Lord laid. One brick at a time, I see it and I step."

"Go back with me, brother. Let's put it right. Let's build up our home again, together. That's what they would want, our folks."

"Go back?"

"Don't we owe it to them to make that place right?"

"Jess. There ain't no going back for us. You's as deep in this as me now. I guarantee you got a bounty on your head. You got to know there ain't no going back for us."

I looked to the ground. "What is we if not that spread?"

"Humble yourself, sister. Be *His* implement, not your own." He touched his hand to my knee. "Think about it. He has delivered you here for a reason, hasn't He?"

"You believe the Lord has delivered me?"

"Admit to yourself you felt the hand of God shepherding you to this moment. You can admit it." He smiled on me with honest warmth.

"Yeah," I said. "I guess. I feel it."

"Oh, sis. I am so happy to see you! This is what they would want. Us together, wherever that might be."

I looked out at the land before us, at the blue sky and wisps of cloud. Above and below like two worlds divided at the horizon. My whole life had been spent watching that place where the two unite.

The birds took flight, and the water rippled and then went still, and there the sky shone back from what lies below.

And my brother slapped me on the back. "Come on now. Let's shoot some, like old times. The Lord does love shooting or He wouldn't have given us a surplus of lead and powder."

I followed my brother to the edge, the whole vast desert before us. Way out in the distance like a gray mushroom was the haze of Pearlsville. I looked down and was breathless to see the sage as one plant. A leap from this height and you might take flight.

Noah withdrew a small red cube from his jacket pocket. "If Jane asks about this, let me do the talking."

"Asks about what?"

"You shoot first. Get that pistol ready." He checked over his shoulder to see that we was alone.

"Ain't you gonna get ready, sister?"

"I am ready. What is that target in your hand?"

"Still a show-off, huh? You remember when you hit that yote at like a thousand yards with Pa's rusty old Sharps?"

"Sure, it was my first bull's-eye. But it wasn't a thousand yards."

"You let me take the credit, you remember?"

"I also let you take the blame," I said.

Noah brought his finger to his ear. It was still scarred all these years later from that blow our pa had delivered with his pistol butt. "I've missed you, Jess. I mean that. There ain't a day that's gone by without a long thought of you."

"You gonna throw that or what?"

He smiled. "But all right, you better not waste this. These ain't easy to come by." He threw that cube over the edge and it glittered red in the evening light. I drew and fired with routine calm. The cube become a flash of light the width of a wagon, and the noise knocked me back in surprise. Noah had thrown a piece of dynamite!

"Yip ha!" he shouted. His hat had been blown off and he drove a pinkie into his ear and wiggled it against the sudden deafness. "Nice shooting! Real smooth. You wasn't lying about knowing a thing or two!"

I climbed up from the ground. I put my

own hat back in place. "Next time at least warn me when we's shooting dynamite."

"But did you see that burst! Holy spirit! I swear I looked right into it! I'm blinded by the revelation!" My brother slapped my back and I stumbled toward the edge. "We's gonna have some fun, you and me. I know it. We's gonna do good together, in His name."

The speed had me laughing. That boom was better than whiskey. "You know it, brother."

"Here, here, you throw the next one. Don't drop it. Serious, Jess." Noah drew his pistol and worked the hammer, and the smile on his face was the same damn smile he'd had that afternoon years before when we stole Pa's Sharps.

"The papers all say you is some miracle with a sidearm," I said in jest. "Yet a real man remains holstered until the throw."

"Them papers don't lie. But what do you know about being a man?"

I tossed him a hard glare and spat. "Not much to know."

This left him laughing. He slipped his pistol back in its holster. "All right, make it a good throw then."

"Don't miss. I'll tell everybody I'm the faster Harney if you miss."

"I don't miss."

"Ha!"

"Just throw it, Jess."

I held the cube to the light. "Pa would've loved shooting these things."

"Yes, I reckon you right on that score. For Pa then."

"For Pa." I threw that cube up off the edge and Noah drew, and it was as it had been before.

That night ended like all nights at Lord's Rock, with music and dance. We ate supper and then wandered with lanterns toward the blazing fireplace and the sounds of strings tuning. Jane was skipping in her dress and the children come from their houses at the sight of her to ask after cookies. She pulled one after another from her pockets and soon a whole flock of the little beings was fluttering toward the fire in her lee.

Men and women alike was there with instruments. Eyes was shut to the light of this world and folks saw only with their sense of song. I heard a mandolin for the first time. I heard the emotions that could come from smart lips on a harmonica. But it was Annette's banjo that seized my mind.

She sat in the firelight with her legs crossed and that banjo upon her thigh and her fingers running wild over them strings. How those fingers could move! All at once that hoarse voice of hers cut in and I could no longer keep still. She sang of white horses coming fast, and I was upon those horses.

I longed for Pa's fiddle, but I was no match for these players. Jane took my hand and I joined the dancing.

A lantern was lit within Constance's cottage. I saw the moment it went out. Jane saw it too. She said to me, "Poor girl. We should make an effort."

"Doubt any effort could help," I said.

"Only the Lord can help but we can be His hands."

The music rose up through the peculiar shape of that rock and returned to us as a humming echo. Each of us heard it, I know. It sounded like a voice coming straight down upon us, the coos of a Maker to its chosen child.

In that place set to song it was easy to be sure.

I awoke the next morning early in my bedding on Noah and Jane's floor and could not return to sleep. My body had grown used to the comforts of whiskey and without adequate supplies my sleep was thin and easily punctured. I dressed and stepped into the dimmest gray and looked upon the stars. The rock was a sewing frame to them and I imaged a needle passing its thread back and forth. A silver tear appeared on the velvet of Heaven and was healed again, quick as water.

When I come back inside Noah was getting ready for the day. Like Pa, he couldn't sleep past dawn's earliest glimmer.

"What you doing?" he whispered. He had the stove open and was setting splinters of pine to last night's embers.

"Rolling up my bedding."

He shut the stove and opened the flue and the wood set about popping. "No, I mean why you up?"

"I'm going with you. Wherever you's going."

"Not this time, Jess."

Jane stirred awake and said while stretching, "Too early."

"Go back to sleep, darling," Noah said. "You too, sister."

"I been hunting you for months. I ain't letting you out of my sight now."

Jane lit the lantern and yawned. "Let me whip up some eggs. You'll need something to carry you through."

"No need," Noah said. "Stay in bed. Both of you." He took his hat from its hook and placed it on his head. "Some hard business today."

Jane and I shared a look. "Take your sister with you. She's come all this way to join you."

"Jane, I'll ask when I need your counsel."

I set my bedroll in the corner. "I ain't no stranger to hard business, brother. And maybe today's the day the Lord calls me in service of His plan."

Noah's jaw tightened. "Come on then. But

you stay behind me, you hear?"

We met by lantern light near the pole barn. It was Annette and Youn and us. They was already saddled and had Noah's Blackie tacked up too. Brother had told me Blackie was his lucky horse, had been with him since his first getaway. Now brother put his open hand to the animal's nostrils and the darkness was filled with the sound of breath.

"What's this?" Annette asked, pointing her chin at me.

"You best leave old Ingrid and take another," Noah said. "Somebody fast."

But I whistled anyhow and feet come thundering out of the aspens and into the common bay. I tacked Ingrid with a spare saddle, seeing as she come this whole way bareback. It was an old cavalry number, too much leather for my liking, but it would do.

Noah swung up on his mount. "Let's get." He gave Blackie the heels and in three bounds they was at full speed.

I followed at the rear and watched my brother's strong back as the day broke and the sun threw mile-long shadows. He'd become a damn fine rider, well balanced and casual, a cattleman through and through. He was no stranger to covering rough terrain at speed, he led his animal with his hips. When down in the pines he ducked limbs rather than brushing them aside to keep them from swinging into me.

I don't think I've ever been so gleeful in all my life as I was in that crystalline dawn, following my big brother down his mountain.

The air was still cool with morning when we come to a pair of buildings in the pines, a saloon and a whorehouse. It was just another outpost of sin in the wilderness. Them pines was tall and squirrels dropped cones from the treetops that bounced down the roof and to the earth.

Youn checked the stable. "Three, Boss, including his."

Noah checked the loads in his pistol. "Good."

We hitched our horses in the trees and Noah demanded I stay with them. He said, "Keep at that there back door. Don't go shooting nobody but don't let nobody go running off neither."

I walked toward the building with them.

"What you doing?" he said.

"I'm a better inside man than out."

Annette was smiling. "His Jane do what she pleases too."

"Yes," Noah confirmed. "I am surrounded by women who think they know better than me. Huh, Youn? What happened to the days when a woman listened to a man?"

Youn shrugged. "Chinese no see those days."

"Used to be a man knew what he was talking about," I said.

Annette laughed, the first time I seen warmth on her face.

Noah nodded toward the building. "I'll do the talking."

We pushed through the front door of the saloon and found a man sleeping facedown on a table and another sprawled on the floor where he landed when his chair tipped. We stepped over that one and made our way toward the barkeep, who left a steaming towel on the counter and lifted an old scattergun. "We ain't open. Not for the likes of you."

"Business ain't with you, Rudy. Where's your master?"

The barkeep cocked his scattergun. He couldn't stop blinking. "I ain't asking twice, Mr. Harney."

Youn and Annette took to opposite walls. Annette held her pistol. I kept my post beside my brother.

It should've been concern I felt then, or some similar affliction. I was looking eye to eye with a big-bore scattergun. But all I felt was speed, as if I was atop a tall horse on a downhill run. The morning light was golden through them windows and my brother was an arm's reach away, and in this world he wrote the rules.

The scattergun come up to Rudy's shoulder and glared its hollow eyes on me. "You think this is funny?"

Noah stepped between the weapon and me. "Now, Rudy. You got two barrels there and four gunmen. You do all right with arithmetic in school or should I break this down for you?"

Rudy just blinked.

"See." Noah held up his fingers. "Four gunmen minus two barrels equals two gunmen and no barrels. What happens then, you reckon?"

"I know my arithmetic. I got through the fifth grade." There was an edge of pride to the statement.

"Where's your master?"

Rudy adjusted his grip on the steel. "Boss ain't here."

"Now we both know that's bullshit, Rudy. Your master is in back. What I mean to ask is could you kindly fetch him for me?"

"He ain't my master."

"Then why you whisper that fact?"

We heard a pistol cock and looked to Annette. She was leveled on Rudy. She said, "I'll kill him now. He ain't of no use to us."

"That ain't no justification for killing, Net. Didn't you get your fill the other night? My partner here is like a fat man for killing."

The scattergun moved from us to her, then back.

"Rudy will do the right thing," Noah said. "He has a wife and daughter up Two Color

Creek. Don't you, Rudy?" Noah pulled his plug and stuck it in one of the barrels of the scattergun.

There come a creaking sound from the back and Youn looked out the window. In a voice as calm as dawn he said, "There he go."

We got to the door in time to see the man and his chestnut go tearing up the road. "See," Noah said, "if 'n you'd stayed out back like I said . . . Now can we give chase before he gets far enough gone to make this an all-day doing? I promised the woman we'd be back for supper."

We rode at a dead sprint and Ingrid did her best to keep up with those bigger horses but after a mile she was some distance behind. She wasn't as young as she once was. "Come on, girl. A little more."

We arrived to the edge of the pines and there was the rider's dust halfway across the plains and between here and there was my brother's crew, gaining. They would have the man soon enough.

Two miles on Noah held up. When Ingrid got to him, he nodded toward our man, who was then limping toward a pile of rocks. In the prairie before us was his wailing horse.

"Poor critter," Noah said. His hands was balanced on the horn, the reins in two fingers. "Must've stepped in a rodent hole. Went down hard."

A bullet cut through the air over our heads and then a half moment later come the sound of its discharge. Two more come by closer yet. The horses sidestepped but we didn't bother taking cover. The man was firing from a great distance with his six-gun. The Lord would have to hate you for you to die so random.

"What's that?" Noah said as another went by. "Four?"

"Five," Annette counted. She pointed a finger toward the heavens. "And that there is six."

We took off at a full run toward the pile of rocks, four horses bearing down on a man as he fumbled with his casings. At a hundred yards I saw the golden gleam of fresh shells. At twenty-five he cocked the pistol and took aim. We split and his shot missed and then Youn leapt from his horse onto him. The two went rolling down the sand and then Youn was up and pounding on the man's face. Annette swung down and lifted the man's pistol and tucked it in her belt. She buried her knee into his neck and Youn bent his arm around until he squealed like a slick pig.

"Tie him up." Noah spat from his saddle.

I recognized him at once from a wanted poster. Even with the blood and snot pouring from his punched nose, there wasn't no mistaking this man was Dizzy Donohue, $250 reward. His hair was still salt and pepper, his moustache still night black. He was one of many the Governor wanted hanged.

Annette set Dizzy in the sunny side of the rocks without his hat. Behind us and in his eyes loomed the red-hot sun.

Off on the trail Dizzy's horse cried with pain. It was trying to stand and failing. Ingrid pranced about with her tail out and then spun to face the sorry creature. She answered its cries.

Dizzy paid his animal no mind. He was cursing about being woke and chased at such an early hour, and for what?

I walked to the horse and saw her leg snapped midshank. A badger hole in the road is what done it. It was a gruesome wound and there would be no recovery. I wasted not a moment in ending her misery.

I holstered my pistol and returned to Ingrid. She watched me with wide eyes and as I drew near she backed away. It was the first time she ever done that. I put my hand to her neck and she froze. "It's just me, girl."

Noah pulled his hat from his head and wiped the sweat from his brow. "The calendar says autumn, but I'll tell you what."

Dizzy was panting. Sweat stained his night-clothes.

Noah was studying his own fingernails now. "You wake up in these cool mornings and think you'll need the long johns but then by

431

midmorning it's damn near July again."

The older man sighed and looked to the dirt. "So this is it for me, then. Dead in my underclothes. After everything." His voice was nasal on account of the broken nose.

"It don't have to go that way," Noah said. He drew his knife and put it to his fingernail and cut free the excess. "Last week your boys hit a wagon as it crossed Thimble Creek. You got a recollection?"

He shrugged. "My boys hit a lot of wagons."

"I guess that's part of my confusion," Noah said. "A private wagon never carries nothing worth stealing, not no more. Why rob families when all the money in this country is in but ten pockets?"

Dizzy was squinting into the light. "So they was friends of yours? The drivers of this wagon?"

"Yes, in fact they was. Good folks. And that's the other part of my confusion. Why kill honest men when you don't have to?"

"Witnesses. The marshals always want witnesses." Dizzy shrugged. "I guess in a manner of thinking, that makes the killing the marshals' fault, don't it?"

"Well, let's test that logic in this particular circumstance, why don't we." Noah put his knife away. "Dizzy, what are you exactly, in this situation?"

He looked about our eyes. "I don't see your point."

Noah smiled. "Maybe you is as dumb as you look."

"A witness?"

"There you go."

"Okay," Dizzy said. "I learned my lesson. I'm reformed. No more killing witnesses."

"If only it was that easy." Noah shrugged. "But a man will always return to his familiar drink, won't he?"

"I promise," Dizzy said. "I won't go killing folks without better cause. And I won't rob from family wagons no more. You done showed me the light on this issue. I been rehabituated."

"That's a big word, Dizzy. But we're just starting here. You can take your rehabituated arse out of this county. No more pines. Not for you or your boys. You clear this county and don't let me see you in them trees again. If I do, it's war. You want to war with the Wild Bunch? You want Noah Harney hunting you in your sleep?"

Dizzy squinted into the light. "Whoa, now, whoa. There ain't no reason to get apocalyptical. Them pines is where I keep my retail operations. Folks enjoy the shade and the pleasant breezes and such. You don't intend I move entire whorehouses into the prairie where the only people is shepherds and off-reservation reds?"

Noah tipped his hat back. He winked at me. "And since we're on the subject, I do

433

take some issue with your use of child whores. Why you got them girls when there's no shortage of proper widows looking for employment?"

"Matter of customers is all. A business these days got to have an edge."

"Those girls don't leave with you. The Lord wants them free."

Dizzy grew fiery all at once. "Goddamn you to hell, Harney! You ain't got no sense of right."

Noah said, "Maybe you'd prefer to sell the whole farm. My partner here is a willing buyer."

Annette drew her pistol. She cocked it and drove the barrel into Dizzy's temple.

"Damn you, you Mexican shitbag! We should've wiped out your kind when we had the chance. You just a two-bit pistol player, Harney. The Lord don't know you from a pile of whiskey shit."

Noah smiled. "Come now, Dizzy. We're all countrymen here. No reason we can't still be friendly and what have you. So long as you keep out of them pines."

"I think I should kill him," Annette said.

"I know you do," Noah responded. "But then his boys would only replace him, and we'd still have all the same problems. So Dizzy? Can I trust you to lead your boys to a new county? If you say yes, you live another day. That's charity at work, right there. That's the Lord's spirit."

"Fine," Dizzy cursed. "Business been slowing anyhow."

Noah nodded, and Youn holstered his gun, drew his knife, and cut the rope from Dizzy's wrists.

"Bless you, Dizzy Donohue," Noah said. "May Jesus show you a brighter path while you still got time."

We returned to the bar where it had begun and this time hitched our horses to the post out front like proper patrons. Annette and Youn went in to drink. I went to follow them but then Noah called to me. We went to the whorehouse next door.

The matron was surprised to see two gentlemen, as she called us, at such an early hour.

Noah pulled a wad of cash from his pocket and placed it in her hands.

"My, my," she said. "That is a heavy roll of money. What kind of party you planning, mister?"

"That's your traveling money. Dizzy is done here. I'm your new boss and that there is a parting gift."

Her smile was gone. "Now wait a minute."

Noah stepped past her. He hollered up them stairs. "Rise and shine, girls! Step out onto the landing and into your new day!" To the matron he said, "Tell them to do it."

"I will not!" The matron clenched her jaw.

Noah took back the cash quick as lightning and drew his pistol with the other hand. I will admit I was impressed with his speed.

"Now you're plain fired. Get. Go on."

"You're that Harney."

He cocked the pistol. "And this here device airs out heathen flesh."

She looked on the barrel. "Can I pack a bag?"

He put the pistol back in its place. "By all means, ma'am."

The doors was open now and little faces peeked out. Noah called, "This business is closed and your lady fired and this is your one chance to come with us to a place of food and plenty. No more whoring. There's mommas where we go."

Once the first emerged the rest did too. Nine in total. They come down the stairs in their little dresses with their little hair done up in little braids and such. There wasn't a one of them girls over fourteen.

That afternoon Jane and the other women tended to the new girls and found them families willing to take them on. Susie, the youngest of the girls, looked to be about ten. She hadn't said a word other than to tell us her name, but she had followed me out into the meadow where Ingrid was grazing. Ingrid trotted close and Susie touched her neck. Ingrid put her nose to Susie's hair and nibbled. Susie giggled. Then Ingrid lowered her face so Susie might rub her brow. I ain't never seen such a quick connection between a horse and girl as that one.

"She trusts you. You been around plenty of horses."

"Seen plenty. Never touched one. Only menfolk get to ride horses."

I plucked some grass and put it before Ingrid and she bent her neck to nibble it. As she done so, I helped Susie swing a leg over Ingrid's neck. It was as we used to when it was just us, and Ingrid remembered. She lifted her head and little Susie slid over her mane and to her back. Susie laughed. At the familiar weight, Ingrid's eyes mellowed to a half blink.

Jane emerged from the door and called Noah out too. They stood by the stone house and watched as Susie rode Ingrid bareback around the meadow. I called instructions and the little girl listened to none of them, but she kept her fists balled in Ingrid's mane and her knees locked tight and she wore a smile as bright as June sunshine. Ingrid too trotted with the lightness of old summer. She kept her head high and her tail out, and I could see she was proud of carrying that little girl. A horse can miss home too.

I turned and there was Annette beside me. "Ain't nothing more natural than a girl on a pony."

"You right on that score."

She reached a hand inside her jacket. Out come a bottle of whiskey.

"Well, then," I said, taking down my first gulp in days. It was wetter and better than I remembered. "So you ain't all gravel."

She shrugged and took a pull for her own self. "Mostly."

Annette was her own critter. She smelled of sweat and horse and her hat was tipped back and dust clung to her wet temples. I will admit my pulse quickened at her sudden proximity. That morning I wondered if we might come to blows, but here she was now sharing her whiskey.

I returned the favor with my tobacco pouch. Annette took a three-finger pinch and chewed the mess and tucked it in her cheek.

I saw Jane resting her head on Noah's chest and his arms wrapped tight around her and the both of the them watching Susie ride circles about that meadow.

"Where you get the liquor?" I asked.

"Stole it. You ever make it your own self?"

"No, but I like that notion. You?"

"Some. Not me but some fools I know. Don't taste, but it'll make you blind."

"Blind is good."

Annette didn't laugh. She spat a black stream upon the grass. "Thanks for the 'baccy."

■ ■ ■ ■

That evening Constance was looking about the meadow. Her hair was fresh brushed and she wore a new dress, this one a standard wifely affair. Even in that humble cotton, she looked royal to my eye. When she saw me, she walked straight to where I was enjoying a large plug. I knew what she was coming to ask.

I told her most everything I knew, that Drummond and Greenie had been ordered by her father to deliver Will to the train depot. But I left out Will's busted knee and the clubs heavy with lead. I told her it was Agent Thorvald who done it.

I was surprised when Constance took this news without a tear. I do believe the version I offered was less troubling than the horrors she had been imagining all this time.

"What happened to his body?" Her voice was barely a whisper.

"They put it on the train."

A long while passed and I offered what I had, my chaw, but she didn't notice.

She said out of the blue, "He came to live at our house when we were eleven. Both of us. Our birthdays are the same day. That has to be a sign, right? I remember everything. They came by train and Father sent a carriage for them at the station. It was Will's first carriage ride. They wore the clothing of servants, but they had been without employment so long their seams were tearing and their knees threadbare. I saw them then only as Father did. I did not understand how Will's people had suffered. I did not understand that he too had hopes beyond the walls of Father's house. I believed what my father taught me, I believed Will only to be grateful for employment and for our charitable offering of it. He was tall even then and I found it challenging to remove my eyes from his dark face. He scared me a little with his darkness, I will admit. Yet I know for certain Will was more scared of my whiteness than I was of his blackness, and for better reason.

"But we were the only two children on the estate. It was only a matter of time before we took to each other. Will loved to drive the carriage for pretend, and I was his favorite passenger, and sometimes we would play for hours before remembering our places.

"We began to play tricks on Charles. Hiding something necessary or replacing something valuable with something earthen. Once," she smiled, "I dressed in Will's tails and he in my gown. I talked in his tone and he mimicked mine. We paraded before my mirror as if we were a couple. I loved him even then."

She turned to me. "Have you ever loved?"

"Ain't had the chance, reckon."

"Love is outside the bounds of chance." Her hair was loose, and she tucked a lock behind her ear.

It was Greenie I thought of then. For wasn't it love I felt for him? Yes, but not love like what I saw now in Constance's eyes.

"Charles did discover our illicit play and reported our insolence to Father. We leaned our ears to his office door. We could hear everything. Charles volunteered to resign his position. But Father wouldn't allow it. He ordered Charles to keep better control of his 'offspring.' I believe Father saw this as a tremendous act of charity. Really, Father counted on Charles too much to let him go.

"By then our course was set. Our games had grown too important to simply be forgotten. We knew each other too well to see what everyone else did in our colors. I was a lonely girl, Jesse. Jesse, is that even your name?"

"My ma named me Jessilyn. Jane is calling me Jess."

"Which do you prefer?"

I shrugged. "Jess, I reckon. Why belabor it."

"I never knew you were a sister. Never suspected it. I knew I saw something different in you, however."

She took a long moment considering me. "Could you have done anything? Could you have warned him?"

"I've been turning that over ever since."

"He was the only person who knew me.

441

And he believed I was the only person who knew him. But did I? Oh Lord, I hope I did. I pray I offered him half of what he offered me. There is no one left who knows me." She wiped her tears and even as more rolled she looked royal and above suffering. "I have spent these days attempting to reconcile this world. How is it that the sun still rises and sets and the seasons still turn and men laugh as they pass? How do these things still occur when Will no longer draws breath?" She shook her head. "I'm sorry. I've been slipping into self-pity."

"You got the right," I said.

Constance dried her eyes. "I will never again utter Father's name. I pray it is erased from this earth forever."

I joined Jane in making supper that night. It was just us in their place. Jane had made potatoes and a roast and the air smelled homey and fine. There was day-old bread, a gift from another house. I gave the stove some juniper and then stirred the meat juice into flour gravy while Jane set the plates.

Jane was telling me of the eligible bachelors among us. "You don't want any of the Wild Bunch, trust me. Sure, a couple of them might catch your fancy, but those boys are feral creatures. Forgive my bluntness, but Lord knows what sins they have perpetrated in the name of lust. Now there's Mr. Thompkins. Have you met him yet? He is a widower and the father to a pair of boys in hard need of a mother. You've seen them about the meadow surely."

Jane was a tough one to sort. She spoke with a highfalutin air, and her back was always straight like Constance's, yet her hands was rough from a life of labor. Sometimes she used the low word instead of the high, as if by mistake. Noah told me she was a schoolteacher before they met, but I wasn't so sure I believed him. Most of all it was her eyes. I saw in them something I recognized, a thirst to be believed.

From an open chest she lifted a pink dress with little white flowers upon it. It was a girl's dress, not in size but in pattern, built for luring in a man. You'd never see no married woman in a dress like that.

"It is mine from before, a lifetime ago, when I was narrower." She held it out between us. "I want you to have it."

I didn't squeal with delight. I ain't sure what look I had on my face but whatever it was sent Jane scrambling.

"I know it suffers from wrinkles, but, Jess, we can smooth those. It does have some wear but wear can be mended." She lifted the hem. "Nothing a few stitches can't solve. I should've done that before I offered it to you. How rude of me. I see now that it looks worn and maybe belongs to an older generation."

"Nah, thank you, Jane. I just taken a liking to trousers is all."

Noah walked in and hung his hat on the hook and pulled out his chair at the head of the table and sat heavy.

"But you're so beautiful!" Jane said. "I know you have those marks and they must give you terrible grief, but those aren't any reason to hide yourself. Jess, the right man won't care about marks."

She placed her hand upon my shoulder. "The right man loves not the shell you show the world but the fiber you keep safe beneath. Right, dear?"

"Right," Noah said. "Supper ready? Smells ready."

"We're discussing womanly matters," Jane said. "Matters of love."

Noah looked at me. "I ain't heard Jess ask for no help on matters of love, sugar."

"Well, that's rather my point," Jane said.

Noah winked at me.

I took a seat near my brother and let Jane bring the food to the table. Noah said, "What is it you want, sister?"

"Supper. And whiskey, if I tell it honest."

"No, I mean the long view."

"I don't rightly know, if we ain't going home."

"Sure you do. I see the resolve in your eyes. You got some notion stirring up your soul."

I hit the spittoon even though I chewed no

plug. "I want to join your crew. I want to be part of your Wild Bunch."

He smiled. "You don't have to. I got plenty of boys. Jane could teach you a few things you missed by the lake. It ain't easy being on the crew."

"I ain't after easy. I want to ride with you."

At this he looked me over. "So this ain't a costume then? You really don't want to dress nice and talk sweet and find yourself a man to call your own?"

"Brother, I want to be at your side anytime you walk into trouble."

He paused to think on it. He looked to Jane. Jane pursed her lips.

He hit my shoulder as he used to when we was kids. "All right then. Well, I guess that makes Annette your new boss. You best pay her a visit after supper."

Annette and a few of the boys was tending to the storehouse. Inside was crates of jarred goods and drums of salt pork and boxes heavy with nails and tools. There was slabs of curing ham and wood crates filled with straw and eggs. On one wall was bag after bag of feed for the horses. There was a great roll of hemp rope long enough to reach the moon. The storehouse didn't have no windows and it was as cool in there as the night itself.

Annette set a box of straw-laid onions on top of another of dirt-crusted potatoes.

"Won't look like this come the end of winter," she said when she saw me at the door.

I offered to help but Annette said they was through. She ordered the boys out and locked the door behind us. She put the key in her pocket.

In the evening light, the boys got to pushing one another and laughing and Annette took a seat on the gate of a wagon. I didn't have the nerve to take the seat beside her, she'd have to scoot over to make room for me.

I leaned against the wagon. "This will be a hard place to winter."

Annette put a match to her rollie. "The only place to winter is upstairs of a saloon, you ask me."

The one they called Mason pointed at Annette's smoke. "Can I roll one, Boss?"

Annette stood from the rear of the wagon, cigarette in her lips. "Come on," she said to me. "I got me a fresh bottle, and these boys is dumb as hell."

I followed her to the entrance of the Rock and beyond. I might've told myself I was following that bottle but it was the shifting of Annette's body that held my attention. I couldn't hardly hear my thoughts for the pounding in my chest.

Annette wore that bear-hide vest in the cool mornings and come the hot afternoons she

rolled up the sleeves of her flannel and unbuttoned it partway. When she rode through dust
she drew up a green bandanna till only her
eyes showed under her black hat. She kept a
pinch of wolf fur in the band.

She walked with the unease of a man who
had spent his days upon a fast horse, and I
couldn't help but make a study of her motions. Everything she done had her brand on
it. Even how she wiped the sweat from her
brow. She lifted her hat and used the underside of a wrist. I'd never seen nobody do that
before. When I was away from eyes, I tried it
for my own self. To feel what she must feel.

In the time I knew her Annette didn't hide
her womanness or find cause to flaunt it. She
didn't tell no man he was right just to end
the fight. She thought what she thought and
did what she wanted to do, and she had my
brother's full respect because of it.

Before us that evening the sage was lit in
red light. Annette leaned on the outside of
the Rock and I done the same and we smoked
and shared a bottle as the light left this world.
She was telling me about some of the dumb
things the boys done. I thought my laugh
sounded too girlie.

Bats come out the rocks and fluttered
overhead like leaves in a storm. For a time
she quit talking and we just watched. All that
silence and I worried over my words. Nothing I thought to say sounded good enough.

But soon the whiskey had me bolstered. "What about Jane? She always so smiley?"

Annette made a farting sound with her lips, and passed me the bottle. "That woman. She done softened him for the worse. She's the reason we's here, sitting still, rotting like some puffed-up beaver.

"Before her your brother rode fast and slept out and played music till dawn and come winter holed up in proper towns with plenty of drink. We was a crew of pure bandits. Done as we pleased. Now we dwell with straight folk who look on us like we's savages. Don't get me started on that woman."

"She's sweet on him though," I said.

"They been together plenty long, you ask me. I'm waiting on your brother to come back to us. She's just a stopping-over point for him. He got a soft spot for the motherly types. He used to take up with one like that each winter."

"He married this one."

"Yes, he did. But Jane ain't cut out for this life. She just trying it on. She likes the way the story sounds, wife to an outlaw."

We passed the bottle.

She asked me, "You just trying it on?"

"I was born his sister," I said.

"That ain't what I'm asking."

I looked at her, the first time our eyes met and lingered. Her face was dark and full of whole worlds. "I ain't the storytelling type."

Her eyes went to the distant north. She was always looking north.

"You ever consider leaving him?" I asked.

"For what?"

"I don't know. Back home or whatever?"

She took back her bottle. "Where I come from sticking a side is your home. Your brother? He's my side. He might get tamed by that woman but he's still my partner."

She pulled up her shirt to reveal the bare skin. The light was just enough I could make out a ragged tear long as a forearm, years ago healed over but all crooked and warped and thick as leather. "My horse was shot out from under me on the run. Spined. I went head-long into the timbers. Got myself skewered out. I was three weeks on my back in a doc's house. Lucky to come through it at all. Your brother stayed on with me. He paid the doc and he didn't leave, even when I cursed him."

"My brother stayed with you?" I admit to thinking of him that night long ago when he'd left me with Pa bleeding on the floor. I swallowed more whiskey.

"Ain't many like that in this world. Your brother, he sticks his side. He's the most home I ever knowed."

Annette had rode south from Canada. Her Blackfoot ma was half French and had passed early. Her pa was a buffalo hunter but he wasn't nobody she ever met. She took to fending for herself at age eleven. By thirteen

449

she took up a pistol and crossed the border. At fifteen she put the barrel to a stranger's back and demanded his cash money. That particular stranger was my brother.

"What was he like as a boy?" she asked. "I ain't never had no big brother, but I bet he was a bully. Was he? Did he beat on you?"

"He made sure I had half the quilt during the night. That was the kind of brother he was."

By now the whiskey had us soaked. We sat on the ground with our backs to the Rock. Annette was cross-legged and took off her hat and set it on a knee.

I was wet enough to ask, "You don't believe in what my brother believes, the Lord and all that, do you?"

She put a new rollie to her lips and sparked it. The match went tumbling through the darkness and we could see its ember on the dry ground.

"Oh, them's just words." She twirled her finger at the stars. "Men is all the time hiding behind words."

Next day at noon I had my first guard duty and took my brother's Winchester up the trail to the rim. I was nearing the top and huffing with the climb when I heard some commotion ahead. The boys was there and they was laughing. Annette was with them. She was laughing too.

The one they called Blister shouted, "Youn thinks he can outwrestle me. What do you think?"

"I pin you in ground like girl," Youn said.

Blister laughed. He was a thick man with a neck that was all muscle and wider than his jaw. When he laughed, a vein rose across his forehead. "See? Wagers. Give 'em to Jeremiah."

Money was being counted out all around and Blister looked to me and said, "You in?"

It was the first time I'd been included among them. Natural enough I dug out the last bills I had in my pocket. "Why they call you Blister?"

Annette answered. "On account he shows up when the work's done. I got a dollar says I can whup the winner."

I pinched my bills. "These here is on Annette."

A chant started and Youn and Blister took off their guns. Youn bent until his palms lay flat on the rock. Blister called him all sorts of names, mostly having to do with his people being short and slow of mind. The words was cruel but the game was in good fun. Youn stood and rolled his neck. "Your tongue run many miles. Wear you down."

Their fight was short. Blister started with a good leg sweep that caught us all by surprise and Youn hit the rock hard. Blister was upon him and shouting as he wrestled, "See? See?

A Chinaman ain't nothing special!"

What Youn did next happened so fast some boys missed it. By a miracle of bending Youn hooked his heel around Blister's neck. The bigger man smashed backward into the rock. Youn rose and embraced Blister in such a manner that the man's knees was about his face. Blister fought but it was already too late. The pain was written upon him. He had no move and the fight was over that quick.

The boys fell down with laughter. I was among them. To see bigmouthed Blister deflated so quick was high pleasure.

Annette handed me her gun belt. She shed her coat and I took that too. She spat out her tobacco.

Youn was collecting his money. "Chinaman win! See! Chinaman best."

Blister was rubbing out his shoulder.

The one they called Carlos called, "These dollars is on Annette!"

"Youn," Annette called. "Put that money on this here fight."

Youn turned and studied her. He put his money in his pocket and said, "No fight girl."

"Bullshit," Annette said. "You fighting me."

He shook his head. "Chinese no hit girl."

"You in America now." Annette punched him in the nose.

All of us gasped at the sight. The men started pushing at one another with the speed of it. A circle formed at once. Blister said,

"Get her, Youn. Hit her back."

Youn wiped the blood from his nose. He spat more blood to the ground. "I no fight Boss." He held his finger at me and said, "You fight her."

The boys erupted in cheers. Boys who had claimed to only hold a nickel in their pockets now pulled wads of cash from their boots and hats. Someone pushed me from behind. I stumbled into the center of the circle.

Annette smiled. She cracked her knuckles. She rolled her neck. She had a few inches on me and every belief she would win.

"How about we shoot?" I said. "I wager you can't hit that . . ." I looked out over the sage for a target.

"No lead," Annette said. "I aim to beat you with my fists."

The boys started a chant.

One of them barked, "Take off your clothes!"

Annette kneed that man in the stones and everyone laughed at his expense. The chanting grew louder. "Fight, fight, fight."

She come to me and put her hand on my shoulder and her lips to my ear and she whispered, "To hell with these nimwits. I'll hit you and you go down and we'll split the winnings."

Something about her assumption that I would throw a fight so she might come out its victor convinced me. I shed my pistols. I shed my coat. I tossed my hat to Youn. I was ready to earn my place among them.

Annette come at me and I ducked and hit her square in the belly. She buckled with the surprise of it and I could've hit her again but I was amazed at what I just done. I hadn't thought of it, I had only witnessed it occurring. Maybe it was the drilling led by Drummond rising now like instinct.

Annette was on a knee. She looked up at me and smiled. There wasn't no anger between us, it was something else. I backed from her. I readied myself. I feared what she might deliver.

She seized me in a grapple and dropped me to the rock. She climbed up my length and I knew then that Annette had won many a rumble with men bigger than me. She drove her forearm into my throat and kneed me and pummeled my abdomen. She was laughing as she done it.

I got a hand free and drove it up under her ribs and she let me roll loose and stand up. But she was ready and her blow hit me square in the jaw and my head rung as if I had fired a pistol in a holehouse. She could've ended it right then. I was staggering and blurred and unsure of the season. Anyone could've called the fight.

But the men cheered.

Annette blurred into four. They all said in unison, "Now that we's warmed up."

I shook the dizzy from my vision and put out my fists. She was right there within reach. When she come with a wide right I delivered a jab to the nose and blood come over her lips. Maybe she let me hit her, I don't know. She licked the blood. She laughed. She made like she would strike again but then swept my leg out and I was down. She was upon me and wrapping me up tight and I couldn't free my back from the earth.

The boys counted it out, and then it was over. I had lost. There come a great chorus from their ranks.

Annette helped me up and put her arm around me and blew the blood from her nose. She was panting and laughing and she said, "You don't fight like no girl."

I spat blood. "What a girl fight like?"

"Loud. Afraid to punch so they claw. Pull your damn hair out if you let them. Ain't a good time. That was a good time."

The boys slapped us on the backs and one ruffed my hair. Another replaced my hat. Blister handed me my pistols. Blister who had regarded me with cold eyes since my arrival now said, "Good show, Jess."

Money was paid out all around and Annette took up her winnings and stuffed them in her pocket and put on her hat. I didn't hear my brother but I saw the boys go straight and turn toward the trail. Their laughter was gone. "Howdy, Patrón."

Noah's thumb was hooked on his holster.

Blister said, "We was just passing some time is all, Patrón."

Noah walked past them and looked on me. He put a pinkie to the blood on my chin. He turned on the boys. "Which one of you was hitting on my sister?"

A raven sailed by and cawed. It was the only sound for a thousand miles.

"Huh?" Noah barked. I will admit it warmed me some to see him take such offense. He looked in the eyes of each man one at a time.

"I just tripped and fell is all," I said.

The boys laughed, then caught themselves. Noah took Blister by his collar. Blister had fresh blood on his brow.

"It was me," Annette said. "I done beat up your sister. And I liked it too."

Noah come to stand before Annette, and the boys backed off. Noah chewed the plug in his mouth and their faces wasn't twelve inches apart. Annette didn't flinch. Finally he spat to the side and offered his hand.

"Well, I guess I owe you my thanks then. That girl's been needing a whupping. Ain't that right, sister?" His eyes was all sunshine. He draped his arm around Annette. "With a face like that, a blow will only improve its symmetry."

A bottle was passed to me then and I took a pull. The boys was laughing and pushing.

Annette's eyes was on me.

After that day I was welcome among the boys, and I took to playing cards with them during the dull hours. I wasn't never no good at poker and so I come to pay out most of the gold nuggets I stole from the Governor. At other junctions I won back some of the nuggets with my shooting, both the quickdraw and the distance. The boys pushed me in ways they didn't Annette and cracked jokes at my expense. But if a bottle was procured, it come my way. When there was liquor enough they was eager to share stories too, most of them about my brother, about funny things he done, or great shots he made, or in hushed voices how he had changed since Jane come around. They was careful not to talk ill of Jane, least not around me.

I believe they was, to a boy, afraid to be without the protections of my big brother. In that, we was the same.

The days turned colder and the nights began to freeze and I knew it was this time of year when Pa had passed, and I suspected the very date of his demise was upon us now or would be soon. I thought often of him. Not often of his body no more, but of the man he was in that brief window without syrup. That was the man I carried now. Yet what name was I to call that man?

One afternoon I tacked up Ingrid and went looking for my brother. It was warm that day and the sky was without a cloud. The wind was gentle from the west. We'd been holed up long enough that I was starting to itch. I was also wondering about the wisdom of wintering so high in the mountains. The Rock would be beset by snows soon and our animals would not have access to graze.

Noah's mount had a peculiar rear shoe which made picking his sign easy enough. I cut it on foot, and then swung up and walked Ingrid along the trail, leaning over the horn to watch the tracks.

They led across the valley and to a canyon cut in the bright rock surrounding us. There we hit aspen and the smell of morning dew. The grass along the canyon floor was still deep green and I could see sign from deer as well as antelope. Overhead, a golden eagle watched from its perch on the wall. All the little critters was hidden and on guard.

I found Noah at the head of the canyon, where the water trickled down a narrow coulee that only a goat could climb. At first I saw Blackie. The animal had a mouthful of grass and was broadside watching us, not chewing. Ingrid liked the looks of that and began to trot, and Blackie put her head back to graze.

Noah called from above. There was a ledge about twenty feet off the meadow. "Nice, ain't it?" His voice echoed like a shot. "Nothing like this back home."

"If you looking for lonesome, brother, say the word."

"Nah. Join me. I've known plenty of lonesome."

I removed Ingrid's bridle so she might eat unencumbered, and then picked my way up the crag toward my brother. It was a hard climb and he met me at the edge with a hand.

"I was just giving thanks to our Maker in my own way. Strong medicine in the artful contours of this world He built us."

Out of habit I reached for my tobacco.

"Annette got you smoking rollies, I see."

"Gives my hands something to do. I prefer working to all this sitting still." I offered him the pouch and he took it.

"Too many idle hours in banditry."

We twisted our smokes in silence.

"I used to be always planning the next heist. I was accumulating bills like I was accumulating pride, and pride is a deadly sin. In truth, what does a dollar buy you anyhow? Nah, in this world a dollar is a fool's bait."

"I think you can only say that when you got plenty of them dollars stashed about."

"Dollars is shallow. I just knew there had to be something deeper than dollars in this world." He flicked a match and sparked his cigarette and then mine. "Second to the Lord's good graces is the freedom to ride

459

unseen."

I thought that one over. It was Pa who come to mind, Pa and his true name, our true name. He had ridden free under a new name. I still hadn't decided if or when to tell my brother the burdensome news that his name was not Harney.

"What's the long view, brother? What happens after winter?"

He drew a breath and nodded. "Well, I ain't sure yet, but I know we must move on from these mountains. Maybe we can return in five or ten years, but until then we got to find something new. But I don't want the newspapers talking like we fled. I need to trust in the Lord on the matter, frankly."

"Brother?"

"What is it? Say it."

"If He's Lord over us, why does it matter if we trust or not? He's still the Lord either way."

He looked on me as if for the first time. "Sister, trust is what opens the gates to our eternal reward in Heaven."

"Heaven," I said. "Someplace outside this place." I drew on my cigarette and watched the smoke move down on the morning chill. "But look about this canyon, brother. Tell me this ain't Heaven enough for one life."

"Praise the Lord," my brother said. "You ever think of them together in Heaven? Ma and Pa?"

460

"I try."

His voice went low. "I don't remember her face no more, Jess. Children born now will have photographs, they won't even need memory to know their people. That'll change this world."

"You always so sure, brother. I wish I was sure like you. My sure comes and goes. Mostly it goes."

He smiled. "I too wavered, for a lot of years in fact. Now I see that even the doubting was part of His vision for me."

I drew a pocket bottle Annette had slipped me.

"Ain't it early for liquor?"

I took a little draw and passed it through my teeth and looked to the eagle on his rock. Just as my eye found him, he lifted into flight. His shadow tracked the canyon wall and then was gone. Not a moment later, a squirrel appeared atop a rock. Birds began chirping from every crack. A rabbit hopped out from its bush. This world waits on the eagle to look away.

"I don't like the notion of us wintering here, brother. Snows could be ten feet deep, you don't know."

"The Lord knows."

"You sure? There's a lot of lives down there counting on you."

"Counting on the Lord," he said. "I am but a humble servant."

I took a pull of the bottle and drew my Peacemaker and dumped the shells and set about reloading them. Something to do with my hands. "I ain't sure about Heaven, brother, but I know for certain we make our own hell."

On Sundays the folks gathered to make a big breakfast of eggs and bacon and biscuits. It was the one meal when the boys and the folks ate together. A young couple without children, called the Cherrys, was always the first outside on Sundays. Mr. Cherry took it upon himself to start a fire in the hearth and Mrs. Cherry would start the children singing. Soon folks would sing hymns and preaching songs and in time the boys would join the tunes with their instruments and little children would get their first lessons on the guitar or fiddle. Dogs put their wet noses to hands and was rewarded with crumbs. Hens too watched us from the edge, and when the dogs and the children was otherwise engaged, them birds rushed by twos toward a bowl left unattended.

It was Noah's arrival beside the fire that commenced Sabbath services. He donned a dark woolen suit and a flat-brimmed hat and a pair of shiny boots. When folks saw him coming they quieted their children and took seats before the fire. The boys put aside their instruments and sat cross-legged upon the ground and snuffed their smokes. There come only the chatter of children and the whinnying of horses at play. Doves cooed from the Rock and swallows careened. The autumn sunlight was welcome on our skin.

Noah began his sermons by taking up a flame from the fire and touching it to a wax candle. Then he produced a small jar of Old World spices from his pocket and this he sent along from person to person. Men and women alike smelled the contents with their eyes shut to this world. As they done so Noah strummed his guitar.

I will admit it was easy to believe when I looked upon my brother before us. His was a powerful tonic. He was quick witted and beautiful and it was easy to think him smarter than the lot of us. If a man of his caliber could be so sure, then we was fools to hold any doubt at all.

Noah turned his face toward the heavens. All us did. He spoke with his eyes wide open. "*Hear* us, Lord, *hear* our humble tribute. We desire only your guidance and your forgiveness."

"Yes!" Mr. Travis proclaimed. "Say it new!"

Annette chipped a scab from her knuckle. When she saw me watching she raised an eyebrow and yawned.

Noah preached, "Remember that *blessed* are ye, when men shall revile you, and persecute you, and shall say all manner of *evil*

463

against you falsely, for my sake. Matthew tells us to *rejoice,* and be exceedingly glad, for great is your reward in *Heaven,* for so persecuted they the prophets which were before you."

"Amen!"

I noticed Constance had not yet joined us on this particular Sabbath. She had been among the first outside on the other Sundays. Her cottage door was shut.

Blister was admiring his pistol. He cocked the hammer and let the hammer down until he felt a presence and looked up to see me watching. He put the pistol back in his holster and looked again upon my brother, hands folded in his lap.

"There is a *valley* in our realm, I walk about it in my dreams, where the *grass* grows overhead and *cattle* have not yet trod. This valley is wide enough to hold us all and our children and our children's children and so forth until the Lord again sends His *son* to us." Noah held out his fist as if it contained this valley. "But we *cannot* enter our valley until we destroy Mammon's army and *seize* control of his gate, for the Lord has saved His *greatest* earthly reward for His bravest and most faithful and most humble servants." He opened his fist and dust fluttered to the ground. "The *Lord* shall reveal our moment."

I couldn't help myself. I asked, "Where is this valley, brother?"

His eyes found me. He stepped closer. He took hold of my arm and lifted me from where I sat.

Annette picked food from her teeth. She was watching this.

He said, "It is inside you right now! It is inside all of us!"

All this time Noah had held the Bible and now he lifted it and thumbed to the page marked with a slip of paper. I had witnessed Jane reading him this passage the night before and the morning before that. He knew some words but his powers of mind lay in memorization. His true gift was in the delivery. Now he held the book before him as if reading the words direct. Even his eyes moved as if he was reading.

After services I visited Constance. She was in bed reading a book. There was no mistaking the fact she was pale in the face with sunken eyes, and when she saw me she tossed the book aside without concern for losing her page.

"Good story?"

"Why does every book end in a wedding or funeral?"

"Which do you prefer?"

"Neither," she said. "Both are beginnings."

"What do you want to read?" I had seen a stack of books in the storehouse. I could get her one. It was something I could offer her.

"I want a love story that doesn't involve a king," she said. Neither of us spoke a time. I took a seat on the bed next to her.

"There is something . . . ," she began in a new voice. "Something I want to tell you. Jane already knows. Jane was the one who understood the signs. But I want to tell someone. I want to tell you."

"I'm listening."

"Jess, I am with child."

"With child?"

"Yes. Will's child."

I couldn't help but smile at such bright news — a new baby coming to this world, Constance a mother.

She told me all about these headaches she was having, about how the old happy smell of horses was now offensive to her nose. She had upchucked one noon, and Jane had known right off what was afoot. "If Will . . . Our plan had been to be married just as soon as we reached New York, married under a new name. They allow such marriages in New York. That was the plan even before. Those nights with him, I believed — it sounds queer, I know, but I believed us to already be married, married in the Lord's eyes. Married in the manner that counts most, by the heart."

I took a breath and pondered. This rock was so very far from any midwife or doctor. The child would be born in May or June.

466

Would the snows this high be melted by then? "Will lives on. So I should be purely happy. . . . I should be, shouldn't I? But I keep thinking, I can't stop. What am I to do now? With this child but without him?"

I thought of them in any town, a dark child with a white woman. Would it be any easier, a dark man and a white woman?

Constance said, "Will would know what to do. If only we had slipped away one night, or on a casual errand. So many times we might have vanished together! Will would know his child. Will would be a father. Will would know what to do. Us, together." She wiped the tears from her eyes. "You know what that house was like. I mean . . . Should I have anticipated what Father was capable of? I think about it instead of sleeping. Every moment that we might have escaped together. Why didn't we escape?"

She looked up into my eyes. "Your brother thought to do it at the ball. He said all the guests would add a level of confusion to the getaway."

For a long minute neither of us spoke.

I said, "You don't think that's the real reason he wanted to try at the ball, do you? I mean, Pearlsville at midday got plenty of crowds to confuse things too."

She looked to her lap. "I don't know. Harney is the one who understands such matters."

"But you doubt," I said. "I can see it in your face."

Constance drew a big breath and let it out. "I don't want to talk about this."

"Okay," I said. I stood from the bed. I put my hat back on.

"Jess?"

"Yeah?"

"I think he wanted an audience. I think he wanted the newspapermen present. I think he wanted the story told."

Jane spent most of her weekly hours with the children in the big house. A pair of mothers assisted but nobody had Jane's knowledge of reading and arithmetic and Bible studies so it was natural for her to be the teacher and the headmaster. There was tablets stacked near the window and chalk enough for a lifetime.

That week the older students used their skills to write a story on a scroll. Jane brought it home and read it to herself in the firelight. She was making notes. Her script was tight and quick and never dipped or climbed from its straight path. When I had asked her about Constance's child, Jane glowed. "Isn't it amazing news! But keep it close, Jess, for her sake. Constance is early yet, and these things don't always keep. The fewer who know, the easier the recovery, should the Lord decide to take that tiny soul home."

Now I said, "Jane, you write like you got

schooling."

She answered without looking up. "Any skill can be learned."

"Where did you learn it?"

"My mother," she said. Her eyes found me. "When my father passed, it was on me to take a job at the schoolhouse. I was barely older than the students."

"Where was that?"

Noah interrupted, "Am I in the story them kids is writing?"

"Here. Read it yourself," Jane said. "You could use the practice."

"You read it to me."

"You will see it soon enough." She smiled. "It is a play. Won't it be nice to see these children put on a performance? They will beam with confidence and joy. They so need confidence, these children."

My brother went back to cleaning his pistol.

I said to him, "Why do you lead them all to believe you can read?"

He looked on me. Then to Jane and back to me. "I can read."

For a long moment our eyes held the other's.

Then Jane said, "Here, I will read it out loud for the both of you. Okay?"

Annette joined me on the rim for my stint of guard duty. We sat upon the stone wall built on the edge with rifles lay across our laps.

469

The breeze was light that day, light enough we could twist smokes without shielding the tobacco with our bodies.

Her match lit both, then we watched that match flutter and tumble into air until it grew too small to see. We drew in smoke.

"What you got in your hop?" Annette asked.

I nodded toward Constance's cottage. Jane was there bringing warm food. I said, "You know she's pregnant."

Annette exhaled from her nose. "I know. You sound surprised."

"You ain't?"

She smiled. "Sometimes you got this streak of being young in the ways of the world, you know it?"

I looked at my hands.

"Oh, quit it," she said. "Don't think so much."

"I ain't thinking."

"You get this look on your face. When you thinking. Like you bit into a sour old beetle." Her hand reached across the divide between us. But she withdrew the hand before it touched my marks.

In the distance our few head of cattle lounged and swat at the flies taunting them.

I asked her, "Do the men you killed ever haunt you? They keep you up at night?"

She didn't answer at first but then she said, "I come up here in the dark, and listen."

"What do you listen for?"

470

She looked at the end of her cigarette. She brushed the ash from it against her chaps. "I ain't sure."

Ingrid and me needed free that afternoon. It was our first romp in some days. We rode across the sage and then along the cliffs till we found a gap that allowed us into a new canyon.

I heard aspen fluttering long before I saw it. When we come into the grove there was a pool of water big as a wagon with all manner of critter sign coming in and out, but not a single boot track. Ingrid drank and I took up a handful and put it to my lips. I shed my hat and passed the water through my hair. I drew a full breath, and it felt like the first time.

A magpie landed in the branches overhead. He didn't call but only turned one eye down on me. He was there to drink.

I looked up at his white belly and his long black tail. He hopped lower, testing me. I wondered why God would make a lowly scavenger as beautiful as them magpies. I wondered what sense that made. I wondered if I still believed there was any sense to this world at all.

The magpie dropped to the water's edge and put his beak to it. I left that girl out to be consumed by his kind. They picked at her until the coyotes come to chase them off. But after the coyotes ate their fill it was the magpie who returned to finish what remained. By then her bones was scattered. Her hair. By then she was everywhere, nowhere.

I was the only person in this world who knew what had come of her. I alone knew the end of her story. But only its final line.

That night Jane suppered with Constance. Constance had hardly left her cottage in days, and Jane herself had fallen into some mood. She wasn't bursting with talk like normal.

So that left Noah and me alone in the house. He was in a spry humor and offered a longer than typical prayer before saying amen and lifting his fork. He said, "I remember you as a baby. I remember the weight of you in my lap. The way you stopped crying when I gave you your finger to chew on. You remember anything about being a baby?"

"No. First thing I remember is you holding Pa's gun."

"First thing I remember," he began.

"What?"

"Her. Her singing to me. She sang to me in Spanish."

We didn't say nothing for a time. We stared into our steaming food. Stirred it about.

He said, "She talked them words when it was just us, when Pa was gone off in the hills. I tried to speak her language with you. I can't recall even a word of it now."

He took a bite, and I did too, but the food

didn't sit right with Ma in the room.

He shook his head. "She would've loved this place. He was the hermit. Ma always missed her people. She would've loved living so close to other families. All these children. That's what she wanted. To live among friends. She was lonesome there in that place. He made her lonesome. Just like he made us lonesome."

"Brother, you worried about that baby Constance is growing? I mean, this is a long way from any doctor. What if the snows ain't cleared by then? What if she sets to bleeding?"

"Let's keep it happy tonight," he said while chewing a mouthful. He was always taking too big a bite.

"I just asking questions is all."

"Well, don't sour a good mood. Don't you see? This here is the start of the golden days for us. Trust me. I've asked all the questions and more, for both of us."

"Brother, did the Lord tell you it's all going to work out?"

"Indeed," he said. "He sang it to me."

"You sure it was the Lord singing?"

He laughed. He rocked back in his chair. He choked a little and coughed and wiped his lips with a napkin Jane had laid out for the purpose. "Oh, Jess. I'll let that one go. But I don't like this talk from you, of all people."

I pushed my plate away. "We's too high in these mountains, brother. It is water that carved this place. Snowmelt. This valley is going to catch the clouds. I been studying the contours. It's clear as day that this place collects snow."

Now he set his fork to the table. "Jess. I warned you. Leave it."

"Brother."

"Sis."

I looked him in the eye. "You sure when you talk to God it ain't your own voice you hear echoing back?"

He swung to slap me, but I blocked his arm. I leapt to standing and my legs bumped the table and my plate slipped to the floor.

"You ain't never once tried to hit me," I said.

He blinked. He seemed more surprised than me even. On his face was a familiar mix of heat and regret.

"You look like him, you know."

He pointed to the door. "Go on. I don't need this."

I bent to clean the plate and food from the floor so Jane wouldn't have to but his voice commanded I leave.

"You kicking me out?"

He blinked. He looked to his hand. I didn't know what he was going to say.

I took my bedroll from the corner and my hat from the peg. I didn't stop at the door.

■ ■ ■ ■

I took my roll to Annette's place and rapped twice. The cabin wasn't much bigger than her bed and a woodstove but she had drug in a pair of chairs and kicked clean one of them now. "Wondered when you'd get sick of them two. They probably go at it like pine squirrels."

She passed a hand through her sleepy hair. She was all the time sleeping when the mood struck, daytime, morning, whenever. Here it was the supper hour and I'd woke her. She lifted a bottle from the floor and took a swig, wiped her mouth with the back of her hand.

"I can sleep in the bunkhouse," I said.

She passed me the bottle. "Nah. Roll out your things. You don't want sleep in that barnyard. This place got plenty of room for two."

Her banjo hung from pegs above the door where most would hang their rifle. Her Winchester lay on the bed. Some flies bumped against the window.

She coughed and spat what come up. "I ain't cleaning the place," she said.

"That ain't what I'm thinking," I said.

"What you thinking then?"

I nodded at the banjo over the door. "You teach me?"

She smiled. "That there is the third-best

thing about this business. Second best is the whiskey."

"What's the first best?"

"Getting loose with a bag of gold. That or killing bastards. The two sorta tie for first." She took back the bottle. "Go on. Throw your bedding aside and let's start us a tune."

Days passed and the wind grew colder with each one. Noah and me kept our distance. It was easy enough to avoid him. I thought of Pa and my brother those years before, keeping to opposite ends of the spread. That saddened me, but I was too prideful to apologize.

I loved that banjo. Only thing I loved more was watching Annette play it with her eyes shut. Those slow days, the Rock was full of song from noon on.

The boys joined us one evening when Annette and me was on her porch playing. There was wind and the sun went down quick and then a nighttime stillness come over the Rock. The Wild Bunch brought chairs and bottles and lit a fire on the ground for light and took turns pulling and playing. We was getting sloppy wet and our songs was turning to howls. The folks shut tight their doors and drew closed the curtains. Lanterns shone from the windows but then those started going out one by one and still we played on. The boys all knew the same tunes, and they could keep the strings humming without cease. Once I finally had too much whiskey in me for keeping pace, I give up and started dancing.

The fire was licking head high and then all at once it was coals. Ash was falling.

I looked to Annette, both of her. She hollered, "Howdy, pardner!"

When I turned, Noah was over my shoulder.

"Quit this mayhem!" he said. "It's near morning and these children are trying to sleep."

Annette done a slow nod. "Berry true."

Noah hit my shoulder. "What you got to say for yourself, drinking like this?"

I looked about. All the boys still awake was watching me. I looked to Noah. "Sorry, Pa?"

At this the Wild Bunch broke into mad laughter. Boys fell backward off their stools. Annette went face-first.

Then it was just two of us, Annette and me, on her porch and dawn was warming the sky. We was twisting up smokes with limited success. Took both us to hold the match still enough that it might catch the tobacco, my hand over hers.

I remember looking over the cigarette in my lips, over the match wavering near it, and into the flame flickering within Annette's eyes. Her holster was against my thigh. I was wet but remember every detail.

We tumbled onto her mattress. Most the whiskey had spilled out, we was already sick with it. I remember the two of us laying there clinging to the mattress like it was some manner of raft and we was cast out upon a violent sea.

That's where she took hold of my hand for the first time. That's how I fell asleep, Annette clinging to me.

The morning alit with the force of dry mouth and headache. For me anyhow. Annette woke as she done any other morning, with cursing and kicking around for a bottle.

"What is it?" I asked.

"I do believe we drank up the last of the whiskey."

"That might be for the better."

"Don't blaspheme," she moaned. "I ain't made for dry."

She put some fresh wood to the stove and then put a pot of water on it for coffee and then she sat down in her chair. "I ain't looking forward to this day."

Annette's hair was ragged with sleep and now she roughed at the tangles dust and dreams had left.

I watched her move about from bed. Even then I was trying to hold on to every moment.

There wasn't no clear sense of what work we was to do that day. I asked Annette if she

might like to ride. I was seeing us making
our way into the forest and maybe having a
meal by some water, and maybe finding our
way to a store of liquor. I didn't think Annette
would have no trouble with this plan, but she
only shook her head. She was watching
Noah's cabin as I asked her.

"Why not?"

"We don't want no tracks on the road."

"So we'll cut through the timbers."

"Nah, best keep close."

"Come on," I begged. "Let's go get us some
whiskey. He won't hardly notice if we's here
or gone."

She looked on me. "I ain't leaving."

I spent that morning with the Wild Bunch
bucking up firewood. The boys was restless
and Annette saw they needed some hard
labor in want of a gunfight.

She and me unbelted our guns and took up
either side of a saw. The chips flew and the
sweat soaked through our shirts. It was good
to sweat out that whiskey. The labor set my
body right again. A bucket come around and
I tinned out some water. Poured one over my
face.

The boys rolled free the rounds and put
axes through them. Others stacked the quarters in waist-high walls against the lees of
each house. They was offerings in a way, for
keeping up the children the night before. The

boys didn't bother stacking their own supply of wood for burning in the bunkhouse, but instead left a heap that near blocked the only entrance.

Annette's shirt was unbuttoned partway down, her hat was off, and wood chips clung to her skin. "Nah," she said, seeing that heap. "Blister, Pale Jay. Stack that pretty. Get it under the lee so the rain don't fall on it."

"Why us?" Blister complained. "You always picking on the white boys."

Annette stood tall and glared. "White or purple, don't step in shit if you don't want to clean it off your boot."

Blister and Pale Jay got to stacking without another word of protest.

After the wood was done, Annette set the boys to cleaning out the bunkhouse and another crew to cleaning and reordering the storehouse. I was grateful when it come my turn for guard duty. Up top it was just a rifle, silence, and a long view.

As the sun set Annette and me was outside on chairs trying to think of something other than whiskey and the shortage of it. We was in a sorry way. All we did was quarrel. We argued about how much snow would fall come winter, about how much feed we'd need for the horses, about the right way to skewer a grouse. We grew weary of talking, and then we grew weary of silence.

480

She said out of nowhere, "We shouldn't have drank it all at once."

"Don't. We promised not to talk of whiskey."

I don't think she thought about it at all. At the word "whiskey" she kicked at me and I fell off my chair.

"Well, to hell with you if 'n you gonna be a rag!" I stood up and dusted myself off

She was standing now too. "Rag?"

"Yeah," I said. "You heard me. Rag." I tried to walk past her. I don't know where I would've gone. I didn't want to be away from her. She kicked my foot in midstep and shoved me.

I didn't tumble but nearly.

I looked back on her there laughing at me. We was both cracked with drought, and the boredom drought delivers. Natural enough I tackled her.

We rolled in the dirt and beat on each other a time. I hit her guts and she drove an elbow into my lip. She punched and I kneed and it was too serious for moaning or crying or anything but gritting your teeth and venting the heat that built up.

But then we was worn out and rolled free of each other and laid there in the dirt too sick to fight, too sore to work, too dry to laugh.

Annette was the first to stand. She offered me a hand, but I didn't take it. I stood my own self up. I wiped the blood from my lip with a knuckle.

"Come on."

I followed her across the meadow. "What you got in mind now?"

I stood guard at the entrance to the storehouse while she poked around for a bottle that might've been misplaced or otherwise hid. She reappeared with something held under her arm. "Hurry," she said.

I followed her to the lee of her cabin. But it wasn't whiskey she carried. It was a small satchel of sugar.

"Damn it to hell," I moaned.

"No," she said. "It helps. Like this." She licked her finger and put it to the bag.

"I'm so thirsty. I need me some water."

"To hell with water," she said. "Water won't touch what you suffer. Our only hope is sugar."

I licked my finger and dipped it, and she was right. Somehow the sugar quenched the desert inside me. "What will we do when its gone?"

She looked about. "Honest? This ain't a situation I find myself in regular."

I poured a pot of water while Annette split kindling.

After, she took off her shirt and then her pants and hung them behind the stove to dry. They was crusted with old sweat. She moved about that room in only her boots. And then she took them off too and sat in her chair. I didn't dare look straight. From the corner of my eye I saw the old chips and divots in her flesh, a thousand wounds healed crooked. Her toes was bent from long days in riding boots. She said, "Ain't you going to strip down? Can't rag off if you still wearing your stinky old clothes."

I didn't want to make no issue about keeping on my clothes. I didn't want her to see that being bare scared me. So I stripped down and hung my things from the wall behind the stove as she done. I pulled up the other chair like it wasn't no big deal and asked after the sugar so I'd have something to busy my hands. It was the first time I'd ever been bare before another.

"Pass me that rag first. Is the water hot?"

I dipped my finger in the pot. "You could try it."

"I don't want to if it ain't hot. I aim to scold off this drought."

"Well, it ain't hot."

Annette sat back. She sighed. "You gonna pass me the sugar or I gotta kill you for it?"

She licked a pair of fingers and buried them in the satchel and then sucked them clean like they was short ribs. I reached and took the bag for my own self and done the same. I sat back in my chair. "Damn it, give me the tobacco."

She tossed me the pouch.

I rolled up one but it broke and so I dumped its guts back in the pouch and started again.

"You a fool at rolling them things."

"I am not. Not on a given day."

"Look at them fingers. They clumsy as clubs. Here." She leaned across me and took back the pouch. I let her take it. My fingers was too nervous for careful work. She rolled us two in no time. "See, ain't hard. You just got to own your fingers is all."

She sparked a match and cupped her hand over it and leaned and lit my smoke and then hers and then waved out the match and flicked it into the corner. She was all the time lighting my smokes. I didn't recall ever seeing her light nobody else's smokes.

That's what I was thinking but what I said was, "Don't you worry you gonna burn down this place flicking matches like that?"

"Nah." She was sitting close enough that I could smell her skin. Like dust before a thunderstorm, with some cedar in the mix. She was going at the sugar, three fingers at a time now, and I wanted it to rain.

Her skin wasn't so different in hue. Not so different from the girl I left out.

"Why you looking on me like that?" she said in that voice of hers heavy with Indian sounds.

Somebody loved that girl I left out.

Without the whiskey to dilute it or the uniform to dam it, what I done flooded through me. Who was I to feel anything joyous in this life after I stole from that girl? After I stole that girl from one who loved her?

Annette frowned. Her cigarette burned unsmoked. She pushed the sugar to me but I was too far gone now. "It's okay," she said. "There's more whiskey in the world. We just got to find it is all."

"I ain't told you this. I ain't told nobody."

"What ain't you told nobody?"

I had spent these months trying never to think of that girl. But she was always there, lurking just out of sight. And all my dodging had done nothing to age or dim her. I know it don't make no sense, but I swear, on that night with Annette, the girl was in the room with us. She was sitting there and she too was bare to the world. Her ribs shown from where the magpie picked. Her eyes was gone, just dark holes, looking.

"I killed her, a girl, younger than us. I shot her from behind. She was stealing Ingrid and I broke open her head."

The girl put her fingers in her sockets and removed the top of her skull as my bullet had.

Annette shrugged. "Some problems only a bullet can solve."

"You don't get it. I left her out for the scavengers. I just left her. No grave or nothing."

485

Annette licked her fingers. "A grave ain't for the dead. They work good, but if you miss your chance, no sense beating yourself over it. It's all the same far as the dead concerned."

"I killed her and I don't know nothing about her."

She waved to clear the smoke between us. She leaned forward and rested her elbows on her knees. "If 'n she was stealing your horse, she was prepared for what might come. She mighta done worse for you, you don't know."

"That don't make me feel no better."

She laughed. "Shit. What makes you think you get to feel better? Listen, you didn't make the rules of this world. You was just dropped in it. What you and me know that the boys out there don't is that we ain't nothing special. Nothing we do will matter either way." She slapped my knee. "That there is good news. That there means you and me is freer than wind. We look after our own selves. We look out for each other."

I remembered the cigarette in my fingers and drew from it. The heat of the ember warmed my fingertips and dried my eyes. "It must matter."

"Folks put too much stock in death. It don't matter. You die, I die, we all die. You wanna die as some old hag all busted up and no teeth? Not me. I wanna die in a gunfight. I wanna die at the peak of living. You know?" She touched my knee. "Only one thing in this world better than a gunfight, and it's harder yet to come by."

"How can you say such awful things?"

"You so damn dramatical when you straight. I ain't sure I like you without whiskey." She winked and leaned past me and dipped her finger in the water upon the stove. "Here, turn around."

"What?"

"Just do it." She dunked a rag in the hot water. "Go on now. Have some sugar and then turn around. This here rag is getting colder by the second."

I done as she asked and she put the hot cloth to my neck. The water run down my front and back at once, its warm streaks splattering on the floor. The cloth passed down my shoulders. Its course was slow and its warmth spread through me.

She dipped the cloth again and wrung it out and put it to my neck. "Now turn around so I can get at your front."

"I'll do my front," I said matter-of-fact as if we was talking about cleaning stalls. In truth my heart was pounding louder than fists on a door. "I can reach my front just fine."

"You sure?" She passed her finger over my marks.

"No, I ain't."

When she was done she dropped the rag in the pot and sat back and drew from a cigarette. Her eyes studied my person.

487

"Your turn. Do my back. And do like you mean it. Do like I done yours. Put some feeling into it. This is what we got. Make it matter. All that out there? It don't matter. Not like this."

I dipped the cloth in the water and then wrung it out and she said, "No. Don't wring it out. I want it to run all over me. I want to feel it everywhere."

She turned and spread her arms and I saw wounds to her flesh old as she was. Craters and faults where I was smooth. I put the cloth to them and let the water run about her and she sighed at its heat. "More," she said. "I want it everywhere." Her fingers come up sparkling in sugar and she took them in her mouth.

"They tell me I was three years old when the soldiers come through camp," she said to the table. "They tell me . . . I don't remember nothing. None of it." She looked at me now. "But sometimes if all goes still and there ain't nothing to chase and no whiskey to drink dry, well sometimes the smell comes back to me, and then I hear everything I didn't see. I hear my ma's voice. That morning never stops chasing me even though I ain't got no memories of it."

I put the cloth back in the pot and brought it dripping to the skin of her chest. I passed it down that most ragged scar and rivers run her length and spilled upon the floor.

"Burn me with it. I ain't afraid of fire," she said.

I put the scolding cloth to her face and passed it over her brow and then about her eyes.

She said, "Make it hot and then open it and lay it over my face. I want sugar on my tongue and I want to feel that heat on my lips and everywhere all at once. Can you do that?"

I done that for her.

"What we gonna do for clothes?" I whispered when we was done.

She tossed the rag into the pot and water sloshed over the edge and went to hissing vapor. Even the air was wet now. She shrugged. "Maybe I should go ask Jane for a dress."

At this we laughed so hard we got to coughing.

We crawled under the warm quilt and listened to the cracking of the wood fire and for a long time neither of us said a word.

"If you ain't afraid of fire," I whispered, "what you afraid of?"

Her eyes opened. Tears glistened in the dark. "Honest?"

"Honest."

"Being without a side."

Even without whiskey, sleep always comes, and when it come for us it come deeper than in all my life before or since.

Annette was curled for warmth, her arms wrapped in the ancient posture of mother and child and lover and loved, and her breath was in my hair and we slept past the dawn and into the day. We rode the same dream from one day into the next.

Annette and me didn't have long together, but we did have deep.

It was Noah who finally woke us. He beat on the door. "You in there, Net?"

"Sure." Annette sat up and yawned, her arms out wide as if taking this whole world in her grasp. "Is it morning already?"

My brother's voice through the door, "It's damn near noon."

Annette looked on me. "Oops," she lipped. "Be right there, pardner."

"You seen my sister this morning?"

I waved my hand to say no. So Annette called, "You wanna come take a peek for your own self?"

There was a pause. "She on duty up top?"

Annette made a joshing face and I nearly laughed out loud. "Must be. Is her shift and all."

"You hurry up, Net. We's got to race Blackie against Youn's mare. I put it off last time but that Chinaman has got to talking madness again. Net?"

"Blackie'll show him." She winked at me. "Ain't nobody luckier than Blackie."

490

After he left, Annette pulled on her sweat-stiff jeans and tied her green bandanna about her neck and belted on her Remington. She smelled my stinky clothes on the line and shook her head.

"What's we gonna do?" I asked in a hushed voice.

"About the whiskey?"

"Yeah, about the whiskey."

"We got to get to town and stock up for winter."

"I'll talk to brother."

"We should wait on rain," she said. "Erase the tracks. Noah was sure about that."

"Might not be any rain this autumn. Might go straight to snow. It's got that feel about it."

She pulled her hat on low and tipped it to me. "All I know about today is I aim to get back here with you."

Nobody ever said nothing like that to me before. I didn't know how to say what I felt, so I punched her in the shoulder.

She made like she might tackle me, but then held up and smiled.

After Annette left I warmed my hands over the woodstove and smelled the brown water that still steamed on top. My mind was clean in a manner I wasn't accustomed to and I took that steam deep. It smelled of her, and it smelled also of the earth that had washed from us.

With my eyes closed I saw a garden, and us barefoot in it.

I found Noah outside the Rock with the boys, preparing to race Blackie against Youn's mare. I pushed him from behind and he turned with his hand on his pistol. "What in the name . . ."

"Howdy, brother."

"Don't go pushing me like that. I shoot too quick. You liable to end up aired out."

"I owed you one for slapping at me them nights before."

The boys was watching. They all had quit their talking and was staring at what I done.

Noah said, "Jess, you can't be pushing me."

"But I got your attention."

"Just say my name and you get my attention."

I spat. "All right, brother. I'm going to town today. These skies smell like snow, and I've seen the supplies and counted the mouths and I know we ain't got enough."

"You and Annette just want whiskey," he said.

"True. And I'll get you some of that rollie tobacco you favor. But it's flour and beans and salt pork we need. Let Annette and me go and we'll come back with a wagon full. We'll need six or eight more loads by my count, if we's to stay fed until that baby comes."

"Ten," he said. "We need ten loads."

"So let us get one, and also a feel for the heat on the roads."

He turned from me and looked toward Youn. "Now he's braiding that goddamn critter's . . . Come on now!" he shouted. "This ain't no beauty pageant! Let's race these animals!"

"Brother, you listening?"

He glanced on me but then give his attentions back to Youn. He hollered, "You think a braided tail will help her run faster? Nothing could help that pony!"

"Brother!"

"Have you seen the reward on our heads? No wagons until the rains come. I ain't bending, sister. Not for whiskey."

"What if the rains don't come? What if the snows come instead?"

"It'll rain any day now," he said, while looking at Youn.

"I don't understand you, brother. How you can game with all these folks counting on you."

He flicked off my hat. "Appreciate me for it, sister. I do the thinking so you don't have to. Now stop jabbering and watch me outpace Youn and that pony he treats like a girlfriend. I promise, you'll want to tell this story."

I found Annette and held the pink dress Jane had given me up to my body.

493

"What's this?" she asked.

"Ain't nothing more natural in the whole world than a husband and wife stocking up for winter."

A big old smile come across her face. "This his idea or yours?"

"The dress is my idea," I said. It was as close as I come to lying to her.

She looked about us. "I'm surprised he folded. You must hold some pretty high cards."

"Sister cards."

She laughed. She pointed with her thumb. "Let's pick me out some attire and do this right."

Annette wore a round hat and waxed coat that made her shoulders appear wider. I offered her a woolen beard but she refused it. She had removed her gun belt and hidden the pistols in the crevices of the wagon. Annette looked me up and down in that dress and bonnet and whistled. "Boy, howdy! Now that there is a lady."

"I hate pink."

"Don't hate it. It don't hate you." She felt the fabric between her fingers. "Don't move just yet. I want to remember this for some time."

We climbed atop the wagon. I wore a quilt over my legs to ward off the chill. I almost told her then, but I didn't. Maybe I worried

494

she'd pick him.

Annette clicked and gave the reins a flick and the wagon rolled. There come the welcome music of metal rims on stone and hooves on earth and the shifting mass of a hearty wagon. We rolled into the windblown sage. I thought of Ma and Pa crossing the mountains all them years before.

Our timing was right. Noah and the boys was off on the back side of the Rock.

"Where's your guns?" she asked.

"A wife never tells."

We was across the valley and out of sight when I said, "Give me some your rollie tobacco."

She looked me over. "That ain't no way for a gal to talk."

I thought on how Jane would ask. "Might I taste those smoky leaves you hard men so fancy? Trade you for a biscuit and jam."

Annette laughed.

I said, "Well, give it to me."

She shrugged. "I'm plum out. Tell me you got a pouch hidden somewhere."

"Plugs. But I'm in the mood for rollies."

Annette flicked the reins and sighed. "Maybe it's a sign. I've been trying to quit them rollies. They get their claws in you deep."

I retied my bonnet so it would conceal my marks. "Quit smokes? Good heavens, why?"

"I kind of think they make me smell a little queer."

"You don't say."

"My fingers mostly. I don't like my fingers smelling queer. I like them smelling like horse sweat or gunpowder."

We rode into the dark and as the moon rose and thrust shadows upon the earth I found myself full of contradictory notions. The wagon rocked and clanked and I spread preserves on bread and fed the bites into Annette's mouth. The lantern swung on its hook and the squeak of its handle set a fine rhythm to our travels.

We kept on without hardly a pause but to water the horses. We took double plugs to keep awake and stared out at the darkness. There come the sound of the creek for a time where it rushed on below. It faded off and then was gone and soon after we broke from the warmth of the pines and into the chill open and saw then the expanse of stars from horizon to horizon.

We needed supplies and we was out of whiskey, but in truth, I reckon, I wanted to know Annette outside the shadow cast by my brother.

"How'd you come to be the boss of those boys?" I asked. "They don't doubt you at all."

Annette shrugged. "They did at first. Doubted hard. But you ever seen a turkey in springtime? That's every boy you ever met."

"I guess I don't see your point."

"There ain't a turkey in the whole world who can stay puffed up all day, now is there? And after he lets down, he's always gonna be a touch unsure of his honest size. So that's when you show him."

"Show him what?"

"Show him that being boss is always knowing your true size."

We rolled into the dawn and come to stop before Pearlsville's limits, having earned no sleep and feeling in hard need of it. The city lay beneath matted smoke. The morning was uncommon still, without no breeze at all. Snow clouds loomed high overhead, and sound carried for miles. A door swung shut with a slam. A far-off dog barked.

I was worried Annette might hear the wild beat of my heart. I will admit I was scared to be back in this place where Greenie or Drummond or Tuss might be waiting around the next corner. This dress couldn't fool them.

"I need a drink," Annette said. "I need to stretch my goddamn legs and give my arse a rest. I'll take twenty days in a saddle to one in a wagon, tell you what. Where's the nearest whiskey anyhow?"

At the saloon Annette ordered a pair to even us out. The barkeep looked on us suspect and I tugged Annette's sleeve and said, "Ain't you gonna order nothing for me?" She had forgotten she was ordering for a lady.

Annette pointed her thumb at me. "And two of whatever you give mouthy women."

"Any grub?" the barkeep asked.

Annette said, "Give us two platters of bacon and fry some eggs in the grease."

We retired to a proper table before the window and watched as the city come alive with the day. When the barkeep turned his back we clanked whiskies and put them down quick. I held the lady's honey gin for a sniff.

"How is it?" Annette asked.

"Sweet," I said, cringing. "In a sorry way."

Annette took down the spare. She flinched. "They sure make women some rusty concoctions."

The liquor settled me and I could then feel my hunger.

We ate every scrap of meat and eggs and we left with all the whiskey he'd sell us, two crates. Annette paid gold though I could tell she wasn't comfortable paying for nothing. She heaved the first crate and kicked open the bat-wing doors. The bottles rattled when she set the crate at the back of the wagon.

"Should've stole it proper," Annette said. "Feel a mite foolish trading money."

"Paying bought us the luxury to dally."

Annette shrugged. "It just feels wasteful is

all to give gold for what you can steal."

She looked about and stiffened. I saw why.

Men was watching. Men riding by and their heads swiveling to study us. Men nodding at their buddy and both of them turning to look. There was a shortage of women in that country and here was one in a pink dress standing beside a darker man.

Annette put her arm about me. "Let's get."

We hit the mercantile and I read the shopkeep our list while his son and Annette loaded our wagon to capacity. We paid gold, and the man said, "Nobody has paid me in gold in near on fifteen years."

Annette's eyes went hard. "Gold a problem?"

"No, sir. Just peculiar is all. I prefer gold in fact. Just wondering how an Indian came to have such a supply."

Annette's lips narrowed. "You asking?"

"No, sir," the shopkeep said. "Ain't none of my business at all in fact. We do appreciate you coming by." He called his boy over and with a nod of his head sent him inside and away from us.

Annette helped me into the wagon.

"Bye, now," the shopkeep said with a wave. As we rode on, he stood on the porch and watched which way we went.

In the street dogs was growling over a bloody bone. A herd of children chased a loose piglet. Out come buckets of wash and worse and they splattered before us. The streets was foul with mud and flies.

We was halfway through a block when out come a whistle from the shade. I turned to it and saw a wide man spat. "You charging for rides, little lady?"

Annette reined the wagon to a stop. The whiskey rattle ceased. "What'd you say?"

"I asked if she was charging for rides, but now with a closer look I see she ought to pay me. Not even pink can make that pretty."

The man was big. When I say "big" I do not convey the size of this man. His britches cling so tight to his legs there wasn't no mistaking his member plumped off to the side. He tucked his thumb in his belt, about all he could fit.

I tapped Annette's knee. "Let's keep about our business, husband."

But Annette only handed me the reins.

The man said, "What you going to do about it, Redskin?"

She leapt down and come around the wagon and stepped onto the boardwalk with the fat man. Her guns was still hidden in the wagon. This man was wearing his own, though it looked tiny as toy on his huge hip. Annette was a good foot shorter than him and only a third his weight. Maybe a quarter. That man could've had a triumphant career as a circus giant.

He looked down on Annette and said, "Ain't you fancy, all dressed like a white man and —"

She spat on his knee.

The fat man leaned to look.

The motion come so fast I didn't see it so much as hear it. His teeth broke with the sound of gravel. Annette had driven the butt end of her knife upward into the man's chin. He fell to his knees, and as he did, Annette swung around behind him and pulled back his chin and put the blade against the tender flesh of his neck. A bead of blood let loose, just one.

Someone shouted, "There's about to be a killing!" A crowd began forming all at once in the street and on the boardwalk.

Annette growled in his ear, "Tell her how beautiful she is."

Blood was bubbling from his lips. The man stuttered. There was crazed fear in his eyes now.

"Tell her!"

Through broken teeth he said, "You is hard fancy to gander at, ma'am. I was mistaken to say otherwise."

Annette cleared her knife and booted the man in the back and he hit the boardwalk with a smack that shook the whole building. Annette pulled his billfold from his pocket, drew out his bills, and threw the rest back upon him.

She took her seat in the wagon and flicked the reins and we rolled on without a glance back. I looked at her with wide eyes.

"Come here."

I scooted closer and she put her arm around me.

The road took us by the sheriff's office. We didn't dare stop but we slowed and I looked careful at the wanted posters. There I was, a man. They had my name as Samuel A. Spartan. They said I might also go by Straight or Landcaster, but they didn't list Harney or Rowhine. I didn't see myself none in the drawing but I saw my marks. There was no mistaking my marks.

All at once my face went hot, and I looked about. How was it these men didn't peg me at once? I was but five yards from them and branded, and their eyes worked at me, at parts of me, parts I didn't much have — how did they not see me?

But I knew. Men looked on me and saw only a pink dress.

"You was up there," I muttered to Annette. "The Moonshine Kid."

"What'd the words say?"

"They call you his sidekick."

She scoffed. "Figures."

Before we left Pearlsville we passed within sight of the Governor's great white estate.

Men was on ladders painting the building.

Before the gate stood three guards in dusters and black hats and not a one was a familiar face. Near the white columns of the house stood yet more men dressed in uniform, and upon the roof I saw three where there was usually one.

I could not tell if Greenie was among them.

In all truth, I missed Greenie. In my imaginings I saw him and Tuss and Drum playing cards and drinking whiskey and I wondered if Greenie loathed me now, if he said cruel things about me, if he wanted me dead. Did he believe I'd played him those nights when it was just the two of us? I was on his side them nights. I was on his side now, his and Noah's. I know it don't make no sense on paper, but I believe a soul can be on both sides.

In the far field I saw Constance's mare looking off toward the east. Her ears pointed forward and her tail did not flick. She was watching something in the sage.

Annette said, "Powerful critter. Like to ride that one."

"Too headstrong for easy working."

"My kind of mount."

As we passed nearest I saw what had Enterprise's attention. A man was sitting in the sage. Only his head was visible above the gray matter. He was black and aged, and as I studied him he turned to me. Our distance was sixty-five yards, but there wasn't no mistaking who this man was. Charles, the butler. Our eyes met and then I looked away and hid my face on Annette's shoulder.

"You know that one," she said.

"I do."

"He's still looking at you. He a problem?"

"No. He ain't no problem."

We rolled until we was took in by the shade of the pines and then reined to a stop near some green grass to rest our hard-driven stock and find some sleep before the long travel ahead.

Annette and I took our pistols up toward some rocks off the meadow, a place we could defend if trouble come, and there we laid out in the pine needles. She tipped her hat over her eyes. "Just five minutes slumber and I'll be born new."

I laid down nearby. "I can't hardly see. My eyes going fuzzy, I'm so wore out."

"Flatter over here," she muttered.

I crawled nearer and tossed a few pinecones aside and then collapsed. I laid my face against the fold of her arm and at once I fell out the bottom of this world, asleep on the arm of my darling.

Some hours later we awoke at the same nothing, and both sat up. Around us there wasn't a bird, not even a chickadee. In the meadow, the horses stood rigid, their eyes on some point off in the trees.

I looked to Annette. She put a finger to her lips.

Just then a pine squirrel got to hollering on the far side of the meadow and we both went for our guns.

We dropped off the back side of the ridge without a word. I followed Annette at a run now. We kept the land between us and the meadow, and when we hit the road we followed it back at a creep, pistols at the ready.

We saw the tracks in the dust, a big horse, and beside them the crisp prints of rounded city shoes. They had walked until they saw our tracks leave the road, and then they had reversed. So whoever it was, was hunting us.

Annette nodded and that said enough. We split and cut through the pines at a stalk. That squirrel was still blowing his warning, and so we knew where this lawman or bounty hunter or Pinkerton had to be. I reckon we both assumed him to be prone over a rifle, waiting to dry-gulch us as we went for our mounts.

I saw him first by a patch of gray fabric, and put a big tree between us while I got in close. I picked my steps with tender care, clearing the earth with my toe before laying my foot into something that might crackle. I drew back the hammer on the Peacemaker with my off hand over top so the click wouldn't carry.

I swung around the tree and leveled the pistol.

The man was laid out watching our stock all right, but he didn't have no rifle. It was Charles. "What you doing?"

"Don't shoot!" he begged, his hands out. "Please!"

I lowered the hammer. Annette was still hidden in the timber. I knew her to now be checking to see that he had indeed come alone and was not followed.

"Awful steep risk you took sneaking up on us," I said. "And I guess I just don't see why."

He rose from the ground and I could see he hadn't been eating much these last weeks. His clothes wore dirt and sage and now pine needles. He had a split in one lip, and a swelling upon his brow. He said, "Is she safe?"

I nodded, and the relief was clear in his face.

Charles rode Enterprise. He had stolen her from the pasture by luring her near the willow where she couldn't be seen by the distant guards and then prying loose the fence boards. He admitted he wasn't much a horseman. He'd fallen hard, but damn if he was leaving that horse to the Governor.

Annette had brought the animal through the timber and tied her to a lodgepole. Charles was off behind us on a log. I told him to relax there while I explained these matters to my partner.

Annette offered me the tobacco.

"You sure the side he's on?"

"I'm sure."

She looked him over. She tapped the ash from her rollie. "Well, reckon Noah will want to know him."

We tied Enterprise by a short lead to the rear of the wagon and made space for Charles on the bench with us. That meant I sat tight to Annette, her body along every inch of mine. When the sun set and the air grew dry with young ice, we spread the blanket upon our laps. We pushed hard to clear through that uncertain country.

If we'd rolled an hour faster or three slower, who knows how things might've gone different.

Charles was asking all the same questions as Constance about what come of Will. It was hard news I was giving him, but he only nodded.

"What did they do with his remains?"

"Put them on a train," I told him.

"Which train? Which direction?"

"I don't know. Must've been the eastbound, given the time."

That is when he wept. His head tipped into his hands and he sobbed with a fury that scared me. Annette went stiff at the sound.

"I fled west for my son's sake. He did not

mature in the same world as I, but it is the same world that stole him nonetheless."

Near the darkest hour of the night we heard voices up the trail. Annette reined the stock to a stop. Enterprise still wore the Governor's brand, there'd be no explaining that. I readied my pistol under the quilt.

Charles whispered, "What are they?"

I put a finger to my lips.

Their voices grew, and we could hear the drink in them. Soon enough we come to see their lantern light through the pines and then we could see their faces. Three men within pistol range before they noticed us, that's how deep they was in the drink. "Whoa, now," their front man said.

The boss among them was some years my senior. His beard was grizzled and cut short, and his nose was red as coal. He hollered, "What business has you got passing this road at this hour?"

"I ask you the same," Annette called. "Last I knew this road don't belong to nobody in particular."

The man shifted in his saddle. He drew his pistol and set its barrel upon the horn. His eyes didn't look drunk no more. "Well, I done asked you first."

"Just passing through is all," I called in my sweetest little voice. "Why don't you put that iron aside, mister, so I don't got to worry none about my husband's health and all."

But the man heeled his horse into a trot and come along Annette. He held the lantern over her. His pistol was now eyeing her at near point-blank. The man squinted on Annette. "Hey, now, hold on. You look hard familiar."

Blood busted from his chest and he went sliding backward off his mount. The echo was the first I heard of the shot. My bullet hit right where I was looking.

So there wasn't no going back. I swung and dumped the man on my side, and Annette put three rounds into the one in back. It was done before they got their guns up.

Charles had fallen sideways off the seat. I thought he must've been hit. But he was fine, only covered in mud. His hands was shaking with ice-cold fear.

Annette held the lantern over the men one at a time. She rolled one with her boot and drew his billfold from his pocket.

Their horses was long gone already. They would ride home empty and then whoever was waiting would come looking.

"You know 'em?" I asked.

"This one here is Dizzy's crew."

"Could be he broke off when Dizzy left the county."

She looked on me. I could see she was doubtful.

She tossed me the billfold of the man I

shot. I caught it out the air, and studied it. But it wasn't the billfold I was noticing. It was my hands. They was stone still. Queer as it sounds, I was calmer than I had been at any point since leaving the Rock in costume. There was something else too. The way the night looked, sounded. Like I'd finally come full awake.

I walked near Annette and looked her over. She had their guns in a pile and was dragging the bodies by the arms off the road. To Annette this was just another day of labor.

She stood and picked at some blood drying on her cheek. "They sure got cash like they still work for Dizzy."

We hid the provisions where another wagon could come for them, and then rolled fast. We went on beyond our turn and all the way to a crossroads and down into a gully. There we cut free the horses and left the wagon out of sight and rode up the creek and then cross-country until we was back to our familiar path up the mountain.

Charles rode Enterprise, and I counseled him to control his heels, to keep straight, to tell her in a sweet voice he was taking her home. But his eyes kept lingering on my gun hand. He said, "The air come out of that man when your bullet hit him. Like he was hit with a board."

"That is the idea."

"I keep hearing the sound of it."

I looked off into the dark timber. I recalled my flask of whiskey and offered the last pull to Charles.

We rode through the gap and into our valley just as the dawn turned the cliffs orange. The antelope lifted their heads but did not break.

Annette and me was on ahead so we could talk in private tones. I asked her, "Did I need to kill those men? Now I ain't sure."

She turned a piece of grass in her teeth. "I like how you done it. Quick as flight. I'm always the one who sends the first lead. I ain't used to being surprised by a shot. I enjoyed the sensation."

"It's his fault for pulling that revolver, right?"

"Oh, for sure," Annette said. "His fault for being ass dumb and riding so close, but those ain't no points worth making. Got to admit it was fun though, right? I like riding with you."

"Killing ain't fun," I said.

"Just got to do right is all."

"I think I wanted to impress you."

"Well, good job then."

We rode for some minutes in quietude. The birds was coming awake. Annette said, "But I mean it. I like riding with you, Jess. You and me could go a long way together."

As we entered the Rock I said, "Annette.

511

There's something I got to tell you."

Hardly any sleep in two days and the action was gone now from my blood. The tired hit me all at once. She was looking at me. "Yeah? Don't tell me you's married."

I couldn't help but laugh.

She smiled on me. "Go on. What got you all twisted up?"

But I didn't get the chance to tell her. Noah was there waiting on us. No doubt the look-out had seen us coming and called to him. I should've told her sooner. I meant to tell her on the climb up the mountain. But killing has a manner of taking up all the room in a mind.

Noah stepped out from a fold in the canyon and Enterprise bucked at the sight. He wore his pistols and his hat on low. We couldn't yet see the meadow and the houses. He wanted us alone.

Annette said, "Got her done, but had to stash the supplies in the valley. Dizzy ain't left the pines. Though he got three less men than he did yesterday."

Noah didn't take his eyes from me.

Annette grew weary of the silence. She shifted.

"It worked out," I said to my brother. "Don't look on me like that."

Noah's eyes was narrow and cold. I never saw those eyes in his head when he was a boy. There was a well of hate deep in my brother and I had found it.

"Hold now," Annette said. She frowned on me. "You said he was game for a run to town."

"I mean . . . Well, I didn't say those words, in precision."

Her brow flickered. "You played me?"

"No, I mean . . ." But that was exactly what I done.

She cursed and heeled her horse from me.

"Annette."

"I thought we was in this together!" she shouted. "I thought it was you and me, no bullshit. I thought you was the type to stick your side!"

I don't know what I thought would happen. I guess I reckoned we'd laugh it off like we done laughed off so much.

She galloped from me and into the meadow.

"You're a fool," Noah said to me. "Hard-headed as Pa." He nodded at Charles. "And who the hell is this?"

Charles walked forward and stopped before my brother. Behind him, the reins still in Charles's hand, Enterprise lipped at blades of grass. Charles said, "Mister Harney."

Noah offered his hand but he looked to me when he said, "No blindfold or nothing?"

"This is Charles, the Governor's former butler. Will's father."

I brought Charles to Constance's door and

rapped. She was slow to respond. When she opened the door, I saw she hadn't yet brushed her hair or changed from her nightclothes. At the sight of Charles, the boiled egg she was holding hit the floor.

I don't know what was between her and Charles before, but now she embraced him about the neck and wept. His arms lived by old rules and kept their place at his sides, but only for so long. Those arms could not hold out against all they mourned.

Noah stomped clean his boots at the door. He hung his hat on its hook and his jacket on another. He left his pistols on. He looked on me. It was just us in his house. I had followed him in. I wanted to set things right.

He put a cigarette to his lips and dragged a match across the table. "He that dippeth his hand with me in the dish, the *same* shall betray me." The flame touched the cigarette and the smoke left his nose.

I took his tobacco pouch from the table. "Why beholdest thou the mote that is in thy brother's eye, but considerest not the beam that is in thine own?"

"You miss the point," he said. "You undercut me. All the boys know. Around here, I ain't nobody's brother."

"Don't say that."

"It is a miracle alone that you made the trip there and back without getting killed, or worse, leading the army to our gates. You ain't learned the lesson in this. I can tell from your face. You just feeling sorry for your self."

"I ain't."

"Neither of you ever trusted me."

"I trust you."

"No, you don't. Pa didn't neither."

I looked to my feet.

"How'd you leave the bodies?"

"We drug 'em down into the brush. Won't find 'em until the magpies do."

Noah took off his guns and stared long at them in their holsters before hanging them on the hook. His hand hung there.

Jane got on supper that night. She asked for my help preparing it, and I was glad for a task to keep my hands busy. Noah left and stayed gone. I knew he was with Annette.

Jane was quieter than I'd ever seen her and I kept my eyes to our tasks.

I put the biscuits to bake and then set the table for five.

Charles and Constance joined us, and Jane was her old self, aglow in the company. She told the story of meeting Noah. She told stories about him helping children. She explained to Charles how Noah was a hero to all these people in the Rock. What she said was all true enough. But it was only part of the truth, and the part that might sway Charles toward favoring Noah Harney.

Noah took his turn, telling of his brothers and sisters here among the Rock, talking of the downtrodden across this country. The money that beats them like a hammer. The money built on the suffering of working folk, money to fill gilded pockets in the East.

My brother stubbed his smoke. He said, "We'll get your revenge, Mr. Marshall."

Charles scoffed. "Revenge is your word, Harney."

Noah sat back in his chair.

There was no doubting the straight-backed Charles. He sat before the most famous gunfighter to ever ride and didn't downturn his eyes. He put his hand over Constance's. "Vengeance belongs to the Lord.

"No, this is all about spectacle for you, Harney. You are not so different from the Governor. You speak of good and evil, and so does he. You speak of Heaven and loyalty, and so does he. You speak of brothers and sisters as he speaks of his constituency. Like him, you spin the world so you may be its savior."

"Whoa, now," my brother said. "You out of line."

Charles raised a finger. "Whose line?"

My brother pushed aside his plate. He leaned over his elbows. He smiled and said in that voice that had always swayed folks, "Listen. I could use a man with your knowledge of the Governor."

" 'Use a man!' We come from Portugal, my

516

people, by way of Virginia. Seven generations we have tended the political class. My grandfather's father was once graced by the pope. I myself was in the room as wealthy men formed armies to war against their Yankee countrymen. You are but a cattleman's son. You witness one breath of life in one destitute state and believe yourself to understand the forces of history and your place among them. I am miles above your uses for me, Harney."

Noah swallowed. Jane put her hand on his arm.

Charles looked at Constance now. "I barely kept my baby fed after the armies razed the estate. I knew what was happening in the free states of the West. They would fill with black men set free, and we would have our new place. Our place. Yet I flinched, I admit it. I wrote a letter to the Governor, for I knew his name from the desk I served. I wrote him not for the salary, but because what substance was mine, outside the esteem expressed by strangers for the man I served? I was a man who could not name himself. But my boy knew God. My boy saw in himself what God sees. *That* is why they killed him. My son knew his God-given name. But, Mr. Noah Harney, it is you who will be remembered as the hero outlaw."

Constance had begun to weep. Charles put his arm about her and she leaned her head upon his shoulder.

"No, Harney. It is not revenge that interests me. That man stole my son. I, on the other hand, have pledged myself to his daughter. This is not about your uses for me. This is about the children who come after. This is about the world we build for them, for *they* are our saviors."

I was on Annette's stoop turning it all over when I finally heard boots approaching. It was late enough most of the folks had turned in, their lanterns blown out. Nobody had lit a fire that night. Nobody played music.

But the boots didn't belong to Annette. Noah sat beside me and from there we looked up on that slice of stars between the roof and the Rock.

He said, "You figure that is the same sky we looked on as kids?"

"Ain't considered it. I got enough to figure down here."

"How can these stars not hold your mind? Look at them up there, so far off and watching us. Every one is like the sparkle in an eye."

"I reckon I don't believe they watch us at all, brother. I reckon they don't watch nothing. If they do, they don't see us way down here on this tiny speck of dirt and wind."

He passed me the smoke he'd just rolled and then commenced rolling another. When it was done, he put it to his lips and sparked a match and I leaned in and he lit them both.

"There's something I want to tell you. I should've told you sooner."

"Well, don't make me ask."

"It's good news. The best kind maybe. See, Constance ain't the only one with child."

Her shift in shape and color. The fatigue about her eyes. Jane was growing my kin.

I punched him in the shoulder. I shoved him near off the bench. "You gonna be a pa?"

He looked on his rollie. "You done smashed my smoke."

"Hell with your smoke. You gonna be a pa! This ain't no josh, is it? I'll kill you my own self if you joshing."

"I ain't joshing. Still trying to wrap my head about the fact. Being a pa, well, that's some heavy business."

I looked on him there and all I ever dreamed for us was at once refigured. I couldn't see his face for the lack of light but I was seeing it now anyhow, seeing what his child would look like, my niece or nephew. I punched him again. "We got to celebrate! Too bad you ain't drinking. If 'n there's ever been the moment for whiskey . . ."

"Calm down," he said. "Don't go making a ruckus. Things still ain't right between you and me."

I looked around for Annette on account I wanted to tell the news. What would she say? "We got to tell Annette!"

Noah cleared his throat. He spat. "She

didn't tell you because I asked her not to."

"Annette already knows?"

"I wanted to tell you myself is why."

At once I decided not to let this fact fester. Jane was growing my kin, and that was goddamn sterling. What did it matter that Annette knew before me? That she hadn't told me?

"It's queer, I'll tell you." He relit his cigarette. "The thing moves about inside her. I can feel it against my hand and such. It keeps her up at night now. She's a good two months ahead of Constance. Maybe you've noticed the bulge."

"When will it be born?"

"April, likely. Jane thinks anyhow. I ain't sure nobody can predict such matters."

"Ma's birthday was —"

"That's right," he said. "Jane didn't want folks to know. See, well, she has been with child before. She ain't never carried one this far. It's clear as day a God-given miracle."

"This changes things, don't it? I mean like we got to find us a spread and go by other names and . . . you got to quit this outlawing business."

He chuckled. "You want me to quit. The Lord offers a miracle and you want me to quit Him because of it?"

"But you gonna be a pa. It's time to put this fighting away and take up the holier path of fathering. Wasn't you persuaded by

Charles?"

"Charles is just in grief is all. He'll come around. Everybody do. This war ain't mine to end, Jess. It's the Lord's war, and this here hand is the implement of His divine will." He stood and opened his hand and turned it over in the starlight.

"I'm damn happy for you, brother. I'm damn happy for us. But a child needs his pa to have his eyes focused on the earth. The heavens don't need no tilling."

"I want to start clean with you and me, sis. I don't want you undercutting me no more. Times will grow hard this winter, no doubt, and we'll need to be as solid as this Rock. The boys need to see that you have full faith in me. I can't have you pulling the dirt from my dikes."

He slid closer to me on the bench. This time our shoulders touched. "It's a magical story, ain't it? All that hardship and suffering and all them close calls was to deliver us here, to the beginning of our lives. We sat on the stoop at home, and now we sit on the stoop here, only we behold a new brightness, a new generation. Ain't that right? Ain't that all the proof you need?"

He laughed and put his whole arm about my shoulders and drew me close. "Whoever thought that you and me would end up so far from the lake. Huh? Think of all that's come to pass that Pa couldn't never have imagined.

Think about all that will come in this child's lifetime that we can't even think to consider now! Ah, Jess. My son will be the one to welcome the dawn of peace in His garden. Peace, that is the next great invention! Peace is the destiny we manifest."

He stood and walked out from the eave and tipped his head back toward the sky. My brother never was the type to sit still.

"Tomorrow," he said, "we will ride to Dizzy's saloon and bring an end to that hellhole, and tomorrow night we will celebrate proper. I'll play Pa's song, and it'll be like he's with us again. And we'll bathe in our good fortune. We'll do the Lord's good work, and then we'll relish in His good cheer. We will *lay* ourselves upon His mercy and thereby beckon our *golden* future."

Peace in my life always come from the long view, the far-off mountains and the green valley, a humble lake at its bottom and the house Pa built beside it, a tendril of juniper smoke rising from the chimney. If I shut my eyes and thought hard I could hear the sound of willows and the wingbeats of doves. Noah would be Pa. We'd be a family, wherever it was we went.

"I'm with your child, brother. All I got is for your child."

"That's the spirit!" His smile was wide and bright as the moon. "You and me, together, for always."

■ ■ ■ ■

I finally found her where the edge of the Rock gave way to the canyon mouth. I saw her by the cherry of her smoke. She sat there with her feet dangling over the edge.

I didn't say nothing. I only sat beside her. She looked sidelong and then returned her gaze onto the starlit desert. She didn't speak but she didn't leave neither.

Far off in the dark yonder a wolf lit up. We both turned toward it. It howled three times and then fell silent.

"She's the last one," Annette whispered. "I hear her some nights and there ain't never no answer. She is alone now in this skinny land. She was born too late."

"I'm sorry, Annette. I mean it."

"Up north the wolves howl all night."

"Is that where you wish to go, north?"

"I don't wish," she said.

"Come with me," I said. "Come sleep. Let me tend to you."

"Nah," she muttered. "You go. I ain't leaving. I want to hear her when she howls. If she howls, somebody got to hear."

So Annette and me spent our last night together without sleep and without whiskey, our boots dangling over thin air.

Together, we waited on that wolf to sing.

■ ■ ■ ■

In the faint dawn when stars fade on the eastern edge, we tacked up and passed about boiled eggs and Noah refilled our cups from a tin brew of coffee. We checked our rifles and slipped them in their scabbards. We checked the cylinders on our sidearms and filled our pockets with shells. The morning was full of the sound of metal.

The boys was hungry for it, and they bolstered their courage with pushing and joshing. Annette and me stood off to the side with our coffees.

"You think this is a good decision?" I asked her. "To go after Dizzy?"

"Always a fresh start in some action."

"Listen," Noah said. "I know you all want in on this, but Annette and me talked and only eight of us is going, the rest will stay here."

"No. Why?" Blister dared ask.

"Our enemies are about, and we cannot risk the people by leaving them unguarded. We'll split our force, and I want those that remain to take up defensive positions. That means all bodies on top, and one man assigned the dynamite. If they charge, you blast it and don't worry about us on the outside. We'll fight them from behind."

"Who goes?" Mason asked.

Noah swung up on Blackie. He looked at me. He was asking if I wanted in.

I tipped my hat.

"Good," he said. "A family affair then."

Eight of us thundered through the canyon and into the morning light and come to full speed and it was my brother and Annette on either side of me, and we rode on point with our eyes squinted into the wind. Our hats was on low and we leaned into our speed and the earth shook under us and behind a great wall of dust rose that had nowhere to blow on that still morn.

When we cut from the plateau and down into the pines, the road grew steep. The animals knew the steps and I remember thinking how quiet it all was down there. How not a bird lifted from its roost, and not a deer broke for cover. The road turned into the canyon and the rocks pinched in tight and in that moment it was Blister up front, and then Annette and me and Noah behind. The others had fallen back as we rode the fastest horses. I was looking at his back when Blister crumpled.

I heard not the shots but the sound of bullets ripping air and smacking flesh. The bay I was riding careened and I was swiped from her back by a limb.

Time and distance and past and future, all the currents of a moment lived, condensed into that gulch. I am four decades from there now but I have never left its confines. To be ambushed is to be ruined for quiet moments. To be dry-gulched is to forever dwell one step from fury.

When I rose there was a shortage of sound but belches of fire and gun smoke and tree limbs falling and dirt bursting and bark flying, all of it slower than the rules of earth. Annette was behind her dying horse firing on the rocks above and I drew both pistols and busted rounds at the flashes of muzzles and I must've been hollering because Annette and Noah saw me there and took their chance to fall back. That's when it happened, as he stood to run.

I saw it. The arm that held his pistol folded at a new joint below the elbow and the gun fell to the earth. Noah paid the wound no mind. He seized the pistol in his left hand and busted off rounds as he ran. Blood was pouring from him but there wasn't no time for nothing but getting to cover.

We caught our breath with our backs to stone and then Noah come up firing with his left and I come up firing with both and Annette took careful aim and the three of us bucked off lead and I broke open a man's face from across the gully and then I saw the man I was about to kill stumble as Annette's bullet center punched his chest. Lead splattered all about us and yet we returned that ore in such volume that Dizzy's boys dove for cover.

Noah sank behind the rock and yelled to time our reloading so they couldn't rush us. But he only had one hand and it was his left and so his casings was slow to find their places. When my pistols went dry I reloaded his first and then mine.

I come up hot now and I fired with both hands and still lead kicked chips from the rocks about us. Youn was on the ridge by then, behind the ambush, and I saw him laying waste to those bastards with his Winchester. Carlos was with him and this fight was going our way. The devils was turning to run.

By then Noah was too weak to stand. He give up firing his pistol.

A last few was behind us now and Noah called it and I spun and winged the first one and then Annette stood to fire. That's when she took her hit.

I heard the whack of lead and I heard the air come out her throat. I finished my cylinders into the man who done it.

She sank to the earth as Carlos hollered down from the ridge. They was done for. The day was ours.

Annette's eyes looked up into mine. I ripped at her jacket and there it was. The bullet had tore through her guts.

■ ■ ■ ■

Still it ain't easy for me to tell it.

She was panting and begging for water. She took hold of my sleeve and drew me close. "Water."

I couldn't look at her, Annette gasping, and yet where else could I look?

My brother was poking at the splintered bone, trying to put it back in his skin. The blood was running from him too fast and his face was going gray. He said, "It don't work no more."

Brass glittered in the dirt. Scuff marks where horses bucked and ran. Limbs still laden with green needles splayed upon the earth. Smoke lingering in apparitions. Youn firing point-blank into a crawling man. Echo, echo, echo.

Good ol' Blister, his eyes open to me. Blood bubbling from his mouth, and he ain't gagging.

Blackie stumbling by without regard for the trail, her breathing ragged and wet, her own internals tripping her feet. She stops and wavers, and then falls sidelong and rolls down the ravine and stops against a tree kicking and sucking for air through all that blood.

At my feet Annette is begging for water.

It was Pa's voice that woke me.

Noah was white as death. Blood rushing out with the beat of his heart. He panted, "It don't work . . ."

I cut a cord of leather from my holster and fed it around Noah's shot arm above the wound. I did this as Pa described it done in the war. I done it without past or future, only the words of Pa and the matter-of-fact destruction of human flesh that finds itself in the path of lead. A stick went between the leather and the arm and I twisted it tight. The blood pouring from my brother's flesh slowed to a drip.

Annette's lips was cracked and bleeding and she gripped my hand and barked, "Water. Please. Water." It is true, her belly bubbled with red and green and the air about her smelled like upchuck and worse. She drew me to her lips. "Water. Water. Water."

That voice. It was not hers at all but the howl of the animal that dies within each of us.

It took three men to lift Annette from the earth and deliver her to the wagon. They had heard the ambush from the Rock and come at once.

Annette fought me when I tried to move her and yet with every breath she begged.

Noah walked, a man on each side. He was too dizzy to balance. His hand was now gray and black below the wound and swung of its own accord and he muttered nonsense. He looked everywhere but at his right arm.

I joined them in the wagon. It bounced upon the earth and their flesh went fluid. The longest ride. Days and weeks and years in that wagon to go two miles.

Noah's arm was all but lost. Two inches different and the bullet would've missed clean. Two inches at fifty yards is half a hair's difference at the muzzle.

If Annette hadn't stood to fire might the bullet have missed?

If Noah had been whole, might he have killed the one who hit Annette?

If I had practiced more, might I have saved us all?

If we hadn't gone to town.

These be the trails unrode, the very ones that will haunt me till I join them in the dirt.

Later the newspapermen asked over and over what made me a killer. I had no words for them.

To kill does not make a person a killer. A killer is born from a womb of shame. A killer believes he is worthless. A killer believes only killing can return worth.

We rolled on in the morning light, the wagon rocking over the uneven ground and their bodies sloshing side to side and their blood tracking the grains of wood and all of it my doing. The same morning but it is a thousand years forward and behind.

Before us the sage sea extended to the foot of the Rock, still a hundred miles distant.

"Hurry!" a voice like mine cried. But hurry where?

Hands like mine put a coat under Noah's head. Hands like mine propped up his knees. A hand like mine wiped the fever sweat from his brow.

Annette whimpers. I promise water but still she whimpers.

Her lips taste like ash.

Hurry to the water.

Still we rumble on, that ride that never ends. On and on we ride to a future that has come and gone and comes again, born anew in its ceaseless passing. We ride broken and hurt and shamed, and we turn our eyes toward the horizon, to the Other that dwells beyond.

All of this is their fault. For it cannot be our fault. It cannot be His doing.

I remember Noah's eyes unblinking. The clouds reflected in them. He is mumbling.

"She's before the fire working on the quilt and I lay my ear to her belly, and listen and there's a great universe inside, and so many ways it can go, so why does it always go the same? I'm wore out, I'm wore out from forgetting. I forget her all my life. Her face is gone, no one remembers her face now.

"I'm so damn tired. She holds her hand over my ear, so warm, she sings to me, even right now I am that music from outside and inside and I feel her hand going cold. Stop the baby from crying! Pa. Pa? Make Ma right again. Pa, you gotta fix her. It is so cold here, Ma, sing me a song. Momma. Don't stop singing, Momma."

Jane will meet us in the sage. She will come running with cloth torn into strips that blow out behind like festivities. I'll take her hand as we roll by and she will swing up into the bed. She will gasp. She will draw a breath of resolve. Jane will sit between them and hold their cheeks in her palms and begin to sing.

Hush and bye,
don't you cry,
go to sleep my little babies.
When you wake,
we'll have cake
and all the pretty little horses.

It is the children I remember upon our return. They stood along the wall of the Rock with their backs pressed to it as if to keep a monster from sneaking up behind. Some wept, others stared in vivid knowing.

Men took up shoulders and legs and we unloaded them. They both was shivering with the fever that comes from hard wounds. Charles held Noah around the chest and another got his feet and they hurried sideways. "Get that door!" Charles shouted.

Annette was carried into her house and passed from the sunlight into the shade for the final time.

I could not bear to carry either of them. I sank to my knees. My lips muttering the primal memory of prayer.

"Get help!" someone hollered.

I was standing inside my brother's house.

Jane was barking orders. Charles took my shoulder. "Fetch a saw. Do it now." I was glad for the task, for I did not have to choose.

They laid him out upon the bed and tied down his feet and good arm. He was dazed and too worn for words. Charles had his white sleeves folded up and was washing his hands in a pot of scalding water. "Set the saw on the table. Candles. As many as you can find."

Noah come to at the sight of the saw and felt his legs tied down and knew then what was under way. He roared for us to stop and leave him. He roared like a bear and thrashed until his good wrist bleed from the rope.

"Spite you!"

Charles did not dawdle. He readied his tools.

"Please, no! Please don't," my brother begged.

"We must." Charles put his hand to Noah's shoulder. "I know of this business. The war landed upon us in Virginia and the estate became a hospital. Your arm must be lost if you are to be saved. Best we do it now before the pain sets in."

"There is no other choice?" Jane asked.

Charles shook his head. "Death by fever is the other choice."

Jane took a breath for courage. "Be done with it then so that the worst may be behind us." She laid beside my brother and helped him brace for what approached.

Charles held his knife to the candles until the blade went red and then he put it to the flesh below the elbow and cut deep all the way around. The saw was made hot with flame. Then it was put to the bone. The resulting sound can be healed by no song.

I talked to myself about what I was witnessing, as if one half of me was an elder sibling and the other was naive to the movements of this earth. I couldn't have told you in that moment how his arm come to be damaged. There was no cause and no effect, no before or after. I was native to that breath and only that breath. I breathe it still.

■ ■ ■ ■

After, my brother lay motionless. He did not whimper or cry or pull at his restraints. He only drew breaths and looked straight into Jane's face and recited Genesis from its first word.

The arm was handed to me by the thumb. Charles nodded toward the door.

"Give it to the ground. Can you do that?"

I held my brother's hand as the flesh turned dark. Already the blood was thickening. The horses fled from me as I walked near, Ingrid among them. Out through the Rock and to the sage, a living hand gone to heavy flesh. We never know what our hands weigh.

I dug as deep as I could with a stone and set the arm into the hole and backfilled and rolled a boulder over top. It was Pa's words I heard, *Flesh deserves quiet rest.* I piled more rocks until I was sure no scavenger could dig it up.

All at once I felt my own pain. My shoulder throbbed and my hip pulsed for reasons I couldn't remember. But none of the blood soaking my clothing was mine.

I did find two places where lead had torn my jacket. How was it that lead could come that close and not rip my flesh?

How could it be that lead had broke them

and not me?

"How could you kill as you have?" the newspapermen would ask later.

"Because I was spared."

Annette was moaning and sobbing from her room. The door was open and Charles was with her.

All about children cried. Mothers shoed them inside and shut the doors. There was no place to go in the Rock that was immune to her suffering.

Charles emerged from Annette's room and wiped the fluids from his hands with a cloth and approached until we stood an arm's reach away. "The bullet missed the blood and so she will live sometime in this pain."

"She will live."

"She will breathe a day, maybe two. The water we give her drains from the hole in her back. The pain from these wounds is the worst kind. It comes from the center, not from the extremity, and there is no excluding it. There is no trick of mind to dodge it or potion to remove it."

Charles put his hand to my shoulder. I was wavering. Just this morning we was together and believing, Annette and me.

"Go see her. Sit with her so she isn't alone in her final hours. She asks for you."

I stood and stared at the black hole that was the doorway to her suffering. Drummond had touched his finger to the center of his forehead and made me promise.

I am not proud. I was too shamed to bear her gaze.

"How could you kill as you have?" the newspapermen asked.

"To kill is easy."

The boys was outside piling wood as if human mouths drink wood.

I joined them and we hacked and sawed and stood to watch dead wood fall. We worked with sweat and not words. We relished the slivers in our flesh, pain that we could amplify or extract at our own choosing.

The strongest men lifted Blister and set him atop the fuel. He was wrapped in white cloth and his blood soaked through. The blood had already gone the color of dirt.

Noah was the rightful one to preach upon this loss but he suffered his own tortures now. I put my hands in my pockets and felt a book. It was Noah's Bible and I've never been sure how it found its way to my pocket. Maybe I reached for it as Charles sawed free his arm.

Now I lifted the book from my pocket and offered it around. No man would touch it. I was the only one among them who could read.

I turned to a page I remembered and was thankful for the lines. I could read and thereby not have to form a thought of my own.

The passage was not right but it was a passage and no man about that pyre questioned it. "Enter ye in at the strait gate: for wide is the gate, and broad is the way, that leadeth to destruction, and many there be which go in thereat. Because strait is the gate, and narrow is the way, which leadeth unto life, and few there be that find it."

Youn put a match to a ball of shavings and blew them hot and then placed the shavings among the kindling. He blew and others did too and the breeze took up the flames and then the wood began to crackle and pop and smoke rose up and blew east. It went from gray to black and we all stepped from the heat. We gathered where there was no smell, and then the wind ebbed and we walked in one mass to the other side. When the wind switched again, we gave up and backed away so as not to be haunted by the smell of dripping flesh.

We still hoped not to be haunted.

There wasn't a bottle of whiskey among us and so we smoked cigarettes one after another.

"Dizzy wasn't among the dead."

"I only counted twelve."

"So what's that?"

"Least four left, and Dizzy."

We smoked until our throats went dry and still we smoked more. Not a man would return to the Rock. I believe they too was afraid of Annette's suffering, for it was a reminder of how small was our own.

I threw a cigarette to the earth. "Let's ride. Let's ride through them and destroy them and set this right once and for all."

I did not have to persuade.

What we did that night will offend you. I do not seek to justify our actions, I do not seek to provoke your forgiveness. What we done is for us to bear.

"How could you kill as you have?"

The same logic lies dormant within all fairy tales and histories, it is as fundamental as our origins, as urgent as our breaths. And yet I will confess the choice was ours.

The choice is always ours.

Ingrid would not allow me near, so covered in blood. I saddled another I did not know.

We rode out into the dusk and past the smoldering funeral fire. Thirteen agents come to see the waters prevail. We did not speak. We rode through the silver moonlight. We rode into the warmth of the pines and past their bodies still strewn about the rocks and then down along the small creek that chilled the air. We rode and our horses panted smoke. We rode in fury so as to dodge our grief. We was His anointed few, His agents of righteousness, His deliverers of balance.

From the darkness come a glimmer and our horses picked up speed. Dizzy's saloon cast its light upon the needles and the boys ran a tornado about the building. The party within was blind with liquor. There was a piano and the sound of glass breaking. I suspect there was fifteen or eighteen souls inside, all them guilty to the logic of our grieving.

Youn gave his horse the heels and the two of them went up the stairs in a bound and through the front doors and the mayhem became general. The pounding of feet and the crackle of bones and the pops of twin pistols. Women shrieked and men pushed through the door. The boys was ready for them and laid them out upon the steps.

A man went through a window and broke for the safety of the darkness and I rode him down and shot him in the back. I did not see him hit the earth but turned back for more.

Youn's horse leapt from the deck and landed on the earth and shook as if he was wet from a river crossing.

Jeremiah come around from the back of the building with a man held stiff at pistol point. There was a ragged and gushing tear along the man's brow, but he was lucid and holding his arms over his head and begging for mercy, begging his innocence. Jeremiah kicked him and the man tumbled forward into the dirt.

Jeremiah took him by the hair and said, "Tell us where!"

"I don't know where Dizzy is. I don't. I swear it! Please."

Jeremiah hollered, "I lobby we show this fool the rope."

Mason said, "I second the motion," and offered a section of hemp and he and Jeremiah went about tying the man's feet with it, one end to each ankle.

"What is you doing to me?" the man cried. "I wasn't there. I swear it!"

Jeremiah nodded to me and I saw what he was after and I tossed him the throwing rope I had around my horn. This one he tied to the man's arms, one end to each wrist.

Now the man understood and he began wailing with a desperation that should've troubled us if it wasn't exactly the antidote we'd come for.

One rope went around Youn's saddle horn. The other rope went around Mason's. They rode opposite directions. The man lay on the ground as the earth quivered with hooves and then he rose up but for a moment before crashing back to the earth, now without arms. He was dragged by Youn feetfirst around that building and out of sight and then back around the other side and he come by us like a rabbit flushed from a thicket and the boys opened up on him accordingly. I heard bullets swatting flesh and punching earth and then Youn took a corner too fast and what had been good sport became less. The man went sidelong into a tree and his head split like a melon.

I insisted the boys coil the ropes so as not to waste the materials and then I followed them through the flesh and pools toward the bar. We held one another for balance so as not to fall among the carnage. Mason poured us shots. A body shifted on the floor and eight bullets made it still again. We finished a bottle and started another. We raised our glasses to the friends not with us. We refilled and looked upon one another.

"Let's bring her a bottle," Jeremiah said.

"Let's bring her two."

We carried all we could from the bar and found still more bottles in crates in back and these we put in feed bags and strapped to our saddles. The bottles clanked and rattled and the boys tested their laughter. The whiskey was its own promise.

When we was done we stood and Carlos held a lantern over our efforts. He didn't say a word of disagreement when I took it from him. I heaved it against the wall of Dizzy's building. Fiery oil splattered over the wood.

The flames rose up and into the pines, and when we rode on it was this light that shown our path.

Come morning the sun was high and the sage

was alive with the calls of birds. I was dizzy and my tongue was so swollen I couldn't swallow right. A lizard lingered on a rock three feet away, he did not believe I could see him.

We had stoked up the funeral pyre and drank the whiskey in its light.

The mess of them lay about slumbering, curled and still clinging to their bottles. I looked on them for some time. It occurred to me then that if I died today, they would deliver war to my killer. If I was dragged off by wolves, they would slaughter those wolves one by one to recover me. We had together done what we done, together and without dissent. We was a republic unto ourselves. So long as we was together, the Lord dwelled no farther away than the nearest patriot.

Susie was standing against the Rock. She was outside and alone and watching me, this little girl who Ingrid so favored.

"You shouldn't be out here without a jacket."

She said nothing. She didn't look away from me.

"Is she alive?" I dared ask.

Susie said, "She wailed all night. She wailed for you. Now she has stopped."

A deep silence smothered the Rock. Folks moved about but no voices stirred the stillness. Men stood together blowing steam from their coffee. Women shook their heads. They faced her house and did not turn their backs toward it, as if the structure contained a lion.

Inside the air smelled of sour meat and worse. Annette's eyes opened and she said, "Water." Nothing was left of her voice but a rasp. Her hair was wet with sweat and she shivered despite the blankets upon her. There was no color but shades of ash. It is a terrible business, dying the gut shot.

I ladled out a cup and brought it to her and held the back of her head as she sipped it. She sank back in exhaustion from the effort. I took up a chair beside her, the same chair that had held her bare, whole, perfect body only so few nights before.

"We cleaned them," I said. "We left nobody."

Her eyes half opened but could not settle on me.

"We burned them down for what they done to you."

Her lips moved and I thought her trying to ask about the events. But when I leaned closer I heard her whisper, "Please don't leave again."

I took her hand in mine. I'm unsure if she noticed. Her hand was colder than Noah's when I carried it into the wilderness. I kissed her hand. I kissed her brow. I laid my lips upon each eye. I so wished I could trade my breath for hers.

"Water."

I gave her water, then some more. I could hear it dripping from the mattress to the stones underneath.

She panted. "No wet . . . for our thirst."

Her suffering followed a pattern as steady as the day. Cringing and seizing. Quick breaths and then none. Her brow furrowed and her eyes pinched shut and no air moved. And then the great release, air and settling and shaky breaths. She whimpered then, for water, for it to end. I thought again of Drummond's finger at his brow.

During a calm her eyes opened. "Am I dead?"

"You live."

Her hand fell to my pistol. "Please."

I kissed her lips and the tears rushed from me, so much water when she had none. I stood all at once and put the barrel to her forehead. My hand shook and I could not steady it. I was point-blank and yet sure I'd miss.

She seized again, and it was the moment to give her the gift of an end.

But I am a coward. I lay down beside her. I put my arm about her. Her cheek was against my breast.

"Jess?"

"Yeah, darling."

"Sing. Don't stop."

No words felt true. So I hummed as she shivered. I hummed Pa's lament until the day faded and the shivering stopped.

I wish I could say there was beauty at her end. I considered just now spinning a yarn about the light coming through the slats and about a hum in the air that could only be the Lord's own voice come to call His child home. But at the end there come only a savage gasp. Her eyes opened, and it was terror within them. Every muscle in her body seized against what she saw. She did not want to go wherever she was headed. She did not want to leave.

Her breath gurgled. I was sure only because of her eyes. As I looked into them. Their black went gray.

That is all.

The night we bathed, Annette put her lips to my marks. Hot water streamed from us and her lips lingered upon my scars. "Who made you perfect?"

I stayed with what remained. I stayed until Charles come to check. I stayed on account I could not bear to rise and speak the words and thereby make them true.

It was Jeremiah and Youn and Charles who drug the straw mattress and the soiled quilts from the room. Her body was still upon them. I took up the last corner and we lifted what remained and walked together through the canyon mouth and to the pile of wood that waited.

She looked small upon that pyre. A person is nothing without her body, yet her body is not the person. There is no divine in the dead.

I was the one who sparked the match and put it to tinder. All the boys had gathered. I did not offer a prayer or a speech. I did not settle the unease with words. I believed the unease was ours to bear.

The boys sent her off with strings. They played to her with fiddle and guitar and Jeremiah played her banjo with his eyes open to her flames. Their song twisted into the air and grew and did not let up even after their fingers bled.

It is what Annette would've wanted, a song that went on with no break, a song not fenced by words.

What to tell?

Noah emerged the following day. He come from his house wearing his hat and his jacket and the right sleeve was tucked into the pocket as if the hand was there keeping warm. He was weak in the knees and Jane held him for his balance. His face had yet to recover its color and he looked to have lost more than an arm.

All of us gathered before him. The children

studied that sleeve. Parents stood in silence, eyes sneaking their glance.

We followed him on a slow pilgrimage up the trail and to the rim of the Rock, all of us, the children too. Jane did not want him walking so far, but he only raised his left and her objections fell away.

So Jane led us in "Go Tell It on the Mountain" and we walked at Noah's pace. No one passed. No one took a step that he hadn't already taken.

We gathered among the defensive positions and flipped up our collars against the cold wind. Charles passed around tins of ash from the funeral fires and those of us who felt so moved took up a handful of each.

I had gathered this ash. I had been the one to parse charcoal from bone with the blade of a shovel. I reached in and took up Annette and held her over the edge.

Noah handed the Bible to Jane, who opened it to a certain page and placed it back in his hand. He looked at the text and pretended to read. His voice was too weak for its typical leaps and flourishes.

" 'They are before the throne of God, and serve Him day and night in His temple; and He that sitteth on the throne shall dwell among them. They shall hunger no more, neither thirst any more, neither shall the sun light on them, nor any heat. For the Lamb which is in the midst of the throne shall feed them, and shall lead them unto living fountains of waters, and God shall wipe away all tears from their eyes.' "

The wind that carried these words dispersed the ash over the waves of sage.

"We let them go," Noah said. "We let them join their Maker and be taken back to their rightful origin. Home is not behind us. Home is not before us. Home is now as it will forever be, above us."

At these words I gripped the ash tighter. I took my tobacco pouch, poured out its meager contents, and put the handful inside.

"We let them go," he said, "because they deserve to be free of their earthly chains. They are due in Heaven with their Father. We let them rise."

I placed the pouch inside my breast pocket.

In the stillness of the room we shared I took the tobacco pouch that held her ashes from my pocket. I remembered the water cascading down her chest, her eyes shut and the hot cloth laid upon her face. It was all so close and yet forever out of reach.

"Who made you perfect?"

I dipped my finger into the ash and put it to my tongue.

I sat alone upon the rim, the sky going from fire to water and to ice. I was looking for any sign of her.

The wolf howled twice near midnight, and I rose to my feet. She was across the night and I was here, and only her song could carry so far.

When it was time to wake the next watch, I stayed. I stayed with no thought of sleep. I was still on the rim when the sky warmed in the east. If she sang again I would be there to hear her.

The following morning there wasn't no mistaking Mr. Travis's voice. He was loading his children into their wagon. The bows was up and the tarpaulin pulled over. His wife was carrying a last basket to the bench seat.

Mr. Travis knocked upon Noah's door, and Jane pulled it open. He took off his hat and held it in his hand. I watched this from the lee of Annette's house. I could not hear their words but I knew all the same what Mr. Travis was saying. Then he replaced his hat and tipped it to Jane and walked back to his family. He helped his wife to her place and then come around and climbed up himself. He flicked the reins and they rolled through the meadow and into the canyon mouth and we did not see them again.

Susie stood with Ingrid in the pole barn. Together, they watched the people go.

The departure sparked a rush among the others. In every house was a discussion of leaving.

Had the Lord tested Noah or punished him? Could they be safe in the proximity of a man who may in truth be in conflict with the Lord? Noah needed to rise from his bed and speak to them. They awaited his confidence. All he needed to do was recite some soothing passage that would confirm their faith in him. For that is the nature of belief, its potency increases with the prevalence of doubt.

One more family left that day. Two left the day following. Noah did not even rise to watch them go. On the third day no one left and those who remained, thirty-two souls in total, seemed determined to stay the duration.

Such discussions was alive among the boys too, but in their own way. They didn't talk of leaving Noah, they talked of what they would do if on their own. No surprise most all the hypotheticals orbited some whorehouse and a limitless supply of booze.

The boys would never leave. They was fearsome warriors all of them, and no strangers to hardship. But to a man, they was more likely to charge headlong into certain death beside their leader than wander into safety alone but for their own mind.

Alone in her cabin, I built up a fire each night and washed myself. I spoke to her as if she was still in the room.

■ ■ ■ ■

Constance took slow walks about the meadow. She and Charles had moved into the two-room house left by Mr. Travis. On her walks Constance pulled up her sleeves to allow the sun upon her flesh and she turned her face skyward and shut her eyes and I found myself unable to look elsewhere. She was proof of something in this world that I ain't never found words to describe. She had put it best herself all them weeks before in the carriage. "I am a promise to them." She was no promise to me then, but she was now. Only a promise of what?

I found her one afternoon with Enterprise in the aspens. She spoke to the animal and it listened.

When she saw me she stepped away from the horse but she did not leave. Enterprise flicked her tail.

Constance touched her fingers to the aspen bark. It peeled from the tree like paper. "These aspens are all one creature. Do you know that? The whole stand grows from one root. They say the roots extend a quarter mile in places, maybe more. Two stands on either side of a ridge can be the same tree. Roots seeking water."

"You gonna leave?" I asked. "You and Charles? Thought you would by now."

She passed her hand down a trunk. "Charles wants to leave. I do too, though with all these armies looking, where are we to go? I can't allow Charles to be found leading me away. . . ." She rested her hand upon her stomach. "I felt her for the first time last night. It was only a flutter but I felt her."

"How do you know it's a her?"

"I have dreams, and in them I have a girl." Her eyes filled. "I do wish to be wrong. A mulatto and a girl? The world is cold enough."

Annette was gone and I would never see her again and yet how lucky we had been for those few moments when we fit. I wiped my eyes dry. "What is it like to feel life inside you?"

Constance put her hand to my shoulder. "Jess. I know what it means to lose the one you've counted with your future. I know how it feels to have the future stripped from you."

I looked to the paints on the walls of the Rock. I looked at the handprints of ancient men.

"One time," she began with lightness in her voice, "Will and I snuck out into the sage by nightfall. We were kids and we climbed onto the hill just high enough that we were above the roof of Father's house. There we sat and ate the slices of cake Will had fingered from the kitchen. I kissed him that night. After the cake. The icing was on my tongue and it was

553

still upon his lips and I leaned across the divide between us and licked the sugar from his face. We were twelve or thirteen, so we didn't know what kissing leads to and it went no further. But I remember how the moon bounced from his eyes after, how it bounced from him onto me and how easy it was to believe. The Lord had united us. The Lord intended us together. How could it be any other way? I still feel as much now. Cling to your certainty. Cherish it. No one can take her from you now."

Constance looked to Noah's house. "We are with child together, Jane and I. What else can the Lord mean but that we should stay together? How are we to live in this world if not by our faith in the omens He sends to us?

"There was a time, those first days here in fact, when I believed my faith to be lost. How could the Lord allow Will's death? How could he intend for me to bring up our child without him? I know, Jess, how easy it is to doubt. But He must be watching. He must. We share a cold world, Jess, and yet as long as heat exists, how can we not trust its source?"

By day the boys grew rowdy. Mason got his hands on a cube of dynamite and he rode it out a quarter mile and tied it in the top of some bitterbrush. From the rim we could see only the faintest red speck. The boys laid down their monies and took turns firing on it. I watched and admired how a target could so direct their spirits.

It was sometime before a bullet found its mark. Pure chance. But there was disagreement about the particulars and soon Jeremiah and I was pulling two of the boys apart. Lips was bloody and a shoulder come out of joint. Charles was sent for to mend the shoulder.

Jeremiah offered me a plug. We stood eyeing the crew as they watched Charles rotate the arm. Jeremiah muttered, "These boys need something to do."

"These boys need their boss."

We shared a glance. He spat.

Some days after her death the boys had a card game going. We lingered in the sun near the pole barn. The winter wasn't that far off now and the boys was arguing. The topic turned to my brother.

"Harney without a woman would still have his arm."

"He was distracted."

"Can't have a woman in this business."

"Now that I can agree with."

"I bet you something." Mason nodded toward Noah's house. "That queen of his is making the decisions."

"Wouldn't touch that bet," Carlos said to

555

his cards. "She is the only reason we ain't left yet."

"Shut up, all of you," I said.

There had been talk among the boys for some days about the fact that I was there with Noah and Annette in the hailstorm of lead and yet I had not been touched. When I started across the meadow the boys ditched their cards to follow me.

Jane saw the mess of us coming and met us at the door. She pulled the wood shut behind her so we couldn't see inside. "Pleasant day, isn't it?" She wore that big smile of hers. Her belly bulged. It was the first I noticed the outward show of child. "How can I be of assistance?"

I said, "Let me see him."

"He's sleeping," Jane said.

The door pulled open. Noah stood there without a hat on. He was hard withered, sunken eyes and dry-flaked skin. His arm wore a fresh bandage. Even so blood stained the wrapping. "Morning, boys," he said with gravel in his voice.

"Come tell us what you want," I said.

Noah found his hat on its peg and put it on. He stepped into the daylight and Jane put her hand to his shoulder. He said to her, "Give us a moment, would you, dear?"

"Of course." She stepped inside but left the door open.

With his left hand Noah took a pouch from

his pocket and handed it to me. "Roll me one. I ain't yet mastered the left-handed spin."

"Patrón, how long you reckon we gonna be here?" Mason asked. "We really sticking it out for the whole winter?"

"What's to stop Dizzy from leading the militia here?" I asked.

Noah took the cigarette I offered and pulled a long drag. I was waiting on him to lead his boys. But he only looked on his stub. "Ugly, ain't it?"

"Si, Patrón," said Carlos. "It's ugly."

"Dizzy," I said. "We got to hunt him up. He knows where we hide. That reward is his for the knowledge."

Noah looked up from his arm. He drew on his cigarette. All the boys watched him.

"Either that or we should move on," I said. "You got this figured, so tell us."

When my brother could've led us with any word at all, he only smoked. He had called that arm an implement of divine will, and now the Lord had taken it back.

"Harney?" Mason belted.

Noah spat a flake of tobacco.

I turned to face the Wild Bunch. "All right, boys. We break into two teams. One finds Dizzy before he turns us over and the other stays here in defense. I ride with whichever team is on the hunt. Sound right, Patrón?"

I ain't sure my brother was listening. But

557

now he gave a little shrug and nodded.

The boys pushed at one another and at once was jockeying for who would ride out first. It was Jeremiah who didn't move. His eyes remained on Noah. "What do you think?"

My brother said, "It's a good idea."

"Go draw cards for the teams," I said. "Patrón and me will talk the particulars."

The boys done as I say. Jeremiah was the last to go. We was sharing a look.

Now I took hold of my brother's shoulder to gain his mind. His eyes passed over my face and then to the rim.

"You got to return to us, brother. These boys is counting on you. I'm counting on you."

"All the lead that has come at me, and I ain't never been hit. And then the bullet that does connect takes my right arm. What do you make of that?"

"It don't change the fact all these lives is counting on you. We's here because of you."

He smoked the last drag of his cigarette and dropped it and toed it out. "The boys listen to you."

"I think we should leave. I want to say that. I believe it is foolish to remain here. They may already be marching toward us."

Noah nodded toward the Rock's walls. He looked into the Indian paint upon them. "The snows ain't far off now."

"What you saying?"

He shrugged. "I don't know."

"You got to know."

"Jess, what do you want from me? I lost her too."

I coughed at what rose in my throat. "What about getting Jane and Constance closer to a midwife? What about getting all these children out of harm's way?"

"I just don't know, Jess. Okay? I don't. I mean, how could He let this happen?"

We passed the last warm days of autumn on the hunt. We traveled by forest to likely crossroads and set up ambushes. I carried Annette with me and set her on the Rock beside the shells I lined up in case they was needed. I wanted to rain lead down upon Dizzy from the silence of the forest. I wanted to punch lead through his guts and watch him flail. I wanted to bring him on a pole back to the Rock and teach him what he'd done to her. My mind was consumed with sour visions.

In time we come to feel ourselves alone in that wilderness. The silence got the boys' spirits down. We could feel the long winter bearing in on us, and the stillness it would bring. We all knew the hardships awaiting us in that Rock. The boys would've been wet all day had I allowed bottles on the hunt.

On the last day warm enough to draw

sweat, they was arguing among themselves anytime we dismounted. Petty matters. I ordered them apart. I ordered them to take up firing positions and not to speak.

I had just put in a fresh plug when I heard Carlos clicking for my attention. I turned and saw that something was coming down the road. Whatever it was, was big, brown, and moving without a sound. It hadn't broke a stick or rolled a rock. The boys readied their rifles.

The great bear took his time. He stopped beside an old broken pine and commenced tearing at the wood. Chunks busted free and the bear dug at the rotten wood inside. He licked the grubs from the chips. He sat on his haunches and ripped out more. He was through too many limbs for a clean shot and we was downwind and so not a finger among them rushed. Annette had taught them well.

I might've stood and scared the bear off. I might've saved his old life. But I only watched. Annette was beside me and a grueling winter was before me and my brother wasn't the man I believed and nothing at all was mine.

He finally rose and continued down the trail and when he crossed our agreed-upon marker, we opened up on him. The great bear spun and roared and charged across the stream and up the far slope. The boys fired on him as he ran and continued firing for some moments after he disappeared. Some leapt to their horses and charged after the animal. A bear is much faster up a hill than a horse but our bear was hard hit. Jeremiah fired the finishing shot from his saddle. The bear roared one final time and then come crashing back down the slope. He rolled to rest in the water.

We drug the bear behind us all the miles back to the Rock and there hung it from the pole barn by its neck. From the long drag the hair had been scraped on one half of the bear's body and the other side was caked in dust and grit. Mason cut the hide at the neck and then the boys took hold and pulled while he worked his blade. They joshed like old times, as if Annette and Blister was still among us, as if the crew was whole.

When the pelt come free there hung the strongest-looking man any of us ever seen. The boys quit talking. They stared. His legs was bear-short and his arms bear-long, but his muscles was thicker than even Mason's and in all the same places. The bear twisted in the breeze, naked.

The fat was cut clean from the muscle and put to render and the meat was cut in great chunks and then diced and diced again. This was packed into meal-sized balls that would freeze down overnight. The bullets had soured sections of the meat and these had to be cut free. The bullets was dropped in a tin pail beside the table and each one landed with a plink.

I bent to that pail and lifted one of them pellets. The lead was bent and flattened and contained in its crevices fat and blood and even a single barb of fur. What remained weighed hardly nothing. It had been driven through hide and flesh and muscle and bone and brought a bear to its knees, and now I held it in my hand, this piece of lead no bigger than my pinkie nail.

So minor a metal had reduced her to an ashen corpse.

Folks always think they know what happened next. I ain't seen the history books for my own self but people tell me what they read. I don't like to hear it, and not on account those books missed some facts. I avoid it because they missed the why. It's all yarn without the why.

We didn't go looking for Dizzy no more, he come to us. Behind him was the Governor's militia and a detachment of the U.S. Cavalry, being guided now to the very place that had eluded them so long.

They was years from any battle worth fighting and drier than dust and sure of only one thing. We was outside the boundaries of soul, outside the protections of God, and no scales would detect crime in our slaughter. They rode with a freedom so potent it could sour a nation.

The watchman's alarm sounded before dawn, before the force had cleared the pines. I was already up and dressed as had become my sober pattern and so I was among the first to the rim. It was Carlos who sounded the alarm. He said he had seen a flash on the edge of the plateau, a match to a cigarette, he thought.

The horizon was a crisp line separating realms. The morning star was fading. For a time we stood and watched and wondered if Carlos had it wrong. But then come the rumble of a storm and we knew at once it was not thunder. They come out of the gray dawn to deliver our death.

The boys took to the mortared walls and firing ports. Carlos was blowing his whistle in the code of imminent attack, and from below we heard the shouting of men and women alike. There come the crying of an infant. The pounding of hooves ever louder.

When the horses was inside a mile I got the match sparked and the fuse traced across the red rock toward the canyon mouth. I hollered a warning to the others and then knelt and covered my ears. The dynamite blew and the Rock shook and there come the cataclysm of boulders cascading to earth. The canyon mouth was now blocked by columns of red rock, pebbles and dust still sloughing free.

There come the sounds of doves ripping by overhead but it was in fact bullets. Lead struck stones and wheezed off into nothing. Lead-painted boulders. Hot shards struck my cheek and drew blood. Lead passed so close I could smell its molten vapors, and I saw Pa again but for a flash as he poured balls before the evening fire. So many hours breathing the fumes of lead. Lead fizzed about us. Lead whispering its death song. Lead, and at its launch, a gray ribbon of smoke. My whole life has been governed by this goddamn metal.

Their charge would've cut right through us if not for the Rock. But with it, they was like a storm to oak panel. We fired on them as they neared. We fired on them as they banked from their planned entrance. We fired on them as they continued their charge in a full circle around our Rock and then back out the way they come.

The mess of them, horse and men, collected together again outside rifle range, minus the wounded and dying who now lay upon the sage. The boys continued to lob bullets.

"Save your lead!" I barked. "They seek to empty our reserves."

"They watch us," Noah hollered. He had been slow to reach the rim but now he knelt among us. He poked his head over the rock then ducked back. Lead hit nearby and I felt foolish for not seeking cover. All the boys who had been standing now knelt behind cover.

"Do as Jess says, boys," Noah shouted. "They's counting our guns."

The fighters churned there in the sage, confused no doubt by the lack of access, and then they dismounted. They was a mile out and too far for even the Sharps and they knew it.

Noah took the brass scope from his pocket. He flicked it open and brought it to his eye. The wind was in our face. He clung to the edge of the rock to shield as much of his person as possible.

"I count six dying horses and two dead men," someone said.

"One of them men is mine," said Mason. "First blood."

"Count it." Carlos nodded. "I saw the hit."

Noah was having trouble steadying the scope with one hand. He cursed. "This thing is hopeless."

I took the scope from him and stood from this ridiculous edge of rock and held it to my own eye with two hands. I counted the living as best I could with all the moving in their ranks. "I got one twenty-two," I said. "That's horses, not men."

I will admit I took a moment longer looking for Greenie's red hair. I didn't see it. But I did spy a small man with a sword and figured him to be the major.

Noah took back the scope. He handed me his tobacco pouch. "Roll me one." Now he sat cross-legged with an empty sleeve in his lap.

I rolled him one. Then I rolled another for myself. I sparked a match and covered it to mine first and then his. We looked off into the distance as the sun rose behind us and threw our black shadow out over the enemy and the sage beyond.

That's when I noticed the calm settling about me, in my breathing, in my hands. It was peace, no other word for it. To have the enemy there, in one known place — there was a queer comfort in it.

"Is they coming or not?" Carlos hollered.

"Try us again!" Mason shouted as loud as he could. "Grow some stones and charge! I wanna get me a few dozen more."

"What do you want us to do?" I asked my brother.

He didn't answer. I don't believe he heard the question. The rollie in his fingers trembled.

The fighting juice faded from the boys with the hours and they got to complaining of being hungry, of being bored, of fighting an

566

enemy too yellow to charge.

Still Noah sat behind the lip of rock. "Somebody go down and get us some grub. This here is a siege. Might as well get ourselves fed."

Nobody moved. Nobody wanted to miss the moment the action started. So I picked out two boys and sent them down.

We ate our breakfast on the rim and then we ate our lunch too. Nothing much changed except for the color of the sky. So long as the enemy remained dismounted we knew any attack was still in planning stage. We passed the time playing cards and gambling on all manner of trivial occurrence. I lost a dollar when a raven didn't land on the rock but instead continued past.

Their dead now swelled in the sun and already vultures circled a mile above us, waiting. We could see them coming from a distance, a chain of them following the smell of death and the promise of more. All the battlefields they'd fed on.

I rolled my brother's cigarettes and checked the enemy through the scope. I was trying to make out faces among them but it was no use. I didn't see no guardsmen's dusters or black hats.

"What they saying, you figure?" Noah asked me.

"They's talking about waiting us out. They

figuring how long it'll be before we expose ourselves for want of water."

"We got all we ever need on that accord."

"They don't know what we got."

Noah smoked his cigarette down to his fingers then flicked it away right quick. "Should've gotten some more rollies."

"How long we gonna wait, Patrón?" Jeremiah dared ask. "Couldn't we bait them close?"

Noah exhaled through his nose. "Winter's coming and they ain't got no break from the wind. We'll wait *them* out."

"You really think they'll leave?" I muttered to my brother.

He was fingering the cracks in the rock he was hiding behind. "I don't know."

I clenched my jaw to keep from saying something I might regret. The boys was watching.

Mason said, "I'd feel a lot better if 'n we commenced killing them now."

Pale Jay said, "I think the injuns had it right. Following the buffalo all year. They didn't get themselves in no siege."

"Men ain't built for sitting still when there's a fight to win."

"Still is bored."

"Bored is worse than death."

"I'm rotten then."

"Quit your whining," I hollered.

The boys looked off. Nobody said nothing

for a long time.

Noah climbed from the ground but stayed hunched.

"Where you off to?" I asked.

"You got it up here. I'm going down to tend to the folks and see if I can't recruit some more fighters from among the men."

He should've left us with a great speech of confidence. But he only turned and walked down the path into the meadow.

The boys watched him go. The boys spat. The boys snuck glances on me.

"Keep an eye for sharpshooters," I said.

Come darkness we was in heightened alarm. We studied their shapes and saw that they ate their suppers before twig fires. We saw too that their horses was set out to graze. Their saddles was off and they was hobbled. We took that as a ruse and sure evidence that an attack was imminent.

Not a one of us slumbered. We pulled up our coats and huddled against the wind. I checked for the thousandth time that I had a shell in the chamber.

"Wish they'd just attack already."

"Somebody find some whiskey."

At dawn I pulled up the scope and found their horses still hobbled. A few of their men warmed their hands against fresh built-up fires. The rest was still in the tents. A full day had passed since the last action. Half our boys was laid out drooling in their sleep.

"What they waiting on?" Carlos whispered. He was beside me now, looking over the length of his barrel as it projected from a firing port.

I noticed then that their dead men had been removed during the cover of darkness. It was the only difference.

Noah hollered for us around midmorning and I come to the edge and looked into the meadow. Ingrid and the other horses was at the feed troughs, their heads lost in delight. "Send three boys down."

"Why?"

"Do it."

I called for volunteers and then joined the two that stepped forward. We found waiting on us not a hot breakfast as we'd figured but three buckets of human waste. The men, women, and children could no longer venture into the sage to relieve themselves and so had taken to sitting on buckets. "Ain't we got enough to contend with?" I asked.

Noah's hat was on low and his sleeve was tucked into his pocket. He spoke to my knees. "Bang 'em out when you do it. No sense in bringing some back with you."

We each carried a bucket and did our best not to breathe or slosh.

"To hell with this," Mason said on the walk

up. "I'm a gunfighter not a shit banger-outer."

"We'll do it," I said, "and we won't complain neither. We's the only ones who can walk up here without pissing ourselves for fear. They do stuff for us too."

"I ain't complaining, I'm just saying."

"No, you's complaining," I said. "And the boys don't need no poison."

But Mason hadn't said nothing I wasn't already thinking. My brother had put us in this bind and now he was staying warm down below.

That night we ate and then took turns sleeping and watching their twig fires. Their men sat up late, and from the sounds of their merriment we guessed they had whiskey. In the stillness of the night air we could hear their music. A fiddle was what we heard best.

"They about as good at playing as they is at shooting," Pale Jay said.

I thought on it and then said, "Let's show 'em up."

The boys liked this notion. Mason and three others went down by lantern light and fetched our instruments. When they returned we sat upon the moonlit rocks and the boys tuned up. I watched through the scope for movement among the enemy.

Jeremiah answered with Annette's banjo. He was playing the very song we heard from their camp, only better.

Rest of the boys joined in at once and I watched through the scope as the enemy stood from their fires and looked out at the night. They watched, and though the distance was profound I imagined them in awe. How queer it must've been to hear their very songs played better from the rock upon which they laid siege. Did it make them want to kill us less or more?

The next afternoon a train of wagons appeared behind their camp. We could not see what the wagons contained but we assumed food and bedding and ammunition. We soon learned we was mistaken. Through the scope I watched as two Gatling guns was unloaded and aimed our way.

When darkness fell we didn't much sleep. Those was big weapons.

We was moving rocks to bolster our firing ports when the sharpshooter scored his first hit.

Carlos was hefting an especially big rock and doing so required he straighten his back. His head come up over the edge of the wall. The bullet hit him above the left eye at a glancing angle. He fell to the earth at once and we gasped at what we assumed was his sure death. Then as a ghost he rolled over and held his fingers to his wound and said,

"Who threw that rock?"

"You done got shot!" Mason yelled. "Holy hell and mayhem!"

Jeremiah helped Carlos to sit. The Mexican was dizzy and sank back to the ground. I felt his skull for myself and determined it wasn't broke. A sleeve was all that was needed to slow the bleeding.

Carlos kept asking, "Shot in the head?"

Mason stood and yelled from the rim, "You can't win! Not even your bullets can kill us!"

Just then the Gatling guns opened up and lead cut the air over us and splattered against the rocks below and we dove for cover. More lead than a whole army could deliver and it come from just two guns. The distance was great enough that we could almost see the lead coming and it piled like hail at the base of our walls, tumbling rocks and ricocheting in every goddamn direction.

By a feat of pure random madness some of those thick rounds ricocheted into the meadow.

Horses began wailing. There was screams of children.

I took a leave from the rim and found Ingrid shivering in the pole barn. All the animals was crowded into the corral now, as if it could offer them any protection at all from the brutalities of flying metal. A kind-faced bay struggled in the meadow, limp in the hindquarters and dragging itself about on its front legs, screaming. A bullet had broke its spine.

Mr. Cherry fired a Spencer point-blank into that poor animal's head, and it fell heavy on its side and quivered.

I put my face to Ingrid's. She threw her head to be rid of my obstruction. She was without wound and yet she was panting and wild eyed. Ingrid wasn't built for no war, she was a horse made for quiet, wide-open spaces and I could do nothing to calm her.

Mr. Cherry held his sobbing wife. I couldn't hear what he said but I do wish I'd gone to him then and talked him out of what they come to do.

The dead horse changed things for the folks below. There was no burying a horse in that hard ground and so the folks could no longer avoid the truth of what awaited outside. They took their shelter in the schoolhouse, which sat in the lee of the rock. If men emerged, they ran with their heads low to the storehouse or the woodpile and then come running back.

For all the remaining days of the siege the Rock was filled with the stench of rot. At least up top we had good air.

Clouds started building the next day. The wind smelled of snow.

Jeremiah shouted, "What in hell?"

I come to the edge to find two of ours walking across the plain of ash toward the enemy camp. I knew who it was even before I drew up my scope. Mr. and Mrs. Cherry. They was plumb wore through and wanted out. Who could blame them? Without consulting my brother they had scaled the rubble in the canyon mouth and now they aimed to give themselves to the militia. The logic was sound enough. Who would want to harm gentle farmers like the Cherrys?

The accounts of the event have it wrong. The books will tell you that it was us on top of the Rock who shot them down. Books is writ by the victor.

Mr. and Mrs. Cherry walked hand in hand under that thickening sky, and we stood to watch them go. They walked toward a line of men with rifles and there wasn't a soul among us who could draw a straight breath at the sight. We believed they would be taken in by our enemy and then bound and beaten until they told all they knew. We believed they would be taken in.

But the sharpshooter saw his chance at us there gandering without full cover and let off a round. The bullet hit Jeremiah in the left shoulder and drew blood though it was only flesh and no bone. We drug him into the cover and was ripping at his jacket and so didn't pay much attention when we heard the enemy riflemen open up.

The Cherrys lay writhing in the flat. Kicking and stomping and even from that distance we could hear the agony. It come across that sage and distance and hit us worse than lead. In his last moment Mr. Cherry took hold of his dead wife's hand, and then he too bled out.

Looking back I suspect it was the sharp-shooter's shot that sparked one of the militia-men, and as soon as one bullet had been fired, the rest of the riflemen believed there to be good cause.

I couldn't stop the boys then. They must've fired a thousand rounds at that far-off enemy. The only effect was to provoke ten thousand rounds fired in return. The Gatling guns rained lead like thunderclouds.

Darkness brought a lull, and for the first time there was no moon or stars to light the night. There was no Noah to give us orders. He hadn't come up all day. I had to deliver word of what happened to his people.

He took the news with shut eyes.

I ate from a tin of beans and watched the enemy about their fires. Too many men was standing up that evening. I fell asleep but I awoke with a terrible knowledge. I had seen the major thinking it through.

I stood and called to the boys. "I need ten of you."

"You got a notion?" Mason asked.

We rushed down the slope by the light of a

single lantern and then ran across the dark meadow as the folks slept. There come only the sound of casings in our pockets and the squeak of the lantern's hinge and the patter of boots on rock and then the ratchet of a Winchester levering in a shell.

The boys took up positions in the canyon mouth as I directed and I blew the lantern out. I gave them strict orders to remain silent and to fire only when I had taken the first shot. "No rollies," I said. "No sparks of light."

"I hope they come," said Mason. "I hope they all come."

The fact that the Cherrys had climbed out meant in the mind of the major that there was indeed a way in. What better time to try it than on this dark night?

The fact their attack come as I predicted was further evidence for the boys.

It was in the darkest hour of night, that hour before dawn, when we heard a single slip of cobble. Then a minute later we heard the scrape of leather and the ting of a barrel on rock. I drew the hammer slow enough to dim its click.

We let them scale the columns of rock and we let them believe the gate to be unguarded. We heard pistols cock and spittle splash and then in a bolt of lightning I dropped the lead man myself. I had aimed for the glow of his cigarette but three feet away.

Boys was perched above and boys hunkered

in the path and all at once they opened up. We saw the enemy in the flashes of our muzzles and we took aim on the shapes burned into our vision and we dropped them in the span of two breaths.

When it was through, Youn sparked the lantern and the boys howled at the sight of the corpses upon the earth. They was strewn in unnatural postures, legs forked underneath and eyes blazed open in surprise. Two still gurgled their blood and they was dispatched at point-blank.

The major was not among them. I did not recognize a face.

One of the boys started pissing on a body. Then they all done it. They was laughing like we was six bottles deep.

It had been a single unit of the militia, eighteen men. But had it been the entire force I suspect we could've held them.

On top in that earliest light I put the scope on the major's double tent and saw him out front in conference with his lieutenants. He had ordered them to try and lost. He would try again.

They was here not to subdue us, but to erase us. What else but our complete annihilation could wrestle back the pen that wrote the Governor's legacy?

The Winchester would never reach but I tried anyhow. I held upon the horizon and lobbed pellets of lead. The boys took this as license and we all threw ore across that sage, over the Cherrys still sprawled where they fell, and yet the major and his lieutenants didn't so much as turn our way.

That afternoon the snows began in earnest and Jeremiah and me smoked with our backs to the wind. His wounded shoulder give him pain enough to grimace but he wasn't the type to mention pain. His arm was back in its sleeve. His riding jacket was tore and the bloodstains had gone brown. He was working out the hand, trying to keep it from going stiff. "Why don't he come up?" he asked me in a voice too quiet to be heard by the boys. Noah hadn't even ventured up top to speak of our victory at the canyon mouth.

"I guess we know what to do but it don't sit right, us up here and him down there." Jeremiah drew from his cigarette. "I ain't never seen him like that. Scared."

"Losing an arm, I reckon."

"Don't got to tell me. But I figured him . . . you know, above such worries."

"Yeah, well."

"I would've guessed we could cut his legs at the knees and he'd still be marching about barking orders and preaching hellfire. I once seen him stand and face four men with rifles and not flinch."

I took the last drag of my smoke and flicked what remained. The snow was pelting us now and sticking about the Rock and the day was fading fast and I was certain there was no way out of this but through pure grit. "You keep an eye on the boys," I said. "I'll go see about my brother."

Noah was in the schoolhouse with the others. He was sitting near the stove with his back to the Rock and his book open before him. Since he couldn't read I knew he was only fending off visitation from his people.

When I entered the room all voices fell silent including those of the children. They turned and looked upon me like I was a saint or ghost. I took off my hat and knocked free the snow and set it on a desk since all the pegs was taken.

Charles and Constance stood together before the window. They looked to have been engaged in conversation, but now their eyes was on me.

The people in that room must've known that I was one of the killers who had left those bodies in the canyon. Now I stood among them, a Winchester in one hand and two pistols on my belt. Children watching my guns. I couldn't remember what I'd felt the first time I saw Drummond. Whatever it was had been in error.

I leaned the Winchester against the wall and come through the room and a path opened before me. I stood before my brother. He said without looking up from his book, "Jess."

"The snow is thick and still falling," I said.

"Winter is upon us." His eyes remained upon the page. "Build up a fire. Build up a windbreak. The boys was born tough."

"I ain't here to complain, brother. I believe the lack of visibility may provide us an opportunity."

His eyes glanced upon me and then back to his pages. "Is that so?"

"They can't see us."

"You want to make a run for it? Where will you go? There ain't no way out of this valley."

"Brother."

Now he looked up and I saw the weary in his face. "What, Jess? What? You always pester me. Since you was a girl, always pestering for answers."

I looked about the room. The people was whispering among themselves, their eyes glancing on us, on me.

"You never trust the answers I give anyhow. Look, I know it ain't easy. But you all is doing good. There ain't nothing for us to do right now but wait. You'll get killed or worse if you leave this Rock. This is the only place we got left. Trust me."

"I'm trying to trust, brother. I am. But the boys up there, freezing and ducking lead, they need you. They keep turning to check the trail to see if you've come up. And when they look around and don't see you, they know you is here sitting in the warmth, your back to the Rock. You got any sense what it's like to watch you ride off and leave us behind?"

His eyes narrowed. "What you really talking about here, Jess?"

Jane stepped near. "Jess, you don't understand what he's suffering. This wound. It keeps him up at night. He has dreams. . . . He is a man who is healing. He can't be out in the cold for long hours, not now. You must understand that."

My voice shook. "These boys put their trust in you."

"Damn it, Jess!" His curse sent a shock through the room. I don't think he noticed. His eyes was wet. "It wasn't me who got her killed. You didn't listen. You didn't trust. You went to town."

At this truth my knees wobbled. All those days I wondered if my brother blamed me. Now I knew. Yet nothing he could say about the matter was more cruel than what I said to myself in every lonely moment.

He said, "Just go up top and do as I say."

"Do you trust yourself anymore, brother? I don't think you do. I think you running on fear, not belief."

He parked his gaze in the Bible.

I took his book and snapped it shut. When he looked up, there wasn't certainty in his eyes. Unsure like that, he looked old. He looked broken and familiar. He looked something like our pa.

"Brother, you asked me if you hit him too hard. I lied to you. His head cracked upon the ground and he wasn't never the same after. You knew you broke him. That's why you never come back. Walking the path the Lord laid for you, shit. Walking a length of yarn, more like it. All these years you knew the truth. Didn't you?"

He took hold of Jane's arm.

"Not now, Jess," she said. "Not here."

But my heart was pounding and there wasn't nothing off-limits. I turned toward his followers. "You stayed because you trust this man to lead you. You trust he has a straight line to the Lord and that he hears what you cannot." I opened my brother's Bible to the book of Kings and bellowed, "Read it to us, Noah Harney. Come now. Show us you know these big words. Impress us with your God-given skill."

Noah didn't move. Jane took the book from my hands and said, "You stop this right now."

"See?" I called to the room. "He don't read. He ain't never read a true word of this book to you. Ain't that right, Noah Harney? Come on now. Be clean with them just this once. Be clean with us." I turned to them. "See, Jane teaches him to memorize the words. Then he holds the book before you on Sundays and pretends. Fools, don't you see? All of us, fools. We've been whiskeyed by this man."

At once their voices rose with objection. Their eyes leapt with light and men waded across the room to confront me. They begged my brother to contradict these crazy indictments. They waved fingers at me as if they was knives. They implored him to read a passage, to right his ship, to put this ugly woman in her place.

When I turned, Constance was in the window's light. Our eyes met. She nodded.

I took up my rifle and put on my hat and stepped into the storm. I felt the snow upon my skin and knew.

Live or die, what come next was on me.

On the rim, I racked the Winchester and Jeremiah passed me a smoke. I waved it away. My eyes was on the distance.

The snows had ebbed and I could see over the plateau. Their fires was smothered and their men hid in snowbound tents. Three guards leaned against their rifles.

Between here and there lie the bodies of the Cherrys, two mounds in the white, left out.

My boys shivered against the rocks. My boys had their collars up against the cold and their hands buried in pockets. Carlos wiped snot from his nose. Mason coughed.

The wind grew to a howl and the snow

pelted us and the enemy camp was again lost to sight but not to knowing. It loomed within, always, a cardinal point.

"Tonight," I called and the boys turned. "Out of the darkness. Knives. Teams of four. We move among them like the wind and leave them to bleed with no voice to call out. We slay them as they so deserve."

The boys looked about one another. They stood from their rocks. Snow hung on the brims of their hats.

"The winter is young and we wither in the cold and we do not have any resupply. There is no escape fast enough and surrender means a fate worse than death. And so what choice do we have but to seize the first advantage offered to us? That advantage is now."

Carlos said, "Knives?"

Pale Jay frowned. "I ain't never killed with a blade before."

"It's good," Mason said. "You'll like it."

I drew my own knife and held it to the light. "We enter their ranks. We embrace them as the snows embrace them. We become them, and we kill them son by son, father by father, brother by brother. We kill them and in so doing we set these people free."

Pale Jay said, "But I guess I don't get why we don't just shoot them dead?"

Jeremiah answered for me. "Gunfire will alert them and they will rise against us in sheer number." He nodded to me. "Right?"

"Tonight we attack as they could never expect. We own our murdering and resolve ourselves to it. For if we fail, they will blot us from this earth forever and write our stories in their name."

"This is what Patrón wants?" Mason asked.

I did not hide my eyes. "If you're moved by what Noah Harney orders, you should remain here. He may even let you inside with him."

Mason spat.

Carlos shrugged. "Some of us won't come through."

"I for one plan to die tonight," I said. "I plan to take a hundred of those bastards with me. Ask yourself, is it death you fear or being the last man alive?"

Youn's eyes narrowed on me.

Mason put a thumb to his blade. He shrugged. "You know I'm in."

Jeremiah tested his stiff arm. "I'm going."

All at once, the boys was checking their knives.

Youn was the last.

Jeremiah said, "When do we go, Boss?"

"Hone those edges," I said. "Eat some grub and make your peace. We wait for them to sleep. We wait no longer."

The folks was asleep in their warm stone houses and the fires in their stoves smoldered and filled the wet snow with smoke. It fell so fast we couldn't see nothing in the lantern light but flakes. The night hummed with ashen landings.

We turned our lanterns on the snowbound bodies blocking the canyon and picked our way through the rocks and helped up the man behind and steadied the one in front and we starved the lanterns and set them in the dry lee of the rock and passed through the mouth and into the sage toward our deaths. We knew the direction by heart.

We didn't see their encampment coming, we smelled it. Wet horse, wet wool, wet smoke. The snows fell so hard we could not see their tents until our fingertips found them. We dispersed into the heart of their village. We broke into our fours and I led mine straight for the double tent that held the major.

We took the guard where he dozed. We drove him into the snow without a grunt and four blades worked him until his muscles quit taunting us.

We felt our way around the edge of the tent until our pushing revealed a release in the canvas.

We stepped into the heavy air of men dreaming. The enemy grumbled and rolled over.

We loomed as shadows within a veil of shadow, towering over flesh and blood bound by the same ties to kin and land, governed by the same codes of order and soul, and yet our fingers searched quilt and fur for the tender opening of neck. When we might've noticed the same textures upon them as upon us, when we might've known the lack of division between their breath and ours, we felt nothing but our lust to finish what we had begun.

The major swatted as if at a mosquito. I drew the blade across his bare throat and in the next motion drove it into his chest and he arched in gasping violence and I bore my forearm into his open mouth to silence him and when he quit trying I pummeled his nose with my elbow and reburied my knife in his guts and stirred.

Tent to tent, geyser to geyser, we sank blades into eyes, slashed at cheeks and bellies, hacked and stabbed. Tendons cut loose and muscles balled, joints unhinged, intestines held in open hands. We found each other by click and whisper and moved as one into that next place from which we could not return.

In the space between killings we grew cold. Yet in each new tent waited a rush of pulsing heat, and we relished that warmth like serpents turning toward the birth of spring.

Gunshots as red bursts muffled by snow.

They rose and leapt upon us from every direction. Only they didn't know who to kill.

I hacked with the major's sword. I sliced a man through his collar. I swung at a shape and felt the gravel of spine. I drove the sword through another and left it and drew my pistols and bucked off rounds.

We put our backs to one another and fired at the sounds of men rushing and shouting and gasping. We fired with our eyes open and yet we saw nothing but the dragon's breath of our barrels and the purples and reds of vision lost to light. We fired through tents and at gasps and we understood our hits by the sounds lead makes against flesh, fabric, air. We, the arms and legs of the same insatiable beast.

It went on in increments not tallied by any earthly measure. For centuries we wander that snow with their blood running from our elbows.

Dawn brought only white but no order. The sky as white as the earth and between was white without distance, gravity the only cardinal point.

In the absence of their agony the silence grew to a roar. We turned our war upon silence. We hollered. We fired only to hear the report. We stumbled over bodies and turned to dig them out and check if they was ours.

We heard nothing but for the falling snow and the hooves of our own hearts.

A tuft of red hair among the white. I dug it out with insane terror.

The hair did not belong to my Greenie.

"How could you kill as you have?"

For as long as we've been the Good, we've invented histories to so convince our children. We heed preachers upon tilted altars. We let them spin this world.

So long as we remain at its center.

■ ■ ■ ■

V

■ ■ ■ ■

I do not recall our return. I do not recall if Noah greeted us or what Jane said or if Constance stared in horror at the blood that turned our jackets to armors of crimson ice.

I have no memory of so much that happens after. For decades now I walk in one place and dwell in another.

Before, I was aware of every turn in the breeze, the fibrous flutter of wind through feather, the heat every blister makes upon a heel. Before, I could wake at night and tell how many hours till the dawn, I could work all morning and know how many minutes until the noon.

Pa's voice across years, *Your ma never lost the time.*

What I remember next is Ingrid keeping her distance. Her nose lifted toward my scent.

Despite the snows and risks of winter travel, families began packing at once. The men found the dynamite and took it upon themselves to blast and then blast again the rubble blocking their wagons. They fought that rubble and the frozen bodies below it, heaving until their heat give off clouds. Jane lifted a panel from her wall and dragged from a cave chests built of hardwood. She handed the families sagging bags of gold.

They rolled out into the white without a call back to the man who had brought them there, or to the killers who had traded life for their freedom. The orphans, the homesteaders and their babies, they rolled out into the sun-blind white.

Before they left, Ingrid stood downwind. She stomped a foot. She blew the scent of blood from her nose.

I tried to shirk my frozen jacket. I struggled against the ice until the jacket fell free with a clatter. She was already backing away. She was looking to the wagon.

Susie clung to the wagon's rear. Pots dangled from the bows and a water jug hung from the panel. The children of the mother sat up front. Susie the orphan held to the only space that remained, the flat top of a trunk.

I had to put a rope about Ingrid's neck and tie her to a post in order to tack her up. She did not trust me about her flank. When I was done I drew the rope from her and let her trot home.

Her Susie swung up into the saddle and

old Mr. James adjusted the stirrups to her short legs. I followed them through the mouth and then I remained inside.

I must've run to the top of the rim, for I remember watching Ingrid cross that plateau.

Susie was so light upon her back. Ingrid always was a little girl's horse.

We too rolled on from the Rock and past the bulge of corpses. Ours with theirs, under piled snow.

Constance, Charles, Jane, and Noah sharing a wagon. The five of us Wild Bunch who lived rode behind, Youn, Mason, Carlos, Jeremiah. I remember rubbing ice upon my flesh. It ran from me in pink tendrils.

In time we again entered green forests and the snows melted into the needles and left only a road burdened with mud and trees dragged down by the weight of snow now melted to water.

We rolled through the mud and wore it as we had snow only days before, sawing logs from our path as we went.

Noah sat upon his seat and held the reins in his hand, and when the next log was cleared, he flicked those reins and the wagon rolled on.

I remember my brother in the fire's light, his hand upon my shoulder and his eyes holding mine. His sleeve dangled at his side and his lips drove for the same resolution our knives had sought those nights before.

"The Lord's chosen survivors. He sent us a miracle."

In my sleep they drove their forearms into my throat and I gagged as their knives cut fire across my belly and blood rose up and rained back and I sank away into the flood, gasping.

We traveled for days and I was never sure of sleeping or waking, only of distance.

I remember their first laugh, the sin of it, the highest crime.

I remember them speaking of Old Mexico.

I remember watching my brother point his finger toward the stars.

We saw posters tacked to trees as we neared the first town. We stood before one. Noah said, "I'd turn me in for that kind of money."

In this town the road split, and they pointed the wagon toward the south without conversation. I spoke for the first time in days and all heads turned toward me in mute surprise.

Annette was in my hand. She was always in my hand now.

Noah said, "The snows are too deep to the north. We'd never make it."

I remember Charles saying, "Sitting Bull has survived in Canada all this time. If that land can hide a whole tribe maybe it can conceal us."

Jane said, "No one would ever expect us to turn north in winter."

On a muddy street Mason, Jeremiah, and Carlos stood before me and asked if I'd given any thought to leaving with them. "We could take up hitting coaches. There's always fun in that," Mason said. He punched me in that way of his, and then he put his arm about me. "You know they'll drive you mad with all their baby chatter."

"Creeks made of tequila in Old Mexico," Jeremiah said.

"Come on, *hermano.*" Carlos handed me a brass casing poured full with moonshine. Each of us now held one. He raised his.

"To the boys," Mason called.

"And to Annette," Jeremiah said.

We took them down. Then Carlos offered me the bottle but I waved it away.

"Catch up later then," Jeremiah said, his hand on my shoulder. He drew me in and slapped my back in that manner of hard men who've bled together. "Read the papers and you'll see our names."

In fact he was correct. I would see his and Carlos's names in the papers a month on. Ambushed in an alley for the bounties on their heads. I don't know what became of Mason.

Youn left the same day. He did so without a word. We was walking together along the wagon as it rolled the muddy street. When I looked next he was missing.

I found him headed up a side street. He turned back to me when I called. He tipped his hat, and was gone.

And so it come to pass that Charles, Constance, Jane, Noah, and me rode north to wait out the winter. Come spring we planned to cross the border and into the safety of mountains deeper than these. I rode with them but I dwelled with Annette.

I would deliver her home to the land where the wolves would forever howl, someplace untrampled and raw.

We bought a wagonload of provisions and took up an abandoned shanty in hills blanketed with larch. It was a summer place open to fierce winter winds and so it was the perfect hide for wanted men. There the five of us passed the cold months burning windfall for heat and frying flapjacks upon the stove.

We had come so many miles yet Noah and me did not know how to move about each other. He stiffened when I entered the room. If I saw him coming, I found labors to take me elsewhere. Ours was a truce built from the quietude of shame.

When we couldn't escape the other's presence, we spoke about matters of utility. Where to fetch our next dry wood, a better method for keeping mice from our food stores, the proper way to repair a broken hinge. We talked too of the weather and the duration of the weather and the new ferocity of the weather. It is the weather after all that proves there's no might to human borders.

It was Jane's growing belly that restored my brother. As she swelled with the only true miracle, he devoted himself to learning the Word. He aimed to build a proper congregation in the north, he said, a peaceful one dedicated to the principles of harmony and fair treatment. He didn't speak of it to me, but I overheard as he preached to them.

Jane was the one who guided his teachings. The daylight hours offered plenty of time for study. Jane retained her patience as my brother's tongue stumbled over those sounds. She had to teach him the same lesson a half dozen times before he could demonstrate the principle himself. But his grit did not slip. Nor hers.

Constance and Charles also found direction in his learning. Constance sparked discussions about my brother's preferred passages from the Bible, and Charles enjoyed deepening their debates with contrary arguments. To these conversations I listened, but never joined. My body was among them, but that was all.

At night I rolled out my bedding in a lean-to beside the cabin and set Annette beside me. I moved through each day on ritual, and this was the last. I pulled up the rifle and checked its chamber, and then turned my eyes to our snowbound backtrail. I never counted on sleep and so was never disappointed when it failed to come.

Constance and Charles took to walking in the afternoons, and so I took to following them with the rifle. They walked through the endless larch and Charles shook the snow from limbs and held back boughs so that she might pass without trouble of ducking or dodging. Her belly swelled now with child. I couldn't understand their chatter from the distance but I trailed its harmonies.

In the snow-blind months after the killings, I found direction in imagined threats. Bandits rushing from the hills with weapons. Soldiers leaping timbers and hurtling dynamite. Raiders come to kidnap the mothers I now guarded. Without these fictions the world was only white. And so in every waving branch I saw a hidden enemy, in every foreign sound I heard a battle cry.

But one afternoon I ventured too close and Charles saw me and waved me up. Of course he didn't guess that I had followed them each day. He only assumed I was out hunting and our paths had entwined.

"We were just speaking of Will," he said. "About the jokes he'd be making at our unlikely situation. Holed up and on the run with the infamous Harney as he soon becomes a father."

Constance wore a wool blanket about her shoulders and her hair was hidden under a scarf. The snow landed on her but melted at once. It wasn't falling from the skies now, only from trees.

"What will you do?" she asked.

Charles brushed the snow from my shoulder.

I looked off at the winter, the black trunks of pine against the white quilts of snow. I tried to recall the dews of spring, and the rushing of mountain water. I sought to conjure the bright sides of trout catapulting over skittering bugs. In all of it, I saw a map with no landmarks, no scale. I looked toward the north.

"You are welcome with us," Constance said. "Wherever we end up, you will have a home with us."

Home. The word tumbled on in echo.

As children one spring in that far-off land, Pa had saddled our horses and the three of us rode across the brown grass sopping with melt and then into the snows and still higher to the basin where he knew our bulls had been trapped by winter storm. We found their shapes in the receding white, their meat strewn about the hill, dragged in all directions by the retreat of scavengers. Pa swung down and took up a handful of red ice and said, "They was crossing the hillside when the snow sloughed loose. They didn't stand a chance."

I recall the heaviness of his voice, the water in his eyes. He was looking at their bones there in snow, and knowing that had he done better, had he come up here in time, the bulls would now be swatting at spring's first flies.

He sat in the snow with no regard for the cold. He put his head into this hands and sobbed. Our pa who had survived a war and buried his true love. These dead bulls set him to weeping.

I believed nothing ever changed, but then the first full moon after the equinox brought on Jane's labor.

She moved about the cabin, about the forest, about herself. For two days Constance stayed with her and held her aloft during the pains. In the evening the air around them tingled as it does before a lightning storm.

Charles and Noah spent the daylight hours fashioning a cradle from wood split by ax. I took to laying in a stash of cordwood, the rifle always within reach.

It was during the last day of waiting that Noah and me finally broke from our truce. I was bucking a fallen log when he said, "Let me have a go."

He took up the saw in his left hand and began working it. Chips and dust scattered over the snow. "Not as practiced as I should be," he said, panting. "As I aim to be."

When the length of wood dropped to the snow, he stood a time breathing and studying the ice as it wafted from the limbs overhead. The sun cut through and turned what fell to gemstone.

Inside we heard Jane working through another pain, and I worried how far that sound might carry in the still air.

"Why the Lord has made bearing a child so hard on a woman I can't figure," he said.

This labor was a fate I couldn't protect her against. Her blood would run but would it stop in time? Jane was sure. She wanted us far off, away from midwives or doctors who might know wanted posters.

My brother said, "Men don't ever know that brand of resolve."

He set the saw aside. His gaze lingered on my knees. Those eyes gray and unblinking. "Oh, Jess. I should've been there. I left you with suffering that wasn't yours to bear."

The snow sloughed from the limbs and the air filled with ice. "We come through it," I said, trying to sound okay. "That's what matters."

He looked at my marks, his mouth half

open with words he could feel but not yet find.

I heaved the maul to my shoulder. I wiped the sweat from my brow as Annette would've, with the inside of my wrist. Sometimes I pretended I was her. It was one of the ways I kept her with me.

He said, "You loved her, didn't you?"

"Yes, brother. I did."

"I should've been the one to catch that bullet."

" 'Should' ain't a word the world knows."

We turned toward the sound of Jane's pain. Her roar rose from someplace hidden and ancient. My brother sighed at all he could not help.

"What will you name the child?" I asked.

He was still looking on the cabin. "Jane won't consider a name until the baby is born healthy and whole. She believes in luck, good and bad."

I took a mouthful of snow to wet my parched tongue. "You ever heard the name Rowhine?"

My brother surprised me when he said, "Did Pa tell you the truth?"

"You know?"

"One day beside the lake, laying over the Sharps. He told me the whole deal. I remember the trout sending rings. I remember wondering what a name means."

"He never told me."

"That don't matter. Sister, Pa kept us from town for good reason. You know what folks called our stream? Coward Creek. Everybody knew he was a deserter. You don't escape that war in no sixty-three with all your parts."

"Did Ma know the truth?"

"I don't know."

I was watching the ice in the air. "I never called our father by his real name."

"Sis, his realest name was Pa. You know that. The rest don't count for nothing."

I drove the maul through the wood and into the block beneath. The maul was stuck and I had to jimmy it out. Finally it come free, but I just dropped it into the snow. I was too wore through to keep fighting that wood.

My brother stepped near and put his hand to my marked cheek. "Oh, sister. What might've been."

The pains come in earnest that night and Noah and Charles left the house to us women.

I started to leave too, but Jane stopped me. "Stay. Please."

So I stayed.

In the gaps of her labor she spoke. "He leaves us to interpret everything but this."

Constance pushed upon the small of her back through the pain. "There now. Your body knows all about this business with no help from words."

When it got close Constance held Jane in balance and blew air upon her wet brow. Jane was soaked through and now she could not stand but with help. She bore down with a strength not possessed by five of me.

I was ready with rags and a quilt. The fire raged in the stove and the air among us was wet as storm. Jane had told us how it would go. Constance was to catch the child, I was to run errands.

But now Constance was held tight by Jane's grip. Jane was on her knees and I was the one before her. I saw the skin of her gates stretching tight. The head drove at that flesh just as I had seen each spring during calving, and I knew to put my hands against it, to slow the descent and give the flesh time to soften and open. And so my hands was the first to touch you in this world.

The cord was about your neck and I slipped it free and your eyes opened and revealed the celestial forever and me reflected against it and I knew then my honest name just as I knew yours. I said, "Rosa."

I gave you to your wide-eyed mother.

Those hours we lingered about you. When your tongue got busy Jane put you to her breast and taught you to take in this life. I cut from a roast of venison and fed the bites to your mother's lips from the point of the knife.

Remember is the name of all children. In

that name is the seed and the thaw.

Noah come to me before the fire. Together we held our breaths not as people stooped before some man's idol but as souls bent before the altar of awe.

He held the guitar by the neck. "I want my daughter to know music on her first day."

"I don't know much guitar."

"Slide over."

Noah put the belly of the instrument against my own, against Annette where she always was. "Like this," he whispered. "There now, you're getting it."

So the first song you heard was the song of your people. Noah held the notes and I strummed the strings. We gave you the song as one, together.

That night as you slept bare against your mother's flesh, I slipped from the room and took my bedding as usual to the lean-to and spread it upon the bark chips and set the rifle within reach. I had been up all night with the labor and had not slept during the day and still I could not lose myself to slumber. My vision was consumed with you. I saw us a thousand different ways, among prairies and wildflowers, upon horseback and mountain trail, raising our eyes to the underside of cranes on the wing and bending our noses to the purple petals of camas. I saw it so clear I could feel your hand in mine and hear your voice call for Auntie.

Noah emerged from the cabin with a lantern.

"Put that out," I hushed. "An easy target."

"No one is hunting us here," he said. "Not today."

He sat beside me.

"What is it, brother?"

"Someday," he whispered. "You must tell her. I do not want there to be lies between us and I do not trust myself to tell this true."

"Then I will tell her, brother. I will tell her the bad with the good."

"She will not be proud of her old man."

"You still have time to make her proud."

I turned out the lantern, and the moonlight cast the world in gunmetal.

His voice from the darkness, "Do you believe sin is handed down, one generation to the next?"

"I reckon it piles like snow."

He began to shake. "She deserves better than me."

"Come near, brother."

He leaned until his head settled upon my lap, and there his tears penetrated the wool and wet my skin. I placed my hand on his cheek. I hummed to him, as he used to me, in a far-off place where the desert met a lake.

April passed and still we did not leave. We knew of deep snows in the passes and so we waited until early May. April might've made a difference.

We left the cabin with little and traveled fast. You and Jane rode in the wagon under a thick quilt. Noah held the reins. Charles and Constance followed in back. I rode some distance ahead, on the same chestnut. I had taken to calling her Solstice. She was jumpy and unsure, and I trusted her ears to hear what I might not.

I wore a dress because the posters had me as a man. I had my preferred pistol concealed in the hem of my jacket. The Winchester was in its scabbard where I might wield it if the need arose.

We spent every dark holed up in the lee of the wagon, a small fire for warmth. That's where I took my time with you, just us sitting on the edge of light. Anytime I put my nose to your mouth to take in your breath you latched on. You had this manner of driving your knuckles into your mouth, and I recall saying you was learning your edges.

But one Montana morning delivered ice from the skies and that turned to hard rain and so come dusk we broke from the trail to test our welcome at a lonely ranch house where smoke rose from the chimney. Its owner met us on the porch. He had a black beard and smoked a long pipe, and he thought too long at Noah's offer of gold coins. It was the woman who swept by her man to welcome us. She took a keen interest in you and dished us deep bowls from a pot of mutton broth and told of her family's recent hardships. Two boys played near the stove as we ate. The man kept staring on me. He looked off anytime I turned toward him. My marks couldn't be hid.

On the last morning we rode to a stop on the ridge above the border town. Fourteen buildings, nearly all built with a front to make them appear two stories when in fact they was one. The only true-built two-story was the whiskey house.

The town looked like so many other little cities built upon that wilderness, some fool's vision crammed into a fold of desert or strapped to a precipice. This was no place to call home but for the divide men had drawn on the 49th parallel. Noah flicked his chin toward the other side. "Today we get born new."

Smoke rose from the chimneys below and I saw horses hitched and swatting at spring flies. We might've cut through the woods but for the wagon. Maybe I knew, maybe I didn't.

You cried from the quilt and Jane opened her breast to you. Still you cried. I always wondered if you knew.

Noah removed his glove and put his fingers to your cheek. I saw he was saying his good-bye. Jane began pleading with him but it was no use. He announced, "Let me check the path. If they're on to us, this is where they'll wait. I won't risk you all, not this time. If you hear gunfire, ditch the wagon and cut through the timber and don't stop. Don't wait for me, you hear? I'll hold them until you're safe, and then follow by the cover of darkness."

"No." I said it firm as Pa. Noah's eyes met mine. "You stay with your daughter. I am a woman and they expect a man. I will signal that it is safe."

"This ain't your doing, Jess. I put us in this bind."

But Jane touched his arm. Their eyes met over your suckling and she made him to understand what she and I already knew. His life was no longer his own.

Watching them together, there was no missing the magic between those two. They knew the other as the farmer knows his earth. Your folks was the real thing. You can always breathe deep and know you grew from the true, honest thing.

I looked out over that new country I still hoped to wander. Those mountains went on till winter and beyond.

I drew Annette from my pocket and gave her to my brother. "In case, take her home for me."

"Take her yourself."

I pushed her into his hand. "Promise you'll leave her over green grass where wolves still

611

roam. Someplace far off and holy."

Jane answered, "We promise, Jess."

They looked on me with no words, and that made it feel like the last time.

I smiled. "No need for all this heaviness. I'll see you again in but a quarter hour." I tipped my hat and wheeled Solstice and we rode down that ridge.

I did not look back. I did not say a proper good-bye. What I'd give to have held you once more, to see your eyes and the forever they contained. To see, one last time, a daughter returned to her mother's arms.

Solstice and I come off that hill at a run and slowed into an alley. I dismounted and led the mare to the post and knotted the reins over the wood so she would not rip free. I sat my hat on the horn and knotted on the bonnet. I unbuttoned my jacket and drew the revolver to check its loads and then slipped it back into place. "Be right back, girl."

The street was quiet, as you'd expect of a frontier town at that hour. I walked along the muddy strip, checking for faces in the windows and doors opened just wide enough for a barrel. All seemed right enough. But then behind the saloon stood three saddled buckskins.

Buckskins could belong to any man, maybe Montana was full of them. But these was the first I had seen since leaving the Governor.

I drew a breath and felt the now familiar

calm spread through me. At least the waiting was over.

I looked to the rooftops. I looked to the edges of the buildings. I made a point of every crack in the glass, each woodpecker hole in the wall. If they was indeed onto me and I turned and rode back the way I'd come, I would only draw their malice to you.

So I took a last plug and walked toward the saloon. I would occupy them while you crossed, to safety. This was the gift that only I could give.

I pushed open the door and saw just one man in the room, the barkeep who was busy at his labors. "Whiskey," I said. "Big as you got."

He avoided my eyes. "Sure thing."

If I didn't before, I knew then. When a woman orders a whiskey before noon, the barkeep don't say, "Sure thing." Not even in Montana.

He set my drink on the bar. He turned back to the glasses he was drying.

The back door was closed, the balcony empty. I turned the whiskey.

A flicker of light caught the mirror above the barkeep and I turned to see him in the street. Drummond. He held a Winchester over his shoulder. His duster was tucked behind his pistols.

Greenie appeared beside him, with a long-bore side-by-side. It is queer to admit but I

613

felt relief to see Greenie in that moment. To have a friend there.

Greenie who wore his hat low. Red hair before his ears and freckles upon his nose. Greenie looked toward me but I don't reckon he saw nothing beyond his own reflection in the window. He was thinner and there was darkness below his eyes. I wondered what he'd heard about the high country. I wondered if he'd lost friends to our knives.

"How'd they reckon it?" I asked the barkeep.

The man looked on me like I was some manner of circus creature. "Is you really Samuel Spartan? Don't shoot me or nothing, but I figured you'd be bigger. You wear that dress womanlike. Damn authentic."

I paid the barkeep for a corked bottle and left it sitting on the counter. "This is for that red-hair out there. Make sure he gets it?"

Then there was nothing left to do. I took down the glass of whiskey and walked toward my due death. I did not shake or shiver, I only walked on my own two feet through that door and into the hard gaze of their barrels.

It was Drummond who spoke, not Greenie, but I could hear nothing that was said. In my ears was the rush of a thousand winds, I was upon a sea which reckons no borders, and my course was set.

I remember a mourning dove upon the roof across the way. I remember it lifting from its perch and falling before it flew.

I had every intention of dying willfully and yet all the practice and drilling rose in me as instinct. When Drummond braced my bullet beat his, a maul to the bridge of his nose. I turned and fired what I had left through the glass to put Tuss on his knees as he come through the back door. I did this and then saw what I had done and saw too what I could never do, and I flipped my pistol to the earth for the final time and offered myself to Greenie.

Hope dies last and I was just two hundred paces from the border and all he had to do was lower that barrel. He could say I'd ridden south. You would cross and I would be to you in minutes, and about you for all these years since. That was the gift only Greenie could give.

But I was in that dress and he'd watched me ride away with Noah Harney and he must've wondered if he'd ever known me at all. His jaw hardened. His voice turned cruel. "You look like a damn fish in that dress." I was surprised to see his hands take new grip of the side-by-side. "Who are you for real?" His voice was shaky. I had never seen him scared.

"It's me, Greenie. You know me."

His eyes darted over the dress. There was time. There was time enough to save us both.

■ ■ ■ ■

They put my body on a train, and I rumbled a two-week ride in a day. It was the first time I was ever on a train and it was the last time I was ever someplace else.

This year marks my forty-fourth summer inside the Federal Penitentiary for Women Convicts in Laramie, Wyoming. There is a mote and in spring the fowl linger about us, and the flowers show their purple tops over the green grass. In some years a pair of cranes dance about the blossoms. Iron bars could never hold their music.

They tell me Greenie's barrels was loaded light, bird shot, a hundred tears of lead. So he had come, then, with the intention of firing when duty demanded it but without lethal result. Yet when he could've said "go," he instead directed his barrels at my face.

My arms saved my vision, for that I am grateful.

You made it across the border in the commotion of bodies in the street. Nobody noticed one strange little family in a wagon when nearby lay a shot-up outlaw in a dress. I know it was hard on your pa to just roll by.

Toward Greenie I hold no ill will. Each day since I have risen and known you to ride free, and that is more life than I deserve.

I hope you understand my brother could

not confess our true origins until his final hours, even to kin. Don't hold his caution against him. You've had more privilege than you knew and profited from crimes that ain't yours. I ask only that you live every year you have left in honest reckoning. Our story is yours to make.

Jane's letters have come every month without fail, and so I know of your childhood, and your family now, and the good work you do. You never knew me, child, but I have always known you.

Constance is in touch less often these days but there was a time. She used to tell me of your trips with little Will. She once sent me the portrait she had taken of you both in some park out east. She wrote in the most perfect little script in the corner, "Rosa and Will in summer. 1894." I can't tell you the pleasure that portrait brings, even now when I know you both to be older.

The other photograph I have is you on horseback. In the background I can see the slab of some great mountain. The little girl is still in your face, but I can tell you ride like your old man. I so wish that just once you and me covered miles together.

You can't know what your gift means. A fiddle in this place is like a horse anywhere else. I play each day until my fingers ache. That music carries me through hills and across plains and into mountains deeper than these. You, child, delivered me home.

So near my own end, I often think of those before us who stared into forever. What did they see within those flowing prairies and toothless mountains? What did they feel when a herd of bison surged across a river or a pack of wolves stood cradled in the valley below? As families gathered on the bows of ships delivering them from persecution, as men and women rose from the cotton to learn their children would be born free — in that forever after, did they see tomorrow or yesterday?

Our founders told different stories, but in the spirit moving over these waters we've all chosen to see our due reward.

Child, do as we have not. Wander this land together and with your eyes wide open. Trust the mountain, not your name for it. Bury your hands in the common loam and feel there the blood sent like a flood upon this place.

Feel too the roots and seeds.

ACKNOWLEDGMENTS

My forever thanks to Team Whiskey: Andrea Schulz, Beena Kamlani, and Emily Wunderlich; David Gernert and Ellen Goodson Coughtrey; and to the team's earliest member, Ellie Rose.

I am also grateful for the guidance offered by many friends and readers who offered their time to these pages at various stages: Al Aronowitz, Thomas Christensen, David James Duncan, Dylan Tomine, Elaine Larison, Gretchen Goode, Jim Larison, Joy Jensen, Nathan Koenigsknecht, Rachel Teadora, Steven Perakis, and Wayne Harrison. Also to the larger crew at the Gernert Company who offered their reactions, including Flora Hackett (who read repeated drafts), Rebecca Gardner, Luke Gernert, Will Roberts, Erika Storella, and Anna Worrall.

Also, a perennial thank-you to my mentors: Tracy Daugherty, Paul Dresman, Ted Leeson, Marjorie Sandor, and Keith Scribner.

I also owe a deep debt to Gillian Welch,

whose music was there the night this book was born and nearly every day after. A lyric from her song "Tennessee" ricochets about the title.

This novel would not exist without public support for city libraries, county museums, and academic historians.

ABOUT THE AUTHOR

John Larison earned an MFA from Oregon State University in 2007. During the eight years he was writing *Whiskey When We're Dry,* he worked as a fly-fishing guide, a college writing instructor, and a freelance contributor to outdoor magazines. He lives with his family in rural Oregon.

The employees of Thorndike Press hope you have enjoyed this Large Print book. All our Thorndike, Wheeler, and Kennebec Large Print titles are designed for easy reading, and all our books are made to last. Other Thorndike Press Large Print books are available at your library, through selected bookstores, or directly from us.

For information about titles, please call:
  (800) 223-1244

or visit our website at:
  gale.com/thorndike

To share your comments, please write:
  Publisher
  Thorndike Press
  10 Water St., Suite 310
  Waterville, ME 04901